A MIDSUMMER'S
Kiss

MEARA PLATT

ISBN-10: 1-945767-06-5
ISBN-13: 978-1-945767-06-7

To Nora and Jacqueline, for being my best friends as well as my sisters

CHAPTER 1

Mayfair District, London
May 1814

"OH, DEAR HEAVEN!" The sound of a sweet, feminine voice reached Lord Graelem Dayne's ears, and a soft hand came to rest upon his much larger, rougher one to draw it off the boot he was clutching. "Sir, you mustn't touch your leg. I think it's broken."

"I *know* the damn thing is broken," Graelem said as he lay sprawled on his back in the middle of Chipping Way on this warm and sunny morning, writhing in agony and glowering at the snorting beast that had just burst through the open townhouse gate of Number 3 Chipping Way at full gallop and knocked him senseless.

That horse, the color of devil's black, had been rearing and fighting its rider while she struggled to bring it under control. As Graelem had tried to roll out of the way, one of its massive hooves had landed with full force on his leg, cracking sturdy bone.

"Hellfire!" An excruciating jolt of pain shot straight up his body and into his temples the moment he tried to move his leg.

He was in trouble.

Serious trouble, not only because the horse was still skittish and snorting, but also because Graelem's now broken leg would make it impossible to complete the business he'd come down to London to accomplish. At the moment, he couldn't walk, and his every breath was a struggle as it came in short, spurting gasps.

What was he to do now?

There would be no balls, soirees, or musicales for him for the next month, that was for certain. He'd never cut a striking figure hopping about on one leg, for he was a big oaf even when on two functioning legs.

He glanced at the angry beast.

Hellfire again! Just as Graelem thought he was about to be trampled once more, the beast lowered its massive hooves, let out a few soft neighs, and finally calmed.

"Pull the boot off my leg!" he ordered the young woman who'd slid off the saddle in a blur of green velvet and rushed toward him a moment ago. He wished she had been a man so he could pound his fist into his face for so recklessly galloping into him and efficiently destroying his courtship plans along with his leg.

"Now!" he commanded, knowing the task would be much harder once his leg had swelled as it was starting to do now. Cutting through leather was no easy feat, and any attempt to do so would be far more painful than one swift tug done immediately.

"Of course. I'm so sorry!" She knelt beside him and braced her hands on the heel of the boot, letting out a sob as she apologized again.

Damn, why couldn't she have been a man?

She sounded young, hardly more than a girl.

He inhaled sharply as those soft hands began to tug at his boot.

"I have it," the young woman said in a soothing voice that flowed over him like warm honey. "Close your eyes and take another deep breath. I'm afraid this will hurt."

He let loose with a string of invectives as another dagger-sharp jolt of pain stabbed up his leg and into his temples. His heart felt as if it were about to pound a hole through his chest.

"Oh, I'm so very sorry!" She set aside the boot and turned to face him. Her lips quivered as she struggled to hold back anguished tears.

"I know, lass." He tried his best to answer gently, for he

suddenly felt quite protective of the girl. Although why he should feel that way when she was the cause of his misery was beyond him. She did appear sincerely remorseful.

But whatever had possessed her to ride that demonic beast? Where was she going in such a hurry?

Before he had the chance to ask, he heard male voices calling out and the sound of hurried footsteps coming toward them. His blurred gaze remained on the young woman dressed in the dark green velvet riding habit. Had she really been the rider on that demonic horse?

"Amos," she said with a shaken breath, "put Brutus back in his stall before Father orders him shot." Then she turned to the other man who'd run out of the townhouse to lend assistance. "Pruitt, please fetch Uncle George at once."

"Right away, Miss Laurel."

As both men left to do her bidding, the girl called Laurel sank onto the grass beside him and took hold of his hand, cradling it in her lap. Her soft hands were shaking. As his vision cleared from the blur of pain, he caught a good look at her face and experienced another jolt. The girl was beautiful.

She was also trembling, obviously overset by the incident. He felt the urge to squeeze her hand and assure her that all would be well. However, he dismissed the ridiculous notion at once. How could the mere touch of a chit who'd almost killed him affect him in any way but cold revenge?

Still, he couldn't deny that his anger was fading… or that his blood was heating.

He attributed that surprising effect to the pain of his broken leg.

"Sir, is there someone we can summon on your behalf? I'll send one of our footmen—"

"Lady Eloise Dayne," he said with a nod. "She resides on this street at Number 5."

"Lady Dayne? Oh, my heavens!" Laurel let out another shaken breath. "Sir, are you by chance her grandson? The baron who lives in Scotland and just arrived in town last night?"

He nodded again. "Indeed, lass. Graelem Dayne."

"You're Graelem... I mean, Lord Moray! And Eloise is your grandmother! Oh, this gets worse and worse."

He arched an eyebrow. "Those men called you Laurel."

"Yes, I'm Laurel Farthingale." She still sounded as though she were about to burst into tears. "I live here at Number 3 along with my parents and sisters, and a horde of Farthingale relations come to London for the season. We're your grandmother's neighbors. Friends, too. Though she won't be too pleased that I've almost killed her grandson. Are you in terrible pain?" She let out a quiet sob. "I wish there was something I could do to ease it."

There was, but she'd finish the job her horse had started and kill him if he told her what he was truly thinking. *Damn.* Was he that depraved? At the very least, his senses were addled. How old was she? Old enough to be out in society, he guessed, but not much beyond her first season.

She was pretty enough to be snatched up quickly, assuming she didn't kill her beaus first.

She eased beside him and let out a mirthless laugh. "I'm in for it now. Probably punished for the entire year," she muttered.

"Sorry, lass."

Her eyes rounded in horror. "You mustn't be! This is all my fault. Truly, it isn't much of a loss. This is only my first year out in society and I'm still quite overwhelmed by it. Everyone is so polite and impeccable in their manners, I worry that I'll never fit in. My parents think I'm too spirited. That's the polite term they use, but they really think I'm a hot-tempered hellion. I suppose I am, as you've unfortunately discovered."

He tried to fashion a response, but couldn't, for he found himself staring into a pair of magnificent blue-green eyes that sparkled like sunshine on a Scottish mountain lake. His own baronial estate was on Loch Moray in the Scottish lowlands near the English border. It was a beautiful lake, almost as breathtaking as Laurel's eyes.

Damn. The girl also had a body that could bring a man to his knees. She sat too close, leaning over him in a way that got his heart pounding a hole in chest again... no, the pain was still addling his good sense.

He sank back, but couldn't turn away from the girl. She was a pretty sight indeed. It wasn't merely her shapely form, for the girl was fully clothed, with the jacket of her riding habit buttoned up to her slender throat and the flowing skirt covering everything else that a man would wish to explore. He liked the scent of her as well, a hint of strawberries and warm, summer breezes.

"Laurel, what's happened here?" An efficient-sounding gentleman approached them, a thoughtful frown upon his face. He carried a black satchel with him, obviously a medical bag of some sort.

"Uncle George, this is all my fault! The gentleman is Lord Graelem Dayne. He's Eloise's grandson and I almost killed him!" She also repeated the details of the accident to Eloise when she came running out and paused with her hand over her heart to stare in horror at his injury.

"Good morning, Grandmama. It's not quite as bad as it looks." He got out little else, for Laurel quickly jumped in to assure his grandmother that she had been completely at fault.

Eloise glanced at him and then her gaze shifted to Laurel.

"All my fault," Laurel repeated with a tip of her chin, obviously determined to endure whatever punishment was to be meted out.

"Now, now, my dear," Eloise said. "I'm sure my grandson will find it in his heart to forgive you. Won't you, Graelem?"

He supposed he would. The girl may have been a little reckless, but she had been honest and had readily admitted her mistake. It spoke of her good character. Or was he too quick to forgive her because she was the prettiest thing he'd ever set eyes upon?

A lock of rich, honey-colored hair spilled over her brow.

He felt a sudden desire to undo the pins from Laurel's hair and run his fingers through her exquisite, dark gold mane.

Laurel's uncle said something about needing to cut through the fabric of his trousers before setting his broken leg. He nodded, not paying much attention, for his head was beginning to spin.

The last thing he recalled as he was suddenly overcome by a wave of nausea was Laurel nudging him onto his side and wrapping her arms around him as he cast up this morning's breakfast onto the grass.

He always was one to charm the ladies.

LAUREL KEPT A hand on each of Lord Moray's shoulders to hold him up because his big body was still heaving even though he did not appear to have anything left inside him to come out. "Perfect," he finally muttered and sank back against her, too dazed to notice he was leaning against her shoulder and not a tree or the ground.

"Do what you must, Dr. Farthingale," he said, lightly rolling each *r* in the way Scotsmen did whenever they spoke. It wasn't a heavy brogue, but one mingled with English refinement, as though he'd spent time in both worlds.

He appeared the sort who moved about easily in both worlds, for there was a quiet confidence about him, even though he wasn't at his best just now. *All my fault.*

Uncle George began to quietly explain what he needed to do to treat his broken leg. "Once properly set, I'll fashion a splint around it. Then we'll help you into Lady Dayne's house."

"Graelem, it's best you stay with me until you recover," Eloise said, wringing her hands in obvious concern. "You'll need looking after for the next few weeks."

Lord Moray closed his eyes a moment and nodded. "I had planned to stay at Gabriel's townhouse, but I arrived late last night and haven't bothered to unpack yet. Will you send word to his butler to bring my belongings here?"

"At once." Eloise appeared relieved. "Gabriel's is a big, empty house anyway. What with him gone off again to who knows where on his latest misadventure—" She broke off, suddenly tense. "No matter. It's settled. You'll stay here."

Lord Moray turned toward her uncle. "Go ahead, Dr. Farthingale. Do what you must," he said again. "Bloody thing hurts like blazes."

Uncle George frowned at her. "Hold him down, Laurel. This

shouldn't take too long."

Since Lord Moray was still leaning against her, she merely kept her hands wrapped around his shoulders and prayed he wouldn't be too much to manage. He was far too big and muscled for her to restrain against his will. "Hold my hands, my lord. I think it will help."

He ignored the suggestion at first. However, as her uncle worked on his leg and the pain appeared to become unbearable, he finally complied. His hands felt warm on hers, and she realized she was still shivering with fear… and guilt.

She might have killed the man!

Her heart broke with each twinge of his body. He refused to cry out despite the excruciating pain he must have felt, and she suspected he was purposely trying to spare her feelings. Of course, he couldn't hide the sudden shift of his muscles at every tug and agonizing twist.

"I'm almost done, Laurel," her uncle assured her, looking up briefly to give her a smile. A mirthless smile, for he was disappointed in her behavior and the tension in his expression showed it.

She was relieved of the need to say anything when her youngest sisters bolted out of the house and stopped beside her to gawk. "Crumpets! Who is he?" Lily asked, while the other twin, Dillie, edged closer to his prone body, for he'd closed his eyes again and appeared to be resting. Or passed out.

The twins shrieked and drew back when he opened one eye. "Who are you?" he shot back.

Laurel quickly introduced them, and then explained to her sisters what had happened. "Eloise knows. She's preparing her guest quarters for his recovery."

Dillie glanced at him wryly. "Welcome to London, Lord Moray."

To Laurel's surprise, he laughed lightly. "Not quite the welcome I had in mind, Dillie."

"But one you'll never forget, I'll wager. I hear you're Eloise's favorite grandson."

Laurel groaned. "Yes, Dillie. He is." Which made what she did all the worse.

"Because if I were going to trample someone—"

"The point is, I shouldn't have hurt anyone," Laurel said.

"That goes without saying," Lily chimed in.

Laurel rolled her eyes. "Stop gawking at him."

However, she saw that Lord Moray was curious about the twins as well, for they were identical and impossible to tell apart. Though only fifteen, they were quite clever for their tender years… usually. Daisy was almost eighteen, and as the middle sister among the five of them, she was always the one to keep the peace.

Where was Daisy when she needed her?

"You're awfully big," Lily said, stating the obvious as she addressed Lord Moray once again. "You won't be easy to carry into Lady Dayne's townhouse, much less up the stairs. But perhaps if you shift your weight and—"

Dillie poked his shoulder. "I agree. You're all muscle." She cast Laurel an impish grin. "But I suppose you noticed that."

Laurel felt her face suffuse with heat. "Who's the doctor here? You two brats or Uncle George?" She truly wished Daisy were here, not only to chase the snoopy twins away. She needed to talk to Daisy in private, but it wasn't possible while everyone was about. She sighed, deciding there was nothing to be done about it now. She wasn't about to send Daisy to Hyde Park on her own to deliver a message to Devlin Kirwood. She would simply have to seek out Devlin at Lady Harrow's musicale this evening and apologize for not meeting him today.

He would understand and forgive her once she explained.

Laurel gave no further thought to Devlin, for she felt the subtle undulation of hard muscle beneath her palms and knew Lord Moray was trying to sit up. Goodness! She'd forgotten she still held him.

The twins were still beside her, inspecting him as though he were an archeological treasure. He squinted a little as the sun glinted through the leaves of the towering oak under which they were settled. "Am I mistaken or do you really look that much alike?"

"No one can tell us apart," Dillie said with a chuckle. "Lily and I confuse everyone, even our parents."

Lily just stood there gaping at him. "We have a few more years before we're fit to come out in society, assuming Laurel hasn't killed off all the eligible bachelors by then."

"Don't jest about it, Lily." Laurel tried to keep her voice from trembling, but knew she'd failed. Her eyes began to tear again. "I almost did. It was a very close thing."

Lord Moray shifted slightly to gaze up at her. "Lass," he said with aching gentleness, "I'm a big oaf. It'll take more than an angry horse to kill me."

Laurel's heart leapt into her throat. He had the handsomest smile and dark green eyes that could lead a girl to mischief with very little provocation. Of course, she wouldn't be that girl. She was loyal to Devlin Kirwood. "Our eldest sister, Rose, married last year," she began to prattle, for his smile was doing odd things to her. In a nice but confusing way. "Her husband is Lord Julian Emory, the current Viscount Chatham."

Lord Graelem nodded. "I know him. Good man."

She liked the way the sun warmed the chestnut color of his hair.

"Done, my lord," her uncle said, regaining their attention. "Don't try to get up on your own just yet. We'll summon help."

Once Dillie was sent off to call for Eloise's footmen, it took only a moment for Lord Moray to grow impatient and attempt once again to sit up.

"What are you doing?" Laurel immediately positioned her body against his back to catch him if he started to fall, for he'd been hurt enough for one day. Indeed, hurt enough for a lifetime, as far as she was concerned.

Lily rolled her eyes and began to jabber about linear planes and angles and some nonsense about gravitational thrust, which Laurel would have dismissed had she not found herself suddenly pinned between the trunk of the oak tree and Lord Moray, whose back was unwittingly pressed against her chest.

Her uncle groaned in exasperation. "Laurel, what are you trying to accomplish? You can't lift him up on your own."

"But I only meant to—" Realizing she was only making matters worse, she tried to slip out from under him. Her breasts accidentally rubbed against his shoulder.

"Lass! You'd better… blessed Scottish saints… er, just don't move. I'll roll out of your way."

She nibbled her lip and tried to hold back the tears threatening to well in her eyes, for he sounded so pained and his gaze was now turbulent and fiery. The blaze in his eyes could only signify anger. "I only meant to help."

"I think you've *helped* me quite enough for one day." He fell back as she moved away, knocking his head against the trunk of the oak tree with a soft *thuck*. "Quite enough."

She placed a hand on his arm to lend aid, but received another fiery glance for her attempt. "Lass, it isn't necessary. My grandmother's footmen will assist me to my chamber."

She nodded, feeling worse for causing him yet more discomfort. "Please, let me do something to make it up to you."

"No—"

"But I don't mind at all." Her tears had held off, but no longer. She let out a sniffle. "Just tell me what I can do for you—"

"Lass, it isn't necessary." His gaze was a dangerous smolder that seemed to intensify each time she tried to touch him.

The tears began to stream down her cheeks. "*Anything.* You have only to ask and I'll do it. You have my promise."

"I don't want it."

She hated feeling guilty. Why wouldn't he simply accept her apology? "You have it anyway. My *sacred* promise. What can I do to atone for the damage I've caused?"

He eyed her for a disconcertingly long moment. "Very well," he said with quiet authority. "Marry me."

CHAPTER 2

"WHAT?" LAUREL WAS certain she'd misunderstood, for no man in his right mind would ask such a thing of the very girl who'd almost cut short his existence. She shook her head and laughed lightly. "Ah, I suppose I deserved that jest. Well done, sir. Marry me? For a moment, you had me believing you were serious."

His gaze never left her face. *Oh, dear.* He wasn't smiling. "We'll be wed by Midsummer's Day."

"What?" she repeated, a numbing cold slowly spreading throughout her body despite the warmth of the day. She clasped her trembling hands and rested them on her lap in a useless attempt to keep them from shaking. At the same time, she let out a nervous titter that sounded remarkably like two squirrels scrambling after the same acorn. She never realized her throat had the ability to make such an inane sound. "Well done again, sir. By Midsummer?" *Titter, titter.* "Why, that's merely a month away." She made those hideous squirrel sounds again. "What a jolly jester you are!"

But Laurel knew by his steadfast green-eyed gaze that he was in earnest. Her heart sank into her toes. *Please! No!* Devlin wasn't going to like this one bit. Nor was her family… she hoped. As for her family, she had the two smartest Farthingales at her side right now. Surely they'd think of something to rescue her from this scrape.

Laurel leaned forward, eager to hear Lily's thoughts as her

young sister cleared her throat and prepared to spout her wisdom. *Please, Lily, come up with an answer.* But her sister's mouth was agape and her big blue eyes were wide as saucers, which did not look promising at all. "You've really done it this time, Laurel. Whatever possessed you to give him your *sacred* promise? And we all heard you—"

"Be quiet, Lily. What do you know of marriage proposals anyway?" Laurel winced at the pettiness in her own tone. Lily wasn't the one who'd blundered her way into this predicament. "Sorry, Lily." She turned to her uncle, whose shocked expression mirrored Lily's.

Oh, no. Not Uncle George, too? He was unflappable, the calm and brilliant Farthingale who always helped incompetent family members out of their misadventures.

She gazed at him with pleading eyes.

Her uncle sighed in resignation and shook his head. "This isn't a matter to be discussed on the street. Let's put off further conversation until you've both recovered from the scare." He studied Lord Moray. "I'm afraid you'll be in quite a bit of pain these next few days, my lord. You'll need laudanum until the worst of it passes."

"So will Laurel, by the look of her," Lily commented.

"Be quiet, Lily," she and her uncle said at the same time.

Lily shrugged. "I was merely stating the obvious."

Dillie returned just then. "Eloise's footmen will be along shortly." She paused a moment to catch her breath and glance at all of them. "What's going on? Have I missed something? Laurel, your complexion is as green as your riding habit."

"She's getting married," Lily said.

"I am not!" Laurel dropped her hands to her sides and curled them into fists, wishing to beat sense into Lord Moray even though she'd already caused him enough harm. If only Brutus had knocked him unconscious! Their conversation would never have happened and he would not have asked her to marry him.

In truth, he hadn't asked.

She had begged him. *Anything. Anything, my lord. Ooh, please! I give you my sacred promise!*

And the cur had taken her up on it!

Said cur now leaned on his elbows and turned toward her, his every movement causing him obvious agony. "Does your oath mean so little, lass?"

"Of course not! I keep to my word, but I... you... it isn't possible." A gentle breeze blew through her curls, but the light wind ruffling her hair and brushing against her hot cheeks did little to calm her down. Nothing would calm her down until that big Scottish oaf released her from her promise. And if he thought he'd just won himself a biddable wife, he'd have a big surprise coming.

"She gave Lord Moray her *sacred* promise," Lily added, "so there's no going back on it without risking eternal—"

"Hot, buttered crumpets!" Dillie gasped. "And I missed all that?"

"You didn't miss anything." Laurel gritted her teeth. "It's all been a silly misunderstanding. I'm not about to give up my life and happiness over a broken leg that will heal in a couple of days."

Lily shook her head. "It'll take far longer than that. And you ought to be grateful that Brutus only managed to shatter his lower leg, the tibia and fibula."

Laurel winced. "Only?"

Lily nodded. "Had he struck the femur, then poor Lord Moray would likely be dead by Midsummer. It has to do with the dangers of blood congealing in the area of the upper leg. Isn't that right, Uncle George?"

For pity's sake! How did Lily know these things?

Her uncle knelt beside Lord Moray. "As my niece said, my lord. You had a very close call. Had Brutus struck you above the knee... well, fortunately he didn't."

All the fight drained out of Laurel in that moment. How could she forget that she'd almost killed Eloise's grandson? She owed him a great debt and had to repay it, even if it meant sacrificing her happiness, setting aside her hopes and dreams, and marrying for reasons other than love. She had opened her big mouth and would now be the first Farthingale to sacrifice herself at the altar of convenience. Although marriage to Lord Moray would be anything but convenient.

Indeed, it was quite inconvenient. Surely he'd come to the same realization once his pain subsided, and then he'd be eager to release her from her promise. She merely needed to be patient and not ruffle his feathers any worse than she already had today. *Ah, patience.* Unfortunately, it was a virtue she had never acquired.

She cast the big oaf a hopeful smile.

He frowned back.

Her smile faltered, but she refused to despair for she had a month to gain her release from the hastily made promise. He would relent.

He simply had to.

She'd do all in her power to help him realize his mistake. No man wished to be stuck with a wife who loved another. That was it, her way out. She'd tell him all about Devlin. Not now, of course. Perhaps in a day or two when his pain had subsided.

"Lass," he said with a wry arch of his eyebrow, speaking softly and with seeming regret, "I can't let you out of the bargain. Don't think to change my mind with tricks or pleading or..." he paused for a lengthy moment, "seduction."

She curled her hands into fists again. "Me? Seduce you? Hah! You need have no fear of that." *Since I wouldn't know how, in the first place.* "And why would I want my freedom from you, an utter stranger who took advantage of my good nature to trick me into a cold and loveless alliance? That's right, an alliance. For you and I shall never have a true marriage."

"Suits me fine, lass. I have no intention of imposing myself on you."

"What?" He didn't want her? Then why propose? She resisted the urge to strike him even though her fingers were still curled into fists and she was angry. No, not just angry. She was blazing, fiery furious!

Although she had a retort at the ready, she clamped her lips shut instead because she needed to think and not merely respond like a prickly hen to his goading. Lack of thinking got her into this predicament in the first place. She studied him again.

Did he have a weakness?

If he did, it wasn't obvious. Drat, he really was quite handsome. There was a brooding intelligence about him, the sort of quiet confidence that other men would trust and follow. He wasn't one for glib words either, but seemed to command attention when he spoke. He certainly had her attention now.

In truth, she could not draw her gaze away and he seemed smugly aware of it.

She didn't wish to like anything about him, but had to admit that he had nice eyes. They were a deep green that drew one in with dangerous appeal. He had nicely formed lips as well. She stole a glance at the rest of him. His clothes were of good quality, or had been until Brutus knocked him to the ground and forced him to roll onto the street to avoid being trampled under his massive hooves.

Lord Moray was a gentleman, being Eloise's grandson and a baron. Yet he did not possess a polished air of refinement. No, nothing polished or refined about him. While of good quality, his clothes were not the height of fashion. He was too big and brawny to cut an elegant line. Quite the opposite, he had the mark of a man used to physical labor.

Others in society would disdain him for it, for a true gentleman never indulged in heavy work. Gentlemen were not required to work at all. However, Laurel never could understand why idleness was so admired by the Upper Crust.

Her own family had elevated their stature through hard work in their mercantile endeavors. For this reason, they had yet to be received in the finer homes, but Rose's marriage to Lord Julian Emory, eldest son of a marquis and holder of the title Viscount Chatham in his own right, had gone a long way toward opening doors for them.

Laurel's gaze drifted back to Lord Moray's face and she was once again captivated by his eyes, the sort of eyes that made her melt a little each time he looked at her. Oh, why was it suddenly so hot? And why couldn't she stop gawking at him?

It signified nothing, of course.

She felt guilty about what she'd done to him, that was all.

Eloise's footmen arrived to carry him into the bedchamber she'd had her staff prepare for him. Her uncle accompanied them, as expected, for he wouldn't leave until making certain his patient was well settled and comfortable. Laurel meant to return home, but instead found herself following them up the stairs and into the guest bedchamber where Lord Moray was to spend the next few days recovering.

Goodness! She hoped it wouldn't take longer than a few days for him to be up and about. She stood quietly while her uncle gave instructions to the footmen to help the patient out of his clothes. "Laurel, dear." Eloise, who had also followed them upstairs, gently took her by the shoulders. "I believe it is time for us to leave."

Laurel nodded, but her feet refused to comply until Eloise gave her a soft nudge toward the door. She managed a quick glance at her victim and noticed that he took up most of the bed. A jolt of heat coursed through her. If they married, she might be required to share that bed with him. Ridiculous! There was no room. She'd have to sleep practically atop him or somehow nestled in the crook of his arm.

Why was she even thinking such thoughts? There would be no marriage. Devlin was the man for her. He'd find a way to rescue her from this nightmare. And he wasn't a big oaf who'd take up most of the bed!

She followed Eloise downstairs into her summer salon, a cheerful room decorated in floral silk wallpaper, yellow silk chairs, and polished mahogany tables. "Laurel, are you all right?" Eloise frowned, obviously concerned as she motioned for her to sit down.

Laurel sank into one of the delicate chairs and moaned. "How can I be? I wish I could crawl back in bed and pretend this morning had never happened."

And since she was thinking of beds, seeing Lord Moray stretched out on his bed made her realize that she'd never given much thought to being a wife. She and Devlin had been best friends since childhood. Their amiable relation had blossomed into something more, and each now believed marriage was their natural next step. But she hadn't thought beyond the wedding celebration.

Would Devlin want her to share his bed?

Why hadn't she thought of this before?

She sat silently as Eloise crossed to the bellpull to ring for tea. Laurel cast her a wincing smile when she returned to her side and settled in the chair beside hers. She waited for Eloise's assurance that her grandson would regain his senses. "Well, unfortunately the events of this morning cannot be undone," Eloise said, reaching for Laurel's hand and taking it in hers with a motherly affection. "My dear, shall we talk about what happened?"

"Oh, Eloise! I can't marry your grandson." She edged forward, practically off her seat. "Please, you must pound sense into him."

Eloise gave her hand a little squeeze before releasing it. "I don't know that I can. You see, his purpose in coming to London was to find himself a wife."

"Then let him find one! Just not me! There are dozens of delightful young women who would leap at the chance to become Baroness Moray. He's not only titled, but handsome. Exceptionally handsome." *Why did that slip out?* "He'll be considered quite the catch."

"All well and good, but Graelem isn't fit to court anyone in his present condition." She raised her gaze to the ceiling as though Laurel needed the reminder that Eloise's wounded grandson was undergoing medical treatment upstairs and presently writhing in agony.

Laurel let out a soft groan. "But he will be soon. Uncle George will see to it, for he's the best doctor in all of England. Then you can introduce your grandson to a flock of sweet, biddable young ladies. A quiet tea or dinner party here at home two or three weeks from now ought to do the trick. That's all it will take for the marriage-minded mamas and their dainty daughters to notice him and give chase. He can sort out the prospects at his leisure. He has the entire season to decide. Longer if he wishes."

"I don't think so. You see, he's determined to have it all settled by Midsummer's Day."

Laurel's eyes grew wide with concern. What was so important

about that day? Lord Moray had mentioned it as well, but she'd dismissed it as an arbitrary date set by a man in ill humor. "But that's only a month away. Do you mean to say he intends to find himself a suitable girl and marry her all within a month? His companion for life, the woman who will bear his children, and he thinks he can find her in this short a time?" She let out a snort of indignation. "Seems I misjudged him. He appeared to have intelligent eyes and a thoughtful demeanor, but I'm sorry, Eloise. Your grandson is an idiot."

"At times, perhaps," she said with a hearty chuckle. "But," she added, a merry twinkle now in her eyes, "I think he made an excellent decision. He chose you, didn't he?"

Laurel was spared the need to respond when Eloise's reliable butler entered with a tray of tea and cakes. "Ah, Watling. Set it down right here." Eloise pointed to the small *demi-lune* table between them. "Ginger cake is Dillie's favorite. You must take her a slice or two, Laurel." She set aside two slices as though all other matters had been resolved and this silly cake was the most important thing on her mind.

Laurel shook her head in confusion. Eloise's lack of concern made no sense. How could she treat this day as any other? Laurel had almost killed her grandson. And her grandson now insisted on marrying her. Wasn't it worth more than a two-minute discussion?

Apparently not.

Eloise remained surprisingly cheerful as she moved on to pouring tea into their cups. Laurel sat in silent horror as her dear neighbor handed her one of those delicate cups and continued to chatter while expertly nipping sugar off the small sugar cone beside the teapot and dropping it in her tea. She was chattering about the latest *ton* gossip as though the matter of Laurel's marriage to the big oaf lying upstairs with a broken leg was a *fait accompli*. "Lady Fawnbridge was quite bereft when the Duke of Edgeware called an end to their affair. But we all knew it was in the offing, for they'd dallied almost a month and everyone knows Edgeware does not stay with a woman longer than a month before moving on. It will take a very special girl to steal his heart and shake him out of his solitary existence. I hope he finds her."

"Why are we speaking of Edgeware? Or ginger cake?" *And what is it about men and thirty days?* Is there something terrifying about that period of time? Or what lies beyond it? She thought of ancient sailors who believed the world was flat and they would fall off it into a terrifying abyss if they sailed beyond the edge.

Eloise gave a casual shrug. "Would you rather speak of my grandson?"

Laurel blurted out a *yes* and another quieter, calmer *yes*. She needed to maintain her composure, for rational thought and conversation would win the day, not stomping and storming about in frustration. "Indeed, I would."

Eloise shrugged again. "I don't know what else there is to say."

Laurel shot to her feet, her heart now beating like a war drum against her chest. *Stay calm. Stay calm!* "There's everything to say! You cannot think the matter is resolved. Eloise, I can't marry him!"

"Can't? Or won't?"

"Must we parse words? Very well, I *can* marry him. I'm quite capable of it and there's no impediment in that sense. However, I *won't* marry him. I don't know him. He could be hot-tempered—"

"As you are."

Laurel blushed. "I… well, yes… I will admit that I am prone to… when I believe passionately about something… but it isn't at all the same thing."

Is Eloise smirking at me?

"Graelem is an even-tempered man. Very slow to anger. In truth, I don't think I've ever seen him angry, even after—"

A yelp of agony from upstairs interrupted their conversation. Laurel forgot all about the tea cakes and *ton* gossip and hurried upstairs. What was Uncle George doing to Graelem's leg? Rather, Lord Moray's leg. She shouldn't be thinking of him as Graelem even though Eloise had been referring to him by his familiar name. No, he could never be Graelem to her, even though they were now temporarily and unfortunately betrothed.

The bedchamber door was closed.

Should she enter?

Obviously, it was closed for a reason. Uncle George knew what he was doing, no doubt still working on that busted leg. What more needed to be done? She had no business being up here, for she wasn't medically trained and could do nothing to help. Nor could she simply march in without causing more scandal.

She stood in the elegant hallway, simply staring at Lord Moray's door. She heard the muffled sound of two men bickering inside. Her uncle and Lord Moray, of course. She couldn't hear much, but her uncle was saying that something must come off… or… he had to take it off… or cut it off.

Is the man I almost killed about to lose his leg?

She knew her uncle carried a hacksaw in his medical bag.

Her hand trembled as she placed it on the knob. Surely her uncle would have said something if that leg was to come off. And he wouldn't have bound it in a splint if he thought the bones would never knit properly back in place. However, he'd been in the room with his patient an awfully long while.

And Lily had said that a break just above Graelem's… Lord Moray's knee would kill him.

Had Uncle George discovered a break above the knee?

No, it couldn't be. Even if it were, Lord Moray was a big, strong man and would survive. His leg would heal. It simply had to!

She released the knob and was about to walk back downstairs when he let out another sharp, anguished yelp.

Laurel changed course and burst in.

"Laurel! Lass, for the love of… get back downstairs now!" Graelem wasn't just scowling at her, his face was at full glower. And that glower was the only thing he wore. *The only thing!*

He hastily grabbed the sheet off his bed and wrapped it around his waist to cover his lower body.

Her jaw dropped open and her gaze moved higher. Was she breathing? She didn't think so. And her heart was no longer calmly lodged within her breast, but violently sinking from her throat into her toes and lurching back upward.

He wore no shirt over his magnificently formed muscles.

A well-bred young lady would have turned away at this point, apologized sincerely, and promised never to… why quibble? A well-bred young lady would never have burst into a gentleman's chamber unannounced in the first place.

He still wore no shirt.

No trousers either, obviously, or he wouldn't have needed to wrap that sheet around himself for modesty. Hers, not his. He didn't seem the sort to be bashful about his appearance. Nor did he have reason to be.

His splinted leg was still exposed, and as he groaned and settled back onto his bed still groaning all the while because his pain was overwhelming, he accidentally gave her a glimpse of body bared all the way up to his naked hip.

She noticed this because she still hadn't turned away.

Her heart was still leaping and sinking and leaping again until she was certain it would spurt straight through the top of her head like a volcano spewing lava.

He sank into the pile of pillows propping his back, then yanked the thin sheet upward to securely cover everything below his chest. He reached for the nightshirt neatly folded beside him and hastily donned it to cover his big, broad shoulders.

But his sheet fell as he struggled with the nightshirt and she caught the ripple of his chest muscles as he worked to put it on. *Saints be praised!* Was there ever a better sight than this?

Now respectably clothed, he scowled at her.

She ought to have been repentant or contrite. Alas, she wasn't. Every girl of marriageable age ought to see such a sight as this at least once in her lifetime. Why not include it in a young lady's grand tour? Visit the Roman Coliseum, the canals of Venice, the palace at Versailles, the Acropolis in Greece, the hanging gardens of Babylon… and Graelem Dayne's chest.

Did that make her a sinner? Most likely. She responded to his scowl with an utterly blank stare. Her senses were in a muddle. She'd *seen* him. All of him. A nightshirt and a thin sheet could not expunge the shock of taut muscle that had been on glorious display a moment ago.

Laurel had never seen a naked man before. Did they all look this magnificent? Big and perfectly sculpted with lightly bronzed skin stretched over hard muscle? His muscles were still rippling beneath his nightshirt as he strained to sit up against his pillows. "Why were you howling?" she demanded to know, deciding it was best to go on the offensive because she was never going to admit to this man that she may have been in the wrong.

May have been?

There wasn't a solitary thing right about what she had done.

Laurel, Laurel, Laurel, you ninny. What other girl would have broken down a gentleman's door and barged in unannounced?

She now returned his glare with one of her own, although he might have noticed her distress since her eyes were bulging and her throat was puffing in and out like that of a bullfrog about to let loose with a croak.

Graelem yanked the spare blanket that sat neatly folded at the foot of his bed and spread it across the sheet, adding another protective layer over himself, as if that would do anything to erase the image scalded into her eyeballs.

Hah! It wasn't nearly enough to hide his splendid body. "Laurel, by all the blessed Scottish saints! *Get out.*"

Her brain was shouting the same thing, only she couldn't move.

How much time had elapsed? It couldn't have been more than ten or twenty seconds, although it felt like an eternity. Her uncle, who had been standing with his back to her while she barged in, washing his hands in a basin set on a table by the window, now faced her and let out an oath. "Laurel... I... what..." He was sputtering and shaking his head in dismay. "Did Brutus kick *you* in the head?"

He started toward her, his hands wet, lathered, and fisted at his sides.

Not that he would ever raise a hand to her. Never, for he was a healer and one of the kindest, most decent men she'd ever met. They were obviously curled into fists to subdue his frustration at her behavior. "Laurel," her uncle said, his voice softer in order to control his barely leashed anger, "there's no coming back from this. If gossip gets out—"

"I didn't mean... I thought you were cutting off his leg! I heard you arguing about something that must come off... or stay off... or be kept off." She turned to Graelem and responded to his continued glower with another one of her own. "We're betrothed, aren't we? And you're in agony, aren't you?"

She took a deep breath. Finally, a much needed breath! "Don't bother to deny it because it's etched in the stubborn contours of your face. I can't be expected to sit quietly downstairs nibbling on cake and sipping tea while my uncle hacks off your leg." *The leg I busted!*

"I have no intention of sawing off his leg." Her uncle rolled his eyes. "We were discussing the reason why Lord Moray should keep *his trousers* off for the next few days."

"His trousers?" Laurel's face suffused with heat.

Lord Moray let out a groaning laugh. "That's all it was, lass. Just my trousers."

She wanted to slink away and hide under the nearest rock. "I... I'm so sorry... I just thought you were about to lose your leg... and I couldn't let you suffer through that agony alone. I thought... if you gripped my hand..."

"You were worried about me?" Her explanation had obviously surprised him, for his anger faded and his expression softened, but only a little.

She nodded, closing her eyes a moment while struggling to hold back tears.

"Lass, you needn't have," he said with surprising gentleness when she once more met his gaze. "As for the cries you heard, I had earlier dismissed the footmen thinking I could manage undressing on my own. I found out the hard way that it wasn't as easy as I'd first thought. But I'm a stubborn dolt, as you've certainly realized by now, and refused to admit to your uncle that I needed help. The yelps you heard were merely from my clumsy attempts to remove my trousers." He shook his head and laughed softly. "I won't make that mistake next time. When help is offered, I'll accept it."

As Laurel watched him shift about in bed, an intense heat suffused through her entire body, not merely her cheeks. "Do you need anything now?" she asked and received an insistent *no* from both men as she took a step closer.

"No, but thank you. Lass, I think it's best if you just go away." He grinned lightly and ran a hand through the thick curls of his disheveled hair. There was something endearingly boyish about the way some strands curled at the nape of his neck and others wrapped around his ears.

She let out a sigh. "Of course. I've done nothing but cause you pain."

He appeared to soften at her look of hurt, which was ridiculous since he was the injured party and she was merely hindering his treatment. "Lass, I'd appreciate a visit from you tomorrow afternoon," he said as she was about to turn away. "Properly chaperoned, of course. Choose a book from my grandmother's library and you can read it to me. I'll enjoy the distraction."

From the pain of his broken leg, no doubt. "Have you taken your first dose of laudanum yet?"

His endearing grin turned sheepish. "Your uncle and I were discussing that as well."

Laurel couldn't help but laugh softly. "Discussing? Or arguing? You'll need it, Lord Moray, or the pain will steal your breath away. Please take it, if not for your sake, then for mine. I would never forgive myself if you endured more unbearable pain tonight because of me."

"Very well, lass. If it will make *you* feel better, then I'll take the laudanum." He arched a dark eyebrow. "Any other requests of me?"

Release me from my promise.

She ought to have asked, for he'd given her the perfect opening. She *wanted* to ask, for this marriage farce could not be permitted to continue for another day. She cleared her throat. Took a deep breath. "No."

CHAPTER 3

LAUREL SLOWLY MADE her way home, although it still didn't take her very long to walk from Eloise's townhouse to the Farthingale townhouse since they were neighbors and resided all of twenty paces from each other. The sun still shone and a light breeze caressed her cheeks as she climbed the front steps to her house.

Daisy must have been watching from the parlor window, for she came rushing out to meet her in the entry hall and caught her in a hearty embrace. "Laurel! The twins told me what happened! What are you going to do?"

"I don't know yet. Oh, Daisy! I've made such a mess of everything." She eased out of her sister's embrace. "Where are Mother and Father? I'll have to break the news to them."

"They already know. The twins tattled." Daisy rolled her vibrant blue eyes, those eyes that marked her sister as a Farthingale. Laurel's eyes weren't quite a perfect blue, but muddled with the lightest hint of green as though to mark *her* as different.

Laurel's hair was lighter as well, a confusing mix of amber, gold, and brown curls. Daisy and the twins had the traditional Farthingale dark hair. Fortunately, Rose's hair was also a mix of amber and gold, so Laurel didn't feel completely like the goose among the swans. And none of the Farthingale girls had proper society hair, those straight, blonde, never-a-curl-out-of-place locks that were the mark of a well-bred young lady. No, they all had thick, wavy hair with curls that were as spirited as they were.

"They tattled?" Laurel shook her head in confusion, for she and her sisters were as close as could be and always protected each other. "Why would they do such a thing?"

"They didn't mean to betray you. I think they believed the family elders would lighten your punishment if they were given the chance to digest the startling news before you returned." Daisy nodded toward their father's library. The doors were closed. "The elders are discussing what to do with you now."

"Oh, dear. Already?" Why hadn't they waited for her to return and mount her own defense? But no, closed doors meant the family council had heard more than enough. "Who's in there with Father and Mother?"

"Everyone, except Uncle George since he's still with the gentleman you almost killed. And Uncle Harrison's off fighting Napoleon, of course. But the other aunts and uncles are in there, Rupert, Hortensia, Julia, and all of Father's cousins who came down to London for the season."

Oxfordshire Farthingales, Yorkshire Farthingales, Devonshire… the pulse at the base of Laurel's throat began to beat wildly. "Everyone? Already? They don't move that quickly even when Mrs. Mayhew's renowned Yorkshire pudding is served." She shook her head. "How can they decide anything when they don't know all the facts?"

"When has that stopped them?" Daisy let out a grim, mirthless laugh. "What are you going to tell Devlin? He'll be devastated."

Laurel's heart, already beaten and bedraggled, sank again. "I can't tell him anything just yet."

Daisy let out a soft gasp. "But you must. It won't take long for gossip to spread among the *ton*. He ought to hear the news from you first. Poor Dev! He'll be devastated. He's so devoted to you."

"I'll tell him this evening at Lady Harrow's musicale, assuming I'm still permitted to attend." She shook her head and sighed. "I think Father would like to lock me in a dungeon and toss away the key. I'm not sure that I blame him." She inhaled lightly as the door to the library opened. "Daisy, if it goes badly for me, I'll need you to get word to Dev."

"Of course. You can rely on me." She gave Laurel another quick hug. "I'll do whatever you ask."

❦

GRAELEM WAS IN a laudanum-induced fog, slipping in and out of consciousness and fighting like hell to stay awake when the door to his chamber flew open and Laurel ran in. By all the Scottish saints! Had the girl never learned the art of knocking? "Lass, what are you doing here?"

Even in his present state, he knew that only a few hours had passed since the accident. He hated being under the influence of laudanum, for it badly clouded his senses. Why else would his heart shoot into his throat at the mere sight of Laurel? Why else would he think her the prettiest girl in existence even though she was modestly dressed, now wearing a simple pale green day gown. The prim white lace trimming along her collar drew his gaze to her heaving breasts and… *hell*… that *thud* was his tongue hitting the floor. She was beautiful.

He forced his gaze upward in a vain attempt to control all manner of improper thoughts now bouncing around his befogged brain. He caught the angry flash of her eyes and their sudden softening, and groaned silently because that softness would be his undoing. But he had to resist her considerable temptation. He needed Laurel and wasn't about to let her go.

He waited for her to say something, because she'd obviously barged in here for a reason. When she didn't, he took his time studying her, noting the gentle curve of her neck and the wayward dark gold curls that clung to her pale skin. Her hair was drawn back in a simple bun that just begged to be unbound.

He'd give his right arm to be the man to set those vibrant curls free and watch them cascade over her slender shoulders in a sultry waterfall of gold.

Great. He already had a busted leg and was now willing to lose an arm over the girl. There would be nothing left of him by the time she was through with him.

Still worth it.

His gaze fell back to her ample breasts because they were still heaving and… who gave a damn why? They were heaving and blessedly exquisite and… no, he had to concentrate. He doubted she was here because she desired him.

First of all, he wasn't at his enticing best at the moment. Second, he was never at his enticing best, being too much of an oaf ever to attract a respectable young lady, much less one as exquisite as Laurel.

He felt for his sheet to make certain he was *under* it and not sprawled atop it. Ah, yes. Good. Safely under it and the important parts securely covered up.

Laurel let out a sob and sank onto the stool at his bedside. "Lass, what's happened? Has someone hurt you?"

She shook her head, and he couldn't tell if it meant yes or no or a little of both. "My father is going to sell Brutus." She sobbed again and followed it with a hiccup. "He didn't mean to run you down. You must believe me. What happened was all my fault and I'd do anything to take back those few moments."

Hell, he didn't know what to do to calm her down. Completely lacking in ideas, he ran his fingers lightly through her hair to nudge the loose curls off her tearful face. "I know, lass. He's a fine horse." *For a beast who almost killed me.*

"He's the best! I picked him out myself and raised him from a foal." She took in a great gulp of air. "Brutus would never harm me or my sisters, and he never meant to harm you. It's just that he's used to a daily exercise regimen and I… we… my groomsman… didn't have a chance to take him for his usual early morning gallop, so he was a little friskier than usual by the time we started for the park."

She took in another gulp of air and continued. "And I was late for… well, it isn't important. The point is, my father will sell him and I'll never see Brutus again. And I'm not certain if by 'sell' he means he'll order Brutus destroyed!"

"Would you like me to put in a word with your father?" Lord, he never realized he was such a fool for a pair of tearful blue eyes! Ocean blue with turbulent swirls of green that had the power to draw a man in and drag him under like a dangerous riptide.

Her lips spread into a smile. "Would you? Just to make sure he won't order Brutus put down. And to be sure he'll find a good home for Brutus with someone who loves horses and knows how to care for them. Someone who'll appreciate and love Brutus as I do. Or perhaps you could convince my father that no one could ever love or care for Brutus as I do and it would be a terrible shame to punish Brutus for my mistake and that's what would happen if he were taken from me. I'd be ever so grateful."

The stream of words took a moment to wend their way through his laudanum-fogged brain. "How grateful?"

"What?" She inhaled lightly, slipped off the stool, and took a step back to stand just out of his reach. Did she think he was going to grab her and force her into his bed? Much as he would enjoy having her beside him… under him… he wasn't so far gone as to believe it would ever happen. Or so far gone as to ever force her.

He'd phrased his question badly, that's all. He wasn't even certain what he wished from her beyond a convenient marriage.

Perhaps he was hoping she'd show him the same care and concern she held for her damn horse. It was a foolish notion, of course. She'd raised the stallion from a foal while she'd known him for a few hours at most. What time was it anyway?

"Because if you think I'm going to sacrifice my body —"

He reached over and drew her back to his bedside, the quick motion sending a blinding slash of pain up his leg and into his temples. "Let's get one thing straight here and now, lass. Unlike your horse, I am not a brute. I will not have you come to my bed other than willingly. I will not have you kiss me other than willingly. I give you this promise now." *Oh, bollocks. Shut up, you fool! Your brain isn't functioning. Don't make her any promises.* "I promise that I will never force you to provide sexual favors to me. Those I will gladly take, but only with your freely given consent."

"Which I shall never give." She jerked her hand out of his grasp and tipped her chin up in defiance. "I ought to have known better than to come to you with my concerns. I had thought… I'd hoped… obviously, I was wrong."

"No, lass," he called out as she turned to storm out of the room as quickly as she'd stormed in. "You came to me for help and that's what I'll give you. I'll speak to your father."

She stopped at his door and stood with her back to him for a long moment, then slowly turned to face him. A look of hope glistened in her eyes. "You will?"

Her soft gaze shot like a lance straight through his heart.

His own lance, the one between his thighs, had jolted to attention the moment she barged in and was now hard and throbbing and in desperate need of easing. The blasted appendage seemed to take on a life of its own and could not contain its joy at the sight of Laurel.

He needed to get his lust under control.

Hell, no more laudanum for me.

"I apologize if I spoke out of turn," he said, glancing at his leg. "I'm not quite myself at the moment."

"I understand. Pain does odd things to one's system." She took another step toward him but remained half a room's length away. Much too far for his liking, but he'd shocked the innocent, a tactical mistake for which he was solely to blame. She'd come to him seeking help and he'd turned it into a bid for a sexual encounter. What was he thinking?

Obviously, he wasn't thinking at all.

He was in too much pain to do anything, much less give her a proper kiss… or a highly improper kiss, which was what he'd wanted to do the moment he'd set eyes on her. Her smile was doing the oddest things to his insides.

Bollocks.

A simple kiss from this girl would never satisfy him. He hungered for more, ached to capture her pink lips and feel their generous give against his mouth. *Don't look lower. Don't, you idiot!*

But he did, because a man would have to be dull as a donkey to resist the allure of Laurel's body. Her curves were heavenly perfection. He wanted to kiss his way down her body, down those firm and shapely breasts, along her slim hips, and long, slender legs that could wrap around—

Damn, he was doing it again. Allowing his lower head to take control of his thoughts and rouse hot sensations when his upper head, also known as his barely functioning brain, needed to remain in firm control. "I'll send him a note within the hour."

Her smile was as bright as the sunshine streaming in through his bedchamber window. "I'll fetch you Eloise's writing paper. She won't mind."

"Lass—"

"Yes?"

"You've won this day. No need for you to do more. I'll take care of the rest. Go away."

She blushed. "Of course. You must think I'm the most meddlesome creature, and you'd be right. We Farthingales can't seem to help ourselves. We see a situation and must jump in, whether or not asked." She gave him the gentlest smile. "I know you'll be true to your word. Thank you. I'll go home now."

Her blush deepened and she began to walk toward him. *What the hell?* Didn't she realize that the door was in the opposite direction? "My parents think I'm repenting in my room, which I will do now that we've settled matters. But first…" She stopped at his side and bent over him. "This I give willingly and with my heartfelt appreciation." She kissed him on the cheek, her lips sweet and warm against the beginning stubble of a beard on his face.

He said nothing, just waited for her to leave his room before sinking back against his pillows and allowing that disobedient lower head of his to spring to attention and express its profound joy over Laurel's innocent peck on the cheek.

He was going to stick a keg of gunpowder under that bottle of laudanum and blow it up before it did more damage to his already addled senses.

He glared at the medicine bottle on his night stand, sitting within easy reach. "No, not taking any more of you."

Which was why he was in agony by the time Laurel's father entered his bedchamber an hour later in response to the note he'd sent over. John Farthingale did not look happy as he greeted Graelem with a politeness he clearly did not feel. "My lord, seems we have a situation."

"Are you referring to your daughter or her horse?" Graelem

realized the question sounded glib and impertinent. "Mr. Farthingale, my situation is such that I cannot let your daughter out of our... er, betrothal... as unusual as the circumstances surrounding it happen to be."

Laurel's father frowned. "Unusual? I would call it alarming. You took advantage of my daughter."

"She almost killed me."

Her father arched an eyebrow, and the hint of a grin appeared on his lips. "All the more reason to avoid her at all costs. Surely, you can't be serious. Until this morning, you'd never set eyes upon my Laurel. And now you want her as your wife? I'm a great admirer of Lady Dayne," he said, referring to Graelem's grandmother, "and am somewhat relieved that she vouches for your good character, but I cannot permit this wedding to happen."

"I hope to convince you otherwise. Have a seat, Mr. Farthingale," Graelem said, motioning to the stool by his bedside, which seemed inadequate for a man of his prominence. "Or shall I ring for a footman to bring you a chair?"

"I'm fine standing." Laurel's father crossed his arms over his chest and tossed him a look of anger mingled with impatience, his momentary humor now faded as they moved on to the more serious discussion.

Graelem noticed a resemblance between father and daughter, especially in their scowls. "I'll ring for that chair, Mr. Farthingale. While I will not relent on the marriage to your daughter, I hope to address some of your concerns in that regard. I would also like to discuss your plans for Brutus. Laurel loves that horse, you know. It would break her heart to lose him. Perhaps we can agree on a solution to that."

The comment obviously surprised Laurel's father. "The beast almost cut short your life. Why do you care what happens to him?"

Graelem ran a hand roughly through his rumpled hair. "I don't, but your daughter does. So that makes it my problem. She doesn't like me much right now. In truth, she probably detests me. I don't know if I'll ever change her opinion of me, but I'll do my best. I'm not very proud of myself either. Despite what she thinks of me, I'm not an ogre. I want to make her happy and saving that horse is a first step in the right direction."

Laurel's father dropped his hands to his sides. "I think I will have a chair after all."

Within moments, one of Eloise's footmen had delivered a suitably elegant, red silk cushioned chair and set it by Graelem's bedside. Eloise's butler delivered a tray of tea and cakes, as though John Farthingale had been invited for a social call and was expected to remain a while.

Obviously, this was his grandmother's meddlesome way of encouraging conversation between the two men. "Help yourself, Mr. Farthingale. I'm afraid I can't join in. The laudanum's still working its way through my system and I don't trust what it will do to me if I attempt to eat." Graelem's gaze darted to his night stand and the medicine bottle and spoon still set atop it. *Must find that keg of gunpowder.* "Can't stand the vile substance. I prefer to wrestle with the pain."

"I'll pass on the tea and cakes as well. Don't have much of an appetite at the moment. Having five strong-minded daughters will do that to a man." He leaned forward and studied Graelem. "You don't appear deranged, so will you kindly explain to me why you are determined to marry my Laurel?"

CHAPTER 4

LAUREL SAT IN the Farthingale parlor on the blue silk settee beside her mother while assorted aunts, uncles, and sisters sat on the sofa and chairs opposite them waiting for her father to return from his meeting with the man who had just taken control of her life. Laurel tried to remain calm, but the task was impossible and she couldn't help but fidget in her seat. "What's taking them so long? Father's been there for over an hour."

"I should think it's a good sign," Uncle Rupert said, giving her an encouraging smile that peeked out from under his enormous black moustache.

"Father is brilliant," Dillie added rather hopefully. "He'll convince Lord Moray that he's made a terrible mistake."

"Your father is brilliant," their mother agreed, brushing back a lock of her dark hair that was beginning to show traces of gray, "but as to fixing Lord Moray's *mistake*, I'm not certain it will be so easy. Laurel, if one overlooks your impulsive behavior of this morning, you have much to recommend you to a man. Beauty, wealth, good manners… usually."

The tall windows opened onto the garden, allowing the gentle scent of budding roses to waft into the room on the warm afternoon breeze. Oh, if only her life were as gentle and easy as this soft breeze! "Farthingales marry for love," Laurel insisted. "I won't break with our family tradition."

"Then you'd better fall in love with Lord Moray," Lily pointed out with a logical sensibility that only she possessed. At the moment, it was not appreciated.

Laurel rolled her eyes. "In less than thirty days? I hardly think so."

The parlor was Laurel's favorite room in the house and had a lovely fireplace that was lit on colder days but was presently clean and hidden behind a fire screen decorated in blue roses. The sofa, chairs, drapes, and oriental carpets were in compatible shades of blue silk and damask that blended warmly with the polished mahogany decorative tables that adorned the room. Gleaming silver candelabra and assorted delicate vases and figurines filled the cozy room.

Unfortunately, the room was also presently filled with Farthingales who were now staring at her as though actually considering Lily's ridiculous observation. "I will not fall in love with Eloise's grandson," she said between clenched teeth.

Aunt Julia moved to her side. "Why not? I hear he's rather handsome."

In a big, oafish way. It was of no moment that the sight of his naked body still sent bolts of heat into her cheeks and other parts of her body that could not be mentioned.

"At least give him a chance," Uncle Rupert muttered. "You owe him that much. I'd expect no less if someone tried to kill me."

Laurel curled her hands into fists. "I wasn't trying to kill the lout."

"Why are you calling him a lout?" Dillie cast her a speculative glance. "You did say he was handsome. Lily and I heard you."

"So what?" She shifted uncomfortably on the settee. "He's still a lout."

"Where's Daisy?" her mother asked, suddenly noticing that her middle daughter was absent and momentarily distracting everyone's attention.

Lily opened her mouth to speak. "She's—"

"—meeting a friend in the park," Laurel chimed in before the snoopy twin slipped and revealed that Daisy had gone to Hyde Park to deliver a note to Devlin. Since Devlin was almost as much a friend to Daisy as he was to her, it wasn't really a lie. "A quick visit. I'm sure she'll return at any moment."

"Amos escorted her," Dillie chimed in, referring to Amos Mayhew, the amiable young footman who'd been in service to the Farthingale family for five years now. He was the son of their long-time cook, Mrs. Mayhew, and nephew to their coachman, Abner Mayhew. Amos also helped out with the horses whenever Abner, who was getting on in years, wasn't up to the task.

Laurel had considered asking Amos to put in a good word for Brutus because he'd always gotten along with the beast. But Amos had scrambled out of the house, all too eager to be kept out of the family unpleasantness. He was a wise young man, apparently much wiser than she.

Laurel's keen ears picked up the sound of their front door opening. She shot off the settee. "It must be Father!"

Dillie gave her a supportive smile. "I hope he has good news for you."

Unfortunately, the frown on her father's face as he strode into the parlor had Laurel's heart sinking. "He's refused to see reason, hasn't he? See Dillie, I told you he was a lout."

Her father crossed the room to stand beside her mother. "He's an unusual man, Sophie. I'm not certain what to make of him yet."

"Oh, dear. What else can we do, John?" Laurel's mother began to nibble her lower lip. "Your daughter simply can't marry this stranger."

"No, she can't," he seemed to agree.

Laurel let out a sigh of relief. "Thank you, Papa! You're the—"

Her father held up a hand to stop her in mid-sentence. "Hear me out, Laurel. Lord Moray has persuaded me not to have Brutus destroyed. But neither will you be permitted to keep him. I'm selling that beast to Lord Moray."

"What? Why, that wretch! Has he agreed to do the dirty work for you?" She marched to the fireplace and picked up one of the heavy irons. "I'll show him. If he thinks to harm a hair on Brutus' mane, I'll shove this thing so far up his—"

"Laurel! That will be quite enough." Her father grabbed the fireplace implement out of her hand. "Sit down and behave. Have all these years of etiquette lessons been a waste?"

"He plans to kill my horse! Am I to smile sweetly and allow

it?" She let out an indignant huff. "I think not!"

Her father set his hands on her shoulders and gently but firmly nudged her back into her seat beside her mother. "Think again, child. He has no intention of destroying Brutus. He plans to take the beast back to Scotland as soon as he's fit to travel and will give him the run of the Moray pasture lands. In exchange for that favor to you—"

"Ha! Do you expect me to trust his motives?" She shot to her feet again because one could not be properly indignant while seated.

Her father nudged her down again. "That isn't my concern. Trust him or don't trust him, that's up to you. But the rest is up to me, so after due deliberation with the family elders…" He turned to glance at her mother and the assorted aunts and uncles gathered in the suddenly stuffy parlor, and received approving nods from all of them. "After due deliberation with the elders and with Lord Moray, here's what is to become of you for the next month."

Laurel opened her mouth to protest, but her father's warning frown silenced her.

"You are not permitted any social engagements until such time as Lord Moray's leg is sufficiently healed to enable him to accept similar invitations."

Her eyes rounded in dismay. "But that could take the entire month!"

"So be it. He's young and strong. Hopefully he'll recover sooner."

"And until he does, am I to be kept a prisoner in my own home?" She wasn't going to stand for that. Nor would Devlin. She'd send him another note and invite him over so they could work out a plan. The situation was impossible. Devlin needed her. Lord Moray would easily forget her.

"Not quite. You'll be permitted out every afternoon to visit Lord Moray. Properly chaperoned, of course. It is my hope that you'll get to know him. If in three weeks' time you still wish to be disentangled from your betrothal, I'll appeal to Lord Moray again."

Her mouth gaped open. "Do you mean to say that you haven't outright refused him?"

"No, not yet." He strode to the small desk in the corner and lifted a decanter off a silver tray. He poured himself a glass of sherry and unceremoniously gulped the whole thing down.

She had never in her life seen her father do such a thing. He was obviously rattled, and it was all her fault. Still, it seemed a harsh punishment for a simple accident. "Oh, and another thing," he said, turning back to her and pinning her with his sternest glare. "You are not to have any visitors in that time. No young lady friends or gentleman callers will step foot in this house for the next three weeks."

"Crumpets," Dillie said in a whisper.

"With sugar on top," Lily added with a nod. "This is worse than the punishment I received when I brought explosives into the house."

❧

BY NOON THE following day, Laurel couldn't wait to be allowed out of the house, even if it was to walk next door and sit with Eloise's oafish grandson for the remainder of the afternoon. The morning rain, little more than a light shower, had passed quickly and the sun now shone brightly amid white tufted clouds. She hated to be trapped indoors on what was turning into a fine day, but Lord Moray was trapped as well.

Perhaps they could settle by the window in his room, open it wide to at least gaze out on the beautiful day.

Perhaps I could shove him out of that window.

"Be nice to him," her mother had suggested over breakfast this morning, catching her in the guilty thought and muttering some nonsense about flies and honey. Or was it bees and honey? No matter. She had tried being nice and wound up with an unwanted betrothal because of it. She was not going to encourage the man. She wanted him to rue the day he'd ever set eyes upon her.

However, she had no choice but to be nice to him today

because he truly had saved Brutus. She would restrain her murderous thoughts. Tomorrow was an altogether different matter.

Tomorrow, her delicate lace gloves would come off.

She had already written a note to Devlin about her ridiculously unfair confinement and hidden it in her chest of drawers. Daisy had agreed to secretly hand it to him the next time she rode in Hyde Park, which was something she often did with their cousin William and Aunt Julia when weather permitted, so no one would think anything of it.

The task was easy enough, and Daisy was a loyal sister, eager to help out in any way she could. Laurel hated to involve her, but there was little risk of her getting caught. William always ogled the young ladies on their fine horses. His attention would be cast everywhere but on his cousin. Julia always enjoyed the latest *on dit* with friends she encountered while out riding. The pair could be counted on to ignore her sister.

Still, Laurel suffered a pang of guilt as she entered the bedchamber she now shared with Daisy to retrieve her shawl and the already penned letter. "Daisy, you don't have to do this for me. I'd feel awful if you got into trouble over helping me."

Daisy spared a final glance in the mirror and smoothed out the skirt of her elegant black riding habit that was a shade darker than her hair. "I want to help out. You've helped me so many times I've lost count." She rolled her big blue eyes. "It's the least I can do for you."

"But—"

She put a gentle hand on Laurel's shoulder. "We sisters are determined to marry for love. Since you love Devlin, I'll do all I can to help you to that end. There's nothing more to be said."

"Thank you." But Laurel hesitated another moment before handing over the note. This was her battle and it somehow felt underhanded to involve Daisy, of all her sisters. Daisy was the good daughter, the perfect middle child who was always obedient and sought to please the family. "I won't be angry or upset if you change your mind."

Daisy slipped the note up the sleeve of her jacket. "I have no intention of changing my mind. I know you all think I'm a paragon of virtue... well, I do love the family and I'm much less adventurous than you, Rose, or the twins. But I'm no coward. And I certainly won't stand by and do nothing while one of my sisters is in trouble."

She gave Laurel a quick hug. "Don't be late for your visit with Lord Moray. You must tell me everything that happens between you. As you know, this paragon," she teased, referring to herself, "loves gossip."

Laurel laughed and kissed her lightly on the cheek. "I love you, Daisy. Do be careful."

They walked downstairs together, and Laurel waited for her sister to ride out with the others before heading over to Eloise's home to visit her grandson. Eloise had agreed to act as chaperone for the next few days, but Laurel wasn't pleased with the prospect. She adored the kindly older woman and knew the feeling was reciprocated. But since Eloise adored her, she was no ally in this campaign. Eloise wanted her to make a match with her grandson.

Eloise also knew her very well, which could pose a problem. Although Laurel planned on being nice to Lord Moray today, she meant to be petty and insufferable the next day and the next. Eloise would know it wasn't her true nature and might assure her grandson that it was only a pretense. She didn't want the kindly dowager undermining her efforts to end the betrothal.

She stood on the front steps of Eloise's home and tipped her face up to the sun for she would enjoy little of it in the coming month and had no desire to rush inside. All too soon, the front door swung open. "Good afternoon, Watling."

"Good afternoon, Miss Laurel." Eloise's butler stepped aside to allow her in. She briefly wondered what he thought of this impossible situation, but the man's face was as set as a thousand-year-old rock and he revealed nothing in his expression. "Lady Dayne is in the library."

She followed Watling, although she knew the house very well and often made her way in on her own, for Eloise had become quite good friends with the Farthingales. She and her sisters thought of her as the grandmother they'd never known. Similarly,

Eloise thought of them as the granddaughters she'd never had. Eloise had two sons and they in turn had only sired sons. Not a single female offspring in the lot.

"Ah, Laurel. You're right on time." Eloise beamed at her. "I'll order refreshments to be brought up to Graelem's quarters. In the meantime, choose a book from my library. I think he'll enjoy Shakespeare's *Henry V* or perhaps—"

"Poetry. He seems just the sort of gentleman to adore poems. Long ones. That seem endless." She trailed a finger along the spine of several tomes until settling on Walter Scott's *Marmion*. She'd never read it, but knew it had been quite popular a few years ago. "Let's give this a try."

"*Marmion?*" Eloise shook her head and chuckled. "You are determined to make his life a misery, aren't you? But my dear, even though Graelem detests poetry, I'm certain he will endure anything that springs from your lips. Men are odd that way."

Laurel frowned. Endure? She wanted him writhing and screaming in boredom. She didn't want him to endure. It wasn't at all what she'd hoped to hear. She leafed through the pages, her eye immediately drawn to a couple of lines. "Oh, what a tangled web we weave, when first we practice to deceive." She slammed the book shut and moved on. "It won't do."

Laurel finally decided upon *The Song of Roland* and its four thousand lines of poetry. Eloise shook her head and sighed. "I do wish you'd give Graelem a chance. It isn't at all nice of you to force poetry down his throat."

Laurel tipped her chin up in annoyance. "It isn't at all nice of him to force marriage down mine."

Eloise sighed again. "I'm not suggesting what he did is right. But it could work out if only you'd give him a chance."

"I'm giving him as much of one as he gave me." Having gotten in the final word, she marched upstairs to his quarters and knocked on the door.

"Enter," he called, and Laurel felt an inexplicable warmth steal through her at the sound of his deep, commanding voice. She dismissed her response as a case of nerves. Or incipient dyspepsia. But as she walked in and saw him in his bed, sitting up with his back propped against six or seven pillows and his broken leg elevated, she felt a twinge of guilt.

More than a mere twinge of it—a hefty wallop.

He looked handsomer than she remembered and obviously in a lot of pain. "Have you been taking your medicine?" She set the book down on the stool beside his bed and reached for the bottle of laudanum on his night stand.

"Leave it, lass. That concoction tastes like the bottom of my boots after a day of mucking out the stable. I'll not be drinking it."

"But how else are you to dull the pain?" It wasn't any fun taking revenge on a man already in agony. Not that she planned to do her worst today. No, she was grateful to him for saving Brutus and had only planned the mildest of tortures. Tomorrow she'd be back in stride.

"I'll concentrate on that pretty face of yours. The sight of you will do more good for me than any medicine known to man." He cast her a boyish grin that seemed to turn up the heat in the room. Or inside her.

"I'll open the window for you. It's a beautiful day and…" His window was already open and a pleasant breeze wafted into the room. "Oh, it's already open." She fussed a moment with the drapes that were already drawn aside to allow in the air and sunshine.

"Still warm, lass?"

She turned to give him a snide retort, but he chose that moment to cross his arms over his chest and she became distracted by the play of his muscles beneath the white lawn of his nightshirt. His skin looked golden in contrast to that pale white shirt. "What?"

He grinned wryly, no doubt noticing the blush now staining her cheeks. "I'm feeling a little warm myself."

Oh, drat! Did he think she was affected by him? So what if she was? He was incredibly handsome, even if he was a big oaf. "I've brought you a book of poetry. It will take us weeks to get through it." That ought to wipe the smug grin off his face.

When she returned to his side, he reached out and grabbed the book she had chosen. *The Song of Roland.* Not a bad choice, but I don't think you'll like it. Do you know it, lass?"

"Everyone knows of it." Did he think she was an uneducated ninny? How dare he consider such a thing!

He set the book back on the stool and trained his gaze on her. "But have you read it yet?"

Was it getting hot again? That warm glint in his eye and the slight upward tilt of his lips, as though he understood her ploy and found it amusing, was wreaking havoc with her composure. "No, I haven't read it. That's why I'm so eager to share it with you." She forced her lips into a cool, responsive smile.

He chuckled and shook his head. "I think you're eager to cleave me in half with a broadsword, that's what I think. But don't do it yet, lass. Show a little patience. Ah, Grandmama. How lovely to see you. Come to protect me from Laurel, have you? She has the look of a bloodthirsty warrior."

Eloise marched into the room and took a seat beside the door. "She's delightful. Stop teasing her, Graelem."

Laurel was surprised that Eloise did not plan to sit beside them. "Won't you join us by the bed?"

"No, dear." She tossed Graelem a warning scowl. "Your father and Graelem may have worked out this arrangement, but you and Graelem will never get to know each other if I'm sitting right beside you. So it's best that I stay out of the way as much as I can."

"Eloise, this is ridiculous." Laurel crossed the room intending to move Eloise's chair, but the stubborn old dowager wouldn't be budged. "You're his grandmother and a countess, not my governess or a serving maid to be shunted into a corner. I don't treat Gladys," she said, referring to her own maid, "this rudely."

In this, Eloise appeared quite stubborn. "I'm merely a dowager countess. Gives me no standing whatsoever."

"You could be a fishmonger's wife and we'd all love you," Laurel said in exasperation, turning to her grandson for assistance. What she encountered was a look of genuine gratitude and admiration. What had she just said to warrant approval from the oaf? Oh, she'd admitted that she loved his grandmother. Well, it was true. She had no intention of hiding it.

"Lass," he said with a gentleness that astonished her, "Eloise can be a disagreeable old battle-axe when she wants to be. You won't win this fight. But thank you. I can see why she adores you and your sisters. You have kind hearts."

Laurel wanted to throw her hands up in disgust. She wasn't special or kind. She simply wanted out of this betrothal. She crossed back to his side, lifted the book from the stool, and sank down in its place. "The Song of Roland," she said, opening the pages and beginning to read.

She'd only gotten four lines in when Watling strode in, rolling a tea cart before him. "Lemonade and pies," he announced.

Laurel slammed shut her book. Her attempt to bore Lord Moray into insanity wasn't working anyway. He was reciting the lines along with her, obviously knowing them by heart. All four thousand of them? It wasn't possible. She turned to Eloise. "I thought you said your grandson detested poetry."

Eloise shrugged. "I thought he did."

"Lass, you simply could have asked me. I would have told you that I do abhor most of that drivel, but this poem is about Charlemagne's campaign to conquer Spain and claim it for his empire. The story is about battle and betrayal. Lots of military tactics and murder for boys to love. My uncle, the Earl of Trent, read it to me and my cousins during a summer I spent with them."

She tipped her head, now curious, and couldn't resist asking, "How old were you?"

"I was all of nine years old," he said with a wistful smile and a faraway gaze as he momentarily drifted back in time. "My cousin Alexander was the eldest and quite grown up at all of ten years old going on eleven. His brother Gabriel had just turned eight. Their father read to us a little each night before we went to bed." He shook his head and chuckled. "The ladies did not approve of us dreaming of blood, gore, and death."

"I should say not," Eloise intoned from her corner of the room.

"But it was one of my fondest memories," he said softly.

Laurel's heart began to beat a little faster, and she stifled the urge to lean close and wrap her arms around him. He'd said that his uncle had read these stories to him. Not his father. And what about his mother? Was she one of "the ladies" he referred to? "I'm sure it upset your mother, as it would any woman who wished their children to have sweet dreams."

Neither Eloise nor Lord Moray responded to that remark, but they did exchange a glance. Had something happened to his mother? Or was she not the caring sort? Had she mistreated him?

"Laurel, would you mind pouring me a glass of lemonade?" There was a sadness in his voice that didn't just tug at her heart, it practically wrenched that beating organ from her bosom and slammed it to the floor repeatedly.

Unable to respond, she simply nodded.

She handed him the glass and turned to Eloise. "Would…" She paused to clear the lump suddenly caught in her throat. "Would you care for some?"

"No, dear. Just attend to Graelem. I'll forage for myself."

"Lord Moray, I—"

"Laurel, there's no need for formality between us. Just call me Graelem. Save that stuffy nonsense for *ton* functions. And I'll not have you referring to me as 'my lord' or 'Lord Moray' in our marriage either. You're to be my wife. My equal."

Her mouth dropped open.

"You're gawking at me again, lass. Ah, it's that 'equals in the marriage' I was just talking about. That's the Scottish influence, I fear. We seem to think more highly of our women than the English do."

Laurel snapped her mouth shut. "But you're English, too."

He nodded. "I was raised in both worlds, which makes me suitable for neither. I'm too Scottish for the English and too English for the Scots."

Laurel clutched the book as though it were a shield designed to protect her heart. She had yet to sit beside him for an hour, and he was fast becoming someone she would consider a friend were circumstances other than they were. "I do understand that sense of not belonging. My father and his brothers raised themselves up from the working class to become the respected men they are today. They hate being called gentlemen because it was hard work and rigorous study that got them their success, not idleness or drinking at their clubs."

Graelem regarded her in a manner that encouraged her to continue, so she did. "My sisters and I were raised in Coniston. That's in the Lake District. We only came to London because my parents felt we ought to have a proper introduction into society." She brushed back a stray lock of her hair and sighed. "No amount of tutoring will ever turn me into a biddable young lady. Nor my sisters, for that matter. Except perhaps Daisy. She's naturally sweet and always behaves." *Almost always.* "I'm sure she'll find a sober judge to marry and raise the most obedient children ever created on this earth."

He glanced over her head at his grandmother and grinned. "Well, if Daisy ever decides to live a little more adventurously, I have a rakish cousin she might like to meet. Gabriel, the scrappy eight-year-old I mentioned."

She was trying to disentangle herself from Graelem Dayne and had no desire to entertain a marriage between her sister and Graelem's cousin, especially if he was an adventurer and a rogue. "I think I'll go downstairs and find some other reading material."

"Stay, lass. No books for now. I'd rather learn more about you."

Laurel ignored him and left the room. She didn't care to know more about Graelem for fear that she might grow to like him. However, she was curious about the look he had given Eloise when she had mentioned his mother. She'd ask Eloise later.

~❦~

GRAELEM EASED AGAINST his pillows and let out an anguished groan the moment Laurel left his quarters. The impudent girl looked so damn delectable that it took all his control to keep from taking her into his arms and kissing her up and down her outrageously beautiful body. The innocent could drive any man to sin.

She wasn't purposely trying to arouse him. Quite the opposite, she was doing her best to wriggle out of their betrothal. As far as he was concerned, she was failing miserably, for the more he saw of her, the more he liked her. She seemed genuinely unaware of her charms and used no artifice to enhance her appearance. Her pale blue gown was simply designed and its only adornment was a bit of white lace fabric at the squared-off collar.

The pale blue of her gown somehow intensified the blue-green swirls of her eyes, and the sun filtering in through the open window made her amber-gold hair glisten. Once again, her hair was bound in a bun that was casually pinned at the nape of her neck. He still ached to pull those pins out and watch her thick curls tumble down her back.

He glanced upward. *Lord, isn't a broken leg punishment enough? Must you also torture me by making her so beautiful?* He could look his fill but never touch, not now that he'd made the girl that idiotic promise never to set a hand on her without her permission.

Had any able-bodied man ever made a stupider promise?

Eloise cleared her throat, reminding him that his grandmother was still in the room and intent on dutifully serving as Laurel's chaperone. There would be no misbehaving, even if Laurel were willing, that was for damn sure. No matter. Laurel would never be willing. Why would she be? No doubt she already had a dozen gentlemen eager to marry her. "Dear boy," Eloise began slowly, her lips pursed in thought—or was it disapproval? "She's right, you know. You cannot force her to marry you."

"I don't have a choice."

"And I know for a fact that you do. She isn't a pet dog. You can't simply train her to sit and obey." Her lips were still pursed, definitely in disapproval.

He laughed lightly. "In the brief time I've known her, I would say that Laurel obeys no man. She listens only to her heart, much to her father's dismay. But I like that about her. She thinks for herself and she has a kind and generous nature."

Eloise's eyes rounded in obvious surprise. "How can you tell?"

"For one thing, she dotes on you, sincerely cares about you. Most young women would not concern themselves with an old dowager unless they were trying to get something out of her. Laurel's quite the opposite. She adores you as though you were her own grandmother and looks to your comfort, not hers."

He laughed lightly again as he continued. "And even though she detests me, she still can't help but leap to my rescue whenever she sees that I'm in pain. As for the rest of it, I don't know. There's something about the girl. She's open and honest, makes her easy to understand. Not that I understand a damn thing about women."

He eased up against his pillows, wincing at the pain that reared its ugly head each time he moved. "As I said, despite wanting to shoot me for tricking her into a betrothal, there have been occasional moments when she's wanted to put her arms around me to comfort me."

"That was only yesterday while you were writhing on the street."

He shrugged, trying to sound casual, but his voice came out gruffer than intended and with a raspy edge to it. "Her touch felt good, Grandmama." *So good.*

"Oh, dear," she said in a whisper. There was a tremor to her voice, as though his words had affected her. He hadn't meant to distress her, but he knew that he had when her eyes began to glisten with tears. "You never knew a parent's love. I should have taken up the slack after your mother died and your father…" Her voice trailed off, for his father—Eloise's youngest son—had abandoned him.

They'd had this conversation before. He'd never blamed her for his situation, but she always insisted on taking the blame. He sighed. "You were always loving and kind to me."

"Not kind enough. I should have done more. I should have asked your uncle," she said, referring to her eldest son, the Earl of Trent, "to take you in. But we never realized how unhappy you were growing up with your mother's family. At the time we thought it made perfect sense for you to live with them since you were to inherit the Scottish barony."

"I would have done the same were I in your position."

"No, you would have been more attentive and noticed that—"

"Stop, Grandmama," he said gently. "Aunt Jenny and Granduncle Silas fed and clothed me and provided a roof over my head. They were severe, but not cruel. It was the only way either of them knew how to be. Perhaps things might have been different if Silas had ever had children of his own. But he never married and therefore depended upon his nieces to care for him."

"And then your mother died, leaving the burden to Jenny alone."

He nodded. "The double burden of a demanding old man and a helpless infant. What's done is done. I wasn't about to dishonor my mother's memory by complaining about her family. Nor could I blame Aunt Jenny for resenting me. She was young and ought to have been attending assemblies and musicales instead of sitting trapped with us on a secluded baronial estate."

Eloise's response was cut short by Laurel's return.

Graelem was relieved to end the conversation. He turned his attention to Laurel and smothered a grin. The girl had an adorably smug look on her face. Ah, he enjoyed looking at her wonderfully expressive face. One day, she might look upon him with tender passion. Right now, he was the only one fighting off passionate urges. Laurel's body was like a siren song calling to him with each graceful sway of her hips. "What deadly dull tale have you selected, lass?"

She tipped her chin upward and cast him a victorious grin. "Your grandmother mentioned that you enjoy Shakespeare, so I chose to read *Titus Andronicus*."

He glanced at the freshly baked pies Watling had wheeled in on the tea cart. They were still hot, which intensified their cinnamon and apple aroma. The delightful scent tickled his nostrils. *Titus Andronicus* had a gory scene with a pie central to the story. Did Laurel know what that tragedy was about? Or know that two of the characters were baked in a pie and given to their unknowing mother to eat?

Eloise resumed her seat beside the door. "Laurel dear," she spoke up with concern, "I don't think this play is appropriate. It—"

"It's one of my favorites," Laurel insisted, plunking herself down on the stool and opening the book.

Graelem smothered another grin. Laurel was the sort of girl who only became further entrenched in her position if told she should not or could not do something. It hadn't taken Graelem long to figure out that quirk in her character, and he was surprised that his grandmother had yet to discover it. Then again, Laurel adored Eloise and always sought to please her.

"Is there a reason you chose this particular story?" he asked. "Other than simply because I enjoy his works?"

She blushed. "Yes."

He waited for her to explain, and when no explanation was forthcoming, he merely arched an eyebrow. "Very well, get on with it. And when you tire of reading, we can simply talk. I'd like to learn more about you."

"I have no wish to learn anything about you." She tipped her chin upward again. "We won't be marrying. I hope never to see you again once my punishment is over." She paused a moment and looked down at her toes. "But thank you for saving Brutus."

She paused again, raised her gaze to his, and opened her mouth to speak. Shaking her head, she clamped her mouth shut. He grew curious when she repeated the process, opening that perfectly shaped mouth of hers that was meant to be kissed often and thoroughly, and then quickly closing it. "What's on your mind, lass?"

She fidgeted a moment, took a deep breath, and then looked him squarely in the eye. "Will you sell Brutus to me once Father calms down and permits me to have him back?"

"No."

She shot to her feet and was about to drop the forgotten *Titus Andronicus* on her toes, but he caught the book in time. "Hell and damnation," he said with a yelp, for the quick movement jolted his leg. He tried to ignore the stabbing pains coursing through his body, but the struggle left him in a cold sweat. Moisture beaded across his brow.

He grabbed her hand when she started to turn away. "I'll *give* him back to you," he explained between clenched teeth, still fighting to subdue his pain. *Blessed Scottish saints! Every movement hurts.* "I didn't pay for him and won't turn a profit at your expense."

She stopped trying to draw her hand away. Instead, she

wrapped her fingers in his and stared at him, trying to decide whether or not he could be trusted. "You *did* pay for him," she said in a whisper of contrition. "You paid dearly with your broken leg."

He may have been physically hurt, but she was hurting too and unable to forgive herself for the accident. *Damn.* When she looked at him in that soft way, he was in danger of giving her anything she wished. "I didn't spend any blunt on him and won't make you spend any either. He'll be returned to you at the proper time. Don't ever offer to buy him from me, lass. He'll be yours once your father gives his permission. You obviously love that beast. I won't keep him from you."

He watched her expressive face, the flash of confusion in her exquisite eyes warring with the relief and gratitude she obviously felt.

She sighed softly and leaned toward him.

Was she about to give him another prim kiss on his cheek?

She leaned closer still, and then suddenly remembered that her hand was still wrapped in his. She hastily removed it and took the book back in her grasp.

The incredible feel of her slender fingers grazing his rough skin remained with him. He fought off the wave of heat now coursing through his body. Could he still blame this hot attraction on the laudanum working its way through him? Or on the fact that he *hadn't* taken any laudanum today to stem his pain?

He didn't want his heart involved in this marriage business.

He couldn't afford to like her.

Stick to your purpose.

"I'm sorry I've been so unpleasant to you today," Laurel said, withdrawing a lace handkerchief from her sleeve and dipping it into the ewer near his bedside that had been freshly filled with water shortly before she'd arrived. After wringing out the moisture, she applied it to his forehead and gently wiped the sweat off his brow. Her light touch felt so good. *Too good.*

He needed a girl to marry, not one to love.

Graelem watched as she set aside the handkerchief and returned to her seat on the stool. She sighed softly, clasped her hands, and then once again stared at her toes. "I chose *Titus Andronicus* for two reasons." She spoke so quietly, he almost missed what she was saying. "The first reason is that I thought Shakespeare's classical tragedies would bore you to tears."

"Because you believe me to be a bull-headed, uncouth lout. My grandmother thinks the same of me, so I suppose I am." He arched an eyebrow. "And the second?"

Although her face was still angled to gaze at the floor, he caught the rosy stain of a blush on her cheeks. "My parents refused to allow any of us to read this particular Shakespeare tragedy. I've been curious about it ever since."

He let out a hearty laugh. "Very efficient of you, lass. Dispatching two birds with one stone. But there's good reason for their admonition. It's a cruel and violent play. Not for tender young hearts or delicate sensibilities."

"I won't be afraid." Her chin shot up again. "It's just a play."

He glanced at the uncut pie on the tea tray. The enticing aroma of cinnamon and apples still filled the air. "Hand me the book."

She hesitated only a moment before doing so.

He began to read her the part where the queen was told her children had been baked in the pie she'd just eaten. Laurel shot to her feet. "Wait! Let me see that." She grabbed it from his hands and began to silently peruse the passage, her eyes widening and gracefully curved mouth now pursed in disgust as she snapped the book shut. "You weren't making it up."

"No, lass. I'm an oaf, remember? I could never write or express myself so eloquently." He leaned over and reached for the cake knife to slice himself a bit of pie. Perhaps it wasn't an appropriate moment, but he was hungry and the scent of apples was tickling his nostrils. "Care for some? I promise, there are no children baked inside."

"Graelem! Really, I must protest," his grandmother intoned from across the room. "That's too, too ghoulish of you!"

Laurel didn't appear nearly as overset, for she was merely shaking her head and laughing. It was a sweet, conciliatory laugh acknowledging that she'd been caught in this scheme of her own making. She leaned forward and inhaled the scent of the pie. "I'd love some. Here, let me help you." She placed her hand over his, the casual act setting off a cannon burst within his chest. *Damn.* Why was he so affected by this girl? The pain, no doubt. It was addling his senses.

He had no intention of falling in love with his wife.

Assuming he and Laurel ever made it to the altar.

He ceded the chore of cutting the pie to her capable hands, and then groaned inwardly when her pink tongue darted out to lick a few stray crumbs off her finger. His entire body caught fire. Fortunately, the girl had no idea the impact she was having on his composure.

Unfortunately, he understood exactly what the girl was doing to his composure.

Blessed Scottish saints! This was only his first day with Laurel. What would tomorrow bring?

CHAPTER 5

THE NEXT FEW days were a disaster in Graelem's mind, for Laurel refused to engage in conversation and spent the entire time reading *The Song of Roland* to him. Over and over again. By day four, he swore that if she walked in with the damn poem again, he was going to toss it out the window. Or toss himself out the window if he couldn't wrest the book out of her hands.

His own grandmother had abandoned him to his punishment by day two. She had been slipping out of his chamber each day shortly after Laurel's arrival, knowing the girl's intent and not about to suffer through hours of that wretched poetry recitation along with him.

So much for being chaperoned.

Laurel's attention had been so focused on her mission to make him rue their betrothal that she'd never noticed they'd been left alone each afternoon. He'd survived these visits by closing his eyes and listening to the soft purr of her voice. While she primly read to him, he fantasized about peeling the fashionable day gown off her splendid body and exploring each delicate curve and perfect line of her warm, pink skin with his lips and tongue.

The innocent would bludgeon him if she ever realized what he was thinking.

He was an uncouth lout and proud of it.

And now they were at day five and Laurel was late. He'd earlier washed and shaved, and then donned a fresh nightshirt because he still couldn't fit his splinted leg into a pair of trousers.

Now restless, he eased from his bed and carefully lowered his leg to avoid putting any weight on his foot as it touched the floor. After some false starts, he'd learned to shift his weight onto his healthy leg without too much difficulty.

Once standing, he reached for his dressing gown and then his crutches. He'd just secured the belt of his dressing gown around his waist and was about to make his way to the window on his crutches when his door flew open and Laurel burst in. Would the girl never learn the art of knocking?

A mere glance at Laurel's reddened eyes and tear-dampened cheeks warned him this was no time for glib remarks. "Lass, what's wrong?" On instinct, he set aside his crutches and opened his arms to her.

She let out a sob and flew into his offered embrace, her riot of dark gold curls unbound and flowing down her back.

"Blessed saints, what's happened?" He wrapped her in his arms, pleasantly surprised and at the same time dreading the news that had put her there. "Is it Brutus?" He didn't know her father very well, but the man didn't seem the sort to go back on his word and have the beast destroyed.

"No," she said between sniffles and great gulps of air. She was a little thing and the top of her head barely reached his shoulder, but there was a liveliness about her—a stubbornness, too—that gave her a presence beyond her slender size.

"Has someone been hurt?" His heart lodged in his throat at her nod, his first thoughts drifting to Laurel's sisters and her parents. Despite their lack of conversation over the past few days, he knew that her family was important to her. He wanted to press her for details, but decided against it. She was distraught and wanted to be held. Indeed, she needed to be held so badly that even his odious touch was acceptable.

"He didn't have to go," she said in a strained whisper, burrowing her soft body against his hard frame as though clinging to him would somehow diminish her pain. Sunlight streamed in through the open window, and a warm breeze lightly blew across her golden curls. The beauty of this day was at odds with her anguish. There ought to have been dark clouds and a tempest raging outside, for the girl was in such torment it was clear something very bad had happened to someone dear to her heart.

Yet in her torment, she'd run to him.

Did it signify anything?

Would she ever admit to herself that it did?

He ran a caressing hand through her soft, silken tresses. "Lass, I'm so sorry."

"He could have bought his way out, but refused." She spoke into his chest so that he felt the movement of her lips against his heart. *Damn.* "Julia fainted when she heard the news. She's Uncle Harrison's wife. They have a young son. Little Harry. Why did he have to go? And now no one knows where he is, only that he was wounded in battle and possibly captured by the French!"

Laurel was talking about her uncle's military service. The Farthingales were wealthy and could have paid to avoid sending any family member to fight in the war against Napoleon. Obviously, Harrison Farthingale was a man of honor who was determined to dutifully serve his country.

Indeed, he was now paying a dear price for that duty. Would the wife and young son he'd left behind ever see him again? Graelem had experienced enough battles during his service in the Peninsular war to know the odds were against Harrison's safe return.

Laurel was still sobbing against his chest as she fitfully continued. "My mother and the female elders are tending to Julia. Daisy's looking after little Harry. The poor thing, he's so scared. He's holding onto Daisy for dear life and refuses to go into anyone else's arms. The men have gone off to the regimental headquarters to find out more information, and the twins were sent to Rose's to spend the night."

She let out a string of hiccups and sniffles. "I... I felt so lost and useless. I didn't know what to do... or where I should be."

"Right here, lass." He gently tipped her chin up so that her gaze met his, although he doubted she could see much through her tears. "I'm glad you came to me. This is where you belong. In my arms."

"No, I can't belong with you," she said in a whispered groan, but her hands slid up his chest and her delicate fingers grazed the nape of his neck as she clung tighter and tighter to him until their bodies were flat against each other.

"You do, lass." He had one arm around her slight waist and the other buried in her wild, tumbling curls without a clue as to what might happen next. He'd take his guidance from her.

She gazed up at him, her eyes at first reflecting her confusion and then subtly shifting to reflect something quite different. Something quite surprising. *Blessed Scottish saints!* He understood what she wanted, what she yearned for in that moment. She was asking him to kiss her. Silently pleading for him to kiss her in the hope it would ease her torment.

"Laurel... lass," he said with an ache to his voice as he lowered his mouth to hers, the touch of his lips purposely restrained and gentle although his need was so raw and hungry that he had to struggle mightily to maintain his control.

His desire for the girl had been building over these past few days to a volcanic tension that needed little encouragement to erupt, but he knew that he had to hold back. Laurel sought comfort, not a quick tumble, no matter how desperately he yearned for it, or how confused and desperate she was to unburden the pain in her heart.

If mere kisses could melt away her unhappiness, he'd kiss her into eternity. But he knew it would take more. It would take love and that was something he couldn't give her.

Not yet.

Not until he'd secured his inheritance.

For now, he'd give her his protection. He'd give her his strength.

But he couldn't risk giving her his heart.

He pressed his lips more firmly against hers and felt the urgency of her own sweet lips against his. *This* Laurel truly was a danger to his heart. This Laurel who needed him fiercely and passionately could unravel all his plans. This Laurel who chose him to heal her and ease her terrible pain could ruin all he needed to accomplish within the month.

He could deny her nothing if he allowed himself to love *this*

Laurel.

He deepened the kiss, allowing the heat of his lips to comfort hers, for hers were cold and trembling. But she responded with eager desperation as he probed with his tongue, opening her sweet mouth and inviting him in as though he belonged. As though he were the *only* man who could ever belong, the only man who mattered to her. It wasn't possible. He'd never, *ever* mattered to anyone before.

Lord, she threw him off balance! It wasn't only because he was leaning on one leg and would topple with her slightest push.

No one had ever made him feel needed or important. Not like this.

Is this what love feels like? This fierce protectiveness now stirring within me?

No, this was merely a foolish, lustful yearning and nothing more.

He refused to believe it was more.

Any female touch would have stirred the fire now raging inside him. If he repeated the thought often enough, he might actually believe it.

Not Laurel.

Any woman will do.

So long as she looks like Laurel and tastes of summer strawberries like Laurel and feels heavenly in his arms like Laurel.

Without breaking their kiss, he angled his body so that his weight rested against his bed's footboard, and then he lifted Laurel by the waist and crushed her up against him. He wanted to swallow her up as badly as she'd wanted to be swallowed up inside him. Her body felt hot and alive against his, her ample breasts molding to his chest and her hands now restlessly roaming over his shoulders and back, then up again so that she wound her fingers in his hair.

"Kiss me again, Graelem," she whispered when he forced himself to end the kiss before matters went too far. He didn't wish to take advantage of her in this vulnerable state. He could have done anything to her and she would not have protested.

Even now, he felt the uneven heave of her breasts against his chest. He wanted to cup one of those lush mounds in his palm and run his thumb across its tip, teasing until it hardened beneath his touch. He ached to move lower and take the rosy tip in his mouth, coax breathless moans of pleasure out of her.

He couldn't. Not now. Not like this.

She let out a whimper. "Graelem, I can't bear the thought of losing him. I can't bear the pain in my father's eyes. I feel as though my heart is being savagely ripped apart and it hurts so much."

"I know, lass."

She'd never forgive him once her pain subsided. In another moment, the kiss they'd just shared would be a humiliating memory for her. He had to keep that in mind, for he'd already given her good reason to detest him.

He wasn't certain what to do. Hold her? Kiss her again? Gently set her aside and step back? He simply didn't know.

He had grown up in a very different family, one that hid all feelings. His mother's family had been a cold, severe lot. Not exactly cruel, although he'd experienced more beatings than he thought justified. But life at Moray was harsh, so Jenny and Silas learned never to show their feelings or concerns, as though to express joy or sadness was somehow a sin.

Laurel was completely the opposite. If she felt something, she let you know it.

In truth, he liked that about her.

He liked so many things about her.

He kissed her again gently and began to ease her out of his arms with great reluctance. "Sit down, sweetheart." He motioned to the chair beside his window. One of the footmen had set it there earlier this morning at his request, for he had been too restless to lie in bed with his damn leg elevated and had wanted to feel the warming touch of the sun upon his face. "Tell me about your uncle." *Or not.* He wasn't certain whether offering to listen was the right thing to say.

She nodded and hesitantly released her grasp on his shoulders, as though fearing she'd drown if she ever did let go of him. There was little water about, only the stream of her tears. She hiccupped, sighed, and nodded once again before moving to the chair.

He grabbed his crutches and followed, but remained standing and leaned against the window's frame for support. He placed his weight on his good leg, hoping it would be enough to stem his discomfort for as long as the girl needed him beside her.

She let out a soft gasp and scrambled off the chair when his lame leg accidentally hit the wall, causing him to wince. "You should be the one to sit, Graelem."

"No, lass. I'm fine." *But you're not.*

"I'll grab the stool. Then we can both be seated." She cast him a hopeful smile. "And talk, if you truly don't mind."

He responded with an affectionate grin, pointing to his splinted leg and the sorry state of his attire. A nightshirt and dressing gown were not in the least fashionable or appropriate for a walk in the park. "I'm not going anywhere. I'm at your service. Go on, lass," he prompted when she seemed uncertain where to begin. "Your uncle sounds like a fine man."

"The best," she said with a heartfelt ache to her voice. She took another moment to pick up the stool and set it by his chair, a task he would have done had he been able to get around without the use of his crutches. He offered to take the stool, but she wouldn't hear of it. "It's too small for your large frame. You need a chair with a sturdy back to prop yourself up. You're too big to catch if you should lose your balance and fall."

He didn't argue the matter, for she was right. He couldn't bend his broken leg and was decidedly unsteady on or off his feet.

They sat a moment in silence until he prompted her again, careful to be gentle for she was still distraught. "Is he your favorite uncle?"

"In some ways," she said with a nod, "but they're all wonderful. Uncle Harrison is the most adventurous, always talking about someday exploring the pyramids and temples of ancient Egypt or traveling to the silk farms of China. The Chinese silks have long fascinated him, especially being in mercantile. His mind was always on whatever splendid new things the Farthingales could introduce to England."

He listened while she spoke and subtly encouraged a shift in the topic to the rest of her family, especially curious about her parents and sisters. He smiled and made short comments as she told him stories about them, and then expanded the topic to include more Farthingale relations since there was so much more to her family than just her sisters and parents.

There were Oxfordshire Farthingales. Yorkshire and Devonshire Farthingales. These Farthingales were a boisterous and loving lot.

Laurel obviously adored every member of her large extended family despite their quirks and shortcomings. He was an only child and had spent most of his life working on the Moray estate. He had rarely left Moray except for that splendid summer at Trent Hall with his cousins, Alexander and Gabriel, when he was nine years old.

He'd also spent a few years fighting Napoleon's army in Spain, returning to Moray when Silas fell ill and could no longer manage the estate and the vast Moray holdings. All of it was to be his, after all. Everything *would* be his, provided he married by Midsummer's Day.

The more he listened to Laurel talk about her family, the more he felt he'd made the right decision in choosing her as his wife. But how would he convince her that his decision was also right for her?

He considered Gabriel and Alexander among the closest of his few friends. Unfortunately, neither cousin was in London at the moment to advise him in matters of courtship. He was on his own, but he'd been on his own most of his life and had managed well enough.

He returned his attention to Laurel as she spoke about her eldest sister and how she'd met and married her husband last year. "Rose wasn't supposed to be abducted with Julian," Laurel explained, as though danger and intrigue were a normal part of the courtship process. Perhaps it was with these Farthingale girls. They never meant to get into trouble, if Laurel was to be believed, but trouble always had a way of seeking them out.

He could tell by Laurel's smile as she spoke of her family that she truly loved them. She was particularly close with her sisters, and he envied that bond. Would she ever feel that same affection toward him?

Bah. Why should he care? Their marriage was to be an amicable arrangement, one of convenience and nothing more. Upon his granduncle's death, he had inherited the title of baron and an entailed manor house that was woefully rundown. Marrying Laurel by the Midsummer's Day deadline would secure him the remaining Moray assets, those that were not entailed and that accounted for the bulk of the baronial wealth.

He had built up the estate and its holdings through toil and sweat, and was not about to allow his profligate, incompetent distant cousin, Jordan Drummond, to destroy all he'd achieved. For that reason, he needed Laurel.

He'd be generous with the girl once they married, giving her independence and financial security for the rest of her life without further obligation to him.

Indeed, he'd do all in his power to make her comfortable.

"And it all started when Rose's kiln exploded," Laurel continued as though such occurrences happened every day. "But fortunately, Lily's cache of explosives was still safely hidden under her bed, so we knew she wasn't the culprit. Father confiscated them immediately, of course. Although I doubt there was any danger of the townhouse blowing up."

"What?" He shook his head. "Never mind. Go on." Her parents obviously had their hands full with five well-meaning but headstrong daughters. Abductions? Explosives? Did they never speak of fashions or dances or summer balls?

Rose had made her debut last year, and Laurel's come out was this year. A few weeks in, and she was already in trouble. Perhaps that was why John Farthingale had been a bit harsh with her concerning Brutus.

Who was he to judge the father? He seemed a decent sort and clearly loved his daughters. Were they all like Laurel? She was like a fireworks display, beautiful and fascinating, but if mishandled, one would get singed by that fiery temper of hers. Her parents' goal, no doubt, was to guide her safely through the London season without further mishap.

Laurel paused after they'd been talking for about an hour, judging by the angle of the sun against the blue sky. "I've been quite the chatterbox," she exclaimed. Still shaken by the news about her uncle, she was clasping her hands on her lap to keep them from trembling. "You shouldn't have let me go on for so long. Your ears must be numb."

"My leg is numb," he said, giving her a tender smile. "My ears are fine. More important, how do you feel?" He reached over and took her hands in his, but held them loosely so that she could draw away if his touch displeased her. To his relief, she didn't.

"I keep hoping that Uncle Harrison's carriage will draw up to our front gate and he'll hop out with a jovial smile on his face and a box of silkworms he purchased to create a new line of Farthingale silks," she said, taking a deep, ragged breath. "I keep thinking that it's all been a terrible mistake and the regimental commander will hurry over here issuing his apologies and informing us that my uncle has been found and will be fit to travel home soon."

Her hands were still resting in his as she took another ragged breath. "I know it won't happen. I dread hearing the worst." She gazed at him in expectation, as though he had it in his power to make things right. He didn't. He couldn't fix anything. Not her marriage plans and not her uncle's safe return. However, he had a few connections in the highest echelons and would seek them out. "Graelem, you've suffered loss and seem to have handled it."

"My leg—"

"No, I mean the loss of a loved one." A light blush stained her cheeks. "Are you an orphan?"

He didn't wish to speak about himself, but Laurel would never trust him if he held back now. "I'm in my mid-twenties, too old to be considered an orphan. I don't know how much my grandmother has told you about me."

"She speaks often of all her grandsons, but mostly in a general way."

He nodded. "Yes, my parents are both deceased, if that's what you're asking."

She shook her head and sighed. "When did they die?"

He squirmed in his chair, not liking the path of their current conversation, but he reminded himself that it was important for Laurel to understand him. He wasn't certain why, only that he had no chance of getting her to the altar unless she knew him and trusted him. He ran a hand roughly through his hair. "My mother died giving birth to me."

She inhaled lightly and gave the hand she was still holding an affectionate squeeze. "I'm so sorry."

"So am I, lass. I've often wondered what she was like." He quirked an eyebrow and studied her. "Her family spoke little about her, but the villagers often told me stories of her. She was friendly and caring, but had a willful streak, so I'm told. I think she must have been a little like you."

Laurel slipped her hand out of his grasp and tipped her chin upward. She grinned as she voiced her mock indignation so that he knew she'd taken no offense. "Nothing wrong with standing up for what one believes in."

"I agree. I meant the comparison as a compliment, of course."

She laughed softly. To his surprise, she placed her hands back in his. "All right then. Thank you." She paused another moment, gazing at him solemnly. "Will you tell me about your father? How old were you when he died?"

It was his turn to hesitate and struggle with his words, but he wasn't going to hide the truth about that bastard from Laurel either. "I was in my early twenties. He only died a few years ago, but I never knew him. He left shortly after I was born."

Laurel's eyes rounded in horror. "He abandoned you?" She sounded forlorn, almost as angry and distressed as he'd felt most of his life.

"He left me in the care of my mother's family." Coming from a family such as hers, of course she would equate his father's leaving with cruelty and neglect. "He knew I'd be well taken care of."

That part was a fable. Graelem doubted his father had ever thought of him after dropping him off with Silas, the then Baron Moray. He'd purposely left Graelem in Scotland and not brought him back to Eloise or to his own brother, the Earl of Trent, knowing they would never have let him go off on his own without a thought for his own child.

Laurel nibbled her lip, her frown a hint that she hadn't liked his response. "Were they kind to you?"

"I was never left wanting. One doesn't get to be a big oaf like me by eating gruel only once a day."

The girl began to study him far too intently to be considered appropriate. If he were ever the sort to blush, he'd be doing so now.

"You are big," she agreed. "But I think I've been the oaf to you these past few days." She spoke in a contrite whisper, but her remorse, if she felt any, lasted only a moment before she remembered that she was waging a campaign to end their betrothal. "In my own defense, it's this marriage nonsense. You can't seriously wish to marry me."

She was wrong.

This so-called betrothal was the best decision he'd ever made. All he had to do was convince her of it. But he was no gentleman with fancy words and witty conversation.

He truly was a big oaf.

And big oafs did not know how to win a woman's heart.

CHAPTER 6

LAUREL KNEW SHE'D made a fool of herself in front of Graelem, but he was doing his best not to show his exasperation. She'd spent the first hour a tearful, blubbering mess. Had he understood a word of what she was saying? How could he amid her sniffles, gasping breaths, and hiccups?

And she'd kissed him!

She'd behaved like a deranged wanton who cursed him one moment and then offered her body to him in the next. What did he think of her now? She couldn't have planned a better way to chase him off. Not that she'd planned any of it. Her heart was broken. Grief had completely muddled her senses. In her grief, she'd run to him.

Him.

Why? And if she were perfectly honest with herself, she hadn't thought to run to Devlin. Of course, Graelem was closer since he was recovering just next door. But proximity hadn't crossed her mind. Shelter. Understanding. Warmth. Those were the things she'd been seeking.

Still, why had she run to Graelem? He was handsome as sin, but there were other men who were just as handsome in their own way. Devlin, for example, with his dark hair, hazel eyes, and London sophistication.

But Graelem was here and he had listened to her. Actually *listened.*

She almost believed he cared.

He didn't, of course. How could he when he'd known her a mere five days, most of their time together spent with him in agonizing pain and her reciting epic poetry? She was now convinced that poetry was the most boring art form known to man. Had the Goths used it to destroy the Roman Empire? Slinging endless verses along with their spears and arrows until the Romans had begged for mercy and surrendered or simply fallen asleep?

Yet Graelem had allowed her to read the entire *Song of Roland* to him. Not just once, but several times. He understood it was her way of torturing him and he'd indulged her. She suspected that it was also his way of atoning for forcing her into an unwanted marriage.

He needed only to take it a small step farther. His atonement would best be served by ending their betrothal now. Today. Immediately.

She sighed and shook her head, knowing he would never end it, not after the way she'd kissed him. Why had she thrown her heart and soul into that kiss? She hadn't meant to, but it had just happened that way.

Nor had she meant to tip her head up and gaze at him in that hungry, I'll-die-if-you-don't-kiss-me-now, pleading way. Or stare at his lips as though nothing else on earth mattered more than their warm strength against her mouth. Or breathe in the scent of lather and sandalwood on his throat as though she'd die again if she didn't breathe all of him in right now.

He smelled so good it was all she could do to keep her distance. Indeed, it was quite a struggle to keep from grabbing him and plundering his lips for another kiss. She could do it and get away with it. Why not? She would blame the wayward impulse on her grief and confusion.

After all, she was grieving and confused.

Kissing Graelem had felt surprisingly wonderful. Never mind that he'd been trapped and unable to run from her because of his hobbled leg.

She glanced down. Her hands were still in his. She'd put them there. Another deranged act, but she loved the roughness of his palms. There was nothing milk-soft or delicate about them, yet he managed to be gentle while holding hers in his grasp.

His touch was rough and exciting, and at the same time soothing.

He made her feel better.

More than better, she had to admit. She was still tingling and aching to be back in his arms. There was a protective strength in the way his fingers entwined with hers, and the light stroke of his thumb along her skin chased the cold and despair out of her heart.

"What are you thinking, lass?"

That she wanted to kiss him again. That she'd never been kissed so ardently by any man before, not even Devlin. That she'd never been kissed by any man before, ever. And now that she had been kissed, how could any man surpass the excellent job he'd done of it? That she'd listened to countless church sermons on the evils of such behavior and still had every intention of kissing Graelem again with exactly that same wanton intensity, assuming he would allow it.

He simply has to allow it.

Oh, dear. What if he doesn't?

"Lass?" He gave her hands a light squeeze, and then smiled boyishly when her gaze met his. "Are you woolgathering? Run out of conversation? Thinking up new tortures for me?"

If left up to him, he might not ever kiss her again, for he'd been the one to put an end to their passionate and misguided first kiss. If left up to her, she would already be telling him to shut up and get down to the business of looting and pillaging her innocent treasures.

There was something about him that made her wanton and willing to forsake her virtue. Not just willing, but eager. She wanted his touch, needed the assuring strength of his hands and the heat of his big body to make her feel alive. "I've stayed too long. I must go." *Before I do something utterly foolish.*

She felt the sudden tension in his body. He drew his hands away from hers. "Then I'll not delay you."

"But thank you for listening to me." Of course, she'd only turned to Graelem because Devlin was not available to her. There was no other explanation for the yearning he roused in her. She was overset and simply misdirecting her desire. Also, Devlin was a gentleman and would never have kissed her back in that shockingly unrestrained manner.

Graelem rose along with her, his movements slow but surprisingly graceful as he reached for his crutches to walk her out.

While she'd always admired Devlin's social polish and courtly manner, this afternoon she'd needed something more, for her heart was bursting with sorrow and she needed a way to let out the ache before it shattered into a thousand pieces that could never be properly put back together.

Kissing Graelem had helped.

She suspected that kissing him again would help even more.

It would not have been the same with Devlin, for their relationship was built on courtesy and friendship. There could be no blubbering or wild kisses with Devlin. She would have frightened him with the intensity of her need, clutching his perfectly ironed lapels and mussing his stylishly curled hair. She could not have run her hands up and down his chest for fear of wrinkling his immaculate white lawn shirt.

No such worries with Graelem. His hair was too long to be considered stylish and he wasn't wearing proper clothes, just his nightshirt and black silk dressing gown that accentuated his broad shoulders. She could have ripped the nightshirt off him and he wouldn't have complained.

She blinked her eyes to banish all thought of naked Graelem from her mind. She'd never seen Devlin in anything other than proper attire and had never thought of him standing before her in his naked glory. She didn't think he'd be nearly as glorious as Graelem.

Nonsense! Surely, he would be. One didn't need to be big or muscled to be splendid.

"Lass, you're still trembling." Graelem's soft rumble cut into her thoughts.

She shook her head. "I'm not cold. Just confused and angry. But you must have felt the same when your father... I'm sorry.

Am I overstepping the proper bounds?"

He surprised her with a short, chuckling laugh that wrapped around her like a soft blanket. "I don't think you know any other way to be. But I don't mind, lass. You're welcome to ask your questions and stay as long as you need. As for that poetry you've been spouting..." He gave a mock shudder. "I'll endure your recitations if it will make you feel better."

She tried not to look at him as he shifted uncomfortably on his crutches, his splinted leg held out in front of him. "Earlier you asked what I thought about my father," he continued. "I was too young to understand his actions back then."

"And now?" How could anyone abandon their child? Especially a newborn? She studied Graelem. Yes, she really liked the way his dressing gown stretched across his broad shoulders. He took extra care to keep it securely tied as though that simple gesture would lend respectability to the fact that she was alone with him in his bedchamber, that she'd practically rammed her tongue down his throat when kissing him, and that he was wearing no trousers. *I really have to leave.*

On the other hand, she'd already seen him in a shocking state of undress the day he'd broken his leg and she'd burst into his room thinking it was about to be sawed off.

She'd seen all of him naked.

Wouldn't mind seeing that again.

His response to her question about his father brought her back to attention, for he sounded quite bitter about their relationship. "I wish the... *bastard*... I wish he'd died long ago."

"You're angry." She wanted to take his hands, but they were now occupied holding the crutches. She was better off not touching him again anyway. Not ever. "Quite understandable."

He shook his head and frowned. "No, it isn't. I don't wish to be angry. I don't wish to think of him at all. He doesn't matter to me. He shared no part of his life with me, and I don't want him to intrude in mine."

"I think it's too late. He has intruded and will continue to do so until you forgive him."

"Lass, I'm not the forgiving sort."

She reached out and placed a hand on his chest. The palm of her hand began to tingle against the heat of his body and the strong, steady beat of his heart. She really ought to stop touching him. "I'm quite the opposite. I've never been good at holding grudges. I'll forgive you as soon as you regain your senses and end our betrothal."

His expression hardened. "That again."

"Yes, that. It's the only thing that matters."

He turned away and limped back to his bed, awkwardly settling atop the covers and muttering a string of oaths as he set aside his crutches and used both of his hands to lift his leg onto the bed, the chore obviously still painful and destroying what little good humor he had left. "Not going to happen, lass."

"It will happen, mark my words. I will not be marrying you on Midsummer's Day or any other day." He'd been so kind to her up until now. Why did their meetings always have to end this way? She ought to have held her tongue and put an end to this afternoon's visit, but she knew her own flaws. She was like a dog with a bone that she couldn't let go. "Despite appearances, my father will never permit the wedding to proceed without my blessing."

He returned her gaze, but his was softer and his frown was one of concern, not anger. "We've had this conversation before. I don't wish to fight with you, lass. Not today. In truth, not ever. If you need to talk about your uncle or any other matter that troubles you, I'll listen. I'll do my best to ease your worry. But I will not release you from your promise of marriage."

She liked so many things about this man, but his stubborn refusal to see reason was not one of them. "Perhaps Devlin will change your opinion."

He had been lying prone and now struggled to sit up. "Who's Devlin?"

"The man I love." She tipped her chin upward in defiance and was about to march out of his quarters when his dismissive laughter stopped her in the middle of her step.

"Lass, I'll wager that you never kissed him the way you just kissed me."

She curled her hands into fists. "So what if I haven't?"

The admission appeared to surprise him, but he also seemed excessively pleased by it. He had an irritating smirk on his face. "I pity the poor bloke."

Men were so confusing. She'd never understand them. "Why?"

"Because you obviously don't love him." He relaxed and settled back against his pillows, tucking his hands behind his head and chortling in such a gloating and possessively superior way that she wanted to pound him into dust. "Lass, you may think you do—"

"I *know* I do."

"You don't. No, indeed. Not after the hungry way you held yourself against my body or pulled my head down to yours to give me a scorching kiss that still has me on fire. I suspect that your hot little body is on fire, too."

"How dare you suggest that I... I..."

"Laurel, you're a molten pool of unexplored desires, and I'm..." *Bollocks, don't say it...* "And I'm just the man to release the steamy tempest hidden within you—"

She gasped. "The only one who is scorching and on fire is you! And I know just how to douse your flames." She stomped over to the ewer on his night stand, saw that it was filled, and unceremoniously dumped the water over his head, leaving him sputtering and howling as she stormed out.

But she paused at the threshold and turned back to shoot him a glower. "That ought to cool your embers, you insufferable ass!"

CHAPTER 7

"WHAT IN BLOODY hell happened to you?" Ian Markham, Duke of Edgeware, asked upon entering Graelem's bedchamber in response to his urgent missive and finding him seated beside the open window with his broken leg elevated, pillowed back propped against a sturdy chair, and crutches at his side. "So this is why you couldn't meet me at White's the other day."

Graelem set aside the instructions he had been writing to his estate manager regarding the Moray farmlands and nodded. "An unexpected complication, Your Grace. I was certain you'd heard all about it by now."

Ian grinned. "In truth, it is all the *ton* is talking about. Your grandmother told her friend Lady Phoebe Withnall, who ran straight to me with the news and then ran off to tell the rest of England. The odds makers are having a deuced hard time keeping up with the wagers."

"Damnation," Graelem muttered, his humor turning as dark as the thunderclouds gathering overhead. The air was thick with moisture and the wind was kicking up, a reliable indicator of heavy rains on the way. His leg was also feeling the changes, for the area around the broken bones had swelled so uncomfortably he was tempted to take the entire vial of laudanum and gulp it down to ease the pain.

He hadn't taken any since that first day and there would be none for him today. It was a vile substance that served no purpose but to dull one's senses while loosening one's inhibitions.

"The bets are running in her favor. Odds are that she will never marry you."

"With all due respect, stuff it, Your Grace." He had important matters to discuss with Ian and pressing Moray affairs to attend to immediately afterward, so his head had to remain clear of all the distracting gossip and drivel. Especially since he was the subject of all that gossip and drivel. The duke was used to this nonsense. He wasn't.

Ian paused at his side and stared down at him. "I refused to believe it at first, it sounded too ridiculous. The girl tramples you with her horse and you propose marriage? Were you hit in the head by the beast's hooves?"

"Nothing of the sort," Graelem grumbled, feeling at a distinct disadvantage and expecting to be mercilessly teased about his present state, for one did not meet with a duke in one's nightshirt and dressing gown with one's leg wrapped and raised and purple toes sticking out from that wrapping without a single comment.

Surprisingly, Ian appeared too willing to go easy on him. "Lady Withnall had the effrontery to suggest that one of the Farthingale sisters might be perfect for me should I ever decide to settle down and find myself a wife. I found the notion terrifying as well as preposterous."

Graelem laughed. "You? Terrified of a slip of a girl? I'd love to see the day that happens. Although those sisters aren't your usual sort. You might find one you like enough to marry."

"Please," Ian said with a mock shudder and a wicked arch of his eyebrow. "I've just had breakfast and you're unsettling my stomach. Why have you summoned me?"

Graelem motioned to one of the two empty chairs beside him. "Have a seat and I'll tell you. I've asked Julian Emory to join us as well since he's married to one of the Farthingale sisters."

Ian nodded. "Rose, the eldest. He did well for himself. The girl has brains as well as beauty. But why is my presence required, and how is it in any way connected to that family?"

"Harrison Farthingale was injured and possibly captured while battling Napoleon's army in France. His brothers are frantic with worry. Indeed, all the Farthingales are. You're needed to—"

He broke off as Julian strode in.

"I've just come from Harrison's regimental headquarters and the news is very bad." Julian hastily acknowledged Ian. "Your Grace, glad you're here." He ran a hand roughly through his hair as he continued. "It's almost certain Rose's uncle is dead, but his body hasn't been recovered yet. The battle was a bloody massacre of our English forces. The dead have yet to be counted, and there are so many injured…" He paused as rage and frustration overwhelmed him.

"I know," Ian said with a bitterness that surprised Graelem, for the duke rarely showed his feelings. But Ian was clenching and unclenching his fists as though preparing to pound someone to dust, and his eyes were ablaze with anger. "Gabriel sent his report weeks ago warning about the French troop strength at Boulogne. He proposed a damned brilliant alternative to General Kellington's battle plan, which wasn't a plan at all, but a death march. That horse's arse! He ignored the advice."

Ian, his expression as stormy as the rain now beginning to fall with a vengeance, rose from his chair and began to pace. "I told Prinny that if he didn't remove Kellington immediately, I'd do it for him. And I'll do a hell of a lot worse to him than a mere broken leg. He's destroyed too many lives because of his stupidity."

Graelem had no doubt that Ian would follow through on his threat, and also had no doubt that Prinny took his words seriously. He expected that within the week, Kellington would be quietly dismissed or *promoted* to some useless ministry where his stupidity could do little damage.

Of course, too late to save the precious lives lost at Boulogne.

Ian's eyes suddenly rounded in understanding. "You want me to find Harrison Farthingale when I slip into France. I'm due to leave tomorrow."

Julian nodded. "We know it's asking much of you. I volunteered to go, but the others," he said with a nod in Graelem's direction, referring not only to him but to all the members in the English spy ring secretly commissioned by Prinny, "refused to permit me the assignment."

"I should hope not." There was a determined glint in Ian's

eyes. "You're married and your wife is with child. You know our rules. No grieving widows and no fatherless children left behind. You're still an important part of this organization."

Julian scowled. "But relegated to a clerk's position."

"We need operatives within England as well. Your work remains vital, just not as physically dangerous as the missions in France." Graelem winced as he accidentally moved his leg. "Bollocks! How do you think I feel? I'm the one who should be sailing across the channel. The responsibility should have been mine."

"Yours?" Both men said at once and stared at him in surprise.

"He's Laurel's uncle, and after what I've done to the girl—"

"Offering to marry her?" Ian shook his head. "Isn't it what every debutante desires?"

"I've *tricked* her into marrying me. There's a difference. She wasn't given a choice. I'm forcing her to the altar because of that damned contingency in my inheritance."

Julian nodded. "Rose is quite up in arms about it. I'm doing all I can to keep her from barging in here and doing away with you in the same way we're all contemplating doing away with Kellington."

Ian coughed. "These Farthingales sound quite bloodthirsty. I'll do my best to avoid them. They seem more dangerous than Boney."

"They are," Julian agreed, but his tone gentled. "However, I have no complaints. I love Rose."

Ian turned toward Graelem in expectation.

What did they expect him to say? That he loved Laurel? "I have no complaints either. But ours is a business arrangement."

Ian sighed. "Another deluded bachelor. I had better warn Gabriel about the Farthingale sisters when I meet him in France. Who's next to be set loose upon society?"

"Daisy," Julian said.

"Right, I'll warn him to keep away from her." He turned to Graelem once more. "I'll do what I can to locate Harrison Farthingale and find out about his condition. England can't afford to lose brave men like him. I sincerely hope I can deliver good news."

Graelem nodded.

But none of them smiled, for they'd all experienced war and knew its harsh reality.

Harrison Farthingale was not coming home.

~⚜~

"COME IN," GRAELEM said when Laurel appeared three days later. Her face was pale, and she was nibbling her lip as though concerned about what he might do to her after the way they'd parted company on her last visit. Her hair was drawn back in a stylishly intricate braided bun, but a few golden curls remained loose to frame her heart-shaped face. Her gown was a soft, sea foam green that subtly enhanced the greenish-blue hue of her eyes.

Unfortunately, her eyes were rimmed in red from the tears she had obviously shed these past few days as her family continued to worry over the fate of Harrison Farthingale. There had been no news and that was probably the hardest to endure.

She remained in his doorway, reluctant to step in.

He grabbed his crutches and hobbled over to her side before she lost her composure and fled. He was dressed now, finally able to wear proper clothes, although his leg was still tightly bound to hold the broken bones in place and he couldn't put pressure on it yet.

His attire was simple, never to be mistaken for fashionable. He wore buff breeches and a plain shirt of white lawn. No finely woven jacket. No silk vest or perfectly looped cravat. No fancy leather boots on his feet yet, just a slipper on his good foot and bandages on his bad one.

But he was dressed and that was a step in the right direction. He arched an eyebrow and grinned in response to her questioning gaze. "I've had the ewer restocked with water."

A small smile crept across her lips despite her efforts to hide all trace of enjoyment or desire to be in his presence. "I'm surprised you aren't wearing your oilskin today or keeping an umbrella beside your bed," she responded, finally surrendering to his teasing. A delightful rose blush stained her cheeks.

"I'm ever hopeful that I'll get through this visit without a thorough soaking." He glanced behind her. "No chaperone?"

Her eyes rounded in surprise and she turned to gaze behind her. "I... Aunt Hortensia is with me... at least, she was with me a moment ago. Oh, dear. Where has she gone off to?"

He stepped aside and invited her in. "She must have stopped a moment to greet Eloise. I'm sure she'll be along soon." Not that he wanted to share his time with anyone but Laurel. It wasn't as though the Farthingale elders were diligent guardians. In truth, they were remarkably inattentive. Almost as inattentive as Eloise had been since the first few days.

It seemed he and Laurel bored everyone but each other.

His heart beat a little faster within his chest. She looked so beautiful. In truth, she grew lovelier with each passing day. He couldn't blame his feelings on his blurred vision, for his vision had cleared shortly after he'd been kicked by Brutus. Nor could he blame them on his pain or the laudanum he'd refused to take for that pain.

He motioned to the chair he now kept beside his open window in order to enjoy the outdoors, for he had never been one to spend more time than necessary indoors. This enforced confinement was not in his nature. Were it not for Laurel's visits and the sack of paperwork that arrived each morning requiring his immediate attention, he would have gone stark raving mad by now. "Won't you have a seat?"

She gave him a curt nod as she glided past, sparing a peek at his bed as she did so. He thought it interesting, but made no remark about it, for she was an innocent and knew that remaining in that genteel state depended on her staying as far away from his bed as possible.

He was not so innocent and ached to have her hot and writhing beneath him, the mattress sinking under the weight of their contorted bodies.

He had to stop these wayward thoughts.

She gazed at his leg. "It appears to be on the mend."

Her uncle had come by earlier to examine him and seemed pleased with the progress. "It's healing nicely. George says I'll be well enough to receive company downstairs within a few days."

Her eyes widened and she smiled, obviously relieved that he was one step closer to returning to society. "Excellent," she said with no effort to hide her feelings.

He supposed that he was relieved as well. Laurel's presence in his bedchamber had been wreaking havoc on his composure. He was no saint and his thoughts about Laurel had been decidedly sinful almost from the moment they'd met.

He had no doubt that he would burn in hell for them.

She'd be much safer once he was able to manage the stairs and meet her each afternoon in Eloise's parlor. Well, perhaps not all that safe.

But it would be easier for him to keep his distance from the girl. He had to not only maintain a physical distance, but keep her away from his heart.

He needed a convenient bride.

No complications.

No romance.

No broken hearts.

He needed a wife in name only. After the wedding, he'd return to Moray, for there was plenty of work to keep him busy, the first chore being to restore the manor house that Silas had allowed to fall into shocking disrepair.

After the wedding, Laurel could settle wherever she wished.

He would take her back to Moray with him if she asked, the choice hers.

Nor would he stint on her comfort if she preferred to remain in London with her family. He'd provide a generous allowance for her as well as purchase a townhouse for her in Mayfair.

He liked that idea, for he'd have a place to drop his bags on those rare visits to London. A large townhouse where they'd each have their own private quarters on opposite ends of a long hallway, but not so far away that they couldn't... if they bumped into each other during the night and the urge... *Damn!* What was he thinking?

"What's it to be today?" he asked, giving her the opportunity to select the topic of conversation. She had no book in her hands, thank goodness.

"I think we ought to talk about marriage. I need to know what you'll expect from me. In turn, I'll set out my list of requirements." That pretty chin of hers shot up again, daring him to dismiss her suggestion.

Quite the opposite, he was cheering. Silently, of course. The mere fact that she'd mentioned the word "marriage" was a victory for him. A small one, to be sure. "I have no expectations of you. You'll have as much freedom as you desire."

She let out a huff. "No demands after the marriage? If my presence is so revolting to you, we can end this farce right now."

He groaned and shook his head, already knowing the doomed path this conversation was headed. "I will not call off the wedding. And you know very well that your presence is not revolting to me in the least."

She rolled her eyes. "Be still my fluttering heart."

He sighed again. "But you do deserve an explanation for our betrothal, lass. Have a seat. I'll tell you why it's so important to me."

～⌖～

LAUREL SETTLED IN one of the two red silk chairs placed beside the open window. The stool was tucked beside his bed, and kept out of the way as it had been for her last few visits. She suspected that maintaining identical chairs beside the window was Graelem's way of keeping them on equal footing. Equals in the marriage. Equals in their seating arrangement. Equals in everything but the decision on whether or not to marry.

She was eager to learn why they had to wed by Midsummer's Day. The more he confided in her, the better the plan she could devise to thwart him. She watched him settle into the seat beside hers, her heart tightening as he held his breath and tensed his shoulders while easing against the bright red silk with slow, painful movements.

She knew that she could never be completely angry or indignant with him. He was suffering and she was the cause of it. "Tell me why we must marry."

"Because I'll lose my inheritance if I don't have a wife by Midsummer's Day."

That was simple and direct. She frowned. "So that's all I am to you? A means to an inheritance? No noble reason? You want the wealth and standing in society."

"I don't give a damn about society. I give a damn about the people who live and work the Moray lands, the families that have called it their home for generations. The title is mine whether or not we marry, of course. So is the manor house since it is entailed. However, that house needs a lot of work to bring it back to its former glory. Silas, the old Baron Moray, was not one to spend on basic comforts."

She tipped her head, confused. "So you're marrying me for my dowry?"

"No. Silas died a wealthy man. He could have left it all to me without restraint or restriction since I'm his closest surviving male heir, albeit through the maternal line. But he wanted to be sure I'd continue the Moray bloodline, hence the requirement for me to marry within the month."

"And if you don't?"

He ran a hand roughly through his hair. He'd obviously washed it shortly before she'd arrived so that it was clean and shining, and yet a few thick curls remained damp and refused to behave. The style was not elegant, but his slightly too-long hair and those few wayward curls suited him to perfection. *Drat!*

He cleared his throat and shifted uncomfortably. Clearly he did not like to speak about himself. "I'll lose the farms and other land holdings, the bonds and investments, the mining and shipping partnerships. I've spent most of these last fifteen years building them up for Silas and I'll be damned if I'm to quietly turn everything over to some worthless popinjay distant cousin who'll gamble through the assets within the year."

"Fifteen years? He put you to work by the time you were, what... about ten years old?" She gasped. "He treated you like an orphan in a workhouse."

"He treated me like a strict, elderly uncle who believed in working for one's supper. That's all. Don't make more of it than that."

But for one brief moment, she saw the loneliness and bitter struggles of his childhood years reflected in his gaze. "So Silas gave you only a month to find a wife?"

Once again, he shifted uncomfortably. "He gave me a little longer than that. He died almost three months ago."

She pursed her lips, struggling to rid herself of all sympathetic feelings for this man. It wasn't quite as easy as she had hoped, but she finally managed to do it. After all, he really didn't need her. Any girl would do. "Three months is still not a very long time to find a proper wife. However, you have a wide field of prospects available to you in London. If you're truly to inherit wealth in your own right, and don't need mine—"

"I don't. Lass," he said, his dark green eyes rounding in surprise, "I'd never touch a shilling of yours. What comes from your family is yours to keep."

She was relieved he wasn't after her trust fund, but that only heightened her confusion. "If you don't need my funds—"

"All I need is Moray." There was a stubborn set to his jaw, a nice jaw that any young lady would be tempted to caress. Just not her, because no matter how appealing he might be under other circumstances, he had unfairly trapped her into a betrothal and she could never forgive him for that.

"Then any young lady will suit your purpose."

He cast her a hard stare that caused her to blush by its heat and intensity. "I won't be meeting any of them for another week or two at the earliest. I can't take the risk of running out of time. Moray means too much to me."

But I don't.

"Can't take the risk or won't?" she asked, repeating the same question Eloise had asked of her when discussing their impossible situation and their not-going-to-happen marriage.

The solution to this problem was so simple that Laurel wanted to grab Graelem by his shirt collar and shake him soundly. "I'll speak to your grandmother and we'll arrange a small tea party right here. I'll also speak to my parents and insist on our hosting a dinner or musicale in our own home. I'm sure you will easily manage to walk next door given a few more days." The ideas continued to whirl in her head. "I have several friends making their come out this season. They'll trip over themselves to meet a wealthy baron."

He arched an eyebrow and leaned closer. "If they're so eager, then why aren't you?"

She tipped her chin upward in indignation, the common ending to most of their conversations. "As I said, I'm in love with another."

"Ah, yes. Devlin, the man who's kissed you with the ardor of boiled socks."

Her face began to heat. "If ever he were to kiss me, I can assure you it would be with more ardor than that of boiled socks!"

"If ever he…" He shook his head as though confused, then gaped at her and laughed. "You mean to say that he hasn't kissed you yet? Not even one stolen kiss under a Yuletide bough?"

She didn't think that her cheeks could grow any hotter, but they did. "No. Not yet, but—"

"Blessed Scottish saints," he said in a husky murmur. "Are you saying that I'm the *only* man who's ever kissed you?"

"In that crude and plundering way. Yes." In that wonderful, fires-of-hell-take-me-I'm-yours way that still had her blushing and wanting to rip the shirt off his body and run her hands along his hot, golden skin? She cleared her throat. "In any way at all? Yes. You're the first."

A solemn quiet came over him, but he shook out of it quickly. "Laurel, lass." He spoke with a gentleness not present before. "You can't possibly love him."

"I knew you were going to say that." She curled her hands into fists and returned his gaze with a scowl of exasperation. "I do love him. I *don't* love you. The kiss we shared was a mistake. I wasn't myself. I was distraught and uncertain."

She paused a moment and swallowed hard. "But thank you for not taking advantage of me. Had you tried, I think I would have let you." Because she was crazed and hurting. No other reason. Certainly not because she felt any desire for the oaf.

Goodness and mercy! Why would she feel anything for him?

"I know, lass," he said with a nod. "But I gave you my promise that I wouldn't touch you against your will and I'll keep to it. You wanted the kiss and it was harmless enough." He leaned closer still. "Granted, you wanted more. But I will not have you shamed or living with regrets for your actions on one of the most difficult days of your life. When you marry me—"

"*If* I marry you. Which I won't." *Drat!* The words sounded uncertain even to her ears.

"I'll make you a bargain."

She shot to her feet, instantly wary. "What sort of bargain?"

"I'll agree to attend these bloody teas and musicales if you stop dismissing the idea of our marriage."

She nibbled her lip in thought and noticed that Graelem's eyes darkened as he watched her. Honestly, why did the oaf have to be blessed with dangerously seductive eyes? They should have been watery or rimmed in red. They weren't. His eyes were clear and magnificent. "No more dismissing the idea of our marriage? I'll agree not to mention it when we chat"—*but I'll still think it*—"so long as you don't dismiss out of hand the young ladies I plan to invite to said teas and musicales."

"Agreed." He gave her a heart-melting smile. "Care to seal it with a handshake?"

No, she'd much rather seal it with a kiss. A lips-locked, tongues-plundering string of kisses to be precise. "*Blessed Scottish saints,*" he said in a hoarse whisper and rose from his chair to stand beside her. "Don't look at me that way, lass."

"What way?" She felt her heart beating faster and the heat in her cheeks was now spreading through her body, blazing a fiery trail through her veins. Graelem stood too close. She put her hand on his chest to nudge him back, but somehow her hand curled against the front of his shirt and she found herself tugging his big body closer instead.

Oh, dear. The wrong way.

"What's it to be, lass?" His mouth felt feather soft against her ear. "Do we seal our bargain with a safe and proper handshake?" His cool breath sent very hot tingles up and down her spine. "Or would you rather we seal it with a dangerously improper kiss?"

She let out a soft gasp. Did the man have no shame?

"A handshake, of course." But her wanton hands moved up to cup the back of his head and draw his mouth down to hers. She rose on her wanton tiptoes and leaned her wanton body into his because... all right... yes, she wanted the thrill of his mouth on hers. He was remarkably good at kissing, and who knew how many more kisses she'd get from this big oaf before they parted ways *before* Midsummer's Day? The two of them *unmarried* because she wasn't going to be leg-shackled to a stranger for the rest of her days.

For now, she loved the way he looked at her in that *I'm-so-hungry-for-you* way. And loved the way he held her as though she were the most precious thing to him on this good earth. *Were all men this good at pretending?* And loved the feel of his lips as they descended on hers, the low groan as he captured her mouth, the deeper groan as he ran his tongue across her teeth and gently parted them to plunge inside and explore her mouth.

He overwhelmed her senses.

She couldn't get enough of him, of his fresh, lather scent. Of his muscled arms and hard chest. Of his—

"Laurel!" Aunt Hortensia called to her in a raspy shriek that shook candles out of their sconces and resounded like a trumpet blare throughout the house. "Step away from that villain at once!"

She didn't want to. The kiss hadn't lasted nearly long enough.

A softer voice penetrated her ears. "Graelem! Have you lost your senses?"

Oh, perfect! Hortensia *and* Eloise had caught them in the act. Laurel's heart shot upward, constricting her throat so that she could not form the words to reply. Well, they had asked Graelem the question.

They didn't need to ask her because it was obvious to one and all that she had lost every blessed one of her senses.

Graelem tipped her chin up to force her gaze to his as they drew apart. He may have wanted to devour her, but she'd wanted to do the same to him. Ten times over!

She pushed out of his arms and turned away in mortification, not caring that her shove had almost tipped him over onto his broken leg. But this was Graelem. Big. Stubborn. Immovable. She'd have to push a lot harder to knock him off balance. The man was as sturdy as a slab of Roman marble.

She glanced back at him.

He was smirking at her, not in the least distressed that her aunt and his grandmother had caught them in a most shocking position and were still gawking at them. Indeed, Hortensia's jaw was open so wide her chin almost touched the ground.

Laurel felt humiliated. Tears welled in her eyes. What was wrong with her? What was it about Graelem that turned her into a demented harlot? She'd shamed herself in front of him, and now in front of her own aunt and his grandmother. Within minutes, every Farthingale in England would know what she'd done because Farthingale gossip spread faster than a raging wildfire.

"Lass, it was just a kiss. No harm done." Graelem crossed his arms over his chest and joined their spectators in gazing at her.

"Just a kiss?" Did she mean so little to him that he could simply dismiss it as a trifle? She was in danger of ruining her reputation over this one kiss, having been caught in a most embarrassing position in his bedchamber. Such behavior would not be excused even if they were betrothed.

Especially since it was a sham betrothal.

No, it was no longer a sham. Her father would insist on their marriage once Hortensia told him what she'd seen.

An ache started in the pit of Laurel's stomach and spread outward to her limbs in a slowly building wave. Her heart was already awash with pain, for she wasn't thinking only of herself. She'd betrayed Devlin's trust.

She couldn't blame Graelem for this lapse. He'd kept to his word and only kissed her because she'd wished it, but she couldn't forgive herself for what she'd just done and he was standing there, gloating over her mistake.

He wasn't completely blameless.

The ewer filled with water beckoned to her from Graelem's nightstand. "Damn it, Laurel. Don't—"

Too late. She poured its contents over his head, and then tossed the empty ewer onto his bed before fleeing the townhouse in sobs.

~❦~

"YOU'RE NOT ADEPT with the ladies, are you?" Laurel's aunt, Hortensia, remarked as Graelem stood in the middle of his bedchamber, dripping wet and quite certain Laurel would never marry him now. He'd had his chance to reason with her. They'd struck a bargain and had only to seal it with a handshake. Prim. Proper. Safe.

But no, he couldn't let it go at that.

"Apparently not." He'd wanted that kiss so badly. He'd wanted *her* so badly. Because of it, he had deluded himself into thinking a kiss they *both* wanted was all it would take for Laurel to end her objections and agree to marry him.

Eloise approached him with a towel in hand. "This isn't Scotland, you know. You can't just grab a girl and pull her into your arms no matter how obviously attracted she is to you."

He took the offered towel with a muttered thanks and began to wring the moisture from his hair and clothes. His leg was throbbing and painful. "I know."

"Poor thing. She was horrified by her own feelings for you," Hortensia remarked. "Not that I blame her. You are a nice-looking man." She harrumphed and shook her head. "Still doesn't excuse your behavior. What do you have to say for yourself, young man?"

He arched an eyebrow and considered his reply. Hortensia was an older woman, closer in age to his grandmother, and although Laurel referred to her as an aunt, Hortensia was actually her father's aunt. But it didn't seem to matter to these Farthingales. If you had a drop of Farthingale blood, you were affectionately referred to as an aunt or uncle or cousin. If you were a friend who wandered in often enough at suppertime, you became a cousin.

"Well?" Hortensia prompted.

Her hair was a vibrant white and she had those striking blue eyes that truly did mark her as a Farthingale. She was of average size but a bit on the portly side. This woman enjoyed her cakes, but there was no doubt she'd been a beauty in her younger days, for she had retained most of her fine features.

He sensed that he had an ally in Hortensia, for had she been as shocked or angry as Laurel had been, she would have been beating him about the head with his crutches by now. "Who is this fellow Devlin?"

"Lord Devlin Kirwood?" She smiled grimly. "Your competition. He's now in London, no doubt intending to offer for Laurel now that she's made her come out."

"Tell me about him," Graelem said while continuing to dry himself off. He wanted to twist his bloody towel around Devlin's throat. He wanted to kill the cur. A bit possessive perhaps, but he didn't want the cur sniffing about Laurel.

He didn't trust Devlin.

Hortensia arched an eyebrow. "Our families are neighbors in Coniston and he has long been devoted to Laurel. He's quite good looking. His father is a viscount and Devlin will inherit the title and likely the estate since he's the eldest son. His father ceded one of his lesser titles to him a few years ago, so he's Baron Kirwood now. An English baron, which as you know places him higher in rank than you since your title is Scottish."

She marched toward him and boldly patted him on his damp shoulder. "Don't let your jealousy of Devlin distract you. He isn't your problem. Laurel is."

"I know." Still, any man who had known Laurel as long as Devlin had and never tried to kiss her was suspect as far as Graelem was concerned. What was his game?

More important, how was he ever going to convince Laurel that Devlin had no use for her heart? Graelem instinctively knew the man had to be lusting after her trust fund and not her. "I'm not jealous of that ass. I'll rip out his entrails and stuff them down his miserable throat if he dares come near Laurel."

Hortensia sighed and shook her head. "Men," she muttered. "I had better go find my niece."

She hurried out, leaving Graelem alone with his grandmother. Eloise seemed none too pleased with him either. "You shouldn't have kissed her."

"She kissed me."

Eloise rolled her eyes. "I didn't see you resisting. No matter, the point is that she ran off humiliated. You're not helping your situation."

He ran a hand through his wet hair. "Damn it, Grandmama. I'm not some mewling boy who needs his grandmother telling him what to do."

"Good heavens, I should hope not! No, I think you must enlist the help of Laurel's sisters."

He groaned low in his throat, knowing his protests would fall upon deaf ears, but he had to try anyway. "I don't need anyone's help. I'm handling things just fine."

She eyed him up and down, making no attempt to hide her disbelief. "I can see that." Nor did she attempt to mask her sarcasm.

He supposed it didn't help that water was still dripping off his soaked hair onto his nose or that his shirt was completely soaked through. "I forbid you to invite them here."

"What?" She placed a hand to her ear, feigning deafness.

"Damn it, Grandmama. Do not invite her sisters here."

CHAPTER 8

BY NOON THE next day, Graelem was seated in one of the delicate yellow silk chairs in Eloise's parlor, smiling politely as he entertained Rose, Lily, and Dillie. His grandmother was not at home, which made him wonder whether she'd extended the invitation and then made a cowardly disappearance to avoid his wrath.

Hah! As if he'd ever raise his voice or—heaven forbid—a hand to his grandmother. Until now, she'd been the one ray of sunshine in his existence and the closest thing to a mother he'd ever known.

It was of no moment that right now he wished to strangle her.

"I hope you don't mind our intrusion, Lord Moray," Rose remarked while she and the twins settled in for what was clearly to be a long visit.

"Not at all," he lied smoothly, praying that Napoleon's forces would choose this moment to invade London, for he'd rather face a thousand battle-hardened soldiers than these three Farthingale sisters.

Rose's stomach had a light bulge to it, no doubt a sign of her condition. However, she moved with a casual grace that he found alarming. Weren't women in her delicate state supposed to stay home in bed and knit tiny booties and blankets with which to swaddle their infants once they were born?

To make matters worse, the twins were giving him eye strain. The same face on two different fidgeting bodies was a little more than his eyeballs could endure at the moment. "Your visit is a most… er, pleasant surprise."

Rose arched an eyebrow to signal her disbelief, but she appeared more amused than offended. "I suppose you're wondering why we're here, my lord."

"Quite the opposite." He responded with an amused grin of his own. "I know precisely why you've come here."

"Good, then you won't mind taking our advice."

Hell, yes, I mind!

Before he could answer, Watling rolled in a tray laden with lemonade, poppy cakes, currant buns, and ginger tarts. Dillie's blue eyes popped wide as she grabbed a ginger tart. "My favorite," she cheered and took a large bite.

Rose shook her head in disapproval before returning her attention to him. "We simply had to come. You see, Mother sent word that Laurel cried herself to sleep last night."

Damn. "I'm sorry, Lady Emory. I know she left here quite distressed. My fault, of course."

Rose nodded. She had lovely, dark gold hair much like Laurel's, and she resembled Laurel in height and slender frame. However, her eyes were a vivid blue with no hint of green in them. "Please, call me Rose. I've only been a lady for a few months and I'm still not used to it."

He agreed. "I hope you'll call me Graelem. Same can be said for my title. The ink's still wet on my Letters Patent."

Rose chuckled at the remark, but her amusement quickly faded. "Laurel is unhappy, and only you can change the way she feels."

Graelem shifted uncomfortably, for he wasn't about to release Laurel from their betrothal. "If Laurel sent you over here to—"

"Oh, dear me. No, she doesn't know we're here." A light blush stained Rose's cheeks. "She'd be appalled to know we've… well, taken on the role of mediators. I suppose that's what you would call us."

Dillie hastily swallowed the last of her ginger cake. "Simply put, we're doing what we Farthingales do best, meddling. If you understood Laurel at all, you'd know she wouldn't want any of us to interfere. But she may as well wish for the moon to turn green because that isn't likely to happen either, is it?"

She smiled sweetly and continued. "Laurel never cries, but you have her filling buckets with her tears. What did you say to her?"

"The usual, that I won't let her out of the betrothal." However, he shifted uncomfortably because he knew damn well that it was the spectacular kiss they'd shared yesterday that had set off those tears.

Lily pursed her lips and frowned. "No, that's not it. You've been spouting that same nonsense since the day Brutus trampled you. Something else happened yesterday."

Hadn't Hortensia told every Farthingale in existence about that kiss by now? Come to think of it, why wasn't John Farthingale at his door with every able-bodied Farthingale male over the age of seven threatening to beat the stuffing out of him?

Or at his door with a vicar and a special license in hand. Were he Laurel's father, he would be more determined than ever to see them married at once. Laurel had been caught kissing a man— *him*—in his bedchamber. The scandal would ruin her chances of ever receiving another offer of marriage.

Damn. Of course, Devlin would still want her. The scandal would only clear the field for him, making it easier for the bastard to get his hands on Laurel's wealth. Graelem was sure getting his hands on Laurel was unnecessary, for Devlin was using their childhood acquaintance as the means to lure the innocent into his trap.

Graelem knew men like that cur, men who used their wives as a lending bank and nothing more. Their marriage would be cold and loveless, a living death sentence for a girl as passionate as Laurel. As for himself, he'd do everything in his power to make Laurel happy every day of their marriage, assuming she kept her promise to marry him.

But how was he to prove his good intentions when the means used to bring her to the altar were heartless and cruel?

He considered exposing Devlin for the fortune hunter that he was, but he doubted the plan would succeed. He needed time to dig up dirt on the man, and he was sure there was plenty to be found. He had even considered engaging a Bow Street runner to gather information, but the problem was, he'd never prove Devlin unworthy before Midsummer's Day.

Devlin wasn't to be trusted, that much was certain. Graelem knew it even though he'd never met him.

But how could he convince Laurel?

The short hairs on the back of his neck stood on end at the mere thought of that bounder.

It wasn't jealousy.

It was instinct.

The man was a disreputable character. He'd just kept it well hidden from the Farthingales.

However, the problem remained. No matter how many secrets and scandals Devlin sought to hide, and even if he could find them before Midsummer's Day, Graelem's bringing them to light and destroying the bounder's reputation would not gain him Laurel's favor. She would never believe ill of her childhood friend, and even if she did, she would then be furious with Graelem for tossing the unpleasant truth in her face.

"Aren't you going to tell us what you did to make her cry?" Lily asked again, regaining his attention. He returned Lily's steady gaze. In truth, all three sisters had edged forward in their chairs and were staring at him.

He felt as though he were a prisoner being marched to a hangman's noose. "I kissed her." There was no harm in letting them know. They were going to find out about it from Laurel or Hortensia soon enough.

He wasn't certain why Hortensia had stayed quiet, for he didn't think the words "silence" or "discretion" existed in the Farthingale vocabulary... except for George's, perhaps.

"I assume it wasn't a genteel kiss on the cheek," Lily remarked with a snort.

"Oh, what fun! You gave her one of those kiss-the-slippers-off-a-girl sort of kiss!" Dillie had a soft expression on her face and her eyes took on a dreamy, far away quality. "That's the way Julian makes Rose feel every time he kisses her. Isn't it, Rose? You've said so many times."

Rose blushed.

"I think I'd want my husband to make me feel that way," Dillie continued. "I couldn't accept anything less than his whole heart, because that's what I would give him in return, all my heart. So, was it that sort of a kiss?"

He shifted uncomfortably, blaming the discomfort on his leg and not on the fact that he'd probably trampled Laurel's heart—inadvertently, of course—just as her horse had trampled him. "She might have taken it that way."

He expected gasps and recriminations. He'd coerced their sister into an unwanted betrothal and imposed himself upon her, but the three merely exchanged glances and smiled. "I told you so," Dillie muttered to her sisters and then turned to face him. "Very well, you've won us over. We'll help you."

He shook his head, confused. "Why? Because I kissed your sister?"

Lily continued to regard him as though he were the stupidest man in London, perhaps the stupidest man alive. "Of course not. We'll help you because you made her cry."

Dillie and Rose nodded in agreement. "Agonized, anguished tears."

What the hell?

He was more confused than ever, but he'd been warned by his cousins that women had the power to confound men and make them appear as witless fools. Women spoke another language. It might sound like English, and a man might recognize each and every word as it was articulated, but that didn't mean he knew what was going on.

Chances were, he didn't, for words held one meaning to women and quite another to men.

He'd never known his mother and had no sisters to confound him, so he'd always wondered what Alex and Gabriel had been talking about. Until this very moment. "Am I missing something here?" *Obviously, I am.* "I thought you liked your sister."

"We *love* her," Lily insisted, now looking at him in the same indulgent manner one might look upon one's not very clever dog when encouraging him to fetch the ball that had just landed at his feet without his noticing.

He held up his hands in surrender. "And yet you're happy that I made her cry?"

Laurel's sisters exchanged more glances and then must have reached a tacit understanding for Rose to explain this universal mystery to him. "No, Graelem. We're happy because it is obvious that she likes you more than she cares to admit. You see," she said kindly because it was also obvious that he couldn't see beyond his own nose, "she's overset because she thinks she is betraying Devlin."

"Laurel is very loyal. She's the best friend anyone can ask for," Dillie continued to explain. "Which is why she'd cut off her right arm before ever betraying a friend, even if it led to her own unhappiness."

"Which it will because she values Devlin's friendship, but she's falling in love with you," Rose added.

"Which is what I suggested she do," Lily said with a nod, "when Father admitted he was inclined to permit your so-called betrothal to proceed to a Midsummer marriage. What did you say to sway Father's opinion of you? He was prepared to bludgeon you to death before he met you."

Hell if I know. He shrugged his shoulders. "We spoke of Laurel's horse."

"Brutus?" Rose asked.

Graelem glanced at his busted leg. "Does she have more than one such beast?"

Dillie shook her head. "No, just the one. He's magnificent, but temperamental."

Just like your sister.

Lily nodded. "Father wanted him destroyed, he was that angry."

"I know. That's why I offered to take Brutus. I'll keep him in my care until Laurel is allowed to have him back." Once more, he shifted uncomfortably at the reminder of that horse. His leg began to twinge. "Laurel loves him, and I—"

"And you love Laurel!" Dillie interjected. "So you protected Brutus to make the woman you love happy."

Her statement was followed by a chorus of *eeps* and squeals and exclamations of *crumpets* that had him silently groaning and wishing Napoleon's army would crash through his door already. "We knew it! Father must have realized it as well. Crumpets!" she squealed again. "You certainly made an excellent impression on him. He never, *ever* likes any of the young men who come around to the house. He's very protective of us."

Lily turned to her twin. "Now that we know Graelem loves her, how are we going to get Laurel to admit her feelings for him?"

Dillie pursed her lips. "I don't know. Rose, what's your suggestion?"

"Stop. All of you." Graelem wanted to be stern and make clear that he wanted no interference, but three sets of big blue eyes filled with hope gazed back at him and the admonishment died before it left his lips.

Their gazes held not only hope, but acceptance of him, as though he were already a part of the Farthingale family. "This is getting out of hand. Before you turn me into a damn saint, which I'm not, you deserve to know the truth."

He'd spent his entire life with old Silas and the rest of his mother's clan and never felt welcome. To this day he wasn't certain why Silas had placed that marriage requirement on his inheritance. He wanted to think it was because the old man loved him after all and wanted to see him settle down and raise a loving family. In truth, Silas was probably thinking only of the barony and the need to carry on the Moray line.

His too small chair creaked as he attempted to lean forward without losing his balance. His leg was not yet able to bend, so he held it out straight and positioned in front of him. "I don't love your sister."

Three sets of blue eyes blinked at him at the same time.

He'd shocked them, no doubt. But they loved Laurel and he wasn't about to lie to them about his feelings for her. Perhaps Laurel did love him, in which case he was willing to commit to a real marriage for her sake, but his heart was not at issue here.

"Oh, dear." Rose shook her head and sighed. "This is more difficult than we realized. You're both stubborn and unwilling to admit what you feel for each other."

"Nonsense, I—"

Another girl, who looked remarkably like the twins and could only be Daisy Farthingale, burst into the parlor. "You'll never guess what happened!" she cried, addressing her sisters and overlooking him, although how anyone could overlook his big, oafish presence was beyond him. "Aunt Hortensia couldn't hold the secret in any longer. I knew she was going to erupt like Vesuvius spewing on Pompeii. I saw her bubbling and brewing and then *boom*!" She paused to glance at Graelem. "Hortensia tattled on Laurel to the family elders."

Dillie groaned as she popped another piece of ginger cake in her mouth. "Oh, no!"

"They're all in father's library discussing Laurel's fate as we speak." She rolled her eyes and sighed. "I listened at the keyhole, of course. Then Pruitt came along and caught me with my ear to the door. He chased me away and berated me for snooping." She turned to Graelem, forgetting that she had yet to acknowledge his presence. "Don't you hate it when your butler interferes?"

Because heaven knows, only Farthingales are permitted to do so.

Since Daisy wasn't really looking for an answer, she wasted no time in continuing. "Hortensia described the kiss as wanton. Now, Laurel is too embarrassed to come out of her room." She glanced at Graelem again. "She and I share a bedchamber now that Rose moved out. I'm Daisy, by the way. It's a pleasure to meet you, Lord Moray."

As an afterthought, she bobbed a curtsy.

"I'll have a word with your father. None of this is her fault." *Bloody hell.* He should have been pleased that Laurel was well and truly trapped, but he felt no joy in making matters worse. He didn't want her to be sad or humiliated. He just wanted *her.*

One of his crutches fell to the floor with a resounding clatter.

No, he didn't want *her.* He wanted the properties that were not entailed and ought to have come with the barony of Moray.

Love and commitment had nothing to do with this arrangement. However, he was no ogre. Unlike Devlin Kirwood, he'd never use Laurel as his lending bank and he was willing to put into the marriage whatever Laurel needed to make her happy.

Rose cast him a wry smile. "Wanton? How delicious! Of course, you were completely at fault because my sister doesn't know the first thing about... well, you know."

"I just said I was solely at fault." He frowned at Rose's smug expression. Dillie was smirking, and Lily was gazing at him so intently he thought she might be plotting to dissect him like a frog and report her findings to the medical societies. *Nothing found between his ears, just a vast, empty cavity where a brain ought to have been.*

The muscles in his jaw tensed. Laurel didn't deserve any of the treatment she was receiving from him or her family. Yet, he couldn't let her go.

Their marriage would stop all the gossip. However, Laurel would be the unhappiest bride ever to walk down a church aisle.

The twins were staring at him as though about to utter more words of wisdom. He wasn't about to take advice from a pair of fifteen-year-olds who looked so much alike they gave him a headache. Nor was he going to take advice from Rose who was... what? Maybe a year or two older than Laurel and had pretty much made a wreck of her own courtship, if what Laurel had told him was true about Rose abducting her husband... or had Julian abducted her?

Graelem had been in pain and not paying close attention.

"What is it about men that makes them reluctant to take advice?" Lily wondered aloud. "Especially from women." She perched on the edge of her seat and began to kick her feet out like a child on a swing.

Graelem sighed and shook his head. "Some of the smartest people I know are women. Most are much smarter than men, for they don't allow pride and arrogance to get in their way."

"See, Daisy," Dillie said with a grin, "We told you he was worthy. That's why we must help him. No promises, of course. The choice is ultimately Laurel's, and we must respect her decision."

"We just hope to nudge it in the proper direction," Lily said.

Rose laughed. "You'd better get used to having a large, meddlesome family around, Graelem. If Laurel chooses you, she'll bring all of us along with her." But her laughter soon faded and she grew serious. "You have competition for Laurel's affections."

"I know. Devlin Kirwood."

"We've known him a long time. Our families have known each other for years." Lily frowned lightly. "He's a 'gentleman'. He and Laurel have had a sort of understanding for several years now."

Graelem noticed the emphasis Lily put on the word as though she considered him anything but a gentleman. "Lily, don't you care for him?"

She swung her feet out again, a hint of her consternation. "There's something cold about Devlin."

Daisy shook her head and frowned. "No, he's very nice."

"Oh, he's nice enough to you and Laurel," Lily replied before turning her attention back to Graelem. "He dotes on the two of them, particularly Laurel. He's polite enough to Rose as well. At least, he was until she married, and now he hardly pays her any attention."

"Because I'm married now," Rose said. "It wouldn't be proper for him to take more than polite notice of me."

Lily pursed her lips. "I don't understand these rules of society. Seems to me that friends should be permitted to remain friends, no matter the circumstances. Isn't that what friendship is all about?"

Dillie shook her head. "You're being logical again, Lily. Unfortunately, society does not work on logic, but on status. Wealth, title, and appearances are all that matter. We've gotten off the point." She turned to Graelem and frowned lightly. "Laurel doesn't care for society's rules either, but she feels a sense of responsibility toward Devlin and won't betray him by marrying you."

Graelem arched an eyebrow. "So we're back to where we started."

"Not at all," Rose said. "But you won't like what you'll have to do to win her over."

Graelem didn't like any of it. Damn Silas and his terms of

inheritance and damn himself for wanting Moray so badly that he was willing to force Laurel into marriage over it. Was he that much of an unfeeling brute? He didn't like to think so, but he was. Moray was his and he wasn't about to give it up.

Nor was he about to give up Laurel… not after the way she'd kissed him.

He leaned forward. "Very well, I'm listening. What must I do?"

CHAPTER 9

LAUREL SLEPT FITFULLY and awoke the next morning dreading the stares she was certain to receive from the family members when she walked into the dining room for breakfast. In truth, she had no appetite, and since she was fast discovering that she was a coward, she remained in her bedchamber and rang for Gladys to bring up some tea and biscuits for her.

She also dreaded seeing Graelem this afternoon, not only because of the kiss she'd instigated for a second time, but because she feared Graelem was right. Why had Devlin never kissed her? Why had she never tried to kiss him? Was it because they'd known each other so long that changing the terms of their friendship was awkward?

She really needed to speak to Devlin and was about to write him another note when the door opened and Daisy walked into the room they shared. "Oh, good. You're finally awake. Laurel, are you all right?"

"I don't know," she admitted, scrambling to sit up and giving her sister a quick hug as Daisy sat on the bed beside her. "But I need your help. Did you see Devlin yesterday?"

Daisy nodded. "No one suspects that I've been handing him your letters. He misses you and can't wait until your punishment is over."

"Did he write back to me?"

"No, he was afraid one of our maids might find where you hid his letters and tattle to Mother and Father. He thought it wiser to convey his sentiments through me."

"Nothing in writing to trace back to him." Laurel frowned. "I suppose it makes sense." Yet it felt as though he were ashamed of his feelings for her, or being too coy about revealing them. She didn't think Graelem would have responded in the same manner had the roles been reversed and she obligated to marry Devlin instead of him.

"Laurel, may I ask you something?" Daisy seemed troubled, which only made Laurel feel worse for involving her in something that might end badly. She didn't want Daisy punished or somehow hurt for helping her out.

"Of course you can." She motioned for her sister to follow her to the cushioned window bench where they could sit more comfortably. Laurel tucked her legs under her and leaned against the window pane that had warmed under the sun's glare now that the rain had stopped. "What do you wish to ask me?"

"If you're so wildly in love with Devlin, then why did you kiss Lord Moray? Rose and the twins are certain that you prefer him to Devlin."

Laurel lowered her gaze and proceeded to smooth her nightgown, concentrating on removing a crease that did not exist. "What do you think, Daisy?"

"I'm not sure." She sighed and shook her head. "I adore Dev. We all do. But I also like Lord Moray… Graelem. I can see why you couldn't help but kiss him. He's awfully good-looking. But it isn't just that he's exceptionally handsome. There appears to be more to him than that. I don't know him really. But you've spent quite a bit of time in his company. Are my instincts about him wrong?"

"No, they're quite on the mark. He's clever, but doesn't make you feel inferior. He's big, but doesn't make you feel small. He's strong, but never makes you feel intimidated. Quite the opposite, one feels immediately comfortable and accepted when with him." She sighed again. "I don't know if what I'm saying makes any sense."

Daisy smiled. "It does."

She had to be honest with Daisy, indeed with all her sisters.

"There is definitely something about him that... I don't know. The first time I kissed him, I did it to prove that I would hate it. But I didn't," she said in a tremulous whisper. "So I had to try again, just to prove that first time had been a mistake."

Daisy leaned closer, awaiting her answer. "And?"

Laurel covered her face with her hands and groaned. "I loved it. But that doesn't mean I *like* him. I certainly don't love him. How can I when he tricked me into this betrothal and now won't let me out of it?" She dropped her hands and met Daisy's gaze. "Rakes are known to be excellent at kissing, but it doesn't mean they care about the girl they're kissing. They never do, which is why they earn the reputation as rakes."

Daisy nodded earnestly. "He didn't strike me as the sort to have casual affairs. So you think he's one of those horrid rakehells?"

"Well, no." Laurel took Daisy's hands in hers. "I'm not sure what he is. Or why I like his kisses. I think I'd like Devlin's kisses even more, but he's never tried to kiss me. Does that mean there's something wrong? Am I worrying over nothing?"

"I know less about such matters than you. There's no help for it, you'll have to ask Rose. She's the only one of us with any experience around men."

"Her only experience is with her husband. No, I have to find a way to sneak out of the house and see Devlin. He and I have been best friends forever. I love him. I do love him... it must be love. Will you help me?"

She noted the shadow of concern in Daisy's eyes, but after a long moment Daisy nodded. "Of course I'll help you. But you must be honest with me, Laurel. Are you forcing yourself to love Devlin out of loyalty to him? Or are you falling in love with Lord Moray?"

Laurel drew a deep breath. "I can never love a man who will force me into an unwanted marriage. I will admit that I'm attracted to him. Very attracted," she said as heat stole up her cheeks, "but I'm sorry I kissed him." *Twice.* "I'm sorry that I liked his kisses." *Loved them.* "But I refuse to be coerced into marriage. I'd rather die a ruined spinster."

Daisy let out the breath she'd been holding. "Don't be silly, that won't happen. Devlin adores you. He'll marry you no matter what you've done."

That didn't feel right either.

She wanted a husband, not a toady who would accept all manner of outrageous behavior simply to remain in her favor.

Daisy gave her hands a little squeeze. "Very well, I'll help you and Devlin. It's time you sorted out your true feelings for him. You and he must be honest with each other. It may be that you are only meant to be friends and nothing more. Where and when should he meet you?"

"I'm not sure yet. I'll come up with a plan."

～❦～

GRAELEM'S HEART SHOT into his throat as Laurel entered Eloise's parlor escorted by Watling. Two days had passed since he'd last seen her, and to say that he'd missed her was an understatement. Every minute of their time apart had passed with agonizing slowness, the girl haunting his inappropriately hot, lewd dreams each night, leaving him a hard, tortured wreck by morning.

Yes, damn it. He'd missed her, even though he'd filled much of these two days reviewing contracts and corresponding on Moray affairs.

He refused to consider that he might lose all of it because he hadn't married by Midsummer's Day.

He arched an eyebrow in surprise as she elegantly glided to his side, looking outrageously beautiful in a simple tea gown that picked up the rose blush in her cheeks. The girl usually bounded in with her eyes ablaze and hands curled into fists at her sides, but today she was the model of propriety.

Proper and demure were not words he'd ever associate with Laurel, but he liked this softer aspect to her temperament. He hoped it boded well, but expected it was merely the calm before the storm, for he had agreed to meet eligible young ladies and this afternoon's tea was to be his first introduction to them and others in London society.

Laurel and her uncle George had been invited, and there were to be three other young ladies and their families in attendance, carefully chosen by Laurel and his grandmother, although he suspected that his grandmother had taken the lead in selecting them. The slight description he'd received of these prospects roused his cautious instincts. They did not seem the sort of girls that Laurel would befriend. More to the point, since these girls came from noble ranks, he didn't think they were the sort to accept Laurel, a merchant's daughter, as their friend.

He disliked them already and would have gladly sacrificed his other leg to avoid this party, for he knew who he wanted and was content with his choice of bride, even if London's elegant society found her lacking.

"Blessed saints," he said in a raw whisper, setting down his delicate teacup with a clatter as Laurel settled in the chair beside his and cast him a petulant smile. What was wrong now? Hadn't he agreed to meet young women of marriageable age even though he hadn't wanted to? She had forced it on him. Was she regretting her decision? "You look beautiful, lass."

Watling had set out refreshments in expectation of the arrival of their guests, a display designed to impress Prinny himself, but Graelem didn't really give a damn about the food or the impending company.

Laurel was all that mattered to him.

He'd come down early to avoid being seen limping in and had bided his time by munching on scones and lemon cake. Although he preferred to wash them down with a smooth, aged whiskey, he knew tea was the safer choice. "Truly, lass. You take my breath away."

The compliment appeared to disconcert her, heightening the rose blush in her cheeks that matched the color of her delicate pink gown. Her golden hair was done up in a prim bun adorned with a matching pink ribbon.

She looked angelic.

In contrast, his thoughts were decidedly wicked.

That pea-sized brain of his was dreaming up exquisite erotic pleasures again, all having to do with Laurel. Naked. Beneath him. *Damn.* What was wrong with him? He knew that his tortured dreams would be of her again tonight.

"Care for some tea?" he asked casually. Not that he cared for anything but her... naked. Beneath him. She could keep that pink ribbon in her hair if she wished. "Or a scone?"

He imagined himself slowly untying the prim ribbon and watching her golden hair cascade over her shoulders and spill down her back in splendid waves. His favorite fantasy was of spending the afternoon with his hands buried in her glorious curls and himself buried between her thighs.

Watling cleared his throat to regain his attention. The old butler was usually discreet, never showing his thoughts, but he shot Graelem a disapproving glance that warned he'd better behave himself around Laurel or face dire consequences.

Was he that obvious?

He had better get himself under control before the others arrived. But it was so hard to behave when all he wanted to do was plant his lips, tongue, *and* hands on the girl. He had no need of tea or cakes—he only wished to gorge himself on Laurel. "You may go, Watling."

The old goat nodded and, still frowning, quietly disappeared.

Graelem struggled to his feet and moved across from Laurel's chair to put some distance between them. He sank onto Eloise's dainty settee, taking up most of it. "How are you feeling today, lass? You look overset."

She was frowning at him, too. "I thought you said I stole your breath away."

"You do. Always. But you're angry and I don't know why. Your lips are pursed in an adorable pout that makes me want to—" *Take your fleshy lower lip between my teeth and kiss the anger out of you, kiss you until I coax a hot moan out of you.* "Never mind, my thoughts are not meant for your innocent ears."

"Just as I am not meant for you. You're a beast. Which is why I've been miserable ever since the day I met you." She tipped her chin up and turned her gaze away.

"Ah, that kiss still bothers you." Obviously, it bothered him as well. He was hungrier for the girl than ever. He wanted to do something about it, but wasn't going to. He could see that Laurel was a powder keg of mixed feelings. One wrong step and he would set her off. "You're safe enough with me. Watling's got his ear to the door. Right, Watling," he called out and heard the old man mutter as he hastily shuffled in.

"Did you call for me, my lord?"

Graelem laughed. "No, just testing the waters."

Watling arched an eyebrow. "I'll be *close* by if you require my services, my lord."

"What was that about?" Laurel asked when they were once more alone.

"Nothing." He eased forward on the settee. "Let me pour you a cup of tea. How about a slice of cake? Or do you prefer a scone? They're quite good. I've had three."

She arched an eyebrow. "I wondered why the plate looked bare."

"I needed a bite after my ordeal."

"Ordeal?" A look of concern immediately crossed her face. "What happened? Are you all right?"

He nodded, amazed by how easily she forgot her anger whenever she believed he might be hurt. "I am now," he assured, "but it took me forever to make my way downstairs. I finally gave up and slid down the banister."

Laurel, her heart already softened with concern, couldn't help but laugh. Graelem watched her changing expressions with fascination. She wanted to frown and remain irritated with him, but simply couldn't. Her pretty eyes glistened with amusement and that kissable mouth of hers curled into a grin. "You did what?"

"I slid down. Wasn't too comfortable hitting the newel post when I reached the bottom," he said with a wince, "but serves me right for going down too fast."

"Oh, dear!" Laurel gave up all attempt to remain distant and indignant. He liked that about her. She couldn't seem to hold onto anger. She'd told him before that she was the forgiving sort. Good thing, for he was an ass in so many ways.

He'd forced her into an unwanted betrothal, couldn't look at her without having impure and carnal thoughts, had no intention of giving her up for any of the young ladies he was about to meet, and also intended to have a few words with Devlin Kirwood.

He needed to confront the man.

They were bound to meet eventually, but he would rather it were sooner. His leg was not yet healed, but he didn't care. If there was to be a fight... two cocks fighting over the prettiest hen... he'd rather have done with it now.

Devlin was going to lose.

The sooner he realized it and disappeared from Laurel's life, the better.

Graelem felt his blood heat, and all manner of churlish, possessive feelings began to war within him. Laurel was his and he wasn't going to give her up.

Laurel would never approve of a confrontation between him and Devlin.

Neither would her father, no doubt turning apoplectic at the idea of said two cocks fighting over his innocent daughter.

But what choice did he have? He was a big oaf who didn't know how to seduce a woman. He didn't know how to flatter or deceive or fill a girl's head with pretty lies. He was a hulking bear who followed his animal instincts. It was those instincts that had led him to Laurel.

Grrr. Pretty girl. Want her as my mate.

Mostly, he wanted her in order to secure Moray. But he was growing used to the idea of having her as his wife, of holding Laurel in his arms each night and waking to the sweet warmth of her body curled against his hard frame each morning.

"I used to slide down banisters, too." She cast him a delicious grin, all trace of anger gone for the moment. "That is, until I wound up with a backside full of splinters."

He was growing like the idea of marriage to Laurel immensely, even if it meant having her family about to pester him, for marrying the lass meant his house would be filled with Farthingales from sunup to sundown. Laurel's sisters weren't so bad—he actually liked them. "Ouch! That must have hurt. How old were you at the time?"

A slight blush crept into her cheeks. "It happened last year."

He burst out laughing. "Surely, you jest."

She winced. "I wish I were, but no. My parents confined me to my bedchamber for an entire week. In truth, it was no loss. I was so sore I couldn't take Brutus for his morning run, nor could I spend my afternoons visiting friends and family. The carriage ride alone would have been excruciating. And then to sit for hours in someone's fancy salon, sipping tea and pretending my *derriere* wasn't throbbing? No, I accepted my punishment without complaint."

He liked that mix of spirit and humility in Laurel. She had the ability to laugh at her antics, which only enhanced her good character in his mind.

"But I did let Father know in no uncertain terms that the banister was a hazard and had to be repaired at once."

He liked her playful honesty, her melodic voice and gentle touch.

That he might want her beyond the marriage ceremony concerned him, but he'd be safe as long as he concentrated on his objective.

Bloody hell. He'd never be safe around Laurel.

"But I didn't come here to speak of splinters or faulty banisters." She clasped her hands together and sat up stiffly so that her back was now straight as an arrow. "I've come to a decision."

He arched an eyebrow. "About our marriage?" By the prim purse of her lips, he knew the decision was not in his favor.

She now had the look of a warrior, not a helpless debutante ready to surrender.

Laurel let out a determined breath and glanced toward the door to make certain they were still alone. "I've decided that you are never to kiss me again."

"That's it?" He smothered a grin. Was she still thinking about that spectacular kiss? Could she not stop thinking about it? That sounded promising. "Very well. If that is your wish."

She had raised her teacup to her lips, but set it down with enough haste to spill some of the tea onto the saucer. "Of course it's what I wish. Why would I wish anything else?"

"Because you seemed to enjoy that last kiss. Immensely." He knew it was dangerous to goad her, but he did it anyway. She felt something for him and it was time she admitted it to herself, even if she wasn't ready to admit it to him yet.

More tea spilled onto the saucer again. "I did not!"

"I see." He stretched his arms across the settee and leaned his large frame against the seat back. "Then we have no problem. You don't want me to kiss you again... ever." He shrugged. "So I won't."

She eyed him with suspicion. "I hate it when you're smug."

"I know." He edged forward and leaned closer. "Next kiss is up to you. Since you've just told me that it will never happen, I have no choice but to take you at your word. I know you're not a liar."

"Of course I'm not!" Her glorious bosom began to heave. "How dare you suggest—"

Blessed Scottish saints! Give me strength to resist temptation. "I just said that I believed you. So let's speak of something more productive before the other guests arrive. Guests that you demanded I see, although I'm pleased with our betrothal and have no wish to break it off. You're the one who wants out."

"So would you if the decision were forced on you."

"It was," he reminded her. "Silas left me with little time to find a wife. But you know my predicament. Did you know that your sisters called upon me yesterday?"

"They did?" She eyed him askance. "They didn't tell me about it."

That surprised him, for it was obvious these Farthingales were incapable of discretion. "Should they have?"

She tipped her chin up and glowered at him once again. "They're my sisters. Of course they should have let me know." She paused a moment as though expecting him to speak up. "Well, what did they say to you?"

"It's private. Not for your snoopy ears, although they're very pretty ears. The point is, unlike you Farthingales, I can keep a secret."

Laurel shifted in her chair and edged closer so that they were practically nose to nose. Or lips to lips if she'd only tilt her head upward and… no, she had better not. "My sisters do not keep secrets from me. What did they say?"

He tweaked her nose. "You'll have to ask them. Later. Right now I'd like you to talk to me."

She gritted her teeth and spoke through clenched lips. "I'm trying to, but you're not making it easy. All you do is gloat. Very well. You've won the day. My sisters like you. Hurrah!"

He took her hands in his and held them lightly. "No, lass. I don't know what they think of me, only that they're willing to give me a chance." *And much needed help to survive today's tea party.* He wasn't a gentleman and didn't know how to behave in elegant company. "But you're not."

Her bosom heaved again as she mustered her indignation. "Can you blame me?"

He forced his gaze from her breasts, practically feeling his eyeballs tear from the effort of ripping them away. He was depraved… in so many ways. "I need you to forget for a moment that we're betrothed. I want you to think of these afternoons together as our courtship."

She slipped her hands out of his. "I can't. We *are* betrothed. Without my consent, I might add. You're not courting me, but coldly securing your inheritance. You can pretend whatever you like, but I'm not your sweetheart. I'll never be your sweetheart while I'm your prisoner."

That went well.

He was relieved when his grandmother entered the parlor and soon thereafter, George and the other guests arrived. He was introduced to a beautiful brunette, Lady Jane Hardwick, whose father was the Earl of Staunton, and then a cheerful redhead by the name of Miss Dora Pertwhistle whose mother was the grandniece of a duke, and Lady Katherine Lowesby, another stunner with pale blonde hair whose father was a marquis.

Their smiles faded as they watched him struggle to his feet to greet them. Lady Jane's mother turned to Eloise. "Will your grandson be crippled for the rest of his life?"

Damnation.

He was standing in front of the old battle-axe. She could have asked him the question directly instead of discussing him as though he weren't in the room. He was about to respond with typical Scottish impertinence, his intent to bring this idiotic party to an end before it had ever started, when he felt Laurel move to his side.

She let out a shaky breath. "No, Lady Staunton. It's a temporary injury. He'll be fit in another few weeks."

But the damage had been done. The sight of his crutches had thrown all three young ladies into a dither. As he responded to the introductions and all heard his Scottish accent, whatever might have been salvaged after Laurel's explanation was completely destroyed. The mothers turned coldly from him and frowned at Eloise, which irrevocably sealed his poor opinion of them.

If not for the private grin Eloise cast him, he would have tossed the lot of them out immediately. But this is what his wily grandmother had expected when choosing these particular guests. She knew that a crippled Scot would never be suitable husband material for their precious daughters. He eased back and allowed himself to be ever so politely ignored for the rest of the afternoon.

Getting the cut direct did not anger Graelem in the least. He wanted to leap up and hug his grandmother for purposely inviting three of the most insufferable families among the *ton* to her party. Laurel, so innocent and trusting of his fiendish grandmother, didn't suspect she had been tricked. At first, she looked confused. Then appalled. Then mad as blazes at the lot of them.

He grinned at his grandmother, wanting to reach over and plant a kiss on her lightly wrinkled cheek. The woman was subtly brilliant and understood precisely the effect that his rejection would have on Laurel. The girl, her protective hackles raised liked a mother bear protecting her cubs, was now seated beside him and glowering at everyone else.

"Did you expect these young lambs to flock to me, Laurel?" he said quietly so that only she would hear.

"Yes," she admitted. "There's nothing wrong with you. You're handsome as sin and you'll be a wealthy baron if one of them marries you by Midsummer."

"They don't see me as you do." He nodded to George as he joined their private conversation. "I was just telling your niece that these families can aim higher for their daughters. They don't need to waste their efforts on a Scottish baron with a broken leg when their daughters have already attracted the attention of English dukes, earls, and viscounts."

George readily agreed. "Perhaps Laurel can introduce you to some of her own friends when you join us for supper tomorrow night. I must warn you, the twins will be entertaining us with their musical talents. Dillie's quite talented, actually. She plays the pianoforte and sings beautifully. Lily butchers the harp, evoking sounds out of that instrument that should not exist on this earth."

Laurel grinned. "That's putting it mildly."

Graelem emitted a genial laugh. "I look forward to it. I'll bring cotton to stuff in my ears."

Laurel joined in with a merry chuckle. "Oh, you needn't go to the bother. We provide it to all our guests."

The party ended by late afternoon, none too soon for Graelem. His leg was throbbing and painful, and although he'd enjoyed having Laurel and her indignantly heaving breasts by his side, he was eager to remove his waistcoat and cravat and elevate his leg.

He escorted his grandmother to the front door to say their farewells to their departing guests, eager to be rid of them. However, the young ladies who had looked down their noses at him throughout the dull affair were not quite finished with him yet. Lady Jane brushed her breasts—unsavory, wrinkled plums compared to Laurel's—against his arm and whispered in his ear. "Lady Ansell's ball."

Blessed Scottish saints.

She was seeking an assignation. He wasn't good enough to marry her, just run his hands up her thighs, push up her gown and—

Miss Dora approached him. She angled herself to hide her

actions from the others while she brazenly stroked his manhood. "Lady Ansell's ball."

Hellfire!

The touch of Dora's hand sliding up his member ought to have excited him, but he felt nothing for the girl other than mild disgust.

Lady Katherine, to his relief, snubbed him. Or so he thought, but as he bent over her hand to convey insincere pleasantries, she whispered in his ear. "Lady Ansell's ball."

Bloody hell, her too?

When George joined them on the front stairs and began a conversation with his grandmother, Graelem took the opportunity to step back into the parlor. He ran a hand roughly across the nape of his neck and was about to let loose with a string of curses when he felt someone standing behind him. He turned to face the intruder and noticed Laurel staring at him. She looked stricken. "I saw them all."

Damnation, she'd witnessed everything. "What did you expect? I'm not husband material, but apparently I'm prime stud."

"But they snubbed you throughout the visit."

"So? Do you find their behavior offensive and hypocritical?" He laughed bitterly. "They aren't interested in talking to me. What did you expect, Laurel?"

She shook her head and lowered her gaze. "I don't know," she said in a ragged whisper, "just not this. Are you angry with me? This was my idea."

He tucked a finger under her chin. "No, lass. Even I was surprised by their actions. Seems none of them are quite the sweet innocents their families believe them to be. The sooner they're married off, the better. There are men who'll gladly shackle themselves to the daughters of these *good* families, and other men who'll gladly, er… service them after they provide their husbands an heir and spare. I doubt any of those lovelies will be faithful to their spouses."

"Will you go to Lady Ansell's ball?"

He let out a groaning laugh. "No, unless you'll promise to stay by my side all evening to protect me." He ran his thumb along her jaw. "It wouldn't be much fun for you. I can't dance in my present condition. Never was much of a dancer anyway. Thank you for your concern, lass. It was misguided and unnecessary, but I enjoyed having you near me, caring for me."

She let out a shaky breath. "I seem to dig myself into a deeper hole every day."

"No, your heart is guiding you to me, but you're resisting. I know that I haven't made it easy for you to like me. Nor did I wish to like you, but I find that you grow more beautiful to me with each passing day. We started off badly. Do you think we can start afresh and try to make a go of it? What do you say, love?"

Her eyes widened in surprise and her lips formed a perfect O as she considered his words. "You just complimented me. And why did you call me that?"

"Love?" *Hell.* It had just slipped out. In truth, after her tender treatment of him during this interminable tea party, the endearment felt right. "I don't know. You were wonderful to me, and although I'm an arrogant and stubborn wretch, I appreciated all that you did for me."

And I'm falling in love with you.

"Well, you kept to your part of the bargain. I owe you my cooperation now. I'll see you tomorrow." She shrugged her shoulders and cast him a weak smile. "I've never been courted before."

His hand was still upon her cheek. "Then I had better make it memorable for you."

CHAPTER 10

GRAELEM WASHED AND dressed, and then spent the morning hours dealing with the usual Moray affairs in the privacy of his bedchamber. As afternoon approached, he grabbed his crutches and was about to make his way downstairs to meet Laurel in the parlor, when she burst into his chamber without so much as an acknowledgment and rushed straight to his window. "Aha!" she cried, leaning precariously out of it. "I knew the twins were up to mischief!"

"Lass, be careful!" Graelem limped after her and then set aside his crutches to grab her by the waist. "What in blazes are you doing?"

"It's what my sisters are doing that worries me." He followed her gaze and saw the twins climbing up an oak tree in the Farthingale garden.

Obviously, they were attempting to sneak into an upper bedchamber in the townhouse, using that tree as their arboreal ladder. He watched with amusement as they crawled along the sturdy branches in their prim gowns, gangly stockinged legs exposed up to their knees. One branch touched against the house and was within reach of an open window. "What are they carrying? It looks like a large, carved head of some sort."

He recognized Lily since she was wearing spectacles. Dillie, her partner in crime, clambered in through the window and then leaned out to help drag the enormous head inside. Laurel groaned. "Oh, dear. Lily read about an African fertility god discovered in the Upper Nile Valley. It's presently on display at the Royal Society… rather, it *was* on display. Oh, dear," she said again. "I'm not certain she has permission to take it."

"She must have." Graelem laughed. "She couldn't have smuggled it out, could she? That fertility god is too big to sneak out under her pelisse or in her reticule."

"Never underestimate Lily. She's quite clever."

He and Laurel watched the twins a moment longer. Graelem ran a hand through his hair. "How did they get the blasted thing home without anyone noticing? Did they take a carriage? I didn't hear one stopping in front of your townhouse. They couldn't have dragged the statue through the streets of London. Or could they?"

Laurel was still leaning precariously out the window, and he was still holding her by the waist to make certain she wouldn't fall. She was soft and slender, and it took little effort on his part to keep her in his arms. No effort at all. Indeed, he already regretted the moment he would have to let her go.

She turned in his arms to glance at him. "Lily knows just how to manage these things. No doubt Dillie created a diversion while she carried that hideous thing out. Perhaps in a wheelbarrow. Is it important? They've stolen it and will be forever branded as thieves if they're caught. I had better go help them… I mean hide it for them… I mean, you know what I mean…"

He didn't. No matter. "I'll help, too."

"You will?" Laurel's eyes rounded in surprise. "And what will you do if we're caught and have to make a run for it?" she asked with a gentle laugh.

"I don't know. I'll count on Lily to think of something."

She eased back inside so that he no longer had reason to keep his hands on her. He cleared his throat and quickly reclaimed his crutches. Laurel was now studying him, looking confused. "You'd help my sisters?"

He nodded. "Of course."

"Why? They're obviously petty thieves."

"Because *you* love them and wish to protect them." He returned her direct stare, not certain why protecting Laurel's sisters suddenly seemed so important to him. But seeing her grief over her uncle's probable capture made him realize that she felt things deeply. There was nothing halfway about Laurel.

"Oh, that was well said." Her heartfelt smile reached into her eyes, those sparkling blue-green orbs gleaming like soft, aquamarine starlight.

She was making him realize how empty his life had been until now. Being tolerated by one's relatives was not at all the same as being loved or accepted. Eloise was wonderful, of course, but he'd only spent a summer in his youth with her and his uncle, the Earl of Trent.

At the time, he'd been too young to understand what made for a rewarding family life or a happy marriage. He was learning fast in the little time he'd spent with Laurel. "And I like the twins. They're clever and lively, never boring. I've never cared for empty-headed geese."

"They like you, too."

He chuckled. "As I said, they're brilliant and obviously have excellent taste… except for that monstrosity they just smuggled into your house. I also like their sister," he teased, referring to her, "although she delights in pouring water over my head."

The delicate blush on Laurel's cheeks turned into a crimson stain. "I'm sorry about that. You were defenseless and I allowed my frustration to get the better of me."

"Lass, I'm never defenseless."

"I suppose." She smiled at him again, casually propping her shoulder against the window and crossing her arms over her chest. She wore a dove gray day gown that covered her up to her neck, but there was no hiding her splendid curves or the lushness of her breasts. "My parents will be furious when they realize what Lily has done."

"We'll find a way to get that statue back to the Royal Society without anyone finding out. Eloise holds sway with the Duke of Lotheil. He's the chairman of their board, and though he's a dangerous man to cross, he has great respect for my grandmother. She'll make certain the twins aren't clapped in irons."

Laurel leaned her head back and let out a merry laugh, the first truly unrestrained moment of joy he'd seen in her. "Oh, my goodness! Can you imagine them locked away in the Tower? I'm sure it would take Lily all of five minutes to wriggle out of her chains, free Dillie, and then proceed to dismantle stone by stone this monument that's stood for almost a thousand years."

He laughed along with her, feeling a contentment he'd never experienced before. In this moment, he realized Laurel meant so much more to him than securing the Moray inheritance. She was someone with whom he wanted to share his life. All of it. The joys and tears. The good times and bad.

'Til death do us part.

He knew what her sisters had advised. They'd told him to let her go, to release her from the betrothal. They'd assured him that she would come to him of her own accord. If only he could trust that she would. Even if she didn't run straight to Devlin, she was smart and beautiful enough to catch the attention of a marquis or duke, and an English one at that.

She had no need to settle on a cripple with little to offer but a Scottish title, so why would she ever choose him?

No, he couldn't let her go, not yet. He'd given her too many reasons to dislike him, but she was softening toward him, of that he was certain. Could she ever love him? Perhaps, in time. But Midsummer was looming and there remained one problem he couldn't overcome in a few, short weeks.

She still had too strong a bond with Devlin.

~~❧~~

LAUREL HEARD HER mother's shriek, and she knew that Lily's fertility god had just been discovered by the poor woman who had a houseful of unruly relatives in residence for the season and a hundred guests about to descend on her for the Farthingale party in less than an hour.

Since Laurel was already dressed and her hair was done up for their party, she hurried next door to the room shared by the twins. Her mother was fanning herself with the pair of evening gloves held in her hand and backing toward the door as though that scowling head were alive and threatening to eat her. "What is that thing? Never mind. Dear heaven, I don't want to know! Just get it out of here now."

"But Mama, it has historical signifi—"

"Lily, it's hideous!" The bejeweled pins in her dark hair glistened as she shook her head in vehement dismay. Her usually rosy complexion now was as pale as the ash gray of her elegant silk gown. Laurel felt a pang of remorse. It was a wonder that she and her sisters hadn't turned their mother's hair completely white by now.

"I don't know how Dillie hasn't had nightmares over it," she continued, obviously distressed. "That *thing* belongs in the dustbin, not in your bedchamber."

Laurel placed a hand on her mother's shoulder to calm her down. "Actually… it's quite valuable. The Duke of Lotheil won't be pleased to learn that it has been tossed out with the table scraps."

"What has he to do with any of this?" Her mother's startled gaze moved from the twins to Laurel and back to settle on Lily.

Lily cleared her throat. "Well, it could be that he owns this relic. It could be that he loaned it to the Royal Society for a featured display." She cleared her throat again. "And it could be that it was shoved into the back of the display so that no one would notice when it suddenly disappeared."

"Oh, dear heavens!"

Laurel thought her mother's face couldn't turn paler. She was wrong. Her cheeks were now as white as alabaster.

"And it could be," Dillie chimed in to defend her twin, unaware that the woman who had carried them in her womb and shown them nothing but love from the moment they'd entered this world was about to faint, "that it has legendary properties that are worth exploring, only those fossils at the Royal Society have no appreciation for its importance, and so it was up to us to—"

"Don't tell me you were involved in the theft?"

Dillie glanced down at her toes. "Very well, I won't tell you that… but I was."

Their mother began to shake, and Laurel suspected it was out of a mix of horror, frustration, and fear that her youngest daughters had turned into hardened criminals. "You needn't worry." Laurel tried to assure her by giving her still-shaking shoulders a light squeeze. "Lord Moray has agreed to help the girls. He'll return it to its proper place without mention of their involvement."

"But how—" Dillie's thought was interrupted by a nudge and an imperceptible shake of the head from her twin. "But how… kind of him to put himself out for us," she said in a rush instead of asking her real question, how did he know they'd stolen the statue?

To reveal the answer also meant revealing their escape route along the sturdy tree that stood just outside their bedchamber. That tree would be cut down by their father's own hands this very evening in front of their hundred guests if he ever suspected.

"You can thank Lord Moray when you see him shortly," Laurel prompted, steering her mother out of the bedchamber and down the hall. "He'll take care of everything. All you have to do is welcome our company and enjoy the party. You've outdone yourself this evening," she continued as they walked downstairs and Laurel inspected the beautiful transformation of their home. "The house looks magical."

She meant it. The house was filled with flowers, shining crystal, and softest amber candlelight. A professional orchestra had been hired to provide music for those who wished to dance, and the tables in the dining room were bowing under the weight of the fish, game fowl, and ice carvings on display.

The opulence and elegance was nothing to the feeling of warmth and welcome one immediately felt upon entering their home. Laurel was proud of her mother. No one threw a better party than Sophie Farthingale.

Were it not for the fact that both Devlin and Graelem were expected to be in attendance, she would have looked forward to this soiree. She needed to speak to Devlin as soon as possible. Of course, they would have no privacy here. But they only needed a moment to confirm when and where they next would meet.

If her father ever chopped down that tree outside the twins' bedchamber, she'd have to find another escape route, but she couldn't worry about that now.

She had no more time to think about Devlin or Lily's fertility god as their guests began to arrive and she was caught up in conversation with friends and acquaintances. One of her best friends, Lady Anne Hollings, an auburn-haired beauty also in her debut season, approached. "Is he here?"

"Do you mean Dev?"

Anne rolled her eyes. "No, silly. I mean Lord Moray. Isn't he the man you wrote about in your letter to me? Will you introduce us tonight? If he's half as good-looking as you indicate, I'll be happy to take him off your hands. Unlike you, I don't give a fig about marrying for love."

"You don't?" Her friend's views on marriage suddenly seemed awfully cold. "But we used to chat and giggle about finding our handsome dukes and earls and making love matches."

"Love matches? You did. Not I. No, indeed. I agreed with finding a wealthy duke or earl to marry. Love never entered into my thoughts." She shook her pert, auburn ringlets. "My parents have been perfectly happy living apart these past twenty years. I haven't suffered for it either. We get together for the holidays and other occasions, and they're most cordial to each other. Never any fighting or tears or hurt feelings."

"Oh." Why did that sound so cold and empty to her?

"Father sends us our allowances promptly on the first of the month. I suppose his solicitor attends to it because Father spends most of his time in York with his mistress. His current mistress, that is." She leaned close and smirked. "However, I believe he'll soon be spending more time in Devonshire. Not that he ever tells me of his amorous adventures, but Lady Withnall seems to know all. I pry information out of her every chance I get."

The problem wasn't to pry Lady Withnall's mouth open but how to plug it up. Laurel stifled her dismay. Until this very moment, she had always thought Anne charming, clever, and a good friend. Well, perhaps she did possess all those qualities as well as beauty, but she was shockingly cynical about marriage.

The realization unsettled Laurel, and she thought it quite sad that a daughter should rely on the town gossip for information about her own father. Laurel's father was quite the opposite, always available to his daughters and filled with love for all of them no matter how much they vexed him, something Laurel did far too often.

Anne's gaze shot to the entry hall. "Mother in heaven! Who's that?"

Laurel swallowed hard. "The gentleman I wrote to you about. Lord Moray." He'd just walked in with Eloise, and although he was on crutches, hardly anyone noticed for the fine figure he cut in his evening clothes. He was tall and muscular, and the black of his jacket suited him to perfection, giving him an air of power and elegance that made him stand out among the crowd.

Laurel's heart leapt into her throat and she couldn't quell her excitement despite her determination to remain unaffected by his appearance. But in that moment, she couldn't recall why it was so important for her to resist marrying him.

"Dora Pertwhistle said he was magnificent." Anne's eyes gleamed and her tongue darted out to wet her mouth. "Perhaps he'll show me just how magnificent tonight."

"What?" Laurel clenched and unclenched her fists. Why should she care? She had been begging Anne to help her out of this betrothal and ought not to be feeling the slightest pang of jealousy.

But she was jade green with it, and seriously considering spilling the glass of ratafia she happened to be holding in her itchy hands all over the front of Anne's gown.

"I'll gladly enter into a business arrangement with him, but it doesn't have to be all business, does it?" Anne went on, completely unaware that Laurel was now looking for a cudgel with which to bludgeon her because spilling a drink down her front didn't seem quite enough. "Surely there are benefits to having such a husband." She was still ogling Graelem.

No, Anne would never do. Graelem deserved better.

Laurel held her breath as he walked toward her. Or rather, limped on his crutches. "Good evening, Miss Farthingale," he said, his voice a smooth rumble that warmed her blood and coated her insides like warm honey.

"Good evening, Lord Moray." She winced at the breathless catch to her voice and willed her heart to stop rampantly dancing within her chest. His gaze dropped to her chest for the briefest of glances as she struggled to regain her composure.

Yes, you oaf. My bosom is heaving because of you.

He knew it and cast her a wickedly appealing grin.

She frowned at him, but that only heightened his amusement. "May I present my dear friend, Lady Anne Hollings?"

Graelem took Anne's offered hand and politely tipped his head toward her. "A pleasure, Lady Anne."

Her dark green eyes were wide and innocent as she responded. "The pleasure is all mine, I assure you." She opened her fan and gave it a seductive wave. "It's rather stuffy in here, don't you think? Would you care to escort me into the garden, my lord?"

Why, that predatory feline!

Had she no shame? Not two minutes in his company and she was brazenly declaring herself available for more than a friendly game of whist!

"Alas, another time gladly. I must see to my grandmother's comfort first." He turned to Laurel and met her frowning countenance. "Miss Farthingale," he said with an irreverent smirk, "will you accompany me? She specifically requested your company."

Laurel was angry enough to kick the crutches out from under him, and might have had she not blamed herself—and only herself—for instigating the shocking exchange between Anne and Graelem.

She simply nodded, still too taken aback to respond without sounding like a shrill harpy.

"Your friend Anne seems lovely." He was smirking irreverently. "A little too forward for my liking, but otherwise quite pleasant."

Laurel made a sound of indignation that came out as more of a snort.

Graelem chuckled. "Do I sense disapproval?"

Laurel's shoulders slumped, and she put a hand on his arm to bring them to a halt. "I like Anne, truly. But I had no idea her ideas on marriage were so… so…"

"In line with those of elegant society?" His gaze was surprisingly affectionate. "You Farthingales are the only ones who hold unusual views on marriage."

"Love isn't unusual. Love is special and magical, something to be treasured. But I suppose you're right. Few families think as we do." Her hand began to tremble on his arm. "Anne would marry you if you asked her."

"Do you want me to, lass?"

In that moment, she realized that a simple nod would set her free. No more betrothal. Not a single obligation toward him. Graelem would move on to draw up the betrothal contracts with Anne's father and marry her well before Midsummer's Day.

And why not? Anne was beautiful and charming and would have no qualms about leading separate lives or allowing for an occasional romp in the sack whenever their paths should happen to cross.

But Laurel was frozen in place, unable to blink her eyes much less manage a nod. "No," she said finally in a raw whisper.

He let out the breath he must have been holding. "It wouldn't have worked out with her. I'm finding that I—"

"Laurel!"

A man's voice cut through the noisy crowd, addressing her with unseemly familiarity. She groaned inwardly, recognizing the voice as Devlin's. This evening was quickly going from bad to worse. First Anne and now Devlin. She knew he would attend, but had expected him to wait for her to approach him at a suitable moment so that they could talk privately.

Apparently he'd decided upon another tactic, for he was coming at her like a charging bull.

"Lord Kirwood, how lovely to see you. May I introduce…" Oh, drat! She refused to acknowledge Graelem as her betrothed even though she was warming to the idea. But to say nothing about their present relation did not feel right either.

"Lord Moray," Graelem said, absolving her of the need to

identify him at all. To Laurel's surprise, he did not appear irritated or angry by her hesitation. Quite the opposite, he appeared concerned and willing to help her out of an awkward situation, which was surprisingly decent of him. He could have established his claim on her by mentioning their betrothal as a warning for Devlin to keep away, but he didn't.

Laurel wasn't certain how she felt about that. His gesture seemed noble, but was she misreading his intent? By his politeness, was Graelem telling her that she could have the sort of fashionable *ton* marriage arrangement Anne had been talking about? She shot him a pained glance.

He stared back, confused.

She was confused as well, for she wanted to be released from their forced betrothal but not released from *him*. None of it made sense to her either. "Lord Moray is the gentleman you've no doubt heard about, the one almost trampled by Brutus."

Devlin eyed him with unmasked disdain, his lips pursing in disgust as he stared at the broken limb and Graelem's crutches. "The news is all over London, of course. So it's true. Your leg appears badly mangled. I'll relieve you of the obligation to dance with Laurel and take her for this first waltz." He extended his arm to Laurel.

Her hand was still resting lightly on Graelem's arm, so she felt his body stiffen and knew Dev's challenge had enraged him. "The next, perhaps," she blurted before the animosity between the two men turned physical. Her mother had worked too hard to make this party a success, and she wasn't going to permit these two preening roosters to ruin it.

"I'm sorry, Dev. This is my mother's party and I've promised to help her settle our guests. I must attend to Lady Eloise first."

His smiling facade quickly crumbled and he turned surprisingly angry. "So that's the way it is to be."

Laurel tipped her chin up in indignation. "To help my mother? Yes, that's the way it is to be. You know that family always comes first to me." She spotted Uncle George moving through the crowd toward her and hastily called him over. "I've been summoned to assist Lady Eloise. Will you please... er, help... I'm sure these gentlemen must be thirsty." Although having Dev and Graelem drunk and angry didn't seem to be a very good idea either. "I'll be off then and leave you three gentlemen to… to…"

She dashed off, knowing Uncle George would know just what to do.

Then again, perhaps not.

She'd taken no more than three or four steps before she heard the clang of a tray against the marble floor and the tinkle and smash of champagne glasses crashing behind her.

She closed her eyes and groaned.

No! No! No! Please let it be a servant who slipped and dropped his tray.

When she opened them, Lady Withnall was standing in front of her and grinning in that predatory, beady-eyed manner of hers that left everyone trembling in fear. "Interesting," the old crone said, tapping her ivory-handled cane twice on the floor and calmly moving on.

Laurel was too surprised to take another step and too much of a coward to turn around until she heard another crash and several shrieks from frightened ladies who shoved her aside as they ran past her.

She ought to have run as well, but she wasn't about to stand idly by while all her mother's hard work went for naught.

She turned toward the clamor and groaned.

Crumpets! as the twins were known to mutter whenever a situation got out of hand. That corner of the room looked like a battlefield. She didn't know whom to attend to first. Uncle George was nursing a bloody lip.

Graelem was clutching his broken leg.

Devlin lay sprawled out cold on the marble floor.

All four sisters came to her side to offer their support, or perhaps they simply came to gasp and gawk. Lily seemed to be the only calm one, adjusting her spectacles and clearing her throat before issuing a typical Lily comment. "And here I thought my harp playing was to be the low point of the evening."

CHAPTER 11

"UNCLE GEORGE, I'M so sorry!" Laurel pushed her way through the gathering crowd to reach the three men she had left only moments ago. "I wouldn't have left you alone with these two oafs if I thought for a moment they'd harm you."

Her uncle stopped dabbing the blood at the corner of his lip and managed a lopsided grin. "Not your fault, Laurel."

"Entirely my fault," she insisted, struggling to hold back tears. "Mother worked so hard to make this a beautiful party and now these two have ruined everything. It's because of me. I've handled this betrothal matter so badly!"

She frowned at Graelem, who seemed to be fully recovered and was collecting his crutches off the floor. "Did you hit Devlin?"

He returned her accusatory frown with a dangerous glower of his own. "Yes."

"How dare you!" she said in a harsh whisper, curling her hands into fists as she contemplated pounding them against his arrogant chest. She wouldn't, of course. She had no intention of giving their guests more of a show.

George put a hand lightly on her shoulder. "Laurel, stop. Lord Moray only hit him after Dev hit me."

She gasped as she stared at his cut lip. "Dev struck you?"

He nodded. "In Dev's defense, meager as it is, he was aiming for Lord Moray but missed. As Lord Moray turned to assist me, that's when Dev came at him again and kicked him in his busted leg."

Laurel gasped again, realizing she'd misunderstood the situation entirely. Graelem had to be in agony! She turned to apologize to him, but he shrugged her off and limped from the room on his crutches.

Anne rushed to his side and he didn't shrug her off.

Laurel felt as though she wanted to die inside. She couldn't tear her gaze from the pair. Anne had her hands all over Graelem, but the fact that he didn't seem to mind is what destroyed her the most. After tonight's spectacle, he'd be eager to release her from their betrothal.

Just when she was coming to the realization that she didn't want to be released.

She turned toward Dev as he groaned and slowly got to his feet with the help of Uncle George, the one man who had every reason not to help him. But that was her uncle, a soft-hearted, generous man who put healing others above danger to himself, above his pride and creature comforts.

Laurel took Dev's other arm to support him until he'd regained his balance. "Dev, you fool. What did you think you were doing?"

Graelem was taller and far more muscular. Next to him, Dev looked like one of those frail romantic poets, and after days and days and *days* of reading nothing but odes and sonnets and *The Song of Roland* to an injured Graelem, she really hated those poets.

"You belong to me, Laurel," he said in bitter frustration. "Who is this man to steal you away from me after knowing you less than five minutes? I've known you all my life. We've been friends since childhood. Does he think he can snatch that from me without a fight?"

Laurel stiffened. "Snatch *that*? And what is *that* exactly?" He hadn't said *snatch you*, and amid all his ire and bluster he'd made no mention of loving her. Then what was he courting? Her trust fund?

"You, of course. What else do you think I'm talking about?" He winced and closed his eyes as she and her uncle helped him to their ballroom and into one of the many chairs lining the dance floor. The chairs had been set there to accommodate dowagers and wallflowers, although her male cousins had been ordered to see to those young ladies and ensure each had a dance partner to properly attend to them throughout the evening.

This was a Farthingale party and all their guests were to be entertained, especially the wallflowers. Of course, their guests had been unexpectedly and most shockingly entertained by flying fists and clattering champagne trays just now.

How was she ever going to make it up to her parents? They didn't deserve to be humiliated like this.

"Laurel, dare I leave this fool alone with you?" her uncle asked. "Your mother must be in a state of shock. I'm certain your father isn't dancing a jig either. I need to help them out."

Laurel nodded. "Of course. I'll be safe." Other guests were strolling back into the ballroom now, fortunately to dance and not to gawk or sneer at them, for the orchestra had resumed playing a lively reel and that seemed more fun than watching Devlin wobble in his chair.

Dev exhaled as Laurel settled beside him. She caught a strong whiff of whiskey on his breath. "You've been drinking?"

He shrugged off the accusation. "You've given me cause."

She scowled at him. "You *came* to the party drunk and intending to cause mischief."

He laughed and shook his head. "I needed the fortification to face you. Don't you realize that you broke my heart?" He paused a long moment, the tension between them at odds with the gaiety of the music and the giggles and chatter of their guests. "I love you, Laurel."

She leapt to her feet, refusing to accept his declaration because her heart was already ripping into little pieces, and because knowing that Devlin had truly cared for her all these years would simply tear it to shreds. "Why didn't you ever tell me before?"

His gaze was hot and angry. "I didn't think I needed to remind you until tonight."

"Remind me of what? Of something you've never once expressed in all the years we've known each other? How convenient of you to wait until the worst possible moment—"

He grabbed her hand and held it tightly. "Are you saying that you don't love me? That you've fallen in love with that ruffian?

That you'll allow him to steal your fortune and leave you to pine away in isolation on his Scottish estate?" She tried to pull away, but his grip tightened. "Anne will have him. She told me so earlier today. Leave them to their business arrangement and come away with me."

"No, my parents won't—"

"Do you love me, Laurel? If you do, then meet me one week from tonight in the mews behind Chipping Way. I'll be there at midnight and we'll steal off to Gretna Green together. No one will catch us if we ride on horseback instead of going by carriage. Brutus remains in your stable. I'll bribe your groom to have him saddled and ready for you."

"Don't you dare, Dev!" She shook her head vehemently. "First of all, Amos is loyal to our family. He cannot be bribed and I'd be so ashamed if you tried." She let out a ragged breath as he released her. "I won't be forced into marriage. Not by you or Lord Moray."

"Forced? Is that what you think I'm doing?" Dev appeared to lose all anger. He rubbed a hand across his face as though to sober himself up. "Laurel, I love you. I'll be at the mews one week from tonight. Meet me there at midnight and I'll take you to Gretna Green. It will all work out. You'll see. I'll make you a good husband."

Laurel nodded, for she hadn't the heart to fight with him any longer. That two lords had come to blows over her was already too much of a scandal to tolerate. She nodded again and was turning to walk away when she noticed Daisy standing behind her, concern mirrored in her eyes.

How long had her sister been standing there?

How much had she overheard?

"Laurel, I was worried about you. Are you all right?" Daisy put a gentle hand on her shoulder.

Laurel laughed mirthlessly. "I don't think so. I've ruined Mother's party, Uncle George has a busted lip because of me, and Dev and Graelem almost killed each other."

Daisy grimaced. "Look on the bright side—you'll make me look brilliant compared to you when I come out next year."

Laurel shook her head and laughed in true merriment this time. "Of course you'll be brilliant. You're the good daughter. What can possibly happen to you?"

They shared a brief, sisterly hug before Daisy drew back and pursed her lips. "You're trembling. I think you need a breath of air. Go on into the garden and I'll look after Dev. He looks awfully wretched."

They both glanced at him.

He was looking downward and gazing at his feet. Everything about him spoke of dejection. Laurel couldn't bear it and rushed off toward the open doors leading into the garden, needing the privacy of the dark outdoors where she could give in to her own distraught feelings and cry.

However, if she thought the gentle breeze and scent of roses or the clear, starry night and full, silvery moon would help to calm her, she was sadly mistaken. Graelem was seated alone on a garden bench in a distant corner of the garden, his broad shoulders outlined in the moonlight. Anne must have been seated beside him only moments earlier, for she suddenly stormed by Laurel with a look of murder in her eyes.

Oh, dear. What now?

"Anne." She reached for her friend's hand to stop her. "What's wrong? What happened?"

"Ask your Scottish lout." She tossed back her perfect curls and marched inside.

Were it not for the disappointment her dear mother had to be feeling, Laurel would no longer be thinking of crying but of laughing aloud and not stopping until her sides ached. The evening that was to be so special and delightful was fast turning into a waking nightmare.

She'd spoken to Dev and left him in Daisy's care.

It was time to speak to Graelem.

"How's your leg?" she asked, sinking onto the hard, stone bench and scooting next to him. Her body, once cold and shivering, instantly warmed as she nestled beside him.

"I think your uncle had better have a look at it," he said quietly.

Laurel gasped and regarded him in alarm. She knew Graelem well enough by now to realize he was in agony. Devlin must have broken the bone again when he kicked Graelem, and it must have been a vicious kick to cause that much damage to bones that were well on their way to mending. "I'll go find him."

"No, lass. Not necessary." He ran a hand through his hair. "He knows to look for me once he's attended to everyone else who needs to be calmed. Your mother. Your father. Your Aunt Hortensia."

Laurel quirked her head to stare at him. "What happened to Hortensia?"

He laughed softly. "I have no idea."

She threw back her head and laughed along with him, her anger fading as she sat beside him and commiserated on the disastrous evening. The breeze felt gentle, and there was a softer silver glow to the stars and moon because she was beside Graelem. "We Farthingales are known to be a bit theatrical when displaying our feelings. I'm sure Aunt Hortensia was afflicted by nothing more than a feigned bout of the vapors."

He arched an eyebrow. "Your family a bit theatrical? That's rather an understatement."

"I know." She took a gulp of fresh air, trying to remain calm even though she caught the scent of lilac against Graelem's throat and chest, and knew that Anne must have been all over him only moments ago. Then why did Anne rush off in a huff? "You'll have no protest from me. I know we Farthingales are a menace to society. But... but... but..."

"What, lass?"

She took another gulp of air. "Anne ran past me as I walked into the garden."

"Ah." He gave a knowing nod.

"She wasn't too pleased with you. What happened?" She placed her hand lightly on his arm and felt his shrug.

"It's what didn't happen that has her madder than a wounded boar."

Laurel's heart began to beat faster. "What didn't happen?"

"The kiss she wanted, for starters." He clutched his leg as it began to twinge. "And everything else she wanted that I refused to give."

"And if I asked you why you refused her, what would you say to me?" She knew that she had no right to cheer, for she was the one who'd purposely introduced them. She had wanted to be free of the betrothal until the moment she realized it might actually come to pass. Then, she'd felt nothing but remorse and jealousy.

He muttered a curse as the twinges grew more intense. "I'd say… better fetch your uncle. I think my damn leg is about to fall off."

"UNCLE GEORGE, HE'S burning up with fever."

Laurel was in Graelem's bedchamber at Eloise's house with her hands clasped in worry. She had been seated beside Graelem for the past three hours, watching him grow progressively worse. The party was still going on next door, at her home, and strains of enchanted music wafted in through the open window.

She and her uncle, with the help of Amos, the young Farthingale groom who was big as an ox and twice as strong, had quietly assisted Graelem from their garden into Eloise's townhouse, where Eloise's footmen had taken over the duty of carrying him upstairs.

"There's nothing more we can do but sit and watch him," her uncle said gently. "I'll order an ice bath prepared in case his fever spikes higher."

"What can I do to help?" Laurel hadn't changed out of her pale rose silk gown, but gave it no further thought. She had several gowns in this same hue, for Madame de Bressard, her modiste, had declared pink was her color. She loved this gown and had been dreaming of the moment she would wear it to the party, but now she didn't care if it was ruined. Graelem's recovery was the only thing that mattered.

"Just sitting beside him and holding his hand is doing wonders for him. I'll be back in a few minutes." He patted her shoulder.

"But shout for me at once if he goes into convulsions."

Convulsions!

"I will." Her heart began to pound through her chest and all she could think of was Graelem and how she couldn't bear to lose him.

As little as an hour ago he'd been alert and grinning as they'd listened to the discordant strains of harp and pianoforte filtering in through his open window. The twins had stunned the Farthingale guests with their recital, and Lily's harp playing could only be described as dreadful. Dillie was splendid, as always. No one understood why she refused to cut Lily from the recital and shine on her own. Perhaps because they were bound to each other, two identical hearts beating as one.

Could she ever have such a connection with Graelem?

Her parents had it, always quietly showing concern and affection for each other. Symbolic of their love, together they had regained control of their party, and everyone now seemed to be having a jolly good time, unaware that Graelem was fighting for his life.

What of Devlin?

She hadn't given him much thought over the past few hours. No doubt he had stomped off to pout, for he used to do just that when they were children and he didn't get his way. Goodness, she hoped the petulant boy hadn't turned into a petulant man. Kicking Graelem in his broken leg had been a cruel thing to do.

She couldn't blame Graelem for fighting back. He'd only done so after Devlin had struck her uncle and then kicked him. One restrained punch from Graelem was all it took to flatten Devlin, her uncle had said.

She knew Graelem had held back, otherwise Dev's jaw would have been broken or worse, he would have been dead.

She couldn't worry about him now. Graelem was foremost on her mind. His leg was swollen and purple, revealing another possible break to one of the same bones first broken, and she feared this time it was much worse than Brutus' trampling.

He was in so much agony not even a healthy dose of laudanum had helped.

She couldn't bear to watch him suffer, but neither would she leave his side until he was on the mend again. *All her fault.* What was wrong with her? She had a penchant for getting into trouble, but the punishment usually fell on her. This was different. This felt awful, for Graelem was the one bearing the brunt of her misdeeds.

She wouldn't blame him if he begged out of the betrothal the moment he awoke. How ironic, for now the last thing she wanted was to be apart from him. Why couldn't she get this marriage business right?

She'd only spent a lifetime training for this moment. Apparently, she'd learned nothing in all those years.

"Lass," Graelem said, his voice a whispered rasp, gaining her attention as he awoke from his laudanum-induced stupor. "What are you still doing here?"

She sniffled. "Trying to look after you, but I'm not doing a very good job of it."

"You're doing an excellent job. You're the only vision I wished to see when I opened my eyes… and here you are." He shook his head slowly and swallowed hard. "Though I don't suppose you'll be permitted to stay much longer."

"Since when have I done what I'm told?" she teased and heard him softly chuckle in response. "I'm not leaving your side until your fever breaks and you're strong enough to get out of bed." She sniffled again.

"Laurel, are you crying?"

"Don't be ridiculous." But she sniffled yet again because he reached out to stroke his thumb along her cheek to wipe away the tears that must have been shining upon it. "I'm the hot-tempered, disobedient Farthingale, remember? I think of no one but myself and wind up hurting my loved ones in the process."

"Don't be so hard on yourself."

Her eyes clouded with more tears and she struggled to suppress the sob yearning to break free. "I can't help it. Look what I've done to you."

"Damnation. You're the oddest mix of tough and soft. I've never… lass, you *are* crying. Blessed Scottish saints, no one has ever cried over me before."

No one? Now she was desperately struggling not to burst into wailing sobs.

She turned away to dip her handkerchief in the basin of cold water on his night stand, busying herself with the task while she fought to regain her composure. She wrung out some of the moisture and then ran the now cold cloth across his hot brow to cool him down. "Your lips must be dry and throat parched. Here, let me squeeze a little of the water into your mouth."

He surprised her with another chuckle. "Lass, this one time I could do with your dumping the entire contents of that basin over my head."

"I will if the need arises, especially since I now have your blessing." She smiled at him as she dipped the handkerchief into the water again and ran the cold cloth along his neck and chest. Her breaths were still shaky, she was still sniffling, and she was completely unraveling on the inside. She was so distraught and worried, struggling not to bawl like an infant with colic. "I've been a fool, Graelem. Can you ever forgive me?"

He caught her hand in his and shook his head. "I've been the fool, love. I should be the one asking for your forgiveness. I—" He shuddered as a blinding pain suddenly tore through him. She realized his leg had begun to spasm, each flex and pull of bruised muscle obviously agonizing for him.

Laurel gripped his hand and held it tightly as she drew it against her pounding heart. "Graelem, what should I do?"

He didn't immediately answer.

"Graelem?"

"Love me, Laurel," he said in a whisper and lost consciousness as pain and laudanum overcame him once again.

Had he meant it? Did he realize that he'd spoken the sentiment aloud? She used the back of her hand to wipe at the tears that were now rolling down her cheeks like rivers overflowing their beds. "I do," she said in a whisper. "I love you so much."

CHAPTER 12

LAUREL REMAINED BY Graelem's bedside, holding his hand.

She understood what would happen if she stayed here until dawn, something she fully intended to do despite the consequences. There would be no ending their betrothal. No doubt it was already too late to end it, for even though nothing improper had happened over these past few hours, or could happen with Uncle George, Eloise, and a dozen servants slipping in and out of the room all night long, the news sure to spread throughout the *ton* was that she had spent the night with Graelem.

In his bedchamber.

She had, of course. But only to help save his life.

Rose's husband had come by earlier, having taken it upon himself to report Graelem's progress to the Farthingale family. Her parents were worried, but as host and hostess, they couldn't possibly leave their party.

She was glad Julian was the one chosen to report the news to them, for he was as steady as Uncle George and could be counted upon to use his good judgement. He wouldn't embellish nor would he minimize the danger, but explain it in a manner that did not alarm her entire family. Didn't they have enough to worry about with Uncle Harrison still missing and the ministry still having no news about him?

What the... She blinked as a glimmer of light caught her eye. And then another glimmer. She shook her head and groaned softly. The twins, in their inimitable way, were using a mirror to catch the glow of moonlight and send her signals through their window. The sweethearts wanted to let her know they were still awake and concerned. *I love you, too.*

She eased away from Graelem's side long enough to cross to the window and wave at them. In return, she received three quick flashes of light which she knew signified their wishes for his quick recovery.

She returned to Graelem's side and stared down at him, unable to remove her gaze from his big, handsome body. She'd been an obstinate fool to wait so long to admit that she loved him. What had Graelem meant by the words he'd uttered before slipping back into his stupor?

Love me, Laurel.

Did he want her to love him because he loved her? If so, those words sounded so sweet to her ears because Graelem had uttered them. She wouldn't have felt the same euphoric joy had anyone else expressed those sentiments. Devlin had declared his love for her tonight, but it wasn't at all the same thing. She cringed, recalling their conversation. "Dev, what am I going to do about you?" she muttered to herself.

He'd behaved abominably, but otherwise had been a good and loyal friend to her over the years. His outrageous conduct could be explained as jealousy and probably forgiven in time, for he was angry and bitterly disappointed by the thought of losing her.

Indeed, the more she considered it, the more she realized that her betrothal must have come as a terrible shock to him. She owed him an apology and would speak to him, but only after she was certain Graelem was on the mend.

She refused to leave his side until then.

Graelem hadn't made a sound since falling into unconsciousness, no doubt because of all the laudanum he'd taken, a dosage strong enough to fell a horse. But shortly before dawn, he began to moan and blink open his eyes. She felt him looking at her, his forest green eyes dark and glistening with fever.

She gasped. "Are you awake?" She couldn't be certain, for the drug was known to induce eye movements that mimicked wakefulness.

"What?" He sounded groggy and confused.

"I was so worried about you." She kept her voice low in order not to wake her uncle, who was stretched out across the three red silk chairs set in a row by the window and softly snoring. He'd been up most of the night along with her and was finally getting some much-needed rest.

Graelem tried to sit up in bed, groaning as he strained his big body in the hope of finding a position that wasn't agonizingly uncomfortable.

He wasn't having much success.

She wanted to help, but was afraid to touch him. Not afraid for him, but for herself. Watching the magnificent flex and pull of his hard muscles was doing shocking things to her insides, sending hot tingles shooting through her body and making her want to hop into bed beside him so that she could feel the flex and strain of his big, handsome body against hers, feel his weight as he wrapped her in his arms and brought her up against his hot, bronzed skin.

Graelem's eyes were now alert and fully open, but still slightly glazed, which meant he was feverish. He studied her for an endless moment and smiled. "Feeling warm? Me too, lass."

A fiery heat suffused her cheeks. How could he know what she'd been thinking? Was she that obvious? "I don't know what you're talking about."

Fortunately, he decided not to pursue the embarrassing matter. Instead, he glanced around the room and then toward the window. "What time is it?"

"Almost morning." When she checked his forehead, he felt much cooler than he had been as little as an hour ago. She rested her palm against his cheek and caressed him. "You gave me a terrible scare, you big oaf."

He frowned lightly. "Did you stay by my side all night?"

She nodded. "I was afraid you were going to die." The words caught in her throat as she spoke. "So I stayed, determined to fight heaven and earth to keep you here and safely on the mend."

He grinned. "No wonder I survived. There's no force stronger than a determined Laurel." He noticed that she was still wearing her evening gown. "You look beautiful, lass. Did I mention it to you last night? I meant to. You stole my breath away when I first walked into your home, the party under way and already a crush. But everyone else seemed to melt away and all I saw was you in that gown. There isn't a prettier debutante in all of London."

She shook her head and laughed. "I think you must be addled, but I do like this softer side of you best."

"I don't." He looked down and saw that his nightshirt was damp and clinging to his body. "I don't think anyone can like me as I am now. I'm soaked from head to toe and so loaded with laudanum I can't put two thoughts together."

"Your conversation isn't the problem. Nor are your thoughts. What you don't like is that your guard is down and you're afraid something you don't wish to reveal might slip out. You don't want me, or anyone for that matter, to see beneath your surface."

He arched an eyebrow.

"But you're too late. I've seen you unguarded." She caressed his cheek again. "And I like what I see."

He laughed and reached out to cup her head in his big hand. "How much do you like it?"

"This much," she said and leaned forward to kiss him on the lips. She couldn't quite describe the kiss she gave him, for it wasn't a light peck nor was it a passionate, desperate kiss given with wild abandon. It was full and rich, conveying a deeper meaning, a kiss that spoke of commitment, passion, and enduring love.

Her breasts pressed against his chest as she leaned forward to kiss him, but she didn't draw away. She wanted nothing to keep them apart—certainly not rules of propriety designed to keep a girl pure until marriage, but allow her to take up as many liaisons as she desired afterward so long as she was discreet.

Her mouth parted against his firm lips as he groaned and drew her closer, enveloping her in his arms and running his tongue across her fleshy lower lip before claiming entrance and rousing sensations throughout her body as explosive and beautiful as fireworks upon the Thames.

Everything about him set her blood on fire. The warmth and strength of his body, the gentleness of his hands as he touched and stroked her with possessive urgency. The scent of heat and sweat and sandalwood on his neck and shoulders.

His kiss was hot and determined, yet also gentle, as though he were purposely letting her know that his attraction to her went beyond a merely physical hunger. In the few weeks she'd known him, she'd grown to understand his wariness and reserve. Having grown up an only child in a cold household, he'd always hidden his feelings to protect his heart. But he wasn't holding back on this kiss, he was offering to take her into his heart.

There was a possessive honesty about this kiss, an admission that he wanted her for longer than a night, that he could restrain his need and allow friendship and caring to blossom between them. He wanted her, but he'd made her a promise when they'd first met. He wouldn't impose himself on her unless she was willing, no matter how badly he ached to have her.

Surprisingly, despite her stubbornness and resentment over these past weeks, she'd come to understand his nature well. He certainly understood hers, although she wasn't very difficult to figure out. She instinctively rebelled against being put on a tether and forced to do something she did not wish to do.

But as her affection for him grew, the tether no longer felt like a restraint but a loving bond.

"Blessed Scottish saints," he whispered against her mouth, bringing their kiss to an end, his voice a raw, hungry ache.

His arms were still around her, gently swallowing her up as though he never wanted to let her go. She had no desire to draw away either, so she stayed wrapped in his loose embrace. The choice to stay or pull away was always hers. Graelem had gotten that much right. She wanted to stay. "What you do to me, lass."

She wanted to stay forever.

He ran his big hands along her back and over the swell of her breasts, his thumbs grazing their already taut peaks. His hands trembled and she knew it wasn't from fever or fatigue, nor was it from bashfulness because Graelem wasn't the bashful sort.

He wanted her and was struggling to hold back his desire.

"You do the same to me." She felt breathless and her words mingled with her exhale of air. "Is this what desire feels like?"

"A burning, fiery craving that can't be doused? Och, lass. That's desire. The same as I feel for you."

No, what she felt was more. She was in love with him, not just a physical ache or tingle, but a sensation that penetrated into her soul and made her cry out for him. She wanted to describe this feeling to him, talk to him about it, but she heard her uncle's snuffling snores, a reminder they were not alone.

She eased away.

He had also begun to ease away, groaning as he fell back against his pillows. "We'll explore this another time, lass. Soon, I promise. I'm not at my best now anyway. I must smell as rank as a drunk after a night in a dockside ale house."

"You're not quite that bad." She smiled to hide her disappointment. She wanted to pursue the meaning of that kiss. She wanted to learn so much more from him, for she'd felt the hard length of him along her hip and knew that she had affected him as well.

She liked that his gaze was hot and hungry, that his body was tense and smoldering, as though he wanted to roll her under him and do whatever men did to relieve that hard heat between their loins.

He thought he smelled rank, but he didn't. Beneath the layer of sweat was a clean, manly scent, a heat and dampness mingling with traces of sandalwood from last evening's bath before the party.

"My sweet, tough Laurel," he said in a reverent whisper.

Yes, she was tough because she wanted so badly to be released from her promise to marry him. It wasn't because she wanted to walk away. She had no intention of walking away now. Quite the opposite, she wanted to be with him for the rest of her life. But he'd never know she felt this way—or be certain of it—unless he trusted her enough to set her free.

When she took her vows, it would not be through forced promises and trickery.

"Your lips are pursed," he said, his brow lightly furrowed in concern. "You have something on your mind."

She nodded. "But as you said, it's best we speak later."

There were loose ends she still needed to tidy up before she discussed the matter of her forced betrothal with Graelem. One of those loose ends was Devlin. She had to see him and let him be the first to know that she intended to become Graelem's wife.

Poor Dev, he deserved more than a cold letter containing a hastily penned farewell. She'd ask to meet him tomorrow or the day after. She dared not wait longer than that.

She also needed to talk to her parents. Graelem and her father had not discussed terms of the marriage contract yet, and she wanted to be sure her own terms were conveyed and accepted. She wanted to marry Graelem, but theirs could not be a marriage of convenience.

She wanted the sort of marriage her parents had. Love, commitment, shared hopes and dreams. Shared bed.

Shared hearts.

She hoped Graelem would want the same. But what if he didn't?

Graelem arched an eyebrow, his expression now one of confusion as she slumped in her chair and sighed. "What is it, lass?"

"I'll tell you later."

He reached out and took her hand. "You can tell me anything, Laurel. At any time. I don't want us to hold back secrets from each other, even if it means hurting the other's feelings or angering the other."

She nodded. "Neither do I. It's just that I'm not certain what it is I wish to say to you yet. My brain is a bit scrambled at the moment." She grinned. "And don't you dare comment that it's always scrambled."

"I wouldn't dare," he teased, laughing as he ran a hand roughly through his hair, which was damp at the ends and curled messily about his nape and ears. All she could think of was that he looked wonderful and approachable, and she wanted to run her fingers through those thick, brown waves and draw his head to hers for another tenderly scorching kiss.

"Right, not while you're weak as a lamb and completely at my mercy," she teased, and then gulped as he shifted toward her, his solid muscles rippling across his chest. He wasn't weak. He was splendid. He wasn't at her mercy either. Quite the opposite, she had lost her heart to him and was utterly at his mercy.

The notion terrified her.

How could they be equals in the marriage when she loved him more than he could ever love her?

BY ELEVEN O'CLOCK that morning, Laurel's father entered Graelem's bedchamber to fetch her home. Julian must have reported to him that Graelem was out of danger. "Come along, child. Your mother is worried about you." He patted her on the shoulder. "She needs to know that you're all right."

"I'm perfectly well. It's Lord Moray who's injured."

Her father shook his head. "But you're her child and she's driving us all to distraction fretting over you."

Graelem nodded. "Lass, you haven't slept a wink and must be spent. My fever's broken—"

"As well as your leg," she said as a reminder that he hadn't fully mended yet.

"I know, but your uncle is taking excellent care of me and my grandmother has a staff of servants to take care of anything else I can't do for myself. Go home. Get some rest."

If they were married, she could have spent the night in bed with him, cuddled against his side. Her thoughts must have been transparent, for Graelem's eyes suddenly widened in surprise and he cast her an affectionate but gloating smile. Fortunately, she had her back to her uncle and father so neither of them noticed the heat in her gaze. "Lass, go. I'll see you later."

He shifted so that he now sat fully upright. "I have Moray matters to attend to anyway. I'll see you this afternoon. Or tomorrow." He glanced at his still swollen leg. "I'll be here. I'm in no condition to go anywhere."

She let out a squawk as Uncle George playfully ruffled her hair. She supposed her fashionable hairdo had come undone sometime during the long evening and she already looked a fright. "Get some sleep, Laurel. That's doctor's orders. I don't want you falling ill, too."

Laurel nodded and walked downstairs with her father.

Eloise's butler, Watling, hurried to open the door. As soon as the door had closed behind them, her father slowed his steps to give them more time to talk during the short trip between the neighboring homes. "I will admit to always wanting a son," he said with a wistfulness to his voice, "but I accepted my lot in life and didn't mind that I was graced with five daughters instead. I knew that with five girls, five *dutiful* daughters, my life would be peaceful."

Laurel grimaced. "Father, I can explain about—"

"What? About almost trampling Lord Moray? About promising to marry him and then doing everything in your power to beg out of it? About Devlin's drunken behavior? Or the brawl that appears to have almost taken Lord Moray's life when that idiot Devlin purposely kicked him in his ruptured leg?" He sighed and shook his head. "Despite all, it appears that Lord Moray remains intent on marrying you. Makes one wonder about the man's sanity," he muttered.

She supposed this was not a good time to let her father know that she'd fallen in love with Graelem and actually *wanted* to marry him.

No, not a good time.

She'd spent the last few weeks angrily stomping and storming throughout the house, resenting his very existence. She'd probably enrage her father if she now told him that she'd changed her mind and all her fuss and feathers was for naught.

However, the problem remained that Graelem hadn't said he loved her. He'd only asked her to love him, which wasn't at all the same thing.

Their butler opened the door to their townhouse as they approached. "Good morning, Miss Laurel."

"Good morning, Pruitt." She held his gaze, wondering what he thought of Graelem. Pruitt was known to have excellent judgement, and in retrospect, it was clear by the subtle blink of his eyes whenever Devlin came around that he'd never liked him.

Pruitt must have known by her expression that she was hoping for some hint about his opinion of Graelem, even though Pruitt had only seen him the day his leg was broken and briefly yesterday at the party. "Your mother awaits you in the parlor," was all he said before disappearing to wherever butlers disappeared to whenever they didn't want to be seen or silently begged for advice about a gentleman's character.

Butlers noticed things because many in what was known as *good society* did not think of them as people and allowed their true behavior to show to them. A truly caring and thoughtful person treated servants in that same caring and thoughtful manner. A rude person, no matter how polite and genteel he made sure to behave toward his peers, was always rude to those he considered of inferior standing.

Her father nudged her toward the parlor. "You can pester Pruitt later. As he said, your mother is waiting to talk to you."

Her mother wasn't the only one waiting for her. Rose and Julian, Daisy, the twins, Uncle Rupert, and Aunt Hortensia were there to keep her company. Her mother's concerned gaze shot to her father. "John?"

He nodded. "Everything's fine, Sophie. Lord Moray is on the mend. Our daughter hasn't killed him off yet."

Her sisters giggled.

Her mother looked horrified. "John! What a thing to say!"

"Thank you, Laurel," Rose teased, a smug grin on her face so that Laurel knew she was not about to receive a compliment.

Laurel rolled her eyes. "And what am I to be thanked for?"

Julian laughed heartily. "For making Rose's courtship look tame in comparison to yours, of course. I heartily thank you as well. Your father no longer shoots daggers at me whenever I enter your home."

Daisy grinned and scooted next to their mother, who was seated on the blue silk sofa with her hands tensely folded on her lap. "Don't you worry, Mother. I've paid attention throughout our years of etiquette lessons, dance lessons, and every other lesson imaginable to train us to catch suitable husbands. I'll have a perfectly dull debut season, accept an offer of marriage from a respectable gentleman with impeccable credentials, and enlist you to plan a traditional wedding that won't be a rushed, patched-up affair."

Her mother patted Daisy's hand. "You've always been a good, sweet child."

Lily and Dillie kept their mouths shut, because although they tried to be good daughters as well, they still had a giant African fertility god sitting in the middle of their room that they'd purloined from the Royal Society. Laurel silently prayed that the Duke of Lotheil would not notice the theft and send his hounds on the scent to track it down before Graelem had a chance to arrange its return.

Julian rose from his chair and bowed to all in the room. "I promised to help Lord Moray with some matters concerning his estate. Since he's apparently feeling better and Laurel is safely back home now, I'll go bother him." He gave Rose a kiss on her lips that lasted a bit too long to be considered polite and evoked *oohs* and giggles from the twins.

Their mother sighed in exasperation at her young sisters. "Daisy, take them upstairs. Obviously *they* haven't been paying attention to their lessons on decorum and genteel manners."

Laurel kept silent.

She'd been worse than the twins, always sneaking off to ride Brutus instead of learning to sew a perfect stitch or make a perfect curtsy.

She was left to face her parents, Rose, who she hoped was an ally, Uncle Rupert, and Aunt Hortensia, who must have dropped a bottle of lilac water on herself and not bothered to wash it off. Laurel put a hand to her mouth and coughed lightly, but didn't have the heart to remark upon it. Neither had the others, even though all of them were struggling not to grin or cough.

"Have you made a decision, Laurel?" her mother asked after a long, awkward silence.

"About Lord Moray?"

Her mother nodded. "Midsummer's Day is almost upon us. Now that our time and attention are no longer distracted by the party—"

"Which was splendid, Mother. A job well done." Laurel came to her side and gave her a quick hug before sinking into the seat Daisy had vacated.

"Yes, dear. But your ploy to distract me with praise won't work." She tried to stifle a grin but couldn't. "Despite your brawling barons and Lily's determination to render us deaf with her untuned harp strings, the party was a success. Don't you think so, John?"

"Indeed, my love." Her father gave her mother a private smile.

Laurel gulped. This was exactly the sort of marriage she wanted. Private smiles, just like her parents. Kisses that went on too long to be proper, just like Rose and Julian. Would she ever share that intimacy with Graelem? She had to be sure before she went through with a midsummer wedding. "I think I'm in love with him."

Oops, didn't mean to blurt that.

The admission brought the others instantly to attention. Uncle Rupert twirled his big black moustache. "Then congratulations are in order, Laurel dear."

Hortensia agreed.

Her parents stared blankly at her for the longest time, until her mother finally spoke up. "You're in love with him, but still reticent. What's wrong?"

She sighed. "I want a love match. It's the Farthingale way and I couldn't be happy with anything less. I love him, but I don't know that he feels the same about me."

Hortensia shook her head in disbelief. "How could he not? You're an angel and he's fortunate to have found you." She shook her hand to wave off Laurel's protests, but the gesture caused the scent of lilac water to waft through the air and further permeate the parlor, if that was possible. "He put up with your reading that hideous poetry to him and never once complained. If that isn't love, then I don't know what is."

No one dared mention that she was a spinster and had rejected almost a dozen suitors in her younger day. In Laurel's opinion, Hortensia didn't know anything about love.

"You're wrong, Laurel," Rupert said gently, obviously reading her thoughts. "Hortensia rejected the young men who offered for her hand because she knew precisely what she wanted in a marriage and none of those clots would provide it." He glanced at her parents. "We aren't all as fortunate as John and Sophie. Sometimes we never find the one mate destined to steal our heart and touch our soul."

"But shouldn't that mate feel the same way? What if Lord Moray doesn't actually want to be burdened with a wife? What if he's content to leave me behind after he secures his inheritance? No matter how fancy a townhouse he purchases for me, it will still feel like a dungeon if he won't be there to share it with me." She turned to her father. "I think I must write a list of my demands. He'll have to accept them all before I agree to marry him."

"What if he won't? Will you turn to Dev?" Rose asked. "Daisy overheard him say that he loved you."

Laurel shook her head. "No, he doesn't really. He was comfortable in our friendship but that isn't at all the same thing. Anyway, I couldn't. Not after..." *Kissing Graelem.* "After all that's happened in the last few weeks."

Her mother took her hand and gave it a light squeeze. "Do you need help drawing up your list? I do have a little experience about matters of the heart and what's needed to form a solid foundation for a good marriage."

"Thank you, but I think I must write it on my own. However, I'll ask you to look it over when I'm done. I do want to know your thoughts, but not before I unscramble my own."

"And me, too?" Rose asked. "I want to look over that list. As a newlywed, I'm certain I can offer some helpful advice."

She nodded. "Yes, I'd appreciate it."

"I will as well," Hortensia stated, giving her no chance to decline the offer. "It's important that you know why I rejected so many suitors."

Rupert twirled his moustache again. "You'll need a man's opinion as well. Someone who can be objective, unlike your father, who loves you more than breath itself."

Since she wasn't going to make it from her bedchamber to her father's study without every Farthingale in residence stealing a look at the list and commenting on it anyway, she agreed to let them all see it.

Secrets did not exist in this family. If she tried to hide the list, the snoopy twins would be the first to steal it. There was no chance it would ever remain confidential.

In any event, she wanted to show it to Daisy, for they'd always been close—not only in age, but in their hopes and dreams and desires. True, Daisy intended to go about reaching her dreams by traditional means. But they still wanted the same thing, desired to be more than a mere appendage on their husband's arm.

"I'll write it out this evening." She yawned and shook her head. "Then you can all make your comments." There was little harm in indulging the family. Nothing stayed secret for long in the Farthingale family circle... also commonly referred to as the Farthingale family circus.

She also intended to write a letter to Devlin, something she could hand to him if he made too much of a fuss when they next met. He needed to understand that there was no chance of them ever marrying.

A chill ran up her spine.

She shook it off.

Nothing bad was going to happen.

CHAPTER 13

"I THINK THIS is a very good list," Daisy said as she perused the requirements Laurel had written down. The hour was late, close to midnight. She and Daisy were in the bedroom they shared, dressed in their nightgowns and preparing for bed.

Daisy had only to help Laurel braid her hair.

"I hope so." Laurel took back the parchment and handed Daisy the hairbrush. "Do you think I've missed anything important?"

"The elders can answer better than I ever could. But nothing immediately comes to mind."

Laurel nibbled her lip in thought as Daisy began to run the brush through her thick waves and gather them in one hand. "Father always tells us that people don't change. What if Graelem doesn't love me? Then this list of demands will feel like a prison sentence to him." She began to read off some of the demands. "Shared bed, no separate quarters for us."

Daisy nodded. "That's what Mother and Father do and it's worked well for them."

"But they've always been in love with each other." She sighed and read another demand. "Be faithful in the marriage." She set the list down and glanced at Daisy. "Do you think I need to be more specific? Men can twist the meaning when they desire to stray. Are there degrees of faithfulness?"

"Father or George or Rupert will have an answer to that."

Laurel read a third demand. "Love and protect our children." She sighed. "I think this one will be difficult for him."

Daisy paused in the middle of braiding Laurel's hair. "Why? He doesn't seem the sort to abandon his children. Quite the opposite, he appears to be the sort who would risk his own life to keep them from harm."

"He does have a wonderfully protective quality about him, doesn't he? But how can I know for certain? You see, his father abandoned him after his mother died."

"Oh, how awful!"

Laurel nodded. "What if something happens to me and he chooses to do the same? He won't speak ill of the former Baron Moray, but I think Graelem had a very unhappy childhood."

"Your children will always be loved," Daisy assured. "If he were ever so foolish as to abandon them, we'd take them in. Bestowing love is one of the few things we Farthingales manage to do right. Look at little Harry's situation. If Uncle Harrison truly is… lost to us, would we ever cast out Aunt Julia or Harry? Of course not. Mother and Father have already invited her to move in with us, and our uncles will manage Harrison's share of the Farthingale business profits so that Julia and Harry never lack for funds."

Daisy quickly finished off the braid. "Your children will be protected. Even if he didn't abandon them, we'd still meddle in every aspect of their upbringing. After all, it's what we Farthingales do best."

Laurel laughed. "You've put my mind at ease." But she sobered a moment later. "What if he rejects these demands? I don't think I can marry him then."

Daisy gave her a quick hug. "He'll accept every last one. I'm sure he adores you. Stop fretting. Get some sleep." She left Laurel's side and climbed into her own bed, letting out a sigh as she slipped under the cream silk counterpane and drew the crisp white sheet up to her neck.

Laurel did the same after dousing the lamp by her night stand. "Daisy," she whispered in the dark, "what if he doesn't?"

"That would be a problem."

GRAELEM WAS EAGER to see Laurel the next afternoon. He was feeling much better, for the swelling in his leg had subsided considerably. He'd felt fit enough to wash and dress and make his way downstairs to Eloise's parlor, where he'd spent a pleasant few hours chatting with his grandmother before she'd gone off with Lady Withnall to make their round of calls and terrify the misbehaving elite.

George had returned to the Farthingale townhouse, declaring him fit enough to be left on his own. Graelem had even managed to accomplish a significant amount of work, attending to Moray affairs and those of greater significance to England in its war effort against Napoleon and his army.

He had spent several years fighting in the Peninsular wars, but for the past two years had been working with his cousin Gabriel and the Duke of Edgeware on secret missions in France designed to chart the French military positions and undermine them whenever possible. Julian and a few other noblemen were also involved in these missions, although Julian's services were primarily used now to combat Napoleon's spies operating within England. That was part of the pledge their little group had taken. When one of them married, he was no longer assigned the more dangerous excursions into France.

Julian surprised him by stopping by on his way to pick up Rose from the Farthingale townhouse. "I can't stay long. Just wanted to report that the regimental commander still has no news on Harrison Farthingale's whereabouts or his condition."

Graelem nodded. "That's not good. The longer this goes on, the worse the outcome is likely to be."

"Ian will let us know the moment he finds out anything. He landed in France only a few days ago. It'll be another week at the earliest before we hear from him."

"I should have been the one to go," Graelem said, not bothering to mask his frustration. He'd made several secret trips to France, but Gabriel had taken his last turn when Baron Moray died, and now the Duke of Edgeware had taken this next assignment because of Graelem's busted leg. The duke was one of the bravest men he'd ever met, but he and Gabriel had been taking on the most dangerous missions and Graelem didn't like having to remain behind and not share equally in the risk.

However, he didn't dwell on his own situation. It was more important that Laurel's uncle be found as soon as possible and smuggled to a safe house at the first opportunity. Afterward, he would be smuggled back to England and reunited with his family.

He fervently hoped Ian would find him alive.

"Now you know how I feel," Julian commiserated, "stuck in England while you bachelors get all the good assignments. Although you won't be a bachelor for long."

"Assuming Laurel agrees to marry me."

Julian frowned. "Do you doubt that she will?"

"I won't breathe easily until the vows are spoken and our marriage is official. Figuring out Napoleon's tactics is easier than understanding the workings of Laurel's heart."

Julian slapped him on the shoulder. "Don't even try. You'll never succeed. Just let her know that you love her and everything else will fall into place. That's the best advice I can give you."

"I'll keep it in mind."

Julian turned to leave but paused at the door. "You do love her, don't you? Because I'll have to kill you if you don't."

Graelem laughed mirthlessly. "You'll have to wait your turn. Her father and uncles will insist on having that pleasure first."

Graelem knew Julian wanted a better answer than the one he'd just given, but Watling walked in just then to announce Laurel's arrival. "Where have you put her, Watling?" Usually, Laurel bounded in unannounced. That she wasn't already poking Watling aside gave Graelem cause for worry. Was she reluctant to see him? If so, that meant she had bad news to convey about their marriage plans.

Or rather, about his insistence on marrying her by Midsummer's Day whether or not she wished it.

Julian, knowing Laurel's temperament as well as he did, emitted a chuckling groan. "Good luck, my friend. You'll need it," he said and then strode out.

Graelem heard a brief exchange between Julian and Laurel which included seemingly pleasant laughter, so perhaps Laurel's reluctance to face him did not bode ill. He rose and slipped his crutches under his arms. That nasty kick Devlin Kirwood had landed against his still broken bones had set him back several days, but he was on the mend now and looking forward to making progress in this marriage business. "Send her in, Watling."

After a long moment, Laurel entered.

His heart shot into his throat and his blood caught fire as it always did whenever he saw the girl. She'd looked particularly lovely in pink on the night of the Farthingale party, but was just as spectacular this morning in a gown the color of apricots, a rosy yellow confection adorned with only a bit of white lace around the scooped collar that revealed the slight swell of her breasts.

He forced his gaze upward before he began to drool like an old hound.

Yet another mistake, for she looked soft and vulnerable, and all he wanted to do was sweep her up in his arms and hold her against his heart forever. She blushed and nervously patted her hair, tucking a loose strand behind her ear. Her hair was done up in a casual bun, and little curls of gold escaped to fall over her forehead and about her adorable ears.

He wanted to shut the door behind them and spend the rest of the afternoon alone with her, slowly exploring her exquisite body, but he knew by the swirls of turbulent green amid the serene blue of her eyes that she was troubled. "Have a seat, lass. You look overset." He reined in his lust, for there was no point in delaying what he expected would be bad news for him.

"Not overset, just unsure of myself." She turned to shut the door, remembered that they weren't yet married and shouldn't be alone in the room without a proper chaperone, and left the door slightly ajar before turning back to face him.

Then she shook her head and closed the door firmly behind her.

She fumbled with a letter in her hand, sighed as though

needing a moment to firm her resolve, and then walked to his side and settled beside him on the settee. He smiled at her, but said nothing, for she was obviously preoccupied.

"You look quite well, Graelem." She cast him a shy smile as she placed a hand on his forehead. "No fever. That's good."

Her mere touch intensified the flames already roaring within him. Fortunately, she quickly removed her hand from his forehead and once again fumbled with the scrap of paper that was clenched between her fingers, too distracted to notice his mounting discomfort. "I've brought a list with me."

He arched an eyebrow. "What sort of list?"

"I'll get to that in a moment." She unfolded and refolded the paper several times. "Daisy read it and thought it was quite thorough. The twins agreed. So did my parents and Uncle Rupert and Aunt Hortensia. Rose and Aunt Julia saw it too."

He threw his head back and laughed. "It might be faster if you told me who in your family *hasn't* seen it."

She grinned and a light blush crept into her cheeks. "Quite so. I'm sure you're right." She stuck her hand out and gave him the crumpled sheet. "Please take a moment to read it, but you needn't rush to give me an answer today. Sleep on it if you must and we can talk tomorrow."

He took her hand to stop her when she rose to leave. "Laurel, stay. Whatever this is, it seems to be important to you."

She nodded emphatically. "Very."

"Then stay by my side while I read it. I might have questions about it that only you can answer."

She nodded again, wincing as she gazed at him. "Or complaints. I'm sure you will."

He unfolded the paper that was now a wrinkled mess and perused it. "What is this?" She'd titled this scrap "A List Of Demands", and there appeared to be at least a dozen of these so-called demands written out in her own neat hand, a page filled with them, all concerning the terms of their marriage arrangement.

Share a bed. Kiss me every day. Love our children. Protect our children. Be faithful. Fall asleep in each other's arms. Share problems. Did she think he didn't want those very things?

He ached to have such a marriage, especially with her, only he never thought it possible. "Laurel—"

"You don't have to say anything just yet. I know there's a lot to consider and I haven't done much to recommend myself to you. In truth, I don't understand why you still want to marry me. You ought to be running from me in fear for your life. It hasn't escaped anyone's notice that you always get hurt when you're around me."

He grinned. "I made it through three years of fighting Napoleon, some of those battles long and bloody, with hardly a scratch on me."

"Precisely my point. After one day with me, your leg was broken and you almost died."

"Are you purposely trying to discourage me?"

She glanced up in alarm. "Actually, no. I'm hoping that… that… the problem is, I like you, Graelem. An awful lot. I think I could… I think we could have a happy marriage if you felt as I do."

He shifted closer, loving the way the pulse at the curve of her throat, that soft spot where her slender neck met her slight shoulder, throbbed whenever he drew near. Her breath came faster as well, he could tell by the quickening rise and fall of her perfect chest. Marvelous invention these scooped collars. Allowed a man a peek at heaven. "Laurel, how do *you* feel about our marriage?"

She lowered her gaze to the floor in a failed attempt to hide the intensifying blush on her cheeks. "That depends."

"On my acceptance of these demands?" He glanced at the neatly inscribed velum still in his hands. In truth, he didn't need any time to consider the terms and accept. "What about you? If I'm to be bound by these terms, so should you."

She glanced up in surprise and he smothered a grin upon noticing the curl of her hands into fists. "Do you doubt that I'd be faithful?" *You ass*, she may as well have added because it was obvious that she was thinking it but too polite to say it.

"No, lass. Never a doubt that you'll be the perfect wife. You're honest and loyal." *And achingly beautiful.* "I also know that you'd love and protect our children till your dying breath. But if we're talking contractual obligations, then it only seems fair that we're both bound to the same terms."

She gazed at him in wonder. "Are you saying that you'd accept these terms?"

He frowned, not liking that she seemed surprised. He hadn't given her much reason to trust him at first. But several weeks had gone by with them in each other's constant company, and although there had been a lot of insipid poetry in between, there had also been long moments of conversation. By now, she ought to know him better than any other woman of his acquaintance. "You make no mention of my providing you an allowance or a carriage. Or clothes suitable for a baroness."

She edged closer to him, no doubt exasperated and wanting to shake him by the lapels of his superfine jacket. "I'm not concerned with your wealth. The Farthingale men suggested I add financial demands, but none of the women did. They understand what I want." She paused and swallowed hard. The pulse at the base of her throat was now throbbing wildly. "I'll leave the discussion of financial matters to you and my father. I don't care what you men decide. What matters most to me is… you. Graelem, I want your heart. Surely it's obvious."

He nodded and tipped her chin up so that she met his steady gaze. "How much of it do you want?"

Her eyes grew wide once again and she licked her lips. "Um… all of it. Isn't it obvious? But it would be a mutual exchange. I won't impose terms on you that I would not meet as well. I ought to have made it clear from the start."

He ran his thumb across her still flushed cheek, wondering why he'd picked the only girl in all of London who would impose these requirements. And why he was more delighted than ever that he had. "So you'll give me all of your heart if I give you all of mine?"

She nodded.

"*All* of my heart," he said softly, knowing that accepting her terms… assuming he accepted them… was not the end of it.

"That's asking a lot."

"I know, but I told you early on that we Farthingales marry for love. I promise you, you'll have mine in return."

"Lass, you aren't the sort to simply sign away your heart. Are you saying that you love me?"

The pulse at the base of her throat was now pounding so violently it threatened to break through her silken skin. She was obviously distressed by the question, for her chest was also rising and falling so quickly he feared she might faint. No, not his Laurel. She was made of sterner stuff. She let out an *eep*. "What?"

He ran his thumb gently across her lower lip. "You heard me, lass. Do you love me?"

Her eyes filled with tears.

He groaned softly. "Blessed Scottish saints, don't cry. You don't have to answer me. I never expected you to love me. It's all right if you don't."

"You oaf!" She smacked him on the shoulder. "It isn't all right. And how dare you not require your wife... your future wife... how dare you not mind if I don't love you."

"Then you don't love me?"

She shot to her feet. "I shouldn't. You're the densest man I've ever met. I would detest you if I thought for a moment that all you cared about was your title and the wealth you'd secure once you were married."

"Assuming I marry by Midsummer's Day." He rose along with her and set aside his crutches, then took her into his arms. "But you know I care about much more than that. What about you, Laurel? Do you love me?"

"Why should I tell you when you've yet to tell me anything? I asked you first." She placed her hands flat on his chest but made no attempt to push away. Instead, her hands slid up the front of his shirt so that she was clinging to his shoulders as her body molded to his.

He loved the way she responded to him even when she was angry. She couldn't hide her feelings for him, and he supposed he was being an ass to require her to admit the obvious while he kept his distance and hid behind the promise he'd tricked out of her.

Still, he wanted to hear her say those words aloud. *I love you, Graelem.*

He'd heard her whisper it when she thought he was unconscious.

It was the last thing he remembered before all went black.

When he awoke hours later, he thought he'd imagined it. But now he knew that he hadn't. Laurel loved him. Could he love her back with his whole heart as she required?

"I will not say it, you stubborn oaf. Not until you do," she said so softly he almost didn't hear her. "I need to know how you feel about me."

He was about to relent and tell her, but she had one more requirement of him. "Graelem, free me from the promise and then ask me again to marry you."

"Damn it, Laurel." He crushed her up against him when she tried to draw away. "My heart is yours for the taking. There's no one else I care to give it to. I'll sign your bloody list of demands and hold true to them. But don't make me release you from that promise. If you truly love me, then it doesn't matter how our marriage comes about, only that it happens."

"And if you truly loved me, then you'd understand that I need you to trust me."

They were alone in the parlor and he was in a dangerous state, angry and frustrated that Laurel loved him and still wouldn't accept him. Angry that she was demanding and persistent and just stubborn enough to refuse him at the altar unless he surrendered to her terms. Mostly, he was angry with himself for wanting her so badly, even though he knew that he'd never have a day's peace if he married her.

He had her promise. He had her love.

And she still bridled at the thought of marrying him.

He should cut his losses and offer for Anne Hollings. Cold, simple, and safe.

But he didn't want safe. He wanted Laurel.

Her face was tipped upward in expectation of a response, one that he was not ready to give, so he did what any oaf in his position would do. He lowered his mouth to hers and poured his pent-up desire and weeks of frustration into one hard, consuming kiss, hoping that if he kissed her long enough and with enough passion she'd forget their conversation and not force him to bare his heart and soul to her.

Perhaps old Silas had the right of it, after all. Exposing one's feelings led to pain and humiliation. Is that what Laurel was feeling now? She'd certainly exposed her heart to him and he was giving her nothing in return. This kiss wasn't nearly enough.

He eased up on the pressure of his mouth against hers, afraid that he was too rough in grinding his lips on hers, but her hands wrapped behind his head the moment he attempted to gentle the kiss, her fingers twining in his hair and tugging him closer.

He loved the way Laurel surrendered to passion, and knew she responded this way only to him. She was eager for his kisses, almost as much as he craved hers. The only difference between them was that he could hide his feelings even as he kissed her into tomorrow, but she didn't know how to hide hers.

He loved her honesty and wished he could toss away his years of caution and emptiness, but he couldn't yet. "Graelem," she whispered in a breathless moan.

He slipped his tongue between her lightly parted lips and probed the sweet treasure of her mouth, pleased when he evoked more breathy moans out of her. Lord, she'd be incredible in bed. *My bed.*

He drew her closer, loving the way her slight, shapely body managed to fit against his hard contours. They shouldn't fit this perfectly against each other, for he was considerably taller and broader than she was, but somehow they did.

His loins tightened and his blood ran hot as Laurel responded to the invasion of his tongue by squirming against him. The feel of her glorious breasts against his chest just about tipped him over the edge. The roof of this townhouse could have collapsed atop them and he wouldn't have noticed, so lost was he in the strawberries and mountain breezes scent of her, in the warmth of her body nestled against his, and in the innocent heat of her passion.

She was splendid, to be sure.

Kissing Laurel meant so much more to him than the mere touch of her lips against his or their bodies wrapped so tightly in each other's arms that they molded into one. Kissing Laurel meant hope and happiness and fulfillment of dreams he'd never imagined possible in his stark Moray existence. He didn't think he would ever experience these exquisite feelings with another woman.

He knew he never would.

What he felt for Laurel went beyond a mere physical need to plunder the riches between her thighs, although he felt that hard need most acutely. No, his passion for this beautiful innocent was a long-burning flame, a yearning that would never fade but would grow more intense as the years passed, burning beautiful and golden as they got on in years, incapable of ever being extinguished.

Blessed Scottish saints!

Was he already in love with the girl?

The possibility scared the hell out of him.

He ended the kiss and drew his lips off Laurel's plump, rosy mouth, feeling quite pleased with himself when she made an O of disappointment. She looked incredible, her lips red and lightly swollen, her eyes those beautiful swirls of turbulent green and azure blue. Her hands were resting on his shoulders as she struggled to regain her composure. "Why did you stop?"

"Laurel," he said, planting a gentle kiss on that wildly beating pulse at the base of her neck, "we're in my grandmother's parlor in the middle of the afternoon. Anyone can walk in and—"

She gasped and shook her head while she fidgeted with her hair and smoothed her gown. She cast him a look of distress. "I seem to forget myself whenever I'm with you."

He grinned. "I'm not complaining, lass. Have we settled your list then? I've accepted all your terms."

"All but one," she said quietly.

His expression hardened and he said nothing in response.

He wasn't letting her out of their betrothal.

CHAPTER 14

CRUMPETS! LAUREL KNEW she'd pushed Graelem to the edge.

He was angry.

He was hungry and possessive.

Despite all, he'd accepted her terms with surprisingly little resistance. Did it matter that he'd refused to release her from their betrothal? Perhaps it didn't now that she actually wanted to marry him. Still, his resistance felt wrong, but not everything worked out perfectly in life, did it? If pressed, she had to admit that she wanted Graelem in her life.

Instead of her usual stomping and storming, she reached up and caressed his cheek. "Thank you for not mocking my list."

The gesture obviously surprised him and softened his frown. "Lass, it's a good list."

"It is?"

He nodded, bending his head to kiss her again, his lips hard and demanding as they covered hers. His hands roamed over her body, and despite the force of his desire, there was a gentleness in the way her held her, touched her, moved his lips over hers.

Had she misjudged him? He appeared to want her with an intensity she'd never expected. It was as though he wanted to lay bare his feelings, but couldn't yet express them with words. Would he ever trust her enough to do so?

Was he trusting her now? She suddenly realized he was speaking to her through his kisses, as though his kisses could reveal what lay hidden in his heart.

Oh, goodness!

Could she be happy with this compromise? She wanted him so badly.

But was this kiss merely one of his cruel tricks to bring her to the altar? No, Graelem may have had faults, but deceitfulness wasn't one of them. He was stubborn and determined and direct, which was not at all the same thing as manipulating her affections or spouting lies. And hadn't he agreed to give her his heart? That it was hers for the asking?

Sometime over the course of these weeks she'd lost hers to this big, stubborn man who was too English for the Scots and too Scottish for the English. But he was perfect for her. She loved the hard heat of his body, loved the possessive way he looked at her and the gentle way he held her.

He roused dangerous sensations within her.

He made her physically ache to be with him.

She must have been obvious in her feelings. "Blessed saints," he whispered, closing his mouth over hers again, and groaning as he slid his hand upward to cup her breast. "Lass, tell me to stop," he begged against her lips.

"No." She leaned into him, arching her back and sighing as his fingers brushed across the taut nipple, amazed by how right it felt to be with him and how perfectly her breast rested in the cup of his palm. His thumb grazed across the hard, swollen peak, arousing hot tingles with every stroke. "Oh, my! Graelem, I love your touch."

He seemed to know just how to touch and tease, and though she knew that one word from her would put an end to this exquisite madness, she was greedy and wanted more, ached for the warmth of his fingers against her skin, ached for the intimacy that ought not be shared until they were lawfully married.

But where was the harm in experiencing it all now? Her heart was his, even if she refused to admit it to him. "Graelem," she said in an aching whisper.

"I know, love." As though understanding her wishes, he slipped his hand beneath the muslin bodice of her gown and freed her breast from its confinement.

She felt an unbearable heat stir within her even as cool air brushed against her exposed skin.

The mix of cool air and warmth of his rough fingers aroused her more than she imagined possible. He mercilessly stroked his thumb across her taut nipple, evoking one exquisitely jolting sensation after another, and then he replaced his fingers with his mouth and began to tease it with his lips and tongue until she could hold back no more. *"Graelem!"*

"You taste so sweet, love." He drew her nipple between his lips and suckled it, sending her into raptures with the unrelenting pleasure of his mouth against her bare skin and the hot flicks of his tongue.

She closed her eyes and wound her fingers in his hair, breathlessly whispering his name over and over. *"Oh, heavens! Graelem."* Is this what they would share each night in their marriage bed? Her legs turned to pudding and she would have fallen had he not been holding her in his arms.

She thought she might expire from the exquisite pleasure, but he wasn't finished yet. He moved his hand beneath her gown and gently tugged it upward to slide his fingers up her leg in one smooth motion. He paused at the junction of her thighs as though waiting for her consent to touch her *there*. "Please," she said, her voice low and breathless as she shifted her body slightly to allow him access to the most intimate part of her.

She felt no shame or fear, for this was Graelem, and despite her demands and that forced promise, she knew there was no other man for her. *She loved him.*

"Lass, you're so beautiful." His fingers were a gentle onslaught against her core, stroking and swirling until she responded to the heat of his touch, a wet heat that evoked possessive groans of delight from his lips and gasps from hers. "So soft and beautiful."

He eased his mouth off her breast to kiss her on the lips, his hand still working its hot magic below. She felt the hard swell of his groin and knew that he was as aroused as she was. Did she dare touch him?

She was hot and wanton and no longer cared about propriety. Nothing seemed to matter but being in Graelem's arms as he carried her off to new realms. She cupped his hard length in her hand. He let out a sharp, laughing oath and almost lost his balance. "Not yet, love. Not here."

He took her hand in his and settled it against his chest. She felt the steady, rhythmic pounding of his heart. Hers was rampant and racing wildly. She moved her hand upward to clutch his shoulder as an intense heat suddenly built between her legs. He continued to stroke her *there*, until an intense pressure built within her and she lost control of her body. *"Oh, Graelem!"*

He cupped her trembling heat and encouraged her release as her flushed body floated upward and exploded in a burst of brilliant starlight. Liquid tingles caressed her thighs. He held her tightly, held her close and lovingly. An exquisite numbness washed over her body in slow, undulating waves. "I never knew it could be like this," she whispered when the wave finally began to ebb and she found her voice.

"We've only just started, love. It gets even better." He smiled and tipped her chin upward, at the same time bending his head down to kiss her lightly on the lips. When he drew away, there was a look of pride and a deep satisfaction of conquest in the soft curve of his mouth. His eyes were warm and expressive, reflecting awe and something deeper, a genuine affection. She knew this moment held meaning for him as well for her.

Merciful heaven! She couldn't steady her breathing, for it was still quick and shallow. Her body was still tingling, no doubt because she was still reveling in the afterglow. She knew her feet were on the ground, but she knew that she was floating. How long before these wondrous sensations faded away? Would they ever?

Graelem already seemed to have calmed. Of course, it was to be expected since this was not his first time and he hadn't been carried along on languid waves or swallowed up by these powerful sensations. She wasn't his first conquest. But would she be his last? Would he abide by their agreement if she married him?

"Sweetheart," he said in a gentle whisper, seeming to read her thoughts, "there will never be anyone for me but you."

"Truly, Graelem?" Her heart was still racing and her skin was hot and damp.

He gave her a long, lingering kiss on the cheek. "Truly, lass."

She rested her head against his chest, suddenly afraid to look at him. Goodness! What had they just done? Why hadn't she stopped him? "I've never felt like this before. I seem to turn wanton whenever I'm with you."

He laughed softly. "And I turn lecherous and possessive whenever I'm with you. Laurel, we're meant to be together. Let's just accept it for now and worry about the next steps after we're married. I don't pretend to understand what's happening, only that it's good. Very good."

"It felt magical."

"It was, lass." He said nothing more, simply held her a while longer and caressed her until her breathing steadied. Then he helped smooth her gown in place, his fingers grazing her breast as he tucked the fabric back over its engorged peak and settled the lace trim back in place. Her skin had yet to cool. It was still moist and flushed from the heat of her desire.

She wouldn't fool anyone who happened to walk in on them now. The parlor door was merely closed, not even locked! Had she completely lost her senses? She seemed to whenever she was around Graelem. Her face suffused with heat. "What must you think of me?"

Anyone could have walked through that door.

"I think you're incredible, Laurel. I *know* you're the only woman on this earth I could ever take as my wife." He gave her an exquisitely soft smile. "Your idea about sharing sleeping quarters is inspired. I want you in my bed, sweetheart. Every night for the rest of our lives."

She laughed in relief, although she was still shocked and embarrassed by her behavior. "I'm glad, because you've turned me into a shameless wanton. After what you did to me with your fingers and lips, I will insist that requirement be moved to the top of my list."

"You'll have no protest from me."

She knew the wisest thing to do was to pull away from him now because she was still enveloped in his embrace and breathing unsteadily. Graelem felt so good against her, his touch continuing to ignite little sparks of pleasure throughout her body. "I don't know why I respond to you the way I do. You seem to drag me deeper and deeper into this betrothal every time we meet."

"Not me, sweetheart. Your heart wants this to happen. I want it to happen, too." He brushed a loose curl off her cheek. "You're still blushing."

"I can't help it. What I did…" The words caught in her throat.

He sighed. "I know you've never allowed any man to touch you this way before. My chest may be puffed out with pride and I may be grinning like an ass, but I understand what's happening between us. I think you do, too. You haven't accepted it yet, that's all. But I have. You're not some conquest of mine. You're the only woman who leaves me breathless and out of control. You're the only woman I want in my life."

She nodded against his chest. "I'm still appalled by my behavior and you ought to be as well."

He tipped her chin up and smiled at her. "Very well, I'm shocked and… do I look sufficiently aghast?"

She couldn't help but laugh. "Not in the least, you bounder. Stop grinning."

"I can't. I'm imagining you naked right now."

She playfully smacked him on the shoulder. "I forbid you to do that!"

"Can't help it. I'd carry you up to my bedchamber right now and do a proper job of ravishing your delectable body, but I don't think I can manage you and my crutches on those stairs." He paused a moment and his grin faded. "You're the most beautiful sight I've ever beheld. From the moment we met, I've been silently thanking the Fates that brought us together. If I'm fortunate enough to get you to the altar, I'll be tossing my crutches in the air and dancing a very ungainly jig."

She blushed again. "What we just did… felt very right because it was with you. Everything feels right when I'm with you."

"Feeling is mutual." He tweaked her nose, but continued to hold her in his arms, enveloping her in his embrace. He hadn't said he loved her, not with words. But being in his arms right now, she could believe that he was saying it with his every caress. "Anything else you'd care to discuss, lass?"

"Other than your seductive prowess?"

"Prowess?" She felt the gentle rumble of his chest against her cheek as he laughed. "I'm just a big oaf! Please, let's speak of anything but that."

She grinned against his chest, liking that modesty about him. Although she'd had no experience in such matters, she'd seen how the young ladies at Eloise's tea party were drawn to him. He hadn't needed to utter a word or toss a smile to render them giddy. She cleared her throat. "Now that we've settled the matter of this list... we have settled it, haven't we?"

He nodded. "Yes, sweetheart."

She breathed a sigh of relief. "Now onto the next problem."

He quirked an eyebrow. "What problem?"

"That fertility god Lily smuggled into her room. How are we to get it back to the Royal Society?"

His appealingly fiendish grin brought a merry laugh out of her. "Out with it," she demanded, still laughing. "You've figured out how to do it, haven't you?"

"Lily isn't the only one with a devious mind," he said, his criminal pride showing. "I've already explained my plan to Eloise."

"Your grandmother knows?"

"She knows, is thrilled about being asked to help, and can't wait to put the dastardly scheme into effect."

Laurel's eyes rounded in surprise. "Never say she has a devious heart!"

"Very well, I won't say it. However, my sweet grandmother not only approves, but is more than willing to participate."

Laurel's curiosity was piqued. "What's your plan?"

❦

SNEAKING THE FERTILITY god back into the Royal Society proved an effortless undertaking, for Graelem's grandmother had no trouble convincing the Duke of Lotheil, a long-time friend of hers, to hold an afternoon tea in the Royal Society exhibition rooms in honor of a new project he was about to announce. Since this new project concerned the addition of a new wing to the building, what better place to reveal the news to the world than the very place where the renovations were to occur?

The duke agreed, even though these halls were a male bastion and no female Fellows had ever been inducted. But this was to be a celebration, not a scientific symposium, so gentlemen and ladies from the best families were invited.

Graelem gave his grandmother all the credit for the success of their ploy, for she had convinced the duke not only to hold the event there but also to permit ladies entrance into all the halls, even the private exhibition rooms and library for the day.

In truth, the festivities required a woman's touch, and Eloise was just the woman to take the reins and act as the duke's hostess. The old darling had a shocking streak of larceny in her heart, but she explained it away with a mere wave of her hand. "The duke and I have been friends forever," she had told Graelem. "But he can be a pompous old goat at times. Not only he, but his entire Royal Society, thinking men are smarter than women. This will show him."

She had invited the cream of society to this exciting event, men and women of the highest ranks… and the Farthingales.

Eloise, as part of their plan, had insisted on commissioning an enormous cake for the grand celebration, one that was too big to simply carry in. The many layers of lemon and cocoa butter were delicate and had to be brought in on a cart, a cloth-covered rolling cart.

While the cake sat atop it, hidden underneath was Lily's fertility god.

Graelem, still on crutches, attended the event with his grandmother. "Eloise, you old pirate," he teased as they stood near the display case where the fertility god belonged, "I always suspected you were a smuggler or a highwayman in your younger days."

"Nothing of the sort," she shot back, but the twinkle in her eyes gave away her delight at the notion.

He laughed and gave her a quick hug. "I'm suitably impressed. I've never met a criminal as calm as you."

The small wrinkles at the corners of her mouth twitched just before her lips curved into an unrepentant smile. "Putting a thing back where it belongs is a worthy project. One might even call it a charitable undertaking. Ah, here are Lily and her family. Do they know the plan?"

He nodded. "Lily and her sisters do. They know it. Love it. And wish they had thought of it themselves. However, we decided it was best to keep the Farthingale elders in the dark, although little escapes George Farthingale's notice. He probably suspects his nieces are up to something since they've been on their best behavior these past few days, and he knows that always means trouble."

Graelem glanced around the filling hall. "But I don't see George here yet. Perhaps he's figured out the scheme and is quietly distracting the duke's attention. Ah, there's Laurel's father. Poor man, I wonder if he knows. He looks happy. No doubt he hasn't a clue what his daughters are about to do."

"Poor Sophie, she's tried so hard to make proper young ladies of her daughters. However, I think she's secretly proud of their spirited natures. No boiled mushrooms for brains with these girls." Eloise laughed and shook her head so that the lilac egret feather matching the color of her fine silk gown bobbed up and down. "Oh, good. Speaking of those little devils, they're coming toward us."

The twins, along with Daisy and Laurel, hurried across the expanse of exhibition hall to greet him and his grandmother. Graelem watched three dark heads with blue eyes approach, but it was the fourth that caught his attention, the soft golden hair and aquamarine eyes that were Laurel's. "Rose apologizes, but she couldn't make it," Laurel said in a conspiratorial whisper.

"We don't really need her for this," Dillie added. "And Julian would be apoplectic if his wife were caught. She can't run very fast in her condition anyway. She'd be more of a hindrance than a help. But she's cheering us on in spirit and wishes to convey her deep appreciation to you and Eloise for all your help. Is the head under the cake cart?"

Lily was already behind it and bent over to take a peek. "If you roll the cart a little to the left, we can sneak it out from the back with no one the wiser. I'll pick the lock to the glass case while Dillie and Daisy drag it out from under there. Lord Moray, thank you for agreeing to serve as our lookout."

Since responding with "my pleasure" seemed to condone the theft and scurrilous return of that object, he chose to say nothing and merely nodded.

Graelem's grandmother gasped. "Lily, you know how to pick locks?"

Lily blushed. "It's quite simple really. One merely needs to loosen the lock spring with a hair pin and—"

"Child, I don't need to know anymore. Just get that monstrosity back where it belongs while Laurel and I create the necessary diversion." Eloise took Laurel's arm. "Come along, my dear. Time for us to get to work."

Graelem winked at Laurel.

Laurel responded with a special smile for him, one that reached into her beautiful, sparkling eyes. She was happy for many reasons other than the most obvious one, that Lily would not be hunted down and tossed in prison. As important was the fact that she was no longer house-bound. Her punishment had ended the moment Graelem had been able to leave Eloise's townhouse. Most important, though, was the fact that she was beginning to think of him as the man with whom she'd share the rest of her life.

In truth, he couldn't imagine his life without her either.

His good humor was cut short by a sudden, painful twinge in his leg. This first excursion was already straining his broken limb, and he needed to find a quiet place where he could stretch out and elevate it. He would do so as soon as his lookout duties were over, once the petty thief twins put the fertility god back where it belonged.

He scanned the crowd, all notion of a pleasant afternoon now fading when he noticed Devlin Kirwood among the guests mingling in the great hall. The unpleasant young lord had not yet noticed him, and Graelem preferred to keep it that way. Coming to blows at the Farthingale party was bad enough. The duke would be in a purple rage if the fight extended into his treasured exhibition halls.

Also, the twins weren't finished yet, and he couldn't risk all eyes turning upon them.

But he knew Devlin had spotted him when the idiot suddenly tossed him a scowl and began to approach with hands curled into fists at his sides.

Damnation. He really didn't want to engage the man here.

However, he had no qualms about flattening him with one punch again if the blackguard refused to back off.

To his relief, Lady Anne Hollings entered the exhibition hall and also noticed Devlin. She hurried to his side, apparently unaware of the direction of Devlin's gaze or his intentions. Anne caught him by the arm and began what appeared to be an urgent conversation.

A shiver crawled up Graelem's spine as the pair suddenly turned to stare at him.

What were they up to? Anne's smiling gaze was more predatory than pleasant, while Devlin kept his petulant scowl firmly in place. "Girls," he quietly called over his shoulder, "hurry up."

Although Laurel and his grandmother were creating a fine diversion that had attracted a large crowd including the duke, neither Devlin nor Anne was looking at them. No, indeed. They were more interested in him than in Eloise's fake attack of the vapors. *Damnation again.*

"Almost done," Daisy assured him. "Come on, Lily. Stop studying the other specimens. You can do that *outside* the glass."

"Fine," the little bluestocking said, emitting a sigh, "but what fun is that?"

"A lot more fun than prison," Dillie, ever practical, assured her.

Within a matter of moments, the twins and Daisy were back at his side looking up at him with triumphant blue eyes. "All done,"

Lily said.

He grinned at them and gave an exaggerated wipe of his brow. "Thank goodness. The foundations of England have been restored."

Daisy shook her head and laughed. "But for how long? One can never be sure with Lily on the loose." She had a sweet, charming laugh, and Graelem wondered how many poor fools would fall hard for this beautiful girl when she had her come out next year.

Too bad his cousin Gabriel wasn't suitable. No, Gabriel traveled with a fast set and would find Daisy too traditional for his tastes.

Daisy took the twins by the elbow. "Let's tell Eloise and Laurel that the deed has been accomplished. I expect that Eloise is eager to miraculously recover from her bout of the vapors. Will you join us, Lord Moray?"

He declined, needing to ease the pressure on his leg, which had gone from uncomfortable to fiercely throbbing. He'd noticed some chairs in one of the smaller lecture rooms and decided to rest there. He didn't need an audience while he attended to his busted limb.

Also, he'd be away from the main festivities if Devlin were so foolish as to confront him again.

He had just stepped away from the noisy hall and was about to slip into one of the nearby rooms when a gentleman cut him off. "Hellfire," he muttered, recognizing his distant cousin, Jordan Drummond, who would be the heir to the Moray fortune should Graelem not marry by Midsummer's Day. "It's you. What are you doing in London?"

"Is that any way to greet your cousin?" Jordan was fashionably dressed, down to his fine silk cravat that was perfectly knotted, and might have passed for one of London's elite were he not as big as Graelem and his shoulders not as brawny. But his cousin's eyes were bloodshot, and his breath reeked of whiskey, not the light champagne punch offered at this celebration.

Graelem tried not to breathe in the stale scent of spirits as Jordan leaned closer. "I noticed your betrothed and came looking for you to offer my congratulations. She's a fine-looking filly. I'm surprised you managed to rein her in." He let out a grunt. "Bet she'll make for an excellent ride on your wedding night... or have you already ridden her?"

He slammed Jordan against the wall, grateful that they were alone and out of sight of the main hall. There was enough scandal surrounding his betrothal to Laurel that he didn't wish to add to it. "Crawl back into your hole, Jordan," he said quietly, but with unmistakable anger. "If I ever hear you talk about Laurel that way again, I'll kill you."

His cousin let out an angry oath. "You bloody bastard! Those Aberdeen properties should have been mine. Uncle Silas promised them to me. Do you think to take them from me? Think again, for I'll have all of the Moray estate soon, all but the run down manor house I've always hated anyway. That inheritance will be mine. Mark my words, for you'll never marry her by Midsummer's Day."

"Is that a threat?"

Suddenly, as if realizing he'd said too much, or perhaps he feared Graelem would finish him off here and now, he stumbled backward and hurried back into the main exhibition hall.

Graelem started to return there as well, for his cousin's words disturbed him and he wanted to be sure that Laurel was safe, but his leg chose that moment to spasm. He had no choice but to get his weight off it now.

He hobbled to the closest lecture room, a small space that held about ten chairs neatly aligned in two rows of five chairs each. Overlooking the sensation of fiery knives stabbing his leg, he set his crutches down along the first row, turned the head chair in the second row so that it was perpendicular to the others, and sank onto the head chair with a heavy grunt. "Damn it," he muttered, suppressing a yelp as he elevated his leg and stretched it out across the others.

He closed his eyes to stem the blinding pain that was in a rampant romp up and down his leg. Would the blasted bones never heal? He closed his eyes and gritted his teeth until the spasms subsided to a dull throb.

When he finally opened his eyes, Lady Anne Hollings was standing in the doorway, studying him as though he were a juicy haunch of mutton. *Bloody hell.* The girl was trouble. First Jordan and now her. Could this day get any worse? "Lady Anne, you shouldn't be in here."

"I saw you step away." She twirled a soft curl and cast him a seductive smile that he found not in the least appealing.

"Only to ease my leg."

"Oh, dear. It must be stiff and throbbing. Is that all you wish to ease?" She moved toward him with a predatory, feline stride, her steps slow and sensual as she approached him, her gaze fixed on the male organ between his legs that she obviously hoped would be stiff and throbbing for her as well.

It wasn't.

He groaned inwardly and quickly rose to grab his crutches, knowing he was about to be set up. This had to be what she and Devlin had been discussing so intently earlier—a plan to stage a sexual encounter. He wasn't a fool and didn't think for a moment that she had any interest in him beyond his inheritance.

She looked at him, confused, as he hobbled his way to the door. "Where are you going?" Did she really believe she had anything to tempt him?

He grinned wryly. "You're a pretty woman, Anne. Don't waste your time interfering in your friend's happiness. You may not believe in love, but Laurel does, and she deserves someone far better than Devlin Kirwood."

"Such as yourself?" She sneered at him and blocked his way when he attempted to walk out into the hallway. "Do you honestly believe she'll marry you?"

"You'll be better served finding someone who will treasure you. I'm certain there's a marquis or viscount who would love you if you gave him the chance. It certainly isn't Devlin Kirwood. He's a bounder and isn't to be trusted."

"And you are? You're the one who's tricked Laurel into an unwanted marriage." She tipped her chin up and set her body at the threshold, as though daring him to push her out of the way.

He wouldn't do it, of course, for he'd never handled a woman

178 | MEARA PLATT

roughly and wasn't about to start now. Jordan was another matter altogether. His cousin had always delighted in causing trouble for him, setting him up to take punishment for things he'd never done as a boy, and laughing when Jenny or Silas inevitably took the switch to him. He'd never forgotten those undeserved beatings.

But Anne was before him now. Unfortunately, he couldn't simply lift her up and set her aside either. He needed his crutches for balance and she was going to fight like the devil to stay in his way. They'd both fall and then he would have to take the brunt of the impact to cushion her landing. Despite her being an insufferable nuisance, he didn't want Anne to get hurt.

So that left him trapped with her for the moment.

Sighing, he resigned himself to hearing her out. The sooner she'd spewed her venom, the sooner she'd be on her way. "Go on, tell me what it is you wish to say."

Her hands curled so that she resembled a cat with claws bared. "You'll never marry her."

He frowned. "Who plans to stop me?" How many more threats was he bound to hear today?

"Not me," she said with a menacing laugh, "but I shall heartily cheer your failure, knowing you stood at the altar and watched your hopes and dreams vanish like morning mist when your precious bride fails to appear. Laurel will make a laughingstock of you. She obviously has you fooled, pretending to be sweet and innocent. You'll find out her true nature soon enough, but it will be too late for you by then."

He didn't know much about women. In truth, he knew almost nothing about them, but he did know about character and there was nothing lacking in Laurel's. If she had a fault, it was that there was too much good in her character, for few women would have struggled so mightily with questions of loyalty and love and friendship as she had. "I'll take that risk."

"You're a fool." She tossed back her hair and sneered at him. "I can prove it to you. She's written Devlin a letter agreeing to elope with him to Gretna Green. She handed it to me and asked that I deliver it to Devlin. I have it right here." She motioned to the reticule dangling from her hand. "Care to read it?"

"No." At one time, Laurel might have trusted Anne and considered her a friend, but Graelem knew it was no longer so. If there was a plot afoot, which he sincerely doubted, Laurel would have slipped the letter to Devlin herself or asked one of her sisters to do it for her.

Anne shrugged her shoulders and withdrew the missive from her reticule. "Then I'll read it to you."

Graelem didn't like that they were standing in the doorway so that any passersby might overhear them, but the hallway still appeared to be empty, and in any event, he had no wish to be in the room alone with Anne. He didn't like Devlin or Jordan and knew each had a plot afoot to undermine his wedding plans. They were obviously afraid of him and not likely to approach him again, but he was worried about what they might do to Laurel. Those toads were not above abducting her.

Bloody hell. He really needed to get back to her.

"Very well," he said finally and with marked impatience, "tell me what the bloody thing says."

Anne proceeded, a look of triumph gleaming in her eyes. "Dearest Devlin." She paused to smirk. "I have always loved you and that hasn't changed. The situation is impossible and I fear my father will not allow me to end the betrothal. We have no alternative but to do as you suggest. I'll meet you at the mews behind my house on Saturday next. Be there at midnight, but we must move quickly or my family will catch us before we reach Gretna Green. You have my heart for always. Laurel."

He'd never heard worse drivel. "Do you expect me to believe that Laurel would betray her family's trust?"

Anne smiled wickedly. "She would, for love. By now you ought to know that love is the most important thing to her."

He took the letter from her hand to peruse it. "What did you hope to accomplish by revealing her so-called plan to elope? It seems to me that you would have been better served keeping your mouth shut and allowing them to run off to Gretna Green, if that were truly Laurel's intention. I might have been angry enough, desperate enough to offer to marry you by Midsummer's Day."

The simple question seemed to stump her. Had she and Devlin

really not thought through their scheme?

She appeared angry enough to spit at him. "I wouldn't have you now. As you said, I can look higher than a mere Scottish baron. I don't want you and neither does Laurel." She snatched the letter from his grasp and then turned on her heels to storm back toward the exhibition rooms.

He shook his head as he watched her walk off in a huff, wishing the afternoon festivities would soon end. Unfortunately, they had just gotten underway. He glanced at the neatly aligned chairs, wanting to while away the long hours settled in them, but that wasn't going to happen.

Was it possible Jordan, Devlin, and Anne had formed a conspiratorial circle to undermine his wedding plans? In any event, he knew for certain that Anne and Devlin were working together and would immediately plot further mischief now that their little note scheme had failed.

He didn't care what those bounders did to him, but what they might do to Laurel concerned him.

He had to find her and stay close beside her for the rest of the affair. She might find his constant presence irritating, but he couldn't risk her falling victim to another one of their ploys. Desperate people did desperate things.

Jordan and Devlin were certainly that. He wasn't certain what Anne hoped to achieve, but it stood to reason that she desperately needed something. Probably money. It often boiled down to that.

As he was about to head back to the festivities, a light rustle from the neighboring doorway suddenly caught his attention. Had someone been listening? If so, how much had they overheard? Did it matter? Laurel wasn't going to run off, and he would stay close to her for the rest of this party to protect her from these unsavory characters, some of whom she'd once considered friends.

But as he was about to continue down the hall, he saw the shadow of that person hiding in the next room, and it was a slender, female shape. He started toward it, then shook his head and reversed his course. Whoever this young woman was, it would do neither of them any good to be seen with each other.

Worse, he'd only bring more trouble on himself if it turned out to be one of the supposedly proper young ladies he'd met at Eloise's tea party. All three young ladies were here today and had already tossed him hungry looks.

He wasn't so full of himself that he believed any of these women truly desired him. What they wanted was a hulking, muscled male to perform the naughty deeds they'd never consider doing with their unappealing husbands in the marriage bed.

Laurel had teased him about his so-called sexual prowess. If he were so damned competent, he'd know how to deal with the likes of Dora Pertwhistle, Lady Jane Hardwick, and Lady Katherine Lowesby. But he wasn't a rakehell or practiced seducer of women. He wouldn't know how to decline an invitation without insulting them, and he certainly wasn't about to accept.

No, better to avoid them and let them find some other fool to accommodate their sexual fantasies.

To them, marriage was a cold business proposition.

Laurel was different. To Laurel, marriage was the perfect expression of her heart.

He started down the hall and once again heard the light rustle of a gown. No, he wasn't going to find out who it was. Finding Laurel was more important.

Still, it troubled him.

Who was the young woman and how much of Anne's theatrical reading had she overheard?

CHAPTER 15

GRAELEM RETURNED TO the exhibition hall to find it even more of a crush than when he'd left twenty minutes before. Even so, it didn't take him long to spot Laurel standing beside the twins and Hortensia. Another young man stood beside them. The lad looked so much like George Farthingale, it could only be the son George had spoken of with much affection during his visits to examine Graelem's healing leg.

Laurel's eyes brightened and a genuine smile crossed her lips as he approached.

Lord, he'd never tire of her smile.

"There you are," she said, eyeing him up and down with obvious concern, no doubt noticing his limp was a little more pronounced than it had been earlier. "I don't believe you've met my cousin William yet. He's George's son," she said.

He and the young man exchanged pleasantries. Like all the Farthingales, William seemed to be clever, jovial, and not one to put on airs. However, he was a young man—not that Graelem was all that much older—and his gaze kept straying away from his cousins to survey the other young ladies in attendance. By the expression on his boyish face, he was enjoying what he saw.

Laurel rolled her eyes and playfully nudged William. "Must you be so obvious? Have you settled on any little dove in particular?"

He grinned. "No, they're all too lovely. I don't think of them as little birds, but as tasty bake shop sweets. A soft creme caramel, or a hot cherry pie, or a delightful strawberry crumpet. It's hard to choose, so I shall remain the carefree bachelor for now."

"You'd better not bring any of your *tarts* to the house or I shall box your ears." Hortensia arched an eyebrow. "A carefree bachelor, what nonsense! Why, only a year ago you were a boy in knee pants."

William looked appalled. "I was not!" Then he relented and chuckled. "It's been almost two years since I've worn knee pants, Aunt Hortensia. Leave me a little dignity, won't you? Besides, every man ought to sow his wild oats. Nothing wrong with a little exploration before one decides to settle down."

His aunt shook her head and sighed. "Women like a man of mystery, not a young pup with his tongue rolling out of his mouth."

"Can't help it. As I said, they're all so lovely. Like little pastries in a bake shop, and I aim to sample as many sweet treats as I can before *the* young lady of my dreams comes along and puts an end to all my fun."

Hortensia gave him a gentle smack on the arm. "True love is the best fun of all, you dolt."

"I know. I know. That's why we Farthingales only marry for love. I wouldn't think of breaking with the proud family tradition. We all except for…" His face turned crimson as he stared at Laurel and realized his *faux pas*. Although everyone knew Laurel had been forced into this betrothal, he'd been ungraciously about to state it aloud.

"Yes, we do marry for love," Laurel said, turning her gentle gaze on Graelem and placing her hand on his arm. He silently thanked The Fates once again for leading him to this beautiful girl. If she was deceiving him, as Anne had suggested, then she had to be the best actress in all of London. She took a step closer, her hand still perched on his arm.

William stared at her, contrite. "Well, you didn't like him at first. Admit it, Laurel."

"You're a nuisance," she muttered. "Run along and sow your wild oats. Just keep your wits about you. There are devious mothers out there just looking to reel in unsuspecting bachelors for their daughters."

Graelem's mind wandered to his own wild oats days. He'd sown a few, but he'd never been the sort to womanize or undertake nightly excursions to the seedier men's clubs, except in furtherance of his espionage duties. Between fighting Boney's armies and trying to keep the Moray holdings running profitably, he'd had little time to spare for such activities. And he had no use for them now that he had Laurel beside him.

Assuming he truly had Laurel.

Was she too perfect to be true? Beautiful, passionate, and in love with him? He didn't know what he'd done to merit such bounty, but it was a hell of a lot better than the cold, lonely years spent at Moray, and he wasn't ever giving her up.

Even her imperfections were perfect.

She had a strong will, but he didn't mind. He wanted a wife with fire and determination, not one who faced him each morning at the breakfast table with cool disinterest.

The gentle warmth of Laurel's hand upon his arm brought him back to the present. He thought of her marriage list and one of her more delightful demands, share a bed. *Oh, yes.* That was at the top of his list, too.

And he intended to take full advantage, *if* he were ever fortunate enough to have her in his bed. Or rather, *when* he had Laurel in his bed, which would be soon if the light blush now staining her beautiful cheeks was any indication.

While Hortensia lectured William and the twins were momentarily occupied teasing the poor lad, Graelem eased back for a private moment with Laurel—as private as one could be with two hundred people milling about them.

"You appear to be in pain," she said with sincere concern. "How are you feeling?"

He shrugged. "I tried to find a quiet spot to sit down and elevate my leg, but there doesn't seem to be anywhere to hide in this enormous building."

She glanced at Lily and grinned. "My sister can show you where to go for solitude. She knows all this building's secrets."

"Not all," Lily assured her, hearing her name mentioned and

hopping to their side. So much for his quiet moment with Laurel. "I'm sure there are a few secrets that I haven't found out yet. Isn't this a grand place? So many interesting artifacts brought here from around the world. Can you imagine? *Around the world.* And we've never been farther north than the Lake District. Never even been across the Scottish border, much less into the rugged highlands. Did you know that Edinburgh is situated on an extinct volcano? One would certainly hope it remains that way."

Hortensia groaned. "Lily, dear. While I adore your lively mind, you'll have to learn to keep it well hidden from your suitors when you eventually have your come out. No man wishes for a wife who's smarter than he can ever hope to be."

Graelem wanted to come to the girl's defense, but Hortensia was right. Few men would encourage Lily's brilliant thirst for knowledge, but he hoped for her sake that the right one would come along for her. The right man *would* come along. These Farthingale girls were special, not cut from ordinary cloth.

"Oh, there's Ashton," Lily said, craning her neck to peer at a slender young man with thin blond hair who was now talking to the Duke of Lotheil. "He's asked me to help him on a monograph he's writing." Her eyes were now glistening with excitement. "And I'm developing an idea for a monograph of my own about the habits of baboon colonies. Did you know—"

"Oh, crumpets! Not that monkey blather again, Lily. It's all you speak of lately." William rolled his eyes.

She playfully stuck her tongue out at him. "I'm going off to converse with someone who appreciates my monkeys. Ashton will listen to me."

"I'll go with you," Dillie said and scampered off with her.

"Oh, dear," Laurel laughingly muttered. "The twins off on their own again? I'm not sure that's a very good idea. It won't take them long to cook up some new mischief."

Hortensia shook her head and sighed. "You're right, of course. Come along, William. You and I shall see to it that these imps cause no more trouble."

As the two of them went off, Graelem was finally and truly left alone with Laurel. Her pretty brow suddenly furrowed and she pursed her lips. "Speaking of trouble, have you seen Daisy? I couldn't find her earlier and I'm a little worried."

"Let me see if she's in the hall." Since he was taller than just about any man present, he had no difficulty searching the crowd. "There she is." *Damn.* "She's speaking with your friend Anne." What was the girl telling Daisy? No doubt spouting the same drivel about Laurel and Devlin and their plans to elope. The thought crossed his mind that Daisy might have been the slender shadow he'd noticed earlier when Anne had been reading the letter to him. Indeed, a bad situation if Daisy believed its content to be true.

Laurel's frown deepened. "Anne and I were good friends once, but she's changed so much this past year. Or is it that I never noticed her mercenary qualities? Would you mind if we joined them? I don't think I like her talking to Daisy alone."

Neither did he. "Not at all. Take hold of my arm. I'll part the crowd for us."

Anne had disappeared by the time they made it across the room. He and Laurel came upon Daisy standing alone and looking perplexed. "Something wrong?" Laurel asked her.

Daisy glanced up with the guiltiest look in her eyes, but she shook her head in denial and quickly averted her gaze. "Nothing," she said, gazing at her toes instead of at her or Graelem. "All's well. Ribbons and roses."

"I hardly think so." A flicker of alarm sprang into Laurel's eyes. "You were talking to Anne."

Daisy blushed. "Oh, that. Yes, a… a moment's chat with your friend, Anne. Dull conversation. Very dull, indeed. Almost put me to sleep. Not interesting at all."

Laurel put a hand on Daisy's shoulder. "She hasn't behaved much like a friend to me lately, so beware of what she tells you. Stop fidgeting and tell me what you two were talking about."

Daisy was obviously still flustered, which told Graelem all he needed to know. Anne had been spouting that elopement nonsense again, Daisy might have been the one to overhear them earlier, and now she believed that fable. But what did Anne have to gain by convincing her? It would take nothing for Daisy to talk to Laurel and straighten out any misunderstanding. After all, she and Laurel shared a bedchamber and could easily chat at length in the privacy of their room.

The short hairs on the back on his neck were standing on end again.

No, he didn't like what was going on at all. He'd speak to Daisy, but didn't intend to do it here. There were too many people standing close by, including Eloise's busybody friend Lady Withnall. That tiny termagant had ears like a bat, able to pick up whispers from here all the way to Coventry. He didn't need more rumors than were already circulating in the scandal rags about him and Laurel.

Lord, he hated those insidious gossip sheets.

He didn't care what was said about him, but they'd been particularly cruel to Laurel, calling her "the baron's biscuit" and other appellations that would make a barmaid blush. Damn. He had much to atone for with Laurel. His only saving grace was that she seemed to have fallen in love with him despite all that had happened between them.

He'd make things right with her, but first they had to deal with Anne's mischief. What had she told Daisy?

He glanced once more at Daisy. Her cheeks were stained with a pink blush and she appeared sincerely distressed. The wonderful thing about Daisy, indeed all the Farthingale girls, was that they were dreadful liars. "Oh, look!" she said, her features suddenly brightening. "The duke is about to give his speech. Shall we go listen?" She took off without awaiting their answer.

Laurel shook her head in confusion. "What was that about?"

Graelem held her back when she was about to start after Daisy. "I think I know."

"You do?"

As the crowd began to move toward the back of the hall where a dais had been set up beside what would be the new wing, Graelem took the opportunity to step to the side and sit in one of the chairs along the wall that was now left empty. "Sit with me, love. In truth, my leg won't hold me up much longer."

"Oh, dear." Laurel's hands were already on him to lend

comfort as he sank into the closest chair.

She took a seat beside him. "I've grown used to us spending our afternoons together. In truth, this party has upset my schedule. Although I chatted with acquaintances and studied some of the exhibits, I wasn't enjoying myself very much. My thoughts kept returning to you."

He laughed and shook his head. "My thoughts never left you, lass."

"But you're not going to like what I must do next." She began to nibble her lip and glanced toward Devlin, who happened to be standing at the back of the crowd, looking sullen. "I've disappointed him terribly. I must speak to him. I owe him that much."

Graelem shifted uncomfortably in the chair that was too small for his large frame. "You don't owe him anything. He and Anne already have a new scheme to interfere with our betrothal. Anne showed me a letter you supposedly wrote to Devlin."

"A letter?" She shook her head and frowned. "I wrote him several in the days immediately following our first encounter. But they were mere apologies for why I couldn't meet him in the park or at a particular ball or musicale. I did start to write him an important one the other day, explaining my feelings for you, but I never finished it."

She paused to cast him a pained glance before continuing. "Everything was happening so fast and I honestly didn't know how I felt about you… or how you felt about me. It's still sitting in my writing desk. I never got beyond the first few sentences."

He'd shaken her comfortable existence by claiming her for his own and giving no thought to her wishes. He was still doing it, the only difference being that she was more accepting of it now. Still didn't make it right. "The letter Anne showed me says you plan to meet Devlin this Saturday at the mews behind Chipping Way."

"At midnight?"

He nodded. "You knew about this letter?"

"No, but that's what Devlin asked me to do several days ago. Well, it was more of a demand, and I must say, I didn't like being ordered about. No, not one bit." A sadness suddenly stole into her eyes. "Just as I don't like being forced to marry you. You and he are both in the wrong."

He ran a hand raggedly through his hair. "I know."

This was the undercurrent that coursed through all of their conversations. He had tricked her into the betrothal and she was bitterly hurt by it. That was bad enough, but he was making it worse by still refusing to allow her out of it.

He knew he had to fix this mess. Devlin's deceit was nothing to what he had done to her.

He *would* fix this mess as soon as Devlin was no longer a threat.

But telling Laurel now would do no good. She wouldn't believe him until he actually released her from their betrothal and he wasn't ready to do it yet. In truth, he didn't ever wish to do it. When it came to letting go of Laurel, he was a coward and an ass.

He could face Napoleon's army without flinching.

Why couldn't he let Laurel go?

Laurel nodded her head as though coming to a decision. "I must speak to Dev. Right now."

She stared at him, daring him to disagree.

He wanted to, but knew she'd go off anyway to talk to the bounder. "Laurel, he isn't in love with you. He never was. Just remember that."

"Because he hasn't kissed me yet? Not all men are like you. We've discussed this before. He's more reserved than you are, that's all. It means nothing that he hasn't tried."

He sat up in his chair, every possessive, protective, oafish instinct now on full alert, for he'd stopped listening after that first sentence had slipped from her lips. "He hasn't kissed you *yet*?"

She rolled her eyes. "I didn't mean it that way. I have no intention of kissing him back. Ever. Is that better? Indeed, I'd crack a chair over his head if he ever tried, as I should have done when you kissed me." She grinned at him, melting his anger. "But I had too much fun kissing you and didn't want to stop, as you well know."

"Lass, you can toss about words like polite and reserved and gentlemanly, but men are men. We see a beautiful woman and we want her. Naked. In our bed. Plain and simple."

"That's ridiculous."

"That's men."

She pursed her lips and frowned lightly. "Is that what you think when you look at me?"

"Hell, yes."

She gasped and blushed furiously, an angry blush. "Why, you big—"

"And I also think of the wonderful wife you'll make, and wonderful mother for our children, and how empty my life had been until I met you. But I still want to take you into my bed and hold your soft, warm body in my arms. Only difference is that I want you beside me for all my days."

"You're still an oaf," she muttered, and while her blush remained, it was clear that her anger had completely faded.

"Ideas of chivalry and nobility are pounded into our male brains, but it isn't our brains that usually do our thinking for us. Certainly not when it comes to women. If Devlin truly wanted to kiss you, he would have found a way to do it long ago. Blessed saints, I've been thinking of nothing else since the moment I met you. Lass," he said more gently, "you wouldn't have responded to me the way you did if you truly wanted him."

Her blush deepened, no doubt because she was recalling her behavior in Eloise's parlor a few days ago. To call it reckless and wanton was an understatement.

He gave her a grin that made her cheeks flame a hot, bright red. Having Laurel speechless was an advantage he did not wish to overlook, so he continued making his point. "This is a conversation we've had before, but he's growing more desperate and you have to be made aware. I know his type. Pampered, self-important. Not one to appreciate what he has until he thinks he's lost it. He isn't a good loser. Quite the opposite; he's angry and doesn't care whom he hurts in retaliation. Anne is helping him out, and I'm not sure why. It could be that they've become lovers, or are both feeling spurned and that has drawn them to each other. Whatever the reason, it concerns me that Anne was speaking privately to Daisy."

Laure paused a moment to digest what he'd told her. "You think she showed this so-called letter to my sister?"

"Or told her about it. Yes, I'm certain."

Laurel nodded. "No wonder Daisy was behaving so oddly. I'll warn her. But I still need to speak to Devlin."

He wasn't going to dissuade her, but he intended to stay close enough to come to her aid if she needed help. He'd do his best not to kill the bounder, even though his hands were already itching to close around his fashionably bedecked throat.

Laurel didn't immediately leave his side, apparently having more to discuss with him before she did so. "Graelem, did you believe I'd written the letter that Anne showed you? Or was it a poor forgery that you saw couldn't have been written in my hand?"

He ran his fingers roughly through his hair. "No, actually the forgery was quite good. That's why I think Daisy might believe you wrote it. But not me, love. I never would. Not because of my so-called prowess with women, which is non-existent, by the way. But because of who you are."

"Me?"

"You're incredible, Laurel. You love with all your heart. You're faithful and honorable and loyal."

She grinned. "And I don't have fleas."

"What?"

She burst out laughing. "Oh, Graelem! You've just described the virtues of a dog. Faithful, honorable, and loyal. I can also be trained to fetch slippers and curl up on your lap on cold, winter evenings."

"Blessed Scottish saints," he muttered, shaking his head dazedly. "I told you I'm no good at this courtship thing."

She laughed again, this time more softly. "I know. You're simply dreadful at it. That's why I know you mean it. Thank you. I'm pleased you consider me as noble as a dog. I'm delighted that you trust me, because now I have hope that you'll do the right thing before Midsummer's Day."

She didn't wait for his response, no doubt knowing it wasn't going to be what she wanted to hear anyway. Trust her? Of course he did. So why couldn't he release her from their betrothal? All he had to do was utter those three simple words, *I release you*. In the next breath, he could ask her to marry him and she'd accept.

It was such an easy fix to the bad start of their betrothal.

So why couldn't he do it?

He knew the reason why. To let her go would be like cutting out his heart and he couldn't live without that vital organ. That's how important Laurel had become to him.

Perhaps she understood it, too. Which would explain why she was no longer spouting that demand with her every breath and storming out in a fury when he refused.

"Are you certain you're all right?" she asked, cutting into his thoughts.

He nodded.

"Good. I'll be back shortly." She rose, all the while staring at him, her expression determined. "Remember, you can't interfere, no matter what Devlin looks like he's about to do. I can handle him. You have to trust me."

"I trust you, lass." It was Devlin that he didn't trust. If she thought he was going to hold back if Devlin so much as put a finger on her, she was sadly mistaken.

No, indeed.

Not likely.

Graelem would break every bone in the bounder's body if he dared to touch Laurel. He understood Devlin's plan. But Laurel had now made it her life's mission to repair their friendship. It wasn't going to work, for Devlin had never valued that friendship.

It was all about Laurel's trust fund. For Devlin, it had only been about the trust fund.

Always.

Graelem ached for Laurel and the hurt she was about to receive. "I'll be here, love. Waiting for you."

Waiting to take her into his arms when she cried her heart out for the shattered friendship between her and that undeserving wretch.

"Graelem…" She began to wring her hands.

"Yes, love."

"I'm glad you're the one... that is, I'm glad you'll wait for me."

LAUREL'S APPREHENSION GREW as she approached Devlin and noted the brooding anger in his eyes. This was a Devlin she hadn't seen before. Outwardly he was fashionably dressed, his stark white shirt collar perfectly starched, his fawn-colored jacket neatly tailored, his silk cravat impeccably knotted and held in place with a gold stickpin... but inwardly, he was in obvious turmoil.

She knew it because they'd long been friends.

His hair was meticulously curled, not a strand out of place, giving his face the fragile air of one of those doomed poets so adored among the Upper Crust, but there was an underlying darkness that sent a shiver up her spine. "Dev, I'm so sorry that I've upset you. These past few weeks have been difficult for me as well."

He laughed mirthlessly. "Am I supposed to forgive you now and assure you that we shall always be friends? You betrayed me, Laurel."

Her heart began to pound, partly out of remorse but mostly out of frustration. "I didn't intend to. You know this situation was forced upon me, and I didn't like it at first. But I won't lie to you. I think I could love Baron Moray. In time, he might come to love me. I hope so."

Devlin glanced toward the dais where the Duke of Lotheil was still expounding on the magnificent plans for the Royal Society's new exhibition wing and laughed mirthlessly again. "And that's it? I'm now to be cast off?"

"I value your friendship." She wanted to put a hand on his arm to reassure him, but there was a palpable tension in his stance and she honestly didn't know what to expect from him, so she kept her hands at her sides.

In any event, Graelem would shoot to his feet if she touched Devlin. He'd pound Devlin into the ground and she didn't want to be responsible for that. She sighed. Better to keep a respectable distance. "There will never be more than friendship between us. I intend to be faithful in my marriage."

Devlin's expression turned to one of disdain. "And what of your oafish baron? Do you truly believe he'll do the same?"

She nodded. "Yes. I haven't a doubt." In truth, she knew for a certainty that she and Graelem would hold to their vows. Perhaps that was why she'd fallen in love with him. Her heart must have sensed his merit. She wasn't the only one who had the attributes of a faithful hound. So did Graelem. She knew that he'd be loyal, honest, and affectionate. Goodness, he'd be far more than affectionate.

Even now, at this completely inappropriate moment, her thoughts were on him, recalling the intensely hot way he'd touched her and roused sensations within her body. She didn't just want Graelem, she craved him.

"He's already carrying on an affair with Anne, you know." Devlin's laugh was bitter and taunting. "Dora Pertwhistle wants him too. Will you spend your life wondering with which young lady he's dallying whenever he slips out of your sight?"

"Stop it, Dev. Obviously, you're the one who's carrying on with Anne. Why else would she be circulating that forged letter and trying to undermine my betrothal? It didn't work. I'd appreciate your ripping up that letter and forgetting about any more underhanded tricks. There's nothing you can say or do to interfere with this betrothal." She sighed and held out her hands in a plea. "Please be happy for me, as I will be for you when you find love."

"When I find love? That's a jest. I did find love… with you. Only now, you won't have me." He glanced over her shoulder as he spoke. Laurel turned and followed his gaze, surprised to realize it was trained on Daisy.

She turned back to him, this time angrily. "You're not to go near my sister. Do you hear me, Dev? If you do anything to harm her, you won't have only Baron Moray to fear. I'll kill you myself."

His icy glower secretly shook her to the core, but she refused to let it show. "Have I made myself clear? Keep away from Daisy. For that matter, keep away from all my sisters."

Too overset to return to Graelem's side, she hurried outside to catch a breath of air. Not that London air was all that clean, but it was preferable to Dev's malevolent stench.

She'd botched that encounter.

Graelem probably knew it and was giving her a moment to calm down before he followed after her.

But as Laurel stood on the street and turned back to look at the Royal Society building, it was Devlin who came toward her, attempting to apologize with a quick "I'm sorry" followed by an overly ardent hug.

She quickly pulled away and stared at the doorway, worried that Graelem might have seen the exchange and misunderstood the reason for it. But it was Daisy who was standing at the top of the steps.

Daisy who was frowning at her.

Daisy for whom that embrace had been staged.

Why?

CHAPTER 16

LAUREL TRIED TO draw Daisy aside once they'd returned home and were back in their bedchamber to dress for supper, but Daisy refused to listen. "Not now, Laurel. I'm busy."

"Nonsense. We're merely getting dressed, not sitting for exams at Oxford. Give me a moment to explain what really happened at the duke's tea." Laurel's head was pounding and her heart was in her throat. Gladys was flitting in and out of their room, setting out their slippers and freshly aired gowns, then hurrying next door to the twins' quarters to help those imps dress. "You must talk to me."

"Must I?" She arched an eyebrow. "I don't think so."

"Please hear me out. It isn't what—"

She turned her back on Laurel. "Gladys, should I wear the lemon silk or the poppy red?"

Laurel sighed, realizing she would not have a decent conversation with her sister this evening. In the brief time they'd been alone, she'd tried to reason with her, and Daisy had interrupted her each time.

Laurel wasn't certain what to do next. She'd always been the hot-tempered sister and Daisy had always been the one to calm her down. The situation was now reversed and she had no idea how to handle it. Obviously, she was making a muddle of everything, doing a terrible job of calming Daisy down.

"Very well," she said, sighing again and feeling quite foolish standing in the center of their bedchamber with her hands outstretched in pleading. "But you can't avoid me forever. I've done nothing wrong and I haven't lied to you."

Daisy gasped. "And you expect me to believe that? You can't lure me into another one of your schemes. I'm sorry I ever helped you out."

Tears began to glisten in Daisy's eyes. She brushed them away with the back of her hand and concentrated on securing the clasp to her cameo necklace, which gave her an excuse not to look at Laurel. "I like Lord Moray. I thought you did, too."

"Here, let me help you with the clasp."

She moved toward her sister, but Daisy darted away. "No, thank you. It's done."

Laurel was almost in tears herself, for she couldn't bear to see her sister so distressed. "About Lord Moray. I do like him. Very much. I wish to marry him." Good heavens, she was so deeply in love with him. Why wasn't it obvious to her sister?

"Just how gullible do you think I am?" Daisy turned to gape at her. "If you're so eager to marry him, then why were you embracing Devlin? How can you think to elope with him?"

"I wasn't thinking about it. There will be no elopement. It isn't going to hap—" She tried to finish her sentence, but the twins burst into their room, their mother and Hortensia following closely on their heels. They were all squealing and chattering at once. Laurel couldn't make out what they were saying. "Good grief, are we living in the Tower of Babel?"

Daisy, who was already dressed for this evening's supper, took the momentary distraction as her opportunity to slip away downstairs. Laurel called out to her, but to no avail. She was left frustrated and forced to shout above the din. "Why are you all in here?"

The twins were now on their knees, crawling along the carpet. Their mother and Hortensia were still shrieking and groaning and clutching their hearts.

Laurel knew the twins had done something to throw them into a panic. "What is going on?"

"Lily's spider escaped again," Dillie said. "We thought he might have wandered in here since that's what he did the last time."

"I want that wretched thing out of the house!" their mother demanded in her sternest voice, which wasn't stern at all. None of her daughters ever trembled in fear, because their mother was softhearted in the extreme. She might shout and threaten, but in the next breath, she'd be hugging them and telling them that she loved them with all her heart and would always love them no matter how sorely they tested her.

"Ah, here he is!" Lily crawled out from under Laurel's bed with a hairy, dark brown object squirming in her hand. "I'm sorry, Mother. I don't know how Romulus managed to escape." She plopped her pet tarantula back into the jar she'd brought with her.

Her mother was still clutching her chest. "Frightening thing. Get rid of it. Do you hear me, Lily? That horrid creature must go."

Lily gave a disheartened nod.

Dillie put a consoling arm about her shoulder. "We'll find a good home for Romulus."

"Well, that's done." Hortensia stood there grinning. "Supper anyone? I think I just heard Pruitt ring the bell."

Laurel's mother rolled her eyes. "Who can think of eating now?"

Hortensia patted her rotund belly. "I can, as anyone can plainly see. Come along, girls. Do try to behave for your mother."

Although the twins had caused this latest mischief, Hortensia's gaze was trained like a hawk's on Laurel as she spoke. Laurel sighed.

This is going to be a long night.

Farthingale suppers were never quiet family affairs, because there were always too many Farthingales about. Tonight their table was set for thirty family members. Since she and Daisy were usually seated at opposite ends of the table, Laurel knew she would have no chance to talk to her during the meal.

She decided to seek out Daisy as soon as she entered the dining room. Pausing at the doorway, she quickly spotted her sister standing off to the side engaged in conversation with their aunt Julia.

Although Daisy tried to appear casual and unaffected, Laurel knew her too well and saw that she was still distressed.

This was all her fault… again.

When the supper bell rang, she waited for Daisy beside her chair. "Daisy, please—"

"No, Laurel," she said in a harsh whisper. "It isn't me you who deserves the apology, but Lord Moray. You must tell him the truth."

"He does know the truth," she replied, her voice also a whisper, "and he believes me. He trusts me. So should you."

The other family members were now taking their seats, so Laurel had no choice but to move away and take her place at the opposite end of the table. There were at least a dozen chattering Farthingales between them, and Laurel knew it was hopeless to catch her sister's attention while they ate.

Daisy refused to glance her way, instead spending most of the evening staring dejectedly into her elegant plate.

Laurel couldn't bear to see Daisy looking so hurt. She silently cursed that forged letter and silently berated herself for ever considering Anne a friend. The sight of Anne maliciously whispering lies in Daisy's ear had made her ill. She still had a sour feeling about it.

Daisy had also seen Devlin embracing her in that staged, apologetic reconciliation.

Drat. She knew the events of this afternoon's tea were now churning in her sister's stomach.

Laurel considered using her spoon to catapult a brussels sprout across the table and gain her attention, but the sprouts were heavily buttered and would ruin the delicate silk of Daisy's new gown.

Too bad.

Perhaps she could just launch the spoon.

"Laurel." Uncle George's voice cut through her schemes. *Drat again.* It seemed as though her uncle could read her thoughts as easily as if she'd printed them in the London newspapers. "Put down your spoon and tell me what's wrong."

"It isn't me," she assured him. "Daisy is overset about something and I think it's all my fault. It's this betrothal business."

"So you considered hurling your spoon at her?" He arched a dark eyebrow and shot her a wry grin. "Is your aim that good? I'll wager five pounds you'll hit Hortensia instead."

Laurel smothered a giggle. "A lady never bets. Besides, you're right. That feathery purple *thing* bobbing out of Aunt Hortensia's hair is most distracting. If you must know, I've already decided to wait until after supper to draw Daisy aside."

"Care to tell me the rest of it?"

She nodded, for her uncle could be trusted to keep her concerns in his confidence if she asked him. "But I need to speak to Daisy first."

"Very well, but I'm always available to talk to you girls. Don't hesitate to ask." He popped a buttered sprout into his mouth. "Mmm, delicious. Mrs. Mayhew has outdone herself this evening. Promise me, Laurel. I want you to come to me if you sense something is wrong. Don't try to handle it yourself."

She frowned. "Don't you think I'm capable of exercising good judgement? No, never mind. Please don't answer the question, for it's obvious I'm not."

"Don't be so hard on yourself. Usually you are quite capable, but you did run down Baron Moray. It was an accident, I know. He's obviously forgiven you."

"He's been most accommodating in that regard. Devlin hasn't been quite as understanding. He's angry and terribly hurt about this betrothal business, and I don't think he'll ever forgive me."

"Has he said something to you?"

She nodded. "But nothing to worry about."

"And what has he said to Daisy? Is that why she looks like she's about to cry into her vegetables? Did the little bast—" He coughed and caught himself before he used an ungentlemanly epithet. "Did he say something to her? Tell me what's going on."

"Nothing, Uncle George. You needn't fear. Some silly gossip has been circulating that distressed Daisy. I'll speak to her as soon as we ladies retire to the salon. As for me, I had an unpleasant encounter with Devlin. I tried to speak to him earlier today at the Duke of Lotheil's celebration, but he was angry and still pouting."

"Pouting? Girls pout. Grown men seek revenge."

Laurel's eyes rounded in alarm. "Not Devlin. He'd never hurt me or Daisy. I know he's been sullen, but that's only because his pride has been wounded. He'll get over it and we'll be friends once again."

"You know little about men and their true natures. We're not kind or gentle like you and Daisy."

"You're the kindest man I know, Uncle George. There isn't a finer one, except perhaps Father." She shook her head and sighed. "He must be a saint, for how else could he put up with his wayward daughters?"

He laughed softly. "We're kind to you because you're family and we love you. But all men wear a thin mask of civility, even we sainted Farthingales. It's only a mask, easily cast off."

"Well, Devlin hasn't done a very good job of keeping his mask on. His hurt is so obvious it breaks my heart. But I've made my choice. At least, I think I have. Are you suggesting that I shouldn't trust Graelem either?"

"Quite the opposite. In my opinion, he's one of the few that you can trust. Now, tell me more about this afternoon."

"And Devlin?"

He popped another sprout in his mouth and nodded.

Laurel shook her head and sighed. "Very well, I suppose I could use some help. I think your assessment of Devlin is right. I'm finally noticing his spiteful nature. Daisy hasn't noticed it yet. But more important, she heard something this afternoon that overset her. She thinks I'm going to run off with Devlin. I'm not, of course."

"Run away? As in elope with Devlin?"

She nodded. "He asked me, but I dismissed the notion long ago. I don't think Daisy believes me." She glanced at her plate, and although the food looked tempting, she had no appetite for it. "Why don't you like Devlin? In truth, you've never liked him. Have you? Pruitt hasn't either."

"I can't speak for Pruitt; however, I can tell you my reasons. You know what your father often tells you."

"Oh, that expression he has about the unchanging nature of people. That a petty, indulged child will turn into a spoiled, arrogant adult."

Her uncle nodded. "That's right. I'm afraid Devlin has become one of those."

The possibility sincerely distressed her. "How do you mean? It's important that I know his current situation."

"Devlin is a heavy gambler. I've seen him at the local gaming dens. I stop by on occasion to play cards or have a drink with friends, but he's a regular at these establishments and he rarely wins."

Her fingers tightened around her fork. "Are you certain?"

"Yes. He sinks deeper in debt with each passing day. His father has been quietly covering his losses, but I shudder to think what will happen to the Kirwood holdings once Devlin inherits them. It won't take him long to destroy all that his father has built over the years."

She set down her fork with an inadvertent clatter as it lightly struck her delicate plate, realizing she'd been a fool to think that her friendship had ever meant anything to Devlin. "No wonder he was so overset about my sudden betrothal. He needs my wealth. His anger was never about me at all."

"Since we seem to be addressing this at the dinner table anyway, I'll add my opinion. No, it was never about his caring for you. Even as a little boy, it was obvious that Devlin cared only for himself. But Baron Moray is another matter. His marriage proposal may have started as a business proposition, but it's turned into something much more important to him. You have become much more important to him."

"How can you tell?"

She studied her uncle's expression as he responded. "Too many years without that important person in my own life," he said with a mirthless smile. "What he feels for you is something to be treasured, Laurel." He glanced down the table. "Hortensia and Rupert will tell you the same thing."

She wanted to reach over and hug her uncle, but knew it would embarrass him. "Did you love your wife very much? You've been a widower for a very long time. You rarely speak of her. Does it still hurt too much?"

A glint of doubt sprang into his clear, Farthingale blue eyes. "We were quite young at the time and I believed myself in love. I think I was, but it's been so long. It's likely that as we grew older our love would have matured. William has inherited his mother's liveliness and joyful temperament. Yes, I think ours would have become a love match."

"Thank you, Uncle George." He'd never spoken about himself like this before, and she was honored that he trusted her enough to speak so candidly now.

"Don't demand perfection, Laurel. I love Hortensia, but sometimes I think her standards were too high. What has she gained by keeping to those impossible standards? No husband. No children. Sometimes I see a look of regret in her eyes, although most of the time she hides it. She isn't unhappy, and for the most part she appears content, but life has passed her by and she knows it."

He paused to lift his glass and take a sip of wine. The red wine glistened in the candlelight like a deep red ruby within the crystal glass. "You aren't anything like Hortensia. You won't be happy if you hold fast to your standards and lose Graelem because of it. And I doubt you'll look good in purple egret feathers."

She chuckled. "Purple was never a good color for me. I must agree with you on that point. I'll talk to Graelem... Lord Moray. I know he won't release me from our betrothal and I'm not happy about it, but I'm falling in love with him. I'll willingly lose this battle because I think in time he'll come to love me and that is much more important."

"I'm glad to hear you say so."

"But I'm still disappointed. I wanted to come to him of my own free will. It's important to me." Her lips curled up at the corners as she grinned. "He'll have a lifetime to make it up to me. I won't let him off easily."

George patted her hand. "He will. He's a good man."

"So now, my problem is Daisy."

George followed her gaze. "Talk to her as soon as possible. I've never seen her in such turmoil before."

LAUREL WASN'T ABLE to catch Daisy alone to speak to her after supper. She had just resigned herself to waiting until they retired for bed when Daisy strode toward her with her chin tipped upward and her expression cool. "I'm going to stay with Aunt Julia this evening. I think it's for the best."

"I'll help you pack a few things. We can talk while—"

"No need." Daisy gave a dismissive wave of her hand. "Gladys will help me."

"There's obviously a need." She lightly took hold of Daisy's elbow to prevent her from turning away. "Please, listen to me. Nothing is going on between me and Devlin. What you saw earlier was my attempt to salvage the friendship, but I know now that it can't be done. At least, not at the moment. Perhaps in a few months, after I'm married and settled in."

"Married to Graelem?"

"Of course. Who else would I marry? I love Graelem."

Daisy arched an eyebrow. "Oh, truly? Have you told him that?"

Laurel felt her face begin to heat. She'd admitted her feelings to Graelem the night he was unconscious with fever and the effects of the laudanum, but that didn't count since he hadn't heard her. "Not in so many words." Although she'd freely given him her body. "You know I haven't yet. But I will."

"Why should I believe you? He's the only one who needs to hear it and the only one you haven't told."

Laurel released Daisy's elbow and held her hands out in plaintive contrition. "Daisy, you don't understand. It isn't that simple."

"You're wrong, Laurel. It is precisely that simple. You can't tell Graelem you love him because you don't really feel it. You're still in love with Devlin." She let out a ragged breath. "Love whomever you wish, but stop deceiving your own family, all of us who love you."

"Oh, Daisy," she said in a soft, shattered moan.

"What really hurts is how you used me. I can't believe I allowed you to do it, serving as your messenger to deliver your scheming posts to Devlin." Tears welled in her eyes, but she blinked them away and continued. "Anne read one of those letters aloud to Graelem. He foolishly thought it was a forgery. I heard everything. He has such faith in you, it breaks my heart. I was next door and overheard everything. I know what you and Dev have planned. What the two of you are doing is underhanded, and if you don't confess to Mother and Father, I will."

Laurel wanted to shake her sister in frustration. "There's nothing to confess. I have never lied to you and never will. Come with me right now to speak to Graelem and we'll sort it all out."

"No. Julia needs me. I'll be back on Friday."

"But—"

"Friday."

Laurel nodded. "Very well, we'll talk when you return home."

She'd hoped for a sign of softening from Daisy, but there was none. Instead, Daisy stiffened her spine and tipped her chin up. Laurel immediately recognized the posture because she'd used it all too often herself whenever she was indignant. "Right, Daisy? We must talk."

"Maybe. I don't know if I will have forgiven you by then."

CHAPTER 17

THE SUN WAS shining and a lovely, warm breeze caressed Laurel's cheeks as she walked the short distance to Eloise's townhouse the next morning. Chipping Way was a quiet street, so she often heard the larks and sparrows chirping in the trees. Their chirps often mingled with the din and clatter of passing carriages along the nearby main street.

Those birds were in full song today.

Their joyful song mirrored her own feelings and she had Daisy to thank for that. She'd thought about Daisy's admonition and realized her sister had been right. She had to tell Graelem how she felt. Allowing his kisses and giving him permission to roam his hands freely over her body wasn't enough. It was merely an admission of lust, not at all the same as telling him that she loved him.

"I love you," she murmured. These were powerful words, ones that Graelem needed to hear.

She was about to walk through Eloise's gate, now resolved to tell Graelem what was in her heart, when all of a sudden he appeared before her, moving with purposeful haste so that he almost bumped into her. "Graelem? I was just coming to see you. I know I'm a bit earlier than usual, but there's something important I need to tell you and—"

"Can it wait until later?" He was frowning and seemed to be in a hurry, although she had no idea where he might be going in such a rush, on his crutches no less.

"I suppose." She walked beside him, admiring the agility with which he got around on those crutches. "What's wrong?"

"It may be nothing. Probably is nothing, but Amos just sent word to me. He says Brutus is more skittish today than usual. I was going to see for myself, but I'm glad you're here. No one knows that beast better than you do."

Laurel began to nibble her lip, already fretting over Brutus. She knew Graelem had been seeing to his proper care, allowing Amos to ride him each morning as well as properly feed and groom him each day. "Perhaps he misses me."

"A heartbroken horse?" Graelem paused and arched his eyebrow. "Possibly. I sure as hell would miss you if I were Brutus."

"You would?" She leapt at the opportunity to ask about his own true feelings. "And if you were *you*? Would you miss me if we were apart and you didn't have to marry me? Would you think of me at all?"

He stared at her, his expression revealing nothing for the longest moment, and then the corners of his lips curved upward in the softest smile. "Och, lass. Every day," he said with a deep, rumbling brogue that caused her insides to warm and the little butterflies in her stomach to flutter their wings in giddy excitement. "Every moment of every day."

Her eyes widened in surprise. Although he'd agreed to her terms of their marriage and been content with the requirements in her list, this was the closest he'd ever come to a declaration of love. "I'd miss you too."

He reached out and tucked a finger under her chin. "What's this about, Laurel?"

"I'll tell you after we've seen Brutus." She was eager to tell him that she loved him, but also wanted to make a quick escape if his response wasn't what she'd hoped. She couldn't escape before making certain Brutus was fit.

She eased away and began to walk ahead of him, but he quickly caught up to her.

They walked in silence the rest of the way, turning the corner and entering the mews, which contained a large carriage house, two smaller ones, and a row of stalls to accommodate the assorted conveyances, riding equipment, sturdy carriage horses, and high-stepping mounts owned by the residents of Chipping Way.

The largest carriage house belonged to the Farthingales. One of the smaller houses belonged to Graelem's grandmother, and the smallest belonged to the reclusive and slightly curmudgeonly General Allworthy, who resided at Number 1 Chipping Way.

Laurel noticed Amos standing beside Brutus and soothingly stroking his nose. "Oh, dear. Amos, what do you think is wrong with him?"

"I can't put my finger on it, Miss Laurel. He just isn't himself."

As Amos drew back, she stepped forward and wrapped her arms around the horse's neck. Brutus immediately responded with a neigh and a soft snort of air against her ear. "How are you, Brutus, my love? Have you missed me?"

She gave him a few more strokes, ran her hands expertly up and down his forelegs, and then began to walk him out of the stable. "His gait seems fine. I don't notice a limp." She blushed as the words left her mouth, for Graelem stood beside her, leaning on his crutches. Once he was off them, he'd still have a limp, possibly for the rest of his life. "I mean… perhaps you ought to ride him up and down the street, Amos. I'll watch his movements as you do."

"I have a better idea," Graelem said. "You do it, and if he still appears to be out of sorts, then we'll know for certain that something is wrong."

Her eyes widened and her heart began to beat a little faster. "You'd allow me to ride Brutus?"

Graelem nodded. "He's yours, Laurel. I've already told you that I won't take him from you."

In that moment, she wanted to throw her arms around Graelem's neck and tell him that she loved him. If ever she'd had a doubt that she could be happily married to him, it was now erased. She smiled at him and was met with a warm smile in response. There was a gleam of affection in his dark eyes. Was it love? "Besides," he said, "it's a perfect day for a leisurely ride in Hyde Park."

She gasped. "Truly?"

He tweaked her nose. "If I recall the terms of your punishment, you're confined to your home so long as I'm confined. And now that I'm able to get around, so are you. I'm sure you've missed your daily jaunts to the park."

"I have," she admitted.

"Then go change into your riding habit. I'll wait for you here."

She didn't know what to say. Once again the urge to throw her arms around him and admit that she loved him seemed most appropriate. However, Amos stood beside them and although he was no gossip, Laurel didn't wish for an audience when she handed her heart to Graelem. "Thank you," she said in a ragged whisper.

Graelem laughed and nudged her toward the house.

She hurried off, Graelem remaining foremost on her mind. She simply had to find the right moment to tell him how she felt. He'd be pleased, and if he were inclined to kiss her long and hard, she wouldn't resist.

Indeed, she wanted his hot, hungry lips on hers.

She ached for his big, capable hands on her body.

Gladys was in her bedchamber, merrily humming a country lilt as she dusted furniture. "Back already, Miss Laurel? Was his lordship not at home? Well, it's a lovely day, isn't it? He might have gone out. Can't blame him, being trapped inside for weeks with a busted leg."

"The loveliest day," she agreed. "I met him on his way to the mews. Will you help me into my riding habit? Lord Moray and I are going for a ride in the park."

Gladys smiled. "Oh, what a nice idea."

She nodded. "The nicest. Something spooked Brutus this morning, but he appears fine now. Nonetheless, Lord Moray insisted we take him out for a trot. It's more for my benefit, I think. He knows how eager I am to get out again."

Gladys laughed. "We all know it. You haven't let any of us forget it since the day you were punished."

Laurel winced. "I suppose I have been insufferable these past few weeks. My apologies if I was rude to you."

Her eyes rounded in horror. "Dear me, no! You're never one

take your anger out on others." She shook her head and *tsked*. "You're always much harder on yourself than on anyone else. But no more talk of that when you have a handsome baron waiting for you."

"He is quite good-looking, isn't he?"

"He's a catch, to be sure. So don't let him slip through your fingers. Stop dawdling and get about your business."

With a little help from Gladys, Laurel quickly changed out of her morning gown and into her green velvet riding habit, the one she had worn on the fateful day Brutus had knocked down Graelem. Goodness, it seemed forever ago. So much had happened in these few weeks.

Tomorrow would mark the end of the third week.

Tomorrow her father would expect her decision, although by now he had to be fairly certain of her answer. She was never any good at hiding her feelings, and she'd already admitted to her family that she loved Graelem.

It was time she admitted it to him.

She hurried back to the mews. Graelem was waiting for her, already mounted on one of the Farthingale horses by the time she returned. He sat astride Galileo, a magnificent roan gelding. He looked very much like a brave Scottish warrior and very much at ease in the saddle, even though his injured leg was out of the stirrup and left to hang down stiffly.

Gladys had referred to him as a handsome baron. Indeed, he was. The handsomest ever. "I hope I didn't keep you waiting too long."

"Not at all, lass. Brutus and I were getting better acquainted." Brutus had been saddled and was now pawing the ground, impatient to trot off. Graelem held out the reins that were loosely clasped in his hand. Her fingers grazed his as she took them from him.

Her body immediately began to tingle at his touch.

She blushed and quickly drew her hand away.

He grinned, no doubt noticing the fire in her cheeks that was now spreading down her body and heating the most inappropriately intimate places. Thankfully, those were primly covered by the green velvet of her riding habit.

She quickly mounted Brutus, requiring no assistance as she hooked one leg atop the saddle and settled herself comfortably in the seat. "Shall we go?"

She stared at the back of Brutus' head as she spoke, desperate to avoid Graelem's knowing gaze. What was wrong with her? Couldn't she contain her wanton impulses long enough to attend to her skittish horse? "Thank you for saddling him, Amos."

"I didn't do it, Miss Laurel."

She turned to Graelem in surprise. "You?"

He nodded.

She laughed lightly. "Brutus allowed you near him? I suppose he still feels badly about injuring you."

"I doubt he has any such sentiments. But he senses your ease around me, so he accepts me. Galileo's a fine horse, too," he said, glancing down at his mount. "Let me guess, Lily named him."

Laurel nodded and pointed to another roan gelding in a nearby stall. "She also named his brother, Copernicus."

Graelem shook his head and chuckled. "Of course."

They rode in comfortable silence to Hyde Park and ambled through the park gate, Laurel concentrating on Brutus and his every step. "I wonder what happened this morning to overset him. He seems perfectly fine now." Just to be sure, she spurred him to a canter as they turned onto Rotten Row. His strides were long and sure, with no hint of any discomfort.

Graelem rode alongside her, his gaze also on Brutus.

But as they turned toward the Serpentine, he suddenly motioned for Laurel to halt. She drew back on the reins and turned to him, worried. "What's wrong? Did you notice something amiss with Brutus?"

When he didn't immediately respond, she followed his gaze to a small group of riders stopped just ahead of them. "Oh, dear. Is that your cousin, Jordan? Crumpets, he's with Anne and Devlin. I wonder what they're talking about."

"Us, no doubt. Nothing good, I'll wager."

"What shall we do?"

"Turn back, I think. I won't have you or Brutus injured in a confrontation." He clamped his big hand over hers, capturing it and the reins she was holding, as though to keep her from charging at the three scoundrels. "I mean it, Laurel. I know what you plan to do, that fire in your eyes gives you away."

"So what if I was going to run them down? Those wretches deserve it."

His laughter was more of a groan. "Save that fiery passion for me when I kiss you, which I plan to do as soon as we return to the stables."

His gaze was a most distracting smolder, one purposely designed to scramble her thoughts and make her heart beat wildly in anticipation. Unfortunately, it worked. Now he was grinning at her. She tried her best to look indignant, but was doing a very poor job of it. "What makes you think I will allow it?"

His thumb gently stroked along the hand he was still holding, evoking shivers of delight from her. "Graelem, you're a wretch and an oaf. You know that, don't you?"

He nodded. "But I'm still going to kiss you."

She glanced around and sighed. He'd distracted her long enough so that the deceitful threesome had ridden off their separate ways. There would be no battle charge. A pity. She and Brutus would have enjoyed knocking those elegant scoundrels to the ground, or better, into the fountain. "Aren't you worried about what they might be planning?"

"Yes."

"Yes? That's it? I deserve a better answer than that." She drew her hand out of his grasp.

He took it back and gave it a gentle squeeze. "Lass, the best solution is for us to marry as soon as possible. I have the special license. I've had it burning a hole in my pocket ever since I arrived in London. But since you're taking a deucedly long time coming around to the idea of marriage—and you're the only debutante in London who seems to have any standards in that regard, to my misfortune—I've had to come up with other means to protect you from that toad you thought you loved, and from my wastrel cousin."

"Such as?"

"I have Bow Street runners watching them, following their movements and reporting back to me daily."

Her eyes widened in surprise. "Are they watching me, too?"

"No, I've always trusted you. It's them I'm worried about."

She had been trying to tug free of his grasp, but stopped. "Always? I think that's the nicest thing you've ever said to me." It was almost as good as telling her that he loved her. Almost.

Still, that he'd trusted her from the first was very special. He'd said it so casually, the words slipping from his nicely formed lips with a natural ease, heartfelt and not at all glib or pandering. Perhaps it was the only way he knew how to tell her that he loved her. "Let's go back to the stable, Graelem. You owe me a kiss."

GRAELEM HAD BEEN aching to plant his lips on Laurel's lush mouth again, driven mad by the memory of her arousal and glorious climax at his hands. He longed to touch her, to run his hands along her soft skin and kiss his way down her delectable body. He put action to the thought the moment they returned to the stable and he saw that they were alone.

In one quick motion, he managed to tether the horses and catch Laurel in his arms as she slid off the saddle. Ignoring the hot jabs of pain that tore up his leg with each step, as any mindless, idiot male would, he carried Laurel to an empty stall. His leg was already in spasms by the time they reached it, and he scattered hay and smacked his shoulders against the wooden boards as he fell against them for support.

He didn't care, only needing the one good leg to stand on anyway.

"Graelem, I—"

His lips closed on hers and his hands cupped her buttocks to draw her firmly up against his arousal, so that she knew how hot and hungry he was for her, how desperate he was to drink her in, to devour her.

She gasped against his mouth. *"Oh, Graelem."*

He loved the sound of his name on her lips, loved everything about her. His hand moved up to cup her breast, his fingers teasing the already hardened nipple through the thick velvet fabric. *"Oh, my goodness! Graelem!"*

"Goodness has nothing to do with it, sweetheart." He would have stopped had she flinched or tensed, but she was grabbing at his jacket to shove it off him and he knew in the next moment she would be ripping at his shirt, sending studs and buttons flying everywhere as she tore it off him to touch his bare skin.

He'd be doomed if she actually knew what she was doing, but there was no seductive art or finesse to her actions. This was Laurel, the wanton innocent who responded with all the passion in her heart.

"Lass," he said, grunting and panting as he kissed her, almost exploding as she kissed him back with a breathless, moaning ardor and began to rub her hip against his hard, throbbing heat. She'd stopped tackling his shirt, the studs too stiff to manage while her fingers trembled, and was now tugging at his breeches.

He was aroused beyond measure by this innocent girl who still didn't know what she was doing and didn't understand the sensations she roused each time her fingers grazed his erect tip—which they did quite often as she fumbled in exasperation with the buttons of his breeches, unaware that her haphazard strokes were driving him over the edge.

He caught her hands in one of his and turned their bodies so that her back was now leaning against the boards of the stall, her arms pinned over her head, trapped in one of his big hands. He used his other hand to explore her body, his fingers sweeping across the lush curves hidden beneath the soft velvet. He traced every sweet swell and curve.

Laurel, as ever, didn't hold back. Instead she responded with a breathless eagerness to each caress, grinding her soft, generous lips against his mouth with ardent desperation.

"Graelem," she said in a whisper, closing her eyes and arching her back so that the hardened tips of her breasts pressed against his chest, the sensation so exquisitely hot and intense that he forgot that his leg was still in spasms and there were still layers of velvet and crisp cotton lawn between them. "Release my hands, I want to touch you."

This was the clumsiest sex he'd ever had, standing off balance and in pain while an inept but exquisitely passionate virgin struggled to get in his pants, and—damn it—couldn't seem to manage it on her own. In her own defense, she couldn't manage to do anything but breathlessly moan his name while she writhed between his legs and he ground his throbbing member against her hip.

Lord, everything about this moment was awkward and perfect. Laurel made it so.

Despite the numerous layers of fabric between them, she still managed to stir him to a roaring heat, one that bubbled his blood and brewed within him until he could bear no more. His pleasure was heightened by Laurel's soft cries as she climaxed, her eyes closed and kissable mouth slightly open as she absorbed the powerful sensations flowing through her body in hot waves of pleasure to match his own.

He drew her shuddering body against his and caressed her until she calmed.

She splayed her hand across his chest, resting it against his heart as it throbbed to a steady beat. He felt hers still beating out of control as she leaned against him. "I love you, Graelem."

She opened her eyes and smiled up at him, a sweet, gentle smile that he didn't deserve, for he had yet to respond to this startling admission just sprung from her lips. In truth, he'd known how Laurel felt about him for a while now, but to hear her say it openly had him raising his eyes heavenward and giving thanks for this miracle.

She felt incredibly good, even though they stood together, both hot and panting and disheveled. He swallowed her in his embrace. "I don't want it to be like this any longer, Laurel. I don't want to be stealing kisses in a stable or in a stately parlor, worried about your reputation if we were to be discovered. I want the right to kiss you, to take you into my arms and carry you to bed. Our bed. Every night. Marry me, lass. Now. Today."

Her smile stole his breath away, as did the sparkle in her eyes.

"Is that your lust speaking?"

He laughed and lowered his forehead to hers. "Hell, yes... and no. You set me on fire, you have from the first. I can't look at you without aching or burning, or turning hot and hard. But at the same time, I can't look at you without wishing you were mine forever. I can't look at you without thinking how hopeless and empty my life would be if I could not wake to find your beautiful eyes, the color of a tropical sea, gazing back at me, or not feel your hand gently resting on my shoulder. This is about starting our lives together." He eased back and ran a hand raggedly through his hair. "I've never forgiven my father for abandoning me, but I'm beginning to understand how he might have felt when losing my mother."

Laurel put a hand on his arm and began to stroke it gently. He doubted that she realized what she was doing, but this is why she'd won his heart, this natural urge of hers to comfort him and soothe his pain. No one's touch was as sweet as Laurel's.

"Perhaps he knew that having to look at me would force him to confront his loss every day of his life and he simply couldn't manage it. She was all that mattered to him, and everything else became meaningless."

She frowned. "You always had meaning."

He laughed mirthlessly. "I might, to you. That's why you have my heart, Laurel. There's about one week left until Midsummer's Day. Say you'll have me. In this I fear I'm too much like my father. If it can't be you, then it will be no other."

Her eyes rounded in surprise. Was he giving her a choice? "Graelem, what are you saying?"

"I want to build a life with you and no one else. Claiming the rest of the Moray holdings won't matter if you're not by my side to share it."

She shook her head, still surprised. "But what of your popinjay cousin? You can't let him win."

"I'll still be Baron Moray, of course. Hopefully, I will exert some power over him to keep him from destroying the Moray assets he inherits. With some guidance he might preserve the livelihood of those who've worked the land for generations. In truth, Silas put him in charge of some farms just outside of Aberdeen, and he seems to have done an adequate job with them. Not good, but adequate. If I were to marry in time to claim the inheritance, I'd consider turning those properties over to him. But I won't shackle myself to just any female to gain the inheritance. It's you or no one, Laurel. What do you say?"

She closed her eyes and swallowed hard. He was asking for her consent again, no longer forcing her to bend to his will. "You know it's the same for me. I think you had my heart from the first moment I set eyes on you, only I couldn't admit it. Yes, I'll marry you, Graelem. Now. Today. Any day ever."

CHAPTER 18

AS THEY MADE their way back to the Farthingale townhouse, Laurel walked slowly beside Graelem, worried about his leg, which was obviously bothering him although the stubborn man refused to admit it. "My leg is old news. Let's discuss wedding arrangements."

She let out a bubble of laughter, for it was obvious by his grimace that he'd rather talk about anything but floral bouquets, wedding pudding, her non-existent bridal trousseau (something easily cured by Madam de Bressard at an outrageous price), or how many Farthingales to invite if they expected to keep the ceremony small. "I'll not torture you with the details since it's something better discussed with my mother. You only suggested it because you're eager to switch the topic of conversation away from your leg. It's still hurting you. I can tell by the pinch of your lips. Nice lips, by the way."

He shook his head and grinned at her. "So are yours. If you keep looking at me that way, I'll have to capture them again right here for the world to see."

"How am I looking at you?"

His grin broadened. "As though I'm one of the gods of Olympus and you worship me."

"Worship you! Hah!" She paused to face him and tilted her chin upward in challenge, but quickly gentled. She couldn't maintain the slightest indignation toward him. "Perhaps I do a little whenever you kiss me."

He reached out and caressed her cheek. "Lass, the feeling is reciprocated." There was a smoky huskiness to his voice that shot tingles through her body.

They were standing in the mews courtyard and about to turn onto the main street so there would be no more stolen kisses, although by the gleam of amusement still in Graelem's eyes she knew he was definitely contemplating the possibility. By the wicked smile on his lips, she knew it would not be a genteel kiss.

She backed away slightly and wagged her finger at him in warning. "But I'm still hot-tempered, so you'd better watch yourself around me. I won't always indulge you just because I like you."

"I should hope not." Although up until this moment they had been jesting and teasing, he suddenly turned serious. "Laurel, you must know by now that dull, simpering mushrooms are not to my taste. I don't wish to change a thing about you. I'm sure it's a mistake to admit it to you, but there it is, I think you're perfect."

She groaned. "Oh, this is awful! You must stop saying nice things to me or I'll never be able to stomp about or stay angry with you. What fun will that be? You'll turn me into one of those dull mushrooms."

He threw back his head and laughed heartily. "I have no doubt that I'll provoke you often enough to prevent that from ever happening. Now let's get back to the safer topic of our wedding. Do whatever you wish, lass. Just tell me when and where to show up." He glanced at the crutches he still needed to get him around.

"A simple ceremony at our home," she said, realizing the beautiful church where her family worshiped had several steps leading up to the altar and Graelem would be too proud to be seen struggling to climb them or attempting to kneel in front of the altar.

The celebration had to include not only her parents and sisters, but Graelem's uncle, the Earl of Trent, and his lovely countess, as well as his grandmother, Eloise. His cousins, Gabriel and Alexander, were away and certain to miss the hastily organized affair. She was sorry for that. Although she had yet to meet either of them, she knew that Graelem loved them and would have wanted them present.

His horrid cousin, Jordan Drummond, would not be invited even if he did do an adequate job managing those Aberdeen farms.

She considered her family as well. Most of them were already in London, filling up the guest rooms in their spacious townhouse. Indeed, every nook and cranny was filled with Farthingales.

Daisy was still visiting their aunt Julia and had to be told at once, for out of all the family members to be included in the celebration, Daisy mattered most to Laurel.

In truth, all her sisters mattered. But she and Daisy were almost as close as the twins were to each other, and their current falling out had been difficult for both of them. Daisy would be pleased to know that she had agreed to marry Graelem and was not going to sneak off to Gretna Green with Devlin.

She was already imagining the hugs of reconciliation and was all smiles as Pruitt opened the door to allow her in. However, her joy was dashed the moment she and Graelem entered the house. One look at Pruitt's face and she knew something was terribly wrong. Then she heard sobs coming from the parlor.

Graelem caught her by the elbow as she paled. "Steady, sweetheart. Let's see what's happened." He nodded in reassurance. "We don't have to say anything about our plans yet."

She made no protest as he nudged her forward even though her heart was now lodged in her throat and she was loath to step into the parlor, for she had her suspicions about what had upset her family.

Uncle Harrison.

It had to be.

Her gaze immediately fell upon the twins, who were seated closest to the door and tearfully gripping each other's hands. Her mother was hugging her father. George, Rupert, and Hortensia were seated quietly with their heads bowed. Uncle George's face was buried in his hands. She understood what George was thinking. His hands had healed so many, yet couldn't save his own beloved brother.

No one said anything as she and Graelem entered. No

explanations were necessary. Their expressions revealed everything. "Papa, I'm so sorry."

Her father was too choked up to speak.

"William has gone to collect Julia and Daisy and bring them back here," her mother said, the tears streaming down her cheeks. "Rose and Julian will be over shortly. Will you help Daisy look after little Harry? I don't think Julia will be able to cope with him right now."

"Of course." She glanced at Graelem, wondering what to do now. They couldn't possibly speak of their own plans. How could they even consider a Midsummer's Day wedding when her household was now officially in mourning?

This was her fault again. She'd fallen in love with Graelem almost from the first, yet had delayed the inevitable marriage because of her pride and willfulness. Now, it was too late. Without a timely wedding, Graelem would lose the bulk of the Moray estate, all but a meaningless baronial title and a worn down manor house.

She couldn't let it happen. But what could she do about it? His earlier words resounded in her numbed brain. Did he mean what he said? Would he truly wait for her?

Oh, dear heaven! He couldn't possibly! There was too much at stake for him to lose.

Despite the noble sentiments he'd expressed earlier in the stable, she wouldn't blame him if he chose to secure his inheritance by marrying another. He'd said that he wouldn't, but those words were spoken in the throes of lust, that was all. She wouldn't allow him to throw away his chance at prosperity.

He put a hand lightly on her shoulder to gain her attention. "Will you be all right? I'll stay if you want me to, but I think I had best go. You need this time alone with your family."

Alone?

So he'd quickly assessed the situation and knew he had to move on. He was going to leave her.

"Whatever you think," she said, trying to hide her heartbreak. She'd lost Uncle Harrison and was now about to lose Graelem.

"I'll come by later."

She glanced at her toes, no longer able to look at him without bursting into tears. "No, you mustn't. You have your own worries to address."

"What?" She heard his sudden intake of air.

"I know you meant to honor our betrothal, but it's impossible now. I won't blame you if you look elsewhere."

The muscle in his jaw clenched. "Do you think me so callow as to beg out of our betrothal and seek a mushroom to marry?"

She glanced at him through the tears now clouding her eyes. "I know you meant it at the time, but there's too much at stake for you. That's why I'm releasing you." She placed a hand on his arm and felt him tense beneath her palm. "You'll lose everything, Graelem. I refuse to be the cause of it."

Her hand still rested on his arm so she felt the anger bubbling inside of him, the hot flood of disbelief coursing through his veins. "You're everything to me, Laurel. Don't you understand that yet?"

"But—"

"No. It's done. There will be no Midsummer wedding. We'll make plans once your mourning period is over, if at that time you still wish to marry me—"

"I will."

"Don't be so quick to say so." He shook his head and let out a soft, mirthless laugh. "I'll be a poor baron and a Scottish one at that. Even if you still wanted to marry me, I doubt your father will approve. I doubt you will either. So when your head clears and you change your mind, if you want out of the betrothal... I'll release you. I give you my promise."

Laurel's jaw dropped open in amazement. Angry amazement. She wanted to grab one of his crutches and club him over the head with it. Of course, she couldn't under these circumstances. She wasn't so hot-tempered as to forget herself and cause a scene while they all grieved for Harrison Farthingale.

"In fact, there's no point in waiting," he continued in a whisper, drawing her over to the window overlooking the garden so they wouldn't disturb the rest of her family. She doubted anyone was listening to them or paying them any attention, they were all so lost in their own grief. "I should have done this weeks ago, but it's taken this tragedy to make me realize how much of an oaf I've been to you. I re—"

"I'll smite you with the largest broadsword I can find if you dare utter those words to me," Laurel warned in a harsh whisper, putting a hand to his lips, those wonderful lips that made her come to life whenever they pressed against her skin. "Don't you dare offer to release me from my promise. My *sacred* promise. It's up to me to willingly release you, and that I do now."

He ran a hand raggedly through his hair. "How is that any different?"

She tipped her chin up and frowned at him. "It's completely different."

"We're both doing the identical thing, trying to be noble and releasing the other from a marriage we both want." He held out his arms to her. "Come here, sweetheart."

"Don't confuse me with the facts," she cried, melting into his wonderful embrace as her heart shattered and sorrow overwhelmed her. Oh, she sounded just like one of the Farthingale elders now, responding with their hearts while ignoring all logic. "I have to be the one to let you go. It's only fair because I've behaved so abysmally toward you."

"You've been wonderful."

"You're only saying that to make me feel better. I wish they'd found Uncle Harrison alive."

"So do I, love. So do I." At the time, he and Julian had believed that finding Harrison, no matter his condition, most important. In truth, all they'd done was crush the family's hope. Now the Farthingales had to come to grips with his death.

Harrison Farthingale was a fallen hero, but to have it confirmed brought no one any pleasure or relief.

Graelem felt every one of Laurel's shivers and shudders as he held her in his arms. Her unrestrained tears moistened the front of his shirt. Perhaps it would have been kinder to allow them to maintain a false dream.

"Graelem, I'm sorry. I've destroyed your shirt."

"Hush, love. It's easily replaced."

"I've turned into a water spout," she said between sniffles and hiccups.

"I have an immense fondness for water spouts, especially hot-tempered ones with golden hair." She was irresistible when strong, even more so when vulnerable. That she turned to him in her darkest moments meant so much to him. It meant everything.

She managed a sniffling laugh.

"I wouldn't want you anywhere else but in my arms. This is where you belong," he said, stroking her hair as he spoke. Laurel's hair felt like silk between his fingers. Gold silk.

His hand moved downward to rub up and down her slender back, hoping the heat of his touch would flow through the soft velvet of her riding habit and chase away the deep chill surrounding her heart.

When Laurel finally stopped crying and regained some semblance of composure, she began urging him once again to seek out potential mushrooms for him to marry. He said nothing, just nodded, because he didn't wish to argue with her or rile her. His decision had been made since the first day they'd met. Laurel didn't wish to hear it right now, but that didn't change matters.

She was the one for him. No one else would do.

So, within a matter of days, his cousin Jordan would take control of the unencumbered Moray holdings.

Old Silas had been right after all.

Falling in love was a sure way to ruin a man.

LAUREL HEARD THE soft click of the door handle and then Daisy walked into their chamber. It was late, and Laurel had already changed into her nightgown and was about to retire to bed, although she doubted she'd get a wink of sleep tonight. No one in the household would. "Daisy, please don't be angry with me anymore."

Her tears began to flow again as she rose and held out her arms to her sister.

Daisy rushed forward and hugged her. "I'm so sorry! I was so rude to you and meddled where I had no right to meddle, but it's in our Farthingale blood, isn't it? We can't seem to keep out of each other's business. I'm truly sorry. Let's never fight again."

They clung fiercely to each other and began to cry even harder. Laurel was the first to draw away. She rubbed the tears off her cheeks with the back of her hand. "I'm the one who owes you the apology. I should have been honest with Graelem from the first. Now it's too late and I've lost him. But none of it matters right now. Helping Aunt Julia and little Harry through their grief is most important."

Daisy also took a moment to wipe the tears flowing down her own cheeks. "What happened between you and Graelem?"

Laurel released a ragged breath. "He needs a wife by Midsummer's Day and I'm in mourning, so I can't possibly marry him before next month. How can I even broach the subject to Father? It would be too disrespectful to Uncle Harrison's memory."

She noticed a glint of uncertainty in Daisy's tear-reddened eyes as she continued. "I told him, Daisy. I told Graelem that I loved him and wanted to marry him. I apologized for being so stubborn and hot-tempered. He was pleased, but didn't say it back to me." She frowned lightly. "He said lots of other lovely things to me. I think he does love me, but he doesn't have a meddlesome sister kicking him forward to make him admit it."

Daisy smiled at the remark. "Good thing my penchant for meddling extends beyond the Farthingale family. I'd be delighted to give him the swift kick he obviously deserves."

Laurel gave her another hug. "You needn't. It's too late for that now. We were about to share the good news with Mother and Father when we heard about Uncle Harrison. They'll be making funeral arrangements instead of preparing for their daughter's wedding."

"I'm truly sorry, Laurel."

She released another ragged breath. "So am I. He'll have to move on. He can't waste another moment securing his Moray inheritance. It breaks my heart, but I made him agree that he would."

"And he actually agreed? Do you think he will?"

"I hope so. I may have to take drastic measures to see that he does." Although she had no idea what she could do to make him move forward to secure that inheritance. What if he did lose it and then asked for her hand? Would her father allow her to marry an impoverished Scottish baron? One who had yet to declare that he loved her?

"What sort of drastic measures?" Daisy was now frowning at her.

Laurel sighed. "I don't know. But isn't that what one does for those one loves? I must consider his happiness above my own."

"But promise me that you won't do anything stupid or rash."

"Such as elope with Devlin on Saturday night as he asked me to?" She shook her head and sighed. "I won't. I've learned my lesson. And do you want to know something else? Even if I did elope with Devlin, I don't think Graelem would move on and find himself another bride. The notion makes me feel awful and wonderful at the same time."

"Are you certain? He struck me as having more common sense than any Farthingale, save Father or Uncle George." She shook her head and yawned. "Well, nothing we can do about it tonight. I'm glad you won't consider eloping with Devlin. Let's not mention it again, ever."

They said nothing more as Gladys carried in the overnight bag she'd helped Daisy to pack before Daisy had gone off to stay with their aunt. Gladys now unpacked it, remaining silent out of respect, although Laurel would have much preferred her chattering away. They all needed something to relieve the bleak sorrow descended upon their household.

Within minutes, the chore was done and Daisy was soon ready for bed. Laurel doused the lamp and climbed into bed. She worried that she wouldn't be able to fall asleep, but the events of the day must have exhausted her, for she fell into a sound slumber before her head ever hit the pillow. She awoke late the next morning, saw that Daisy was still asleep, and quietly washed and dressed before heading downstairs.

When she entered the dining room, she was surprised to find it empty. This was a Farthingale first, no one occupying a seat at the dining table. The breakfast salvers had all been set out and steam escaped under several of their shining silver lids. She lifted one lid and found the kippers sitting untouched. She lifted another and found the sausages had not been touched either.

She let out a sigh and moved away. Like the rest of her family, she had no appetite.

"Miss Laurel," Pruitt said as he entered, regarding her in a gentle, fatherly manner. He set down another tray of something else no one would eat this morning. "Is there anything I can get for you?"

"Thank you, Pruitt, but no." She met his gaze. "Where is everyone?"

"Your father and uncles went off to the regimental headquarters to make arrangements." He glanced upward. "Your mother and aunts have asked that breakfast be brought up to their rooms. I doubt any of them will come down before noon. The twins are still upstairs. I'd say they are still abed, but one is never quite certain what they might be up to." He arched an eyebrow. "I have not seen them climb down the tree outside their window, so I would hazard a guess and say they are still in their chamber."

"Thank you, Pruitt. That is a thorough and no doubt accurate report." She cast him a wan smile. "I'll have a cup of tea in the garden. This way I can keep my eye on the twins when they do scamper like squirrels down the tree, off to wreak whatever well-intentioned mischief Lily concocts."

"I think they'll behave themselves today. Are you certain I can't send you anything other than tea?"

"Nothing else. I don't think my stomach will tolerate more just yet." She walked to the double doors that led into the garden and settled into one of the wrought iron chairs beside the flower bed. It was a lovely morning, warm and sunny, with enough of a breeze to keep the day from getting too hot. The sky above was a bright, deep blue and the clouds were as white and soft as lamb's wool.

She lingered over her tea, too distracted to read a book or newspaper, yet bored as she sat alone with only her thoughts. When the clock chimed eleven o'clock, she decided to walk to the mews to see how Brutus was faring. He seemed well yesterday, but one could never be sure with horses.

Abner greeted her as she arrived. "My condolences, Miss Laurel."

"Thank you, Abner." She noticed that the Farthingale coachman was polishing the family carriages and realized it was in preparation for the funeral that would take place within a matter of days. "I've come to look at Brutus."

"He was skittish again this morning, but I can't figure out what's wrong."

Laurel entered the stables and walked to the stall where Brutus was kept. He calmed as soon as he saw her. A few gentle strokes to his nose and a short walk around the mews courtyard had him right again. "I can't find anything wrong either."

She handed the reins to Abner's nephew as he approached. "Good morning, Amos. We were just discussing Brutus."

He nodded. "I'll take him out for a ride this afternoon, Miss Laurel. We'll figure out what's ailing him. Miss Daisy was asking after you."

"Oh, good. She's awake. Do let me know how he does this afternoon. Have you noticed any rats or other feral creatures sneaking into the stalls or carriage houses?"

"No more than usual," Amos said, and the same was confirmed by his uncle.

"Abner, you bring your terriers into your rooms at night. What if we leave them loose and roaming the stables these next few nights?"

"Aye. I can do that, Miss Laurel." He ran a hand across the back of his thick neck. "It troubles me, too. Brutus isn't one to spook easily."

Laurel returned to the townhouse and went in search of Daisy. She found her seated in the garden along with Lily and Dillie, sprawled on the blanket they'd spread atop the grass. The three of them were entertaining little Harry and several other young cousins. Harry was smiling and giggling at their antics, too young to be aware he'd just lost his father.

Daisy glanced up. "Where did you run off to?"

Laurel knelt beside her and lifted Harry into her arms to hug him. "I was at the mews. Brutus has been acting odd lately and I was trying to figure out what's wrong." She shrugged her shoulders. "He calms whenever he sees me. Amos and I thought it might be rats scaring him. Brutus is big, but he's still a temperamental baby."

She kissed Harry's belly, her heart tugging at his joyful squeal, and played with her other little cousins, tickling them and chasing them around the blanket. Young Charles popped one of his marbles into his mouth, but Dillie noticed and got it out before he could swallow it. Lisbeth asked Laurel if she liked to kiss boys. "It depends on the boy. Yes to Harry or Charles," she said and kissed Harry's belly again.

She remained outside with her sisters and cousins enjoying the peaceful interlude, but as the clock chimed twelve o'clock, she decided to pay a call on Graelem—kissing him was nice, too. Very nice.

She knew that she shouldn't visit him, but knowing that she shouldn't or couldn't made her want to do it all the more. He had to find himself a new bride. He wouldn't do it while she hovered over him like a hummingbird.

Still, she missed him.

They hadn't been apart a full day and already her heart felt heavy.

Daisy looked up in surprise as she rose. "Where are you going? We're not supposed to leave the house today."

"Must I report my whereabouts to all of you? May I not have even a moment to myself?" Had it been just Daisy seated beside her, she would have confided that she was on her way to see Graelem. But the twins and their giggling cousins would no doubt say something ridiculously embarrassing about her and Graelem, teasing and talking loud enough so that their voices carried into Eloise's garden.

Missing him was not reason enough to see him. It was completely illogical. She needed to keep out of his way and give him the chance to move on.

But she had never been in love before, and it was no easy chore to force herself to fall out of love with him. She didn't have to be logical at a time like this.

How else was she to make certain he had moved on?

She walked next door and knocked.

While waiting for Watling to open the door, she quickly patted down her hair, hoping the curls hadn't blown out of place. Of course, little Harry had managed to tug on a few with his pudgy fingers. Well, Graelem would overlook a few curls out of place.

She smoothed her gown, a pale gray with white lace trim at the neck and sleeves. No happy colors for her this next month. *Oh, dear.* She'd just been to the mews and hoped the scent of horse sweat didn't linger on her gown. She had washed her hands and face with lavender soap before coming over.

"Miss Laurel," Watling murmured, stepping aside to allow her in. "I'll escort you to the parlor. Lady Dayne and Lord Moray are entertaining in there."

She let out a small gasp and stopped as her heart sank into her toes. "I didn't mean to intrude." Had Graelem moved on already? Would she find a salon full of elegant debutantes eager to land an eligible baron, even if his was a Scottish title? Tears welled in her eyes. "I shouldn't have come."

She turned to walk away—actually, run away in sobs—but Graelem stepped into the hall just then and saw her. "Laurel?"

She tipped her chin up, hating that it was still wobbling as she struggled with tears that had yet to burst free, but were about to.

"Laurel," he said tenderly and started toward her, quite agile on his crutches. She hated that he still had to use them. She'd done this to him.

She tipped her chin up higher. The darn thing still wobbled. "I don't wish to intrude. I understand you're entertaining."

He nodded. "I am indeed. I'm most eager to have you meet them."

Her eyes rounded in horror. Did he truly believe she could behave herself while he casually introduced her to the next Baroness Moray? One of them was not likely to make it out of the room alive, probably him. She knew where Eloise kept her fire irons and she meant to use them as weapons. If he had the gall to introduce her, she'd poke him so full of holes he'd have blood pouring out from every open cavity in his body. "How could you?"

He shook his head, now obviously confused. "What? Don't you wish to meet my aunt and uncle? They're eager to meet you."

It was her turn to gaze at him in confusion. "What?" she mimicked. "Your aunt and uncle? As in the Earl of Trent?"

He nodded.

"And who else?"

"Lady Trent, his wife. Who else do you think is in the parlor?" He suddenly arched an eyebrow and let out a hearty chuckle. "Blessed Scottish saints! Did you think I had a roomful of marriage-minded debutantes parading before me?"

She refused to respond, but her blush gave her away.

"Lass, you have a fertile imagination. No wonder you looked like you were ready to bludgeon me." He handed Watling his crutches and took her into his arms.

She was too embarrassed to protest. Besides, she loved the protective warmth of his arms, loved the hard feel of his oak-hard muscles enveloping her. "Forgive me," she said in a whisper against his chest. "I want you to move on and yet I behave like a demented wet hen whenever I think you actually might."

"I'm little better." He sighed and eased her back a step in order to inspect her features. "There are so many good reasons why I should move on, but none of them matter if it means losing you. You're stuck with me, sweetheart. Will you allow me to properly introduce you to my aunt and uncle?"

She looked down to inspect her simple gown. "I'm not suitably dressed."

"And you've been crying," he said softly.

She nodded.

"Lass, you look beautiful. You always do. There isn't a lovelier girl to be found in all of England." He reached for his crutches and thanked Watling. "As for your tears, they're all aware of the loss your family has suffered. Will you allow me to escort you in?"

She nodded. "I'll stay, but only for a moment. I'm sure my mother will have need of me."

"I know, lass. Let me know if there's anything we can do for your family."

The "moment" turned into an hour spent in enjoyable conversation with Graelem and his relatives. His aunt and uncle were charming and thoughtful, which ought to have come as no surprise because Eloise was the earl's mother and she was the same way. That's why she was beloved by all the Farthingales. As always, Eloise went out of her way to make her feel welcome.

But Laurel had stayed too long and would be missed at home. She cast Graelem a glance to gain his attention. "I must go."

He nodded and rose along with her. "I'll escort you home."

"You needn't trouble yourself. I was going to look in on Brutus again. I may not have the chance to do so for the next few days."

Graelem pursed his lips in contemplation. "He's still not himself?"

"No, but I can't seem to find anything wrong."

"I'll accompany you." He turned to his aunt and uncle, who had also gotten to their feet.

Lady Trent smiled and took Laurel's hands affectionately in hers. "Miss Farthingale, we'll stop by your home tomorrow to pay our condolences to your family. We don't wish to impose on them today, but we're so glad we had the opportunity to meet you."

"My mother," the earl said, turning to Eloise, "adores you and your sisters. I see her admiration is not misplaced. My nephew chose well. We look forward to welcoming you into the Dayne family, although I know under the circumstances, it won't be right away."

That Graelem had no intention of moving on, and had already told his family as much, left her elated but at the same time saddened. "Yes, well..." She didn't know what else to say.

Would Graelem grow to resent her if they married?

After all, she was the reason he would lose his inheritance.

CHAPTER 19

LAUREL AND GRAELEM walked out of Eloise's house and turned onto Chipping Way just as a carriage drew up in front of the Farthingale residence. There were several sleek black carriages already drawn up there, but she recognized this one as belonging to Lord Kirwood. She placed her hand on Graelem's arm to hold him back.

"What's he doing here?" Graelem muttered, a growl of displeasure escaping his lips as a footman opened the carriage door and Devlin descended. He stood off to the side, staring at Laurel's house as though he were inspecting it for its riches and stamping his kid leather gloves impatiently against his thigh while one of the Farthingale footmen assisted his parents.

Laurel liked Lord Kirwood and his wife, but they'd certainly indulged their only child. Lord Kirwood, closer in age to Eloise, had married late in life to a much younger wife and had not expected ever to have children. Devlin was a surprise and joy to them, a more elegant version of his good-natured father who enjoyed the simple country life. Unlike his father, Devlin enjoyed the fashionable salons and bustle of London.

Since they'd been good friends and neighbors for as far back as Laurel could remember, the Kirwoods were considered family, so their condolence visit was not at all out of place. However, she knew Devlin had another purpose in paying the call. Now that Graelem couldn't possibly marry her in time to save his inheritance, Devlin would no doubt offer again to marry her. After a suitable mourning period, of course.

She studied him from a distance. He seemed quite confident for a man in bad financial straits. Did he believe that he could still win her over? He belonged in Bedlam if he did. She would never accept him. "Let's wait until they've gone inside. I don't want them to see me."

Unfortunately, The Fates were conspiring against her. Devlin's father dropped his monocle and as Devlin turned to one of the footmen to command that he retrieve it—Devlin would never stoop to do it—he spied her standing beside Graelem.

He frowned at her and shot Graelem a menacing scowl.

Oh, dear.

Both of them looked ready to come to blows again. She couldn't allow it. "Don't you dare raise your fists to him, Graelem."

His gaze was trained on Devlin and remained on him even as he responded to her. "I won't. I'll just kill him."

Ordinarily, she might have enjoyed watching two suitors vie for her hand and might have taken Graelem's comment as a jovial, possessive jest. But Graelem wasn't one to jest about this sort of thing. She trusted him not to launch the first blow, but he'd make certain his was the last. "Don't hurt him, Graelem."

"I won't. He'll die painlessly."

She shook her head and sighed. "Ugh, men! Go home before this escalates into war. I'll stop by once our guests have all left. We can check on Brutus then."

"What about Devlin? I don't trust him. I'm coming with you."

She turned to him and rolled her eyes. "You mustn't. I have every faith that you'll act the gentleman, but Devlin won't. My household is in mourning. I won't upset my parents more than I already have. You know what will happen the moment you and Devlin are in the same room. You're a lit match to his gunpowder."

Graelem frowned at her, but she knew he was merely frustrated. He didn't want Devlin sniffing about her. His protective instincts were on alert. "Don't let him get you alone. He's a desperate man."

How desperate could Devlin be? He might be heavily in debt, but he was a handsome baron and there were other wealthy families who would gladly trade a hefty dowry for a noble title. "You needn't worry about him. The house is filled to the rafters with Farthingales. There isn't so much as a mouse hole that isn't occupied. I'll be quite safe in my own home."

She left Graelem's side and started toward the house, wishing that Devlin would follow his parents inside and not wait for her to reach him. But Devlin was too busy glowering at Graelem to bother keeping up with his parents or show any consideration for the somber occasion.

"You've been crying," he commented, hurrying to keep up with her as she whirled past him on her way inside. "Has the brute upset you? No doubt he's broken off the betrothal now that there's to be no wedding by Midsummer's Day."

She curled her hands into fists but held them behind her back to keep from poking him in the nose. His was an elegant nose attached to a handsome face, but one she was growing to detest. How had she not seen his petty and insolent nature before?

Devlin continued before she could respond, which was a good thing since he would not have liked her answer to his impertinent question. "But you needn't fret. I'll marry you, Laurel. You know it has always been my wish," he said with such sincerity she might have believed him had she not noticed his gaze straying toward Daisy, who was standing alone by the staircase holding what seemed to be an unopened letter in her hand. A condolence note from a friend? Or more mischief plotted by Devlin?

"Say you'll marry me, Laurel."

"What?" She drew back from him with a scowl. "I'll say no such thing. I'm sorry, Devlin, but I won't. I will *never* marry you. My decision won't change, no matter what happens between me and Lord Moray."

She strode away from him before she gave in to the urge to do him bodily harm. After taking a moment to calm down, she meant to join Daisy. Where did she go? Her sister was no longer standing by the stairs.

Before Laurel had the chance to look for her, Hortensia

clamped a hand on her elbow and drew her forward to greet more close friends and family. "We weren't supposed to have any callers until tomorrow, but seems people are stopping by anyway. I'm going to check on Mrs. Mayhew and her staff. They're scrambling to put out refreshments. You need to stay by your mother's side. The poor dear, she's exhausted and stretched to the end of her patience."

"Of course." She'd find Daisy later.

Laurel hurried into the parlor and groaned softly. Her mother was attempting to pour tea for their guests, but her hands were shaking so badly that Laurel feared she'd drop the teapot. "Let me help."

She settled beside her mother and began chattering to distract everyone as she took over the hostess duties.

"Thank you, sweetheart," her mother whispered, now seemingly back in her usual good form.

Laurel turned her attention to Julia, who hadn't eaten since yesterday and appeared so gaunt and pale that Laurel feared she would faint in front of everyone. And not one of her usual theatrical fainting spells, where she happened to land gently upon the soft sofa pillows with balletic grace.

A few hours later, her fears were realized. Julia's face turned ashen and her eyeballs rolled upward so that only the whites were showing. She dropped like a stone, her head aimed straight for the marble edge of a small table, and would have done serious damage to herself had Laurel not caught her in time.

But Julia's limp body was too much for her to handle on her own and she began to fall backward, her own head about to hit the marble edge. Thankfully, Uncle Rupert caught both of them in time. "Bloody hell, she wasn't faking this time," Rupert muttered. "Laurel, are you all right?"

She nodded and managed to mumble a sincere thanks.

Rupert shook his head and sighed. "Hortensia will tend to her. You had better go back to helping your mother. She's nibbling her lip. Something is amiss."

The unexpected bit of excitement now over, Laurel saw that her uncle was correct. Her mother was fretting again. "Where are the twins?"

Laurel went in search of them. They couldn't have slipped out of the parlor very long ago. She ran upstairs and looked in their room. Not there. She checked all the bedrooms and then searched throughout the house. "Crumpets," she muttered under her breath. They weren't hiding in their favorite tree or anywhere in the garden either.

Had they sought refuge with Eloise? She hurried next door. "Good afternoon, Watling." She cast Eloise's stoic butler a hesitant smile. "I do hate to be a nuisance, but we seem to have misplaced the twins. Are they here by any chance? Mother's quite worried about them."

"Good evening, Miss Laurel," he corrected, for it was almost eight o'clock in the evening. She'd been so busy that she hadn't realized it was so late because the days were longer near Midsummer. Their endless stream of guests, none of whom were expected to visit until tomorrow, had kept her distracted. But Uncle Harrison was beloved, not only by his family but by the many whose lives he had touched. They would not be kept away from paying their respects. "The girls are here. You are never a nuisance. Do come in."

She released the breath she had been holding. "Thank goodness. We aren't afraid for them, so much as for others who accidentally get in the way of their mischief."

A gleam of amusement shone in Watling's eyes. "I completely understand."

He led her through the parlor and into the rear garden, where the twins were seated with Eloise and Graelem. Lemonade and ginger cakes had been set out for them. The twins smiled at her, obviously unaware they'd thrown the household into an uproar.

Graelem rose to offer his chair, but she politely declined. "I can't stay."

"The ginger cakes are delicious," Dillie said. "You must have one."

She didn't frown or admonish her sisters, for her own behavior this past month had been much worse... well, except for the commotion surrounding Lily's fertility god. But Lily hadn't almost killed anybody or caused a brawl in the middle of an elegant party. "Mother was worried about you. She didn't know where you were."

The twins lowered their heads in contrition.

Lily spoke up first. "We didn't think anyone would notice. Everyone was so busy and…"

"We only meant to stay a few minutes." Dillie glanced longingly at the platter of cakes. "Then Watling brought these out. We couldn't be rude and refuse Eloise's generosity."

"Indeed not," Eloise added with a chuckle. "But run along now and let your mother know you're safe. Laurel, are you certain you can't stay? You look tired, my dear. Rest here a moment and I'll follow the girls to make certain they head straight home."

Laurel wasn't tired so much as overwrought. She offered little protest and collapsed into one of the chairs vacated by her sisters, glad for a moment alone with Graelem. "It's all spun out of control. You would have been proud of me. I was the responsible one for a change. Patient, amiable. Tolerant."

He chuckled lightly. "Blessed Scottish saints. What have you done with the hellion I've come to know?"

She grinned at him. "You mustn't fret, she's still here. Just subdued for the moment."

He shook his head and reached for her hand. "Lass, I should have gone home with you earlier. I was worried about you. Is Devlin still there?"

"No, he and his parents left about an hour ago. His parents are quite nice, but I was glad to see them go. They were hoping for a marriage between the families and are terribly disappointed that it won't happen. Anne stopped by earlier as well."

He glanced upward at the sky. "Heaven protect us from bored debutantes who create mischief for their own amusement."

She laced her fingers between his, liking the gentle strength of his touch. "In that moment I wished I were a twin so that I could keep watch on both of them. They were prowling like predators around the edges of the parlor and then splitting up to walk into the dining room, or entry hall, or who knows where else, then returning to the parlor. A little chill ran up my spine each time I caught them staring at me. They're plotting something."

He sat up in his chair and frowned. "Damnation, that settles it. I'm not letting you out of my sight again."

"You'll find no argument from me. They have me worried." She released his hand and clasped her own hands together as they suddenly grew cold. "I think I know what Devlin's planning. He means to harm Brutus. It would explain why Brutus has been so skittish lately."

Graelem held her back when she rose to leave. "Laurel, where are you going?"

"To the mews, of course."

"Not without me. In fact, let me go instead of you. If he's nasty enough to hurt Brutus, he won't hesitate to hurt you."

She regarded him with astonishment. "Devlin wouldn't dare. He wants to marry me, or rather, he needs to marry me to fund his gaming habit."

"He's foolish and desperate. He'd dare anything, though I doubt he plans to harm Brutus. There's nothing to be gained by it. He could have been scouting out the stable though."

"To what purpose? Oh, dear! He wanted to elope with me at midnight tomorrow night. I was supposed to meet him at the mews... er, not that I ever agreed to his plan. I didn't. Not even in the beginning when I didn't like you. Do you think he's still hopeful?"

"The idiot. I hope not, but he may be determined to carry out the elopement with or without your consent."

Laurel shook her head and laughed mirthlessly. "Are you suggesting that he plans to abduct me?"

"It's a possibility." His gaze turned cold and hard, and his expression lethal. "He won't succeed. I'll kill him first."

"No, it's too ridiculous." She shifted uncomfortably, not liking the direction of their conversation. She'd known Devlin all her life. He might be petty and spoiled, but he wasn't evil.

Graelem gathered his crutches and rose. "I hope I'm wrong."

So did she. "What a mess. I still don't understand why you want to marry me. I seem to be nothing but trouble for you. We may as well walk to the mews together. It'll be safe enough with

Abner and a dozen other coachmen hanging about there. Only a fool would try anything now. If Devlin has a plan, he'll wait until nightfall when all our visitors are gone and Abner has retired for the evening. How would his plan work? Even if he lured me out, I still wouldn't go with him."

"You're assuming he'll be alone. Gentlemen don't like to get their hands dirty. He'll hire some dockside ruffians to do the deed, while he's off making certain that he's seen elsewhere." He ran a hand roughly through his hair. "No doubt he'll have my cousin's help. They both gain in preventing our marriage from taking place."

She frowned. "Let them try. I'll make them regret the day they were ever born. I love you, Graelem. There isn't a force on earth strong enough to keep us apart... except you. If you don't wish—"

"That's what I like about you," he said with a grin. "One always knows where one stands with you. There's no hiding when you're angry or when you're hot and wanton."

She gasped and poked his shoulder. "Don't look at me with that gleam in your eyes. I'm feeling neither hot nor wanton toward you right now, and that will not change once we reach the stables. If you think I'll allow you to seduce me there again, you'd be wrong. Terribly, terribly wrong."

He grinned wickedly. "Care to wager on it?"

She poked him again. "No." She'd lose the bet because she was never able to resist him or his kisses. "You're an oaf for forcing me to admit it."

"Lass—"

"We've gotten off the topic."

Graelem folded his arms over his chest and straightened to his full imposing height. "No, we haven't," he said, towering over her and looking impossibly handsome. "I'll assign one of my Bow Street runners to watch the mews tomorrow night. We'll walk over there now, you and I. But you're not to go near there tomorrow. I mean it, Laurel. You're not to get in the way. If there is a plot afoot, I want you safe."

She understood the danger and would do as he asked, but he must have noticed her bridling under the restraint, for he continued his warning. "I have years of battle experience and can judge how a man handles adversity. I know Devlin's type. He'll back down and run away from superior strength. But he's also a sneak, and not above putting you in danger if he thinks it will serve his purpose."

She wanted to disagree, but in her heart she knew he was right.

"If he dares to put a hand on you, I'll kill him. No jest, Laurel. That's how we've been trained to eliminate any threat. If he draws a weapon, I'll kill him. If he so much as reaches for you, I'll kill him."

She dropped her hands to her sides. "You've made your point."

"Good."

"How many men have you killed?"

He turned away and started for the stable, purposely ignoring the question. "Are you coming with me?"

She hurried to keep up with him. "You wouldn't really kill Devlin or your cousin, would you?"

"To protect you?" His gaze turned cold and hard once more. "Without hesitation."

CHAPTER 20

IN A REMARKABLE show of good behavior, Laurel stayed home the following day and several days after that. Time sped by in a blur, her hours filled with helping her mother and Julia as friends continued to visit to pay their condolences. She'd seen little of Graelem other than their daily walks to the mews to check on Brutus, but Graelem hadn't come by today and she already missed him terribly.

Tomorrow is Midsummer's Day.

Graelem had been busy working with the Moray estate manager to ensure an easy transition of ownership of the unentailed properties to his cousin, Jordan Drummond.

If Graelem was despondent over the situation, he didn't show it. Quite the opposite, he seemed calm and confident of earning back all that was about to be lost. "I'll have to finance most of the purchases, but I have backers, and I know which Moray properties make sense for me to acquire. I built up much of Uncle Silas' wealth and can do it again for us."

However, she had no chance to think about it. Today would be their busiest day yet, for Uncle Harrison's funeral had taken place this morning and most of the mourners had followed them back to the house from the churchyard.

Hundreds more were expected to stop in throughout the day. She and her sisters would have their hands full looking after all of them in addition to worrying about Julia and their mother, who had been up before dawn organizing the household for today. Her father and uncles were exhausted as well, the toll of losing their youngest brother weighing heavily on their hearts.

Daisy had been quiet again this morning, stealing glances at her as they readied themselves. When those odd looks persisted into the afternoon, Laurel had finally had enough and caught up to her sister in the entry hall, taking her aside beside the staircase. "What's wrong now, Daisy? Please don't turn away. I know you're worried about something and it has to do with me."

Daisy's chin began to wobble, a sign that she was fighting to hold back tears, so Laurel knew this was serious. She took Daisy's hand in hers. "I won't stop asking until I have my answer. What is it? You know you can tell me anything."

Daisy let out a ragged sigh. "Why did you go to the mews again last night?"

"I told you, Brutus has been skittish again. We can't figure out what's wrong with him. I didn't go alone, Graelem went with me. I've seen so little of him lately." She tipped her head in confusion. "Daisy? What's going on?"

"Nothing. I'm just sorry that Graelem's about to lose everything and you don't seem to be doing anything to help him."

Her eyes rounded in surprise. "First of all, he won't let me do anything to help. He's even more stubborn than I am, if you can believe it. Second, we've all been busy taking care of laying Uncle Harrison to rest." She sighed and shook her head, then released a long, deep breath as the spirit seemed to drain from her. "I know what this is about. Devlin's come around every day this week and you think he and I are planning something. You were reading a note by the stairs the other day, no doubt some more mischief concocted by Devlin. I can assure you that we're not eloping, no matter what this latest note suggested. I love Graelem and will marry him... eventually. Why don't you believe me?"

"I want to, it's just that—"

"Daisy, there you are! Your mother is waiting for you." Hortensia swooped between them on a lavender-perfumed breeze and drew Daisy away, leaving Laurel to stand alone, now worried and frustrated. Why didn't her sister believe her?

And where was Graelem? He ought to have stopped in by

now. Eloise had arrived almost half an hour ago. She started toward Eloise, but Pruitt intercepted her as she made her way through the gathering crowd. "Miss Laurel, it seems we have a situation in the kitchen. Mrs. Mayhew needs your assistance."

"Of course." She hurried to the kitchen and came to an abrupt halt. "What's this?" There was a line of forty or fifty men standing outside the kitchen door.

"These men served under your uncle and have come to pay their respects," said Mrs. Mayhew, wringing her hands. "Where am I to put them? There's no room in the kitchen and they're not... they don't belong upstairs. They'll startle your guests. Yet, your parents would be appalled if we turned them away."

"Do we have food enough for everyone?" She glanced around and saw that every table was laden with pies and cakes, and every nook and cranny taken up with assorted savories ready to be delivered upstairs.

Mrs. Mayhew wiped her brow. "As you can see, there's food enough to feed all of London. That isn't the problem. Miss Laurel, I don't have the heart to turn these soldiers away."

Laurel agreed. "We'll set out tables in the garden. I do hope the weather holds up. I'll grab some fresh linens. Pruitt can spare a few footmen to help me. I'll enlist my sisters. My family should be able to move easily between the parlor and the garden to greet everyone."

It didn't take long to put her plan into effect with everyone pitching in. Laurel was still in the garden talking to the soldiers and some of their well-heeled guests who had come outside to greet them as well when Graelem arrived. He came to her side. "Lass, you did all this?"

"Everyone helped. It's wonderful, isn't it? A fitting tribute to Uncle Harrison."

"Indeed," he said in a gentle murmur. "Nice work. I see that some of your finer guests have wandered outside."

Laurel nodded. "Almost all of them have. But Julia won't come out. I hope these soldiers understand she means no disrespect. Her loss is a raw, open wound, and she can't cope with Uncle Harrison's death yet. She can't abide anything remotely military at the moment. It isn't the fault of these men, it's the dreadful toll this war has taken."

Graelem put a hand to the small of her back, his touch a comforting warmth. "They understand."

"I hope so. My parents came out to greet them all, but my mother had to return to Julia's side. Father and Uncle Rupert are still out here somewhere talking to a few soldiers. Uncle George can't stop being a healer, so he's taken some of the men aside to look at their wounds. Lily's over there." She pointed to the corner of the garden where her sister stood surrounded by a dozen soldiers. "She's explaining ancient Roman battle tactics to them."

Graelem shook his head and laughed. "She has a rapt audience."

"Too bad none of our generals will listen to her," Laurel said with a nod. "She would have defeated Napoleon years ago."

"I have no doubt." Graelem chuckled again as he glanced at the other twin and shook his head in confusion. "What does Dillie have in her hands?"

"A ginger cake she swiped earlier. She intended to hide it for herself, but brought it out and cut it into squares to give to these men." She sighed. "Daisy's been wonderful, too. Most of these men are already in love with her."

"I sense a 'but' in there."

Laurel nodded. "But she still thinks I plan to elope with Devlin. We had a talk the other day and I thought we'd settled matters. She's behaving oddly again today. I tried to draw her aside earlier, but couldn't manage more than a few words before we were interrupted. Graelem, will you please talk to her?"

He shifted on his crutches. "I'll do my best. I doubt it will help, especially if she thinks I'm the dupe in your tawdry love triangle."

She poked his shoulder, her finger gently striking solid muscle. "I'm wanton, not tawdry. However, I'm glad you believe me." She cast him a worried glance. "You do believe me, don't you?"

He slid his hand around her waist and drew her closer. "Yes, love. I still believe you. Never had a doubt. Other women may know how to fake their feelings, but you don't." His lips twitched upward in a grin. "I know your wanton desire for me is genuine.

Ooh, Graelem. Kiss my hot body."

Her cheeks suddenly felt as though they were on fire. "You wretch! How can you be sure I wasn't faking? It would serve you right." She poked his shoulder again. "I could be a brilliant actress."

He laughed. "You could be, but you're not. Any seductress worth her salt would have used her finely honed tricks of persuasion to rouse my desire, her every move calculated to pleasure me with efficient precision in her learned art. You, my sweet, wanton Laurel, didn't get a blessed thing right during our... er, interlude in the stables the other day. You didn't even know what you were groping for."

Laurel was too appalled to utter a word. The best she could do was sputter.

He put a finger to her lips. "I think that was the moment I fell in love with you."

Did he just say that he loves me?

He shook his head and sighed. "No, that isn't quite right. I've been in love with you all along, but convinced myself our betrothal could remain as nothing more than a business arrangement. Our first interlude in the parlor shot that plan to pieces. Despite your obvious lack of knowledge about men, that second time in the stable was incredible, too. After that, I could no longer deny the truth. You have my heart and always will. I love you, Laurel."

She closed her eyes and swallowed hard. The sun suddenly felt warmer and the breeze felt gentle and sweet. Even the birds seemed to be chirping a merrier song in the trees. "Oh, Graelem. Please say it again."

"I'll say it often and always, sweetheart." He drew her behind the trunk of the twins' escape tree. "I love you," he said, wrapping her in his arms as he lowered his mouth to hers for an ardent and lingering kiss.

To say that she was swept away was an understatement.

She kissed him back with equal fervor, wishing for this moment never to end. He loved her! No matter what happened tomorrow, she knew all would be well. They'd deal with any problems and disappointments together.

She was still clinging to his shoulders as he ended the kiss and slowly eased away. "Lass, I can't stay long. Jordan asked to meet me at his club this afternoon. I don't know what he wants, but I'll listen. Perhaps he simply wishes to gloat over his impending victory."

She put a hand on his arm. "He hasn't won yet, so be careful. After all the fuss I made about our betrothal, I'd hate to see it end because of a nefarious scheme of your cousin's. Please, Graelem. Promise me that you'll be careful."

"I always am, love." He kissed the tip of her nose. "And I promise to talk to Daisy before I leave here. Ah, there she is."

She watched him walk toward her sister, then went inside to check on her mother and Julia. Graelem didn't return to bid her farewell, but it mattered little. He loved her. He'd told her so. She glided through the rest of the day as though on angel's wings. All would work out. She knew it would. Graelem's confidence was contagious.

The last of the guests left late. It was after eleven o'clock by the time the family was finally alone, and everyone was too exhausted to linger in the parlor to chat. Her mother and aunts excused themselves and headed upstairs to their chambers. The men retired to her father's study, leaving her alone with her sisters—all but Rose, who had gone home earlier with Julian.

Finally! The chance to speak to Daisy. But Pruitt walked in with a note for her at that moment. "For me?" Curious, she opened it and read the one sentence. *Meet me outside. G.*

She shook her head, finding it odd that Graelem wouldn't simply stop by to see her even though the hour was late. The family usually stayed out well after midnight when attending balls or other social engagements. Of course, condolence visits weren't quite the same thing. Today's stream of visitors had exhausted them all, and Graelem was aware of it. He was just trying to be discreet.

She could ignore the request, but what if it was urgent? He'd met with his cousin today. Perhaps something important had happened that he wished to discuss with her outside of prying ears.

"I'll be right back," she told her sisters and hurried out of the room. She opened the front door and started down the steps to the gate. It was now dark outside, quite dark with the moon hidden behind gathering clouds. There was a dampness to the night breeze that signaled rain.

Laurel paused, her hand unmoving on the gate's heavy knob. Suddenly, the note did not feel right. Graelem would have come to the door, not asked her to sneak around in the dark even if he sought privacy. Hadn't he already warned her not to leave home alone?

She was about to turn back when she heard a crunch of leaves behind her. Before she was able to scream, someone clamped a big hand over her mouth and, with his other, pressed a foul-smelling handkerchief to her nose. She felt dizzy and couldn't seem to push the fiend away. As her vision began to blur, a second man dropped a sack over her head, rolling her in it so tightly that she couldn't breathe.

She tried to kick her assailants, and was still kicking and squirming and letting out muffled screams as the two of them attempted to carry her off. One held her by the legs and the other by her shoulders, which suggested these men were not used to lifting, for anyone with a little strength would have simply hauled her over his shoulder.

She kicked one of them and heard his cultured yelp in response.

These were gentlemen. Desperate gentlemen, as Graelem had described Devlin and Jordan. Had Graelem's cousin formed a scoundrel's alliance with Devlin? Their situations were entirely different now that Jordan was about to inherit the Moray assets.

What was to be gained by stealing her on the eve of his victory?

The sickeningly sweet scent of whatever had been poured onto the assailant's handkerchief surrounded her and made her dizzy. She had to find a way out of this sack and breathe in fresh air before she passed out.

She kicked again with all her might and struck the same

assailant in his soft belly. "Bloody hell! I thought you drugged her." He tried to grab her ankles, but she managed another kick, this time a little lower, landing a blow at the junction of his thighs. He yelped again and fell to his knees groaning.

Her victory was short-lived, for a third assailant quickly took his place. Were there more?

She managed to kick this new man as well. "Bloody hell, why is she still moving?"

He grabbed her legs, his grip painful as he carried her through the gate to a waiting carriage. Oh, no! She was dumped onto the floor of the carriage and stepped on as her abductors hurriedly climbed in. What did they intend to do with her?

The driver snapped the reins.

Laurel's eyes welled with tears. How could she have fallen for such a stupid trick? In her own defense, the events of the day had heavily burdened her heart. She'd been so eager to seek Graelem's comfort again that she had let down her guard.

"I'm raising my price," said the gentleman she'd earlier brought to his knees. "The girl's rich, so why must Dev have all of it? He can spare another thousand pounds for me."

"Shut up, you fool! No names! Do you want to give us all away?"

These were definitely educated men, no doubt schooled at Oxford or Cambridge. They might have been taught Latin and philosophy, but had learned nothing of honor or character. She'd give them a good lesson. They'd be bruised and bloodied by the time she was through with these wretches.

She would be bruised as well, for the carriage bounced and clattered as it tore through Mayfair at a reckless speed, tossing her against the floor boards and rolling her under the boots of her abductors time and again.

She was about to give up hope of ever being rescued when the horses suddenly stopped their mad gallop and reared. The abrupt halt caused her to slam hard against the boards. "Crumpets!"

What was happening? She heard gasps and curses and then the door opened. More gasps and strangled oaths as it sounded like her captors were flung out of the carriage and tossed to the ground—except for one of those wretches who fell atop her with a grunt. She tried to shove him off her, but couldn't. He was a crushing, motionless weight. "Help! Help me!"

Could anyone hear her above the scuffle?

She heard more thuds and grunts as fists connected to bodies.

Then all fell silent. In the next moment, she was lifted out from under the crushing weight and hauled out of the carriage to be set down gently on the grass. The confining sack was lifted off her. "Blessed Scottish saints, lass! You might have been hurt!"

Graelem! I'm in for it now.

She took a deep breath, coughing at the sudden surge of cool air against her cheeks and into her lungs as she inhaled. "Damn it, Laurel," he said, his voice raspy with concern as he drew her into his arms and hugged her fiercely.

"I can explain." Overwhelmed with relief, she threw her arms around his neck and hugged him back just as fiercely, her heart pounding against his warm, solid chest.

"It's all right, lass. What matters is that you're safe."

"No, you can't think I ignored your warning. I was tricked. They delivered a forged note supposedly sent by you and were waiting for me as I stepped outside my door. Had I been thinking clearly, I wouldn't have gone. But the note looked real and I thought you had summoned me." Her voice was weak and she was shaking as she prattled. Still, she had to explain it all to him before he overcame his worry and became angry.

She took another deep breath, not yet recovered from the foul scent of the handkerchief, the odor stubbornly clinging to her nostrils. "The note was written on Eloise's stationery and the handwriting resembled yours."

She expected an outburst from Graelem, but he merely sighed and ran a hand through his hair. He looked over her shoulder and spoke to the barrel-chested man who was holding down one of the assailants. "Mr. Barrow, haul these fools to the nearest magistrate. My cousin will assist you."

Laurel regarded Graelem quizzically. "Who precisely is Mr. Barrow?"

"He heads the team of Bow Street runners I engaged to follow

Devlin and Jordan, although it seems I had no need to worry about Jordan, as it turns out."

A big man with broad shoulders chose that moment to kneel beside them. "Is the lass all right?" She noted his brogue by the slight roll of his *r*.

Graelem nodded. "Laurel, the timing isn't the best, but I'd like to properly introduce you to my cousin, Jordan Drummond."

The wastrel popinjay? He didn't appear to fit the description.

"Och, lass. Glad you're safe." Jordan shook his head and sighed. "That Kirwood fellow confided his plan to me and… seems I have a conscience after all. Graelem and I have never been close, but we're family of a sort. So are you, now since you're betrothed to the undeserving oaf."

"He isn't an oaf. He's wonderful," she insisted, scowling at the man, and feeling quite remorseful for ever referring to Graelem that way herself.

Jordan grinned at his cousin. "In any event, I can't stomach a man who'd put a lady at risk. I had to warn Graelem."

She rested her head against Graelem's shoulder, still scowling at Jordan. "You knew his plan all along?"

"I wasn't in it from the start and never knew all of it, unfortunately. I'm sorry that I didn't warn Graelem sooner, but it seems he already suspected a plot and took measures to protect you. It doesn't excuse my behavior, of course."

Laurel sensed Graelem's tension and realized he was still troubled by something. "It isn't over yet," Graelem said. "Where's Devlin? Jordan, you said he was supposed to join his friends, but they went ahead with the plan without him."

Laurel looked at Devlin's so-called friends, three well-dressed men moaning beside the carriage. "Who are they?"

"Wastrel lords. Heavy gamblers, no doubt cut off by their fathers and left desperate for funds."

"Bribed by Devlin to abduct me?" She drew away and curled her hands into fists. "I can't wait to get my hands on that cur. I'll teach him. Do you know where he is, Mr. Drummond?"

"I dinna, lass."

Graelem frowned and repeated the question to the burly Bow

Street runner.

"Hiding from Miss Farthingale, no doubt," Mr. Barrow said with a chuckle, eyeing her fists as he responded to the question. "But one of my men is following him. He'll report back to me within the hour. I have another man waiting at the mews. We were about to set up watch there when these fancy coves drew up to your gate in their fine carriage. We knew they were coming for you, but they arrived early."

Laurel noticed Graelem's swollen hand. "Oh, dear. Did you break a bone?" She reached out to touch it delicately. His hand felt warm and deliciously rough, his long fingers winding with hers as he gave them a gentle squeeze.

"No, love. It's no more than a minor bruise." He kissed her on the forehead to reassure her.

"What's next?" she asked. "Do you really think Devlin had second thoughts about his plot and ran away?"

Graelem frowned. "No, and I don't like that he isn't yet accounted for. Jordan, help Mr. Barrow with these *gentlemen*. I'm going to the mews as soon as I deliver Laurel home. It's almost midnight. Might as well make certain the vindictive ass isn't planning to harm Brutus."

"Oh, no. You're not leaving me behind. I'm going with you." She scrambled to her feet, but her knees suddenly buckled and she fell against Graelem. "Oh, dear."

"Easy, sweetheart." He swallowed her in his arms. "You need to go home and lie down."

"But—"

"You can beat Devlin to a bloody pulp another time. I need to get you home. Mr. Barrow and Jordan need to get these three scoundrels to the authorities. It's over, Laurel. Just a few loose ends to tie up. Devlin may be close by, but he'll soon be running out of London as fast as he can with his tail between his legs. He'll keep running because his friends have been caught and will surely betray him to spare their own hides."

Laurel sighed. "Is there no honor among thieves?"

"No, love. There never is." He grabbed his crutches, which had fallen to the ground during the short-lived brawl. "Let me help you home. Lean on me and walk slowly."

She nodded and grabbed his arm, loving its massive strength. "I'm going to talk to Father right now," she said as they made their way home and got out of his cousin's hearing, "and insist upon an immediate wedding. I don't care if he's shocked or angry. You may have reconciled with Jordan, but I don't trust him yet. And now Jordan thinks he's about to come into the Moray wealth when he can't possibly be more deserving than you. And did you notice the whiskey on his breath?"

"There's whiskey on mine, too. We shared a bottle while discussing you."

Laurel let out a soft *harrumph*. "He may have acted honorably in this instance, but who's to say he isn't a drunken wretch who will destroy all you've helped your Uncle Silas build? No, it's safest if we marry right away… assuming you still want me."

"Blessed Scottish saints, you have a strong opinion on the matter." He smiled wryly and then began to chuckle. "I've never wanted anything more than to marry you, but I'll not make such a demand on your father tonight. Still, I'm pleased by your suggestion. Never thought I'd hear you say you're eager to marry me."

"And I never thought I'd hear an *I love you* from your lips, so I guess that makes us even." She felt drained, but at the same time exhilarated by what the future held for them. She understood that she and Graelem would not be married by tomorrow evening. At this point, it was a hopeless dream. Her father would never allow it, nor would Graelem ever ask it of him.

Still, a tingle of anticipation shot through her, for marriage had been foremost on her mind these past weeks, and she couldn't imagine anyone else but Graelem standing beside her at the altar. By the smoldering glances he tossed her way, it appeared that he wanted the ceremony to take place as much as she did. It would, perhaps a quiet ceremony sometime next month.

Oh, goodness! Could she keep her hands off Graelem for that long?

They walked through the gate toward the front door, which was now closed. She was about to reach for the knob, hoping it had not yet been locked, when the door flew open and her father was standing there raking a hand through his hair. "Thank goodness! You girls scared the life out of me. Where did you disappear to?"

"It's a long story, but Graelem can explain everything." She felt herself begin to swoon and once again leaned her head against Graelem's shoulder. "I had better sit down."

"Girls?" Graelem asked as they started to walk into the parlor. "What do you mean, sir? Who else is missing?"

George had now joined them. "You mean to say that Daisy isn't with you?"

"What?" Laurel's heart shot into her throat. "Oh, Graelem! She's gone to Devlin!"

He tore out of the house toward the mews at a hobbling run that had to be excruciatingly painful. She hurried after him and heard the heavier footsteps of her father and uncle trailing behind her. "Laurel, what's going on?" her father demanded to know. He caught up to her in three long strides and took her by the arm to hold her back.

"I'm not sure. I hope I'm wrong." Her heart was wildly leaping within her chest as she shook out of his grasp, but her father took hold of her arm again.

"Tell me," he insisted.

Graelem had hopped the high fence to save himself the trouble of running down the street and around the corner, but she was too short to follow him and doubted that her father and uncle could either, although they were remarkably fit for men of their age. They were wasting precious time standing here talking while Graelem ran headlong into who knew what danger.

"I think Dev means to elope with Daisy to Gretna Green." The words took a while to get out because she was out of breath and dizzy once again, not quite recovered from her own near abduction. "I refused him, so he shifted his attention and planned to—"

"Marry Daisy? The cur! She's young and impressionable, not even out in society yet. I'll kill him if he's taken advantage."

She'd never seen her father angrier or more determined.

They reached the mews and saw that the doors to the stable were open. She could hear Brutus snorting and nervously pawing the ground. Devlin was here. Who else was with him? "Laurel, stay back," she heard Graelem urgently caution her, but she'd already drawn up beside him.

He shoved her behind him.

"She's my sister. If anyone is to—"

George grabbed her and dragged her behind one of the stalls. "Stay put, you're only distracting Graelem. Don't you realize the danger?"

Danger?

She peered over the stall and saw Devlin with his arm firmly around Daisy, pinning her to his side. He held a pistol in his other hand aimed directly at Graelem's chest. Daisy was in tears. "Please, just step away and let us go," she pleaded with Graelem. "I don't want anyone else to get hurt."

Else? Oh, heavens! She noticed a man lying unconscious beside one of the stalls, no doubt one of the Bow Street runners. Devlin's pistol was cocked and his hand was shaking. Had he killed the man? No, they would have heard the shot or noticed blood. He wouldn't dare fire, would he?

Laurel slipped away from her uncle, who was too busy staring at Devlin to notice her disappearance. Her father was doing the same. She hurried to the carriage house and grabbed one of the horse whips, not yet certain if it had a use, but she needed a weapon and this would do quite nicely. She crept back in, intending to get closer to Devlin for a chance to crack the whip over his wrist and yank the pistol out of his hands the moment it was no longer trained on Graelem.

Her father had other ideas. "Give me that thing," he said in an angry whisper, grabbing it out of her hand and setting it aside. "Are you mad? Let George and Graelem handle this. I don't want you anywhere near that frightened idiot," he said, motioning to Devlin. "George will calm him down."

But what if her uncle couldn't calm him? There was nothing to stop Devlin from shooting Graelem unless she stopped him. But how? The whip might not have been the brightest idea, but Daisy and Graelem were in danger because of her, and she had to do something to protect them.

Devlin began to sidle out of the stable with Daisy still trapped in his grasp and that pistol still trained on the man she loved. All she needed was a moment to grab Devlin's arm and draw it upward so that if a shot went off, it would harmlessly strike the hayloft above them. But she couldn't risk it while Graelem and now her uncle were still in his line of fire.

"Put down the pistol, Dev," she said, her voice filled with a steady confidence she didn't possess. "It's over. The Bow Street runners have taken your accomplices into custody. You're only making matters worse for yourself."

She saw his eyes go wide in panic, and he began to wave his pistol recklessly. *Oh, dear!* "Let Daisy go. Take me as your hostage instead."

Daisy gasped. "No! Laurel, it's all my fault. I should have believed you, but I allowed myself to be duped."

"No, you're not to blame. He meant to marry me first."

Daisy sniffled. "But I allowed myself to—"

"Both of you shut up!" Devlin shouted, his outstretched arm now shaking from the weight of the pistol held too long. "I can't think with both of you chattering."

"Dev, there's nothing to think about," her father said, stepping out of the shadows to stand beside Graelem and George. In the next moment, he stood between Devlin and Graelem, in the exact spot she'd hoped to be in order to obstruct Devlin's aim. "You can't have either of my daughters. Laurel's given her heart elsewhere and Daisy is too young to know her own mind. Put down your weapon, son. We'll work this out with your father. This can all be kept quiet. We won't call in the authorities. No criminal charges pursued against you or your friends."

Devlin's hand wavered and Laurel noted the doubt now in his eyes. "Do I have your word on it, Mr. Farthingale?"

"You do." Her father appeared calm, but she felt the angry heat radiating off him and knew that no matter what happened, she and Daisy were in big trouble. Huge trouble. Their punishment would be as bad as any Devlin would face. "I give you my word. Hand me the weapon and release my daughter."

He released Daisy but kept the pistol aimed at Graelem.

Daisy flew into their father's arms.

Devlin began to back out, his gaze fixed on the men and seeming to forget about Laurel since she had been shunted off to the side. She waited for him to exit the stable and lower his arm, which now dangled tiredly at his side, the pistol loose in his grip. He started to run, but unlike her father, she'd made him no promises and wasn't about to let the wretch get off so easily.

She grabbed the whip her father had set aside and flicked it about Devlin's ankles, tripping him as he ran. He fell forward, his body hitting the dirt hard and the pistol skating out of his grasp. She kicked the horrid weapon out of his reach and then turned him over and grabbed him by his neatly tied cravat. "You bounder! How dare you endanger Daisy!"

His only response was a strangled gurgle.

Was she choking him? She didn't care. "She was a good friend to you. A dear friend. She trusted you!" She curled her hand into a fist and was about to smash it into his nose, but a big, warm hand fell over hers and she was suddenly plucked off Devlin.

"Laurel, it's over," Graelem said gently against her ear, drawing her into his arms and holding her tight as she still struggled. It might seem a loving, protective gesture to all, but she understood his true purpose, to protect that good-for-nothing Devlin from her wrath.

She tried to squirm out of Graelem's arms but he wouldn't let her, so all she could do was scowl down at the little toad who was now whimpering at her feet. She dared not raise her voice and alert the neighbors, for her father was right to keep the matter as quiet as possible for Daisy's sake. Even though she was innocent in this affair, she'd be scalded by the gossip and her reputation tarnished if hint of this incident ever got out. Everyone would believe Daisy planned to elope with Devlin.

George knelt down and untangled Devlin's legs from the whip. "Tell your father that Mr. Farthingale will call upon him tomorrow afternoon at four o'clock."

Devlin nodded as he struggled to his feet, and then with

another whimper scurried away.

"Dirty, deceitful scoundrel," Laurel muttered, her hands still curled into fists at her sides. "If he so much as glances your way, Daisy, I'll cleave him in half."

Her father groaned. "Enough, Laurel. Everyone back to my study. I'm not nearly done with any of you yet."

Nor am I. But Laurel knew better than to open her mouth and say anything until they were all safely back home. Her uncle took a moment to make certain the Bow Street runner wasn't seriously injured, all of them emitting a sigh of relief when he groaned and rolled to his feet.

Everyone was overset, especially Daisy, who continued to sob against her father's shoulder. How much distressing news could her father handle in one night, Laurel wondered? She had to tell him about her near abduction. It wouldn't do to have a magistrate appear at their door tomorrow morning and her father still in the dark about that unfortunate incident.

"Pruitt, summon my wife," her father said as they all returned and headed into the study. "George, please stay. I think I'll need your steady guidance."

Her uncle nodded. "Of course."

It took only a moment for their mother to join them. She took one look at Daisy, who had yet to stop crying, and rushed to her side. "Hush, sweetheart. All will be well. You're home now."

George closed the door behind them and stood off to the side, knowing this was a conversation to be had between parents and their wayward daughters. "It's my fault," Laurel said before any accusations were leveled at Daisy, who was still too distraught to defend herself. "Daisy had no intention of leaving the house, but when she saw that I wasn't in our bedchamber, she thought I was eloping with Devlin and went to the stables to stop me."

Her father sighed and shook his head. "I appreciate your attempt to protect your sister, but what happened is obvious."

Laurel shook her head. "Not to me. What are you talking about?"

"Daisy planned to elope with Devlin," her father said. "The bounder knew he'd lost your affections and turned his efforts toward the next sister… who didn't have the sense to see through his lies."

The breath was stolen from Laurel's lungs. "No!" Is this what the family thought of Daisy? "She knew what he was and tried to protect me. She was brave and caring and everything wonderful, just as she's always been."

Daisy struggled to her feet. "Laurel, it's all right. You don't have to defend me."

"Of course I do. You only meant to protect me."

Daisy glanced worriedly at Graelem. *Oh, dear!* Did she still think he believed the lies Devlin and Anne had been spewing? "And now you're trying to protect me. But I won't have your happiness put at risk for something that I did." Daisy turned to address Graelem. "Laurel truly loves you. She wasn't lying to you or planning to deceive you. Pay no attention to what she's saying. She had no intention of dashing off to Gretna Green with Devlin. I was the one he meant to take."

Laurel rolled her eyes. "Don't do this, Daisy. Graelem knows. He trusts me. You don't need to worry about us. Our betrothal isn't in jeopardy, although his wretched cousin—"

Graelem suddenly took hold of her hand and squeezed it. He gave an imperceptible shake of his head, as though telling her to stop. He meant to be honorable, but her family needed the reminder about his circumstances. Jordan would inherit most of the Moray properties within a short twenty-four hours if something wasn't done about it.

She cast him a determined glower.

He rolled his eyes and sighed, not exactly forbidding her to speak since he knew that wouldn't work anyway, but merely suggesting that she shouldn't. But how could she keep silent when there was so much to tell, not just about his inheritance, but her own abduction. Keeping silent would be the same as lying to her parents. In any event, she was never good at keeping quiet. "I wasn't in our bedchamber because Devlin's scoundrel friends abducted me shortly before Devlin took Daisy hostage in the stable."

She paused a moment for their reaction. Not even Daisy

appeared to believe her.

A wiser young woman would have stopped and reassessed at that moment, but she was overset and never that wise, especially when indignant. She knew her limitations and would never make a good wife for a diplomat. Goodness, she wasn't certain she'd make Graelem a good wife... or if he'd even want her as his wife once she was through with her speech. "It's true! They held a foul cloth to my nose and tried to knock me out, but I fought and kicked, even though they threw a sack over my head and tossed me into their carriage. Then Graelem and Jordan and a burly man with a bulbous red nose intercepted the carriage and rescued me."

"Graelem's cousin has a bulbous red nose?" Daisy asked.

"No." She paused only to take a quick breath and glance at their faces. They still didn't believe her, and Graelem was standing with his arms crossed over his chest doing nothing to help. "Someone in this household must have heard the commotion. The horses reared and the carriage clattered to a noisy halt just down the street. Graelem had his Bow Street runners take the scoundrels to the local magistrate. That's where we ought to have taken Devlin, since he was obviously the one who paid those vermin."

She could see that her parents were growing impatient.

Graelem reached over to squeeze her hand again.

She gazed at him in confusion. "Say something, anything, so they'll believe me."

Graelem sighed and turned to her parents. "Laurel is telling the truth, as implausible as it may seem. She was abducted. Both your daughters were in jeopardy this evening."

"Which is why I must be allowed to marry Graelem as soon as possible. I know we're in mourning, and Graelem is surely tossing daggers at me as I speak, but after what took place tonight I think the matter of our betrothal must be discussed and resolved immediately. You're scheduled to meet Lord Kirwood tomorrow at four o'clock. We can schedule our wedding ceremony for two o'clock."

Her mother paled and sank into the closest chair. Her father went straight to his wife and put an arm about her shoulders. "Sophie, dearest."

"I'll be all right, John. Just give me a moment to catch my breath." She inhaled deeply several times and slowly exhaled each time. "Both daughters in danger, you say?"

Graelem nodded. "I've had Bow Street runners following my cousin as well as Devlin, worried that they would conspire to keep me and Laurel apart. It would have served both their interests, allowing my cousin to secure his inheritance when I failed to marry by Midsummer's Day, and giving Devlin the heiress he needed to marry to maintain his profligate ways. Jordan refused to be a part of it and warned me. None of us counted on Daisy getting caught up in their scheme."

He sighed and ran a hand through his hair. "But Devlin must have known that Daisy was an easier mark. I doubt he intended to marry Daisy—he probably wanted to hold her hostage to secure Laurel's cooperation. He knew that Laurel would not marry him even if he held a pistol to her head, but one held against Daisy... well, Laurel would have done anything to save her sister."

George groaned.

Her father looked more haggard than Laurel had ever seen him. "Are you certain you still wish to marry Laurel?"

Graelem chuckled. "Incredibly, yes. Never had a moment's doubt, sir. Although she's quite fierce with a whip. I'll have to remember not to anger her."

Laurel huffed. "I'd never hurt you."

"I know, lass. I was just teasing." He reached out and tucked a finger under her chin, his expression now serious. "I know you'll be as protective of our children. They'll be well loved and cared for."

Well loved and cared for as Graelem never was. She knew that's what he really meant to say and it made her heart ache for him all the more. "By both of us."

He nodded. "I love you, Laurel."

Those magic words seemed to lift everyone's spirits. "I love you, too. I know I haven't made it easy for you, Graelem. But I promise to—"

"Hush, lass. I don't need assurances or promises to reform your hellion ways. I've told you before, had I wanted a wife with boiled mushrooms for brains, I would have chosen her weeks ago. Such women are available by the hundreds. But there's only one of you."

"And one is quite enough," her father intoned, mopping his brow. "Two o'clock you say?"

Laurel gasped.

Graelem nodded.

"Sophie, set out your prettiest dress. We're going to a Midsummer's Day wedding."

CHAPTER 21

LAUREL REMOVED HER wedding dress, unbound her hair, and slipped on her bedclothes with the help of a maid.

Once alone, she wasn't certain what to do while waiting for Graelem to enter their bedchamber. This would be a night of magic, if her married sister was to be believed. She wanted it to be true, but didn't think it was possible. Graelem had teased her about being an inept lover.

Did he mean it?

Oh, dear. Of course he did. She was inept and inexperienced.

She glanced around the well-appointed room, her gaze settling on the large four-poster bed in the center of it that was covered by a lustrous emerald green counterpane. The chamber wasn't really theirs, but merely one of the many guest rooms in Gabriel Dayne's unoccupied townhouse. Graelem had intended to reside there during his wife hunt, but that was before Laurel had trampled him while riding Brutus and effectively put an end to his marital plans.

The house had been readied for them this morning.

All thought fled as Graelem entered the chamber and softly closed the door behind him. *Hot, buttered crumpets!* He looked good. Incredibly good in his black dressing gown. From what she could see, he had nothing on beneath it.

She wore a delicate, pale pink nightgown borrowed from her married sister, Rose, who'd grinned wickedly and wagered that she wouldn't keep it on for more than two minutes after Graelem entered the room. "I'd wager one minute," Rose added, "but Graelem's broken leg might slow him down a bit."

Laurel's heart tightened at the recollection of Rose's remark. Her distress mounted as she watched Graelem stride toward her on his crutches, still needing them to get around. It was a grim reminder of how badly his leg had been injured. "Lass, I've never seen you look so scared," he said in a husky murmur. "We have a lifetime together. I'll not force you to—"

"It isn't that." She blushed as he set aside his crutches and reached out to caress her cheek. She loved his touch. "I don't wish to disappoint you. And you said it yourself, I don't know what I'm doing, so how can I possibly please you?"

He groaned as he gazed at her with a tenderness that warmed her heart. "Is that all? Sweetheart, you will please me. You *do* please me. Making love isn't meant to happen with the precision of a Swiss clock or a perfectly rehearsed waltz. It's best when awkward and unrestrained, especially good with a dollop of wantonness thrown in."

She laughed softly and shook her head, forgetting that her gold curls were unbound, so that the unruly strands swayed and tumbled over her shoulders with each shake. "I'm not lacking in that. Even now, my fingers are itching to fling the dressing gown off you so that I can admire your naked body." She blushed. "I shouldn't have said that."

His eyes were gleaming with a mix of amusement and heat. "Do you mean it?"

She nodded. "Of course I do. I've been curious ever since I burst into your room on that first day and caught you with your clothes off." She traced a finger along his exposed chest, absorbing the heat of his lightly bronzed skin and the tickle of his dark chest hairs against the pad of her finger.

He responded in kind, his finger sliding across the mound of one breast and then the other in a languid motion that immediately stirred her blood and caused the private recesses of her body to pulse and throb. The silken fabric between them seemed to heighten the sensation of his rough skin against her breasts.

She closed her eyes and leaned back in the cradle of his arm while he continued to stroke her breasts, his palm now cupping one and gently kneading it. His thumb now rubbing across the hardening nipple. *Sweet Mother of All Crumpets!* He'd barely started and her body was already a hot, wanton flame of desire.

He lowered his head and replaced his fingers with his mouth, teasing the taut peak as he suckled her through the silk and then flicking his tongue across it, mercilessly heightening the unbearable heat now coursing through her body like a river of hot, fiery lava. In the next moment, her gown was off and pooled at her feet, and his mouth was on her breast again, this time without the fabric barrier.

"Oh, Graelem!" She buried her fingers in his hair and then clutched his shoulders, for her legs had turned to butter and she hadn't the strength to stand up. She would have fallen had he not held her in his arms.

She was naked and she wanted him that way, too. She tugged at his dressing gown, too late realizing she had tugged the knot at his belt the wrong way and now she'd hopelessly tightened it. He looked up and grinned. "Let me help you, love."

She grumbled. "I told you I'm no good at this."

"Do you hear me complaining?" He released her to quickly loosen the knot and shrug out of the garment. No barriers existed between them now.

She took the opportunity to study his big, muscled, male body, her breath hitching at the unmistakably hard and erect bulge between his well-formed legs. "What shall I... am I supposed to...?"

He took her hand and led her to the bed, lifting the covers so she could slip between the sheets. He joined her there and nudged her onto her back while he settled atop her, propping on his elbows in order not to crush her, although she liked the weight of him on her body. "I'll show you, sweetheart. There's no rush. We have all night." He stroked his hand through her hair that was splayed across the pillows. "Honey and silk," he murmured, running his fingers through the strands once more and gently brushing them off her shoulders for an unobstructed view of her breasts.

He liked her breasts. A lot.

"You're beautiful, Laurel," he said in a reverent whisper.

"So are you, my love." She raised her head off the pillow to meet his lips in a kiss that was unrestrained, for they wanted each other and neither wished to hold back. He certainly wasn't. His hand slid down the length of her, coming to rest atop her breast and teasing it once again until she bucked beneath him, she was that hot and wanting.

He kissed a trail starting from her lips, down her jaw, to the soft arch of her shoulder, to the taut bud of her breast, taking it gently between his teeth and rousing more exquisite sensations as he nipped and licked with his tongue until she couldn't recall her name or her country of birth or anything but Graelem. Then he moved lower, kissing her stomach, the inside of her thighs, and finally nudging them slightly apart to place his mouth on her nether lips.

Mercy!

He felt so good against her. She felt shameless, but had no desire to stop him even as he tucked his shoulders under her legs for a better angle to probe and swirl and—the moans tore from her throat before she could stop them as a tingling heat began to wash over her body and threatened to sweep her away on a hot, pulsing tide. "Graelem," she whispered, stroking his hair. "I love you."

She was still hot and throbbing when he drew his mouth away from the intimate part of her body only to replace it with his erect member. He positioned himself between her legs and rubbed it along her slick opening, then slowly began to push inside her, ever so gently at first, then a little harder. "I love you, too."

He thrust into her, still careful not to hurt her, but he was big and hard and she'd never experienced this sensation before. She thought it would hurt much more than it did, but the discomfort was only at first. As she curled her legs around his waist, any sensation of pain was quickly replaced by wonderfully intimate waves of heat that increased in intensity as he began to thrust in and out of her.

The building desire she'd experienced a moment ago stirred

again. She began to move with him, arching upward to meet him and clinging to his shoulders as he pulled away and then came back to her. Like waves rolling toward her shore, some of them hard and pounding, while others were gentle. His thrusts came in steady intervals, once again like waves cresting and ebbing, and then they were only cresting, so that the two of them were lifted so high they floated among the stars, their bodies joined, their hearts entwined forever.

She cried his name over and over. She kissed him on the mouth, kissed his jaw, pressed her lips against the hard curve of his taut, muscled shoulders. Whispered his name until they collapsed, moaning and their bodies damp, in each other's arms. "How do you feel, love?" he asked, easing out of her and rolling her atop him as he fell onto his back, sinking into the soft mattress.

Her long hair fell over his chest and shoulders as she rested her cheek against his heart, but he didn't seem to mind at all. Indeed, he seemed to like the feel of her hair between his fingers and the way it fell in unruly waves over her shoulders and onto his body. "I feel…" *Wonderful, spectacular.* "I feel like a baroness. An enchanted baroness caught up in a magical dream that I hope never ends. Graelem, thank you for waiting for me. I'm so glad you didn't give up on me and marry someone else."

He let out a throaty laugh. "I would sooner give up my heart than ever give you up." He absently stroked his hand along her spine as he seemed to sober. "No one has ever fought for me as you have, Laurel. No one has ever loved me as you do. When you came to me with your list of demands and told me what they were, I wanted to sweep you into my arms and kiss you into forever. They weren't demands. They were confirmation that I existed, that my life had meaning. That someone cared if I lived or died."

She hugged him, wanting to cry for all the joy he'd missed as a child. Loving him all the more for becoming the wonderful man he was today, the man who'd stolen her heart. "I hope you remember these words the next time I do something headstrong and foolish and you wish to throttle me."

"You may be headstrong, but you're not foolish." He kissed the top of her head. "I'll remember, and always be grateful for finding you. I'll remember our wedding and especially this wedding night."

A grandfather clock chimed in the downstairs hallway. Laurel gasped. "It's almost midnight."

"So?"

She scrambled to her knees. "The day is almost over."

He quirked an eyebrow, still obviously confused. "I repeat, so?"

"You have to kiss me, Graelem."

"Haven't I been doing just that? And won't I continue to do that in about thirty seconds because your pink, naked body is making me hot and wild again?"

She nodded. "But before that happens—"

"Too late."

"Before that happens, I'd like you to make it a pure kiss, one that is from the deepest recesses of your heart, one not guided by lustful thoughts, although I'd forgive you if you failed to keep it completely pure. I'm having trouble ridding my mind of lustful thoughts, too. You're excessively handsome in your naked splendor."

The clock continued to chime. Eight. Nine. "Quick, Graelem. A kiss I'll never forget."

"A midsummer's kiss," he said as the clock chimed ten. Eleven. He took her into his arms and closed his mouth over hers. More important, he took Laurel into his heart forever and completely as the clock chimed twelve to mark the end of Midsummer's Day.

THE END

Dear reader, if you enjoyed *A Midsummer's Kiss*, I would really appreciate it if you could post a review on the site where you purchased it. Also feel free to write one on Goodreads or other reader sites that you peruse. Even just a few sentences on what you thought about the book would be most helpful! If you do leave a review, send me a message on Facebook because I would love to thank you personally. Please also consider telling your friends about the FARTHINGALE series and recommending it to your book clubs.

Up next is Rose, the eldest of the Farthingale sisters. Her best friend's brother, the dashing Viscount Julian Emory, has just saved her life and she is eternally grateful. So how can she refuse to return the favor when his family begs for her help, even if it means abducting the gorgeous man?

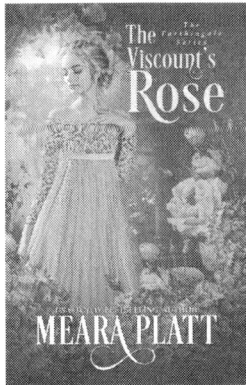

Keep reading to enjoy the first chapter of *The Viscount's Rose*, and don't forget to grab your free Farthingale novella after the sneak peek.

SNEAK PEEK:
THE VISCOUNT'S ROSE
CHAPTER 1

Mayfair District, London
June 1813

"JULIAN, *PLEASE*. I wish you'd meet Rolf."

"Enough, Nicola! I'm not interested." Lord Julian Emory, the tenth Viscount Chatham, stifled a groan as he assisted his sister down from his carriage in front of Number 3 Chipping Way, the stately residence of her best friend, the one whose given name he couldn't recall at the moment because Nicola always referred to her as Rolf. Who would call a young lady that anyway? It was the sort of name one gave to a dog.

Nicola frowned at him. "She's wonderful, as are all the Farthingales. You'll agree once you meet them. Rolf is so much more clever than any debutante making her come-out this season. Much nicer than those supposedly elegant ladies you keep fast company with. Please come in with me, Julian."

He was about to decline, as he had every day this past week, when a small explosion suddenly rocked the quiet street. "Nicola, get back in the carriage. Now!"

"But Rolf—Ack!"

He tossed his sister inside without waiting for her to obey and ordered his coachman to drive a safe distance away before leaping over the gate, for he'd heard several high-pitched cries for help coming from the garden of the very townhouse his sister was about to visit. He ran toward the screams and noticed a small funnel of black smoke rising from a makeshift structure in the far corner of the garden.

Two young girls were being held back by two older women, but the girls were obviously struggling to break free and run toward the danger. He couldn't allow that to happen. "Is anyone in there?" he demanded to know, removing his jacket. He intended to use it as a blanket to extinguish any spreading flames, although the fire appeared to be contained and dying out on its own.

"Our sister's in there," one of the girls replied, gazing at him through tearful blue eyes.

"Her kiln exploded," the other girl said, gazing at him through identical blue eyes. Had his vision suddenly blurred? He was seeing identical faces.

No matter, he'd sort it all out once he'd rescued their sister.

Julian placed his jacket protectively over his nose and mouth, dropped to a crouch, and nudged open the door, which had almost blown off but was still hanging on one hinge. The black funnel of smoke quickly dissipated as it wafted outside, confirming the fire had burned itself out, leaving only smoke in its wake. He had only to find the sister.

Don't let her be dead or injured.

He'd engaged in enough battles on the Peninsula to understand the damage that wounds caused. The remnants were not only visible scars but invisible ones as well, the sort that pierced deep under one's flesh and festered. *Damn.* He didn't even know the young innocent's name to call out to her. "Miss? Can you hear me? Where are you?"

His eyes watered as smoke and dust enveloped him. He wasn't halfway into the small enclosure when he heard a soft moan coming from behind an overturned table. The girl was alive but in what condition? He approached and saw that her ankle was pinned under the table, so he quickly righted it and then knelt to check her for broken bones before he dared move her. The bigger risk now was a break, a bump on the head, or other unknown internal injury.

He brushed a few stray locks off her forehead and spoke gently, relieved to feel no lumps forming on her brow. "Can you move your fingers?"

"I... I th-think so." She appeared to do so without much effort.

"Now raise your arms, one at a time." Again, she managed with little effort. "I'm going to touch your legs, don't be alarmed."

"Nothing will alarm me after this," she said, punctuating each word with a cough. Even so, the gentle amusement in her raspy voice sent an unexpected warmth coursing through his blood. There was a sweet, melodic quality to her voice.

"Good, because I need to make certain you have no spinal damage and then get you out of here before the roof collapses atop us." He touched her leg. "Can you feel my hand on you?" Because he sure as hell could feel her soft, shapely leg, and that warmth flowing through his blood had just turned fiery.

"Yes, I can."

He cleared his throat. "I'm going to take off your slippers and I'd like you to wiggle your toes, one foot at a time."

She was able to do as he asked but winced as she tried to move her injured ankle, which appeared to be the only damage she'd sustained. Of course, she'd inhaled some smoke. That was worrisome depending on how much she'd taken in. "Put your arms around my neck."

He lifted her into his arms while she did so and carried her out into the cool, fresh air. She coughed again as her lungs took in the cooler air and—*merciful heavens*—he felt each heave of her ample breasts against his chest.

Fiery did not begin to describe the heat now raging through his body.

Bloody nuisance.

"Who are you?" he asked. The question came out more sternly than intended, but it couldn't be helped. She was turning him inside out, and he didn't know who she was nor could he see her clearly because smoke still stung his eyes. She did not reply.

A cool, gusting breeze surrounded them now that they were outside. The bright sunshine caused his eyes to tear up worse than they had done in the shed, but he managed to set her down on the grass under a shade tree without stumbling. He wiped his eyes with his sleeve, which wasn't the cleverest idea, for his sleeves were covered in soot and now so was his face.

He knelt beside her, and the little girls with identical faces fell to their knees on the opposite side of their sister, excitedly chattering and obviously relieved she was safe and relatively unharmed. "I didn't hide my box of explosives in your kiln, Rose," one of them said. "I'd never do anything so foolish."

What?

He now knew the name of the girl he'd just carried out. But what were her young sisters going on about? Military ammunition? In elegant Mayfair, no less? He'd question the young girl later, but right now his attention was focused on the one he'd just carried out. He cleared his throat. "Your name is Rose?"

She nodded. "It is, sir. Thank you for saving me. May I ask—" That was as much as her raspy voice managed before she erupted in a fit of coughing that alarmed the small crowd of servants who must have run out of the house when they heard the noise and saw the fire. They were now gathering around him and Rose.

A tall, older man seemed to be in charge of the worried staff and was, no doubt, the Farthingale family's head butler.

"Pruitt, she needs something to drink," one of her sisters said, wringing her small hands together in worry. "And wash cloths to clean the grime off their hands and faces. We mustn't track soot all over this lovely new house after Mama worked so hard to put it in shape."

"Right away, Miss Lily." He sent one of the maids to attend to the chore and then sent two others to the kitchen to bring out refreshments. "Will tea and cakes do for all of you? Sir, shall I send out something a little stronger for you?"

"Tea will do for me." He needed to keep his wits about him, for he had yet to regain control of his body despite the fact that he was no longer holding Rose.

Pruitt assigned several footmen the task of securing the rubble now that the fire was out, and once assured that Rose was all right, he ordered the others back into the house. Only the governesses and Rose's sisters remained beside them. "I'm Dillie," one of the girls said, smiling at him. "This is my twin, Lily."

He grinned. "I guessed as much. Identical blue eyes and dark hair. Identical faces." Same thin, gangly bodies. "Lord Julian Emory, at your service."

"Emory? As in Viscount Chatham? Lady Nicola's brother?" Rose attempted to raise herself to a sitting position, but the movement caused her to cough again.

Alarmed when the coughs suddenly mingled with wheezes, he drew her into his arms and placed a hand on her chest to feel her heart, which was beating wildly but not in a haphazard pattern that would signal something more serious than a cough. Her intake of air, despite her wheezing, appeared adequate.

After a frighteningly long moment, she calmed.

Dillie stared at him and then turned to her twin. "Why is his hand still on Rose's breast?"

"To check her lung capacity, of course." Lily frowned. "What did you think he was doing?"

"Girls, I'm right here. You can ask me… er, no. Lily just answered the question." Although it didn't explain why his hand was still on Rose's breast or why he was reluctant to draw it away. "Who is Rolf?"

Perhaps he ought to meet that sister after all. Nicola had been urging the introduction for several weeks now. Was the girl anywhere near as beautiful as Rose? Not that he'd actually taken a good look at Rose. No, his body had responded to hers in the dark. Quite another matter to study the girl by the bright light of day when her flaws would be glaringly obvious.

He finally managed to move his hand off her chest, but kept it loosely poised at her waist, easily convincing himself that she required his attendance while still unsteady and trembling from her ordeal.

He required something altogether inappropriate.

Why her? Why now? No matter, his inexplicable bout of lust for the girl would soon pass. Even if it didn't, he was never going to act upon it. Still, he was curious to study the face attached to that exquisite body. He spared her a glance... more than a glance.

Merciful heavens!

Despite the smudges of soot on Rose's cheeks and tip of her nose, there was no mistaking her beauty. She had lively blue eyes, a deep, ocean blue that glistened with mirth and intelligence. Her hair was a riotous tumble of honey-blonde curls. She had a generous, sensual mouth. "You asked about Rolf," she said, interrupting the wayward thoughts he ought not be having.

He nodded. "Is she your sister?"

Rose's full lips curled upward in a radiant smile.

Her sisters began to giggle.

Bloody nuisance.

"I'm Rolf. Didn't Nicola tell you?" Rose shook her head lightly.

Yes, his sister had told him repeatedly, only he hadn't been listening. His heart slammed into his chest. "You?"

She nodded. "Rose Olivia Lorelei Farthingale. Rolf to my friends."

"Lorelei, as in the siren who lures men with her irresistible beauty and plaintive song onto the rocks to their watery graves?" He arched an eyebrow.

She managed a soft, still raspy laugh. "At the moment I sound like a bullfrog and I've never lured any man, so I don't think your siren and I are related in any way."

"I suppose not." Clearly, Rose was far more captivating than any mythical creature ever could be. That she was modest about it only added to her allure. No! She couldn't be alluring to him. Not now. He couldn't afford the distraction.

Rose pursed her lips. "Where's Nicola? Didn't she come with you?"

He winced. "I'm afraid I tossed her rather ungently into my carriage when we heard the explosion. I ordered the driver to take her a safe distance from your home."

"Of course. That was the sensible thing to do, while you ran toward the unknown danger. Nicola's often spoken of your military service, and I see that her glowing description of your bravery is well deserved."

"I did no more than anyone else would do." In truth, he was feeling quite cowardly right now. Rose had him quaking in his boots. Nicola had spoken of her in glowing terms, and that description seemed wholly inadequate now. But he'd braved Napoleon's army, had spent the last few years on dangerous spy missions within the heart of enemy territory. Surely he could resist Rose's innocent charms until this latest mission was completed.

He had to.

Pruitt returned with wash cloths and refreshments. He handed Julian a damp cloth and another to Rose, and then set the refreshments out on a nearby table. Obviously, this is where Nicola and Rose had planned to sit during their visit, for it was quite pleasant outdoors if one overlooked the lingering wisps of smoke.

One twin grabbed slices of cake and set them out on plates for him and Rose while the other twin poured lemonade. "Rose, come sit with us."

Julian reached out to lift Rose into his arms. "Your ankle looks swollen. You had better not walk on it yet. I'll carry you to your chair."

Rose became flustered, her cheeks stained a bright pink. "Oh, I'm sure I can manage on my own. You needn't... oh, dear." She cried out softly the moment she rose and attempted to put pressure on her ankle. She fell against his chest. "Ouch! It really hurts."

He wrapped his arms about her and carried her to her seat. "Let me have a better look at that ankle." He reached out to take it very delicately under his inspection. "It could be broken." All three sisters and their two governesses gasped as he raised Rose's gown to examine it.

"I'm sure it isn't," Rose insisted and nudged the hem lower.

"And what if I'm right and it is broken?" He frowned at her, although he was more annoyed with himself for desiring to see her ankle for reasons other than medical. He wanted to see a lot more than her ankle. The pale blue muslin gown she wore did little to hide her curves. Even though his eyes still stung, he could see well enough through them to know that she was nicely shaped. "At the very least it's badly bruised and must be attended to at once. Why won't you let me do it?"

"It's most improper," she grumbled.

"He's already touched your breast," Lily pointed out. The twins were still hovering over them, curious as kittens.

"What?" Apparently, Rose had been too dazed to notice at the time. Her face was no longer pink but crimson. She gazed at him in confusion. Or was it unbridled horror? *Bloody nuisance.* Most women liked having his hands on their breasts. Why should she be any different?

"You were having trouble breathing," he explained, once again annoyed with himself for wanting her to... never mind. He shouldn't be thinking about her or her body. Done. No longer in his thoughts... well, only a little.

Perhaps more than a little.

He was about to insist on attending to her ankle when Nicola entered the garden. Julian frowned. "I thought I told you to wait in the carriage."

"I was worried about you." She started to mimic his frown, but when she saw Rose beside him her expression suddenly lightened and she couldn't stifle her knowing grin. "I see you've met Rolf."

Rose was still blushing. "In a most unusual way." She pointed to her foot. "Your brother rescued me. My work table fell on my leg."

"But I heard a blast. It couldn't have been just the table toppling. What happened? And you both have soot on your faces and all over your clothes."

Rose nodded. "Someone sabotaged my kiln."

"Oh, dear! You said this pottery business was run by scurrilous knaves. I never dreamed they'd behave so badly. Rolf, you might have been killed!"

"They only meant to destroy the kiln as a warning to me," Rose said with a stubborn set to her jaw and a passionate blaze in her eyes. "Well, they've warned me and now it is done. But they won't stop me."

Julian groaned inwardly. The girl was beautiful and strong-willed, a great combination if one were seeking a debauched night of… but never with Rolf. No, indeed. Not with his sister's best friend. "What makes you believe these knaves are done with you? Assuming this was more than a mere accident."

"I can assure you, I am always careful with my kiln. It was no accident." The swirls of blue in her eyes shone as brightly as gemstones.

Julian frowned. He was already caught up in a mission and didn't have time to protect Rose, but he wasn't about to turn his back on her if she was in any danger. "What if they try again? If what you say is true, I can't imagine your parents allowing you to continue this enterprise." He glanced at the twins. "Think of your sisters, if not yourself. They might have been standing near the kiln or by the door as it blew off its hinges."

Her mouth was drawn in a taut, thin line. "Are you through lecturing me?"

"Not nearly through." After all, he'd earned the right to speak his mind by pulling her out of the rubble, hadn't he? "What of your season? It's hardly under way and you're already hurt. I'm sure your parents put a lot of time and effort into launching you into society. They'd much rather see you married than injured… or worse."

Nicola was nodding as he spoke, a rare moment when he and his sister agreed on something. "My brother's right, Rolf. You can't put your life at risk for the sake of a dish or vase, no matter how beautiful. We're in our debut season. We promised to get through it together, so you ought to be thinking of balls and courtship and handsome eligible bachelors, like Julian, for example."

He glowered at his sister. "But not me."

Rose's eyes rounded and she blushed in obvious embarrassment. "Of course not, Lord Emory. I wouldn't presume. I'm most grateful for your assistance and promise to be more careful. You're right, of course. It galls me to have them win, but I suppose they have for the moment. My family will be relieved. As you said, they brought us to London in the hope we'd find suitable husbands." She glanced at her ankle and then looked up and cast him a wan smile. "There'll be no dancing for me for a while. In truth, I was never very good at it anyway."

Perhaps he'd been a little too stern with her. "I'm sure you're an excellent dancer. I'll claim the first waltz once you've healed." *Oh, hell.* He shouldn't have said that. Now Nicola will think her matchmaking scheme had worked when nothing was further from the truth.

Rose shook her head and laughed lightly. "Prepare to have your toes stepped on, my lord."

He arched an eyebrow and grinned. "I'll wear my thickest boots."

"OUR UNCLE GEORGE is a doctor. He'll properly tend to my ankle when he returns." Rose didn't mean to appear unappreciative, but she sorely wished Lord Emory would leave before he lifted her into his arms again and insisted on carrying her into the house. She'd rather manage on her own even though her ankle was sore.

It wasn't broken, but Lord Emory had not given ground on tending it. He'd put a cold compress on it and then bound her foot and ankle with the bandages Pruitt had retrieved from her uncle's quarters. She was in as good a shape as could be expected; even Uncle George would commend him on the admirable job he'd done. "My uncle's an excellent doctor. The best in London."

Lord Emory, who was still kneeling beside her, arched an eyebrow and looked up at her, his expression a mix of cynicism, tender indulgence, and something else she didn't quite recognize. Whatever it was, it made her heart beat a little faster. "So you've told me three times already, Miss Farthingale."

"Well, he is." In truth, Lord Emory had taken excellent care of her, his medical knowledge obviously learned in the midst of battle, which only made her like him all the more for the attentive care he must have given the soldiers under his charge. He was smart and brave, and now that he'd wiped the grime off his face she could see that he was irresistibly handsome. His dark blond hair fell in thick waves almost to his shoulders, and the appealing glint in his dark green eyes made her melt a little each time he smiled.

She liked his smile.

He was muscled, too. She'd felt the sinewed tension along his arms when he'd carried her out of the shed and again when he'd insisted on carrying her to the tea table. Being a damsel in distress wasn't so bad when one's savior was as handsome as Lord Emory.

She studied his graceful movements as he rose from bended knee and took a seat beside her, noting the muscled ripple of his broad shoulders clearly outlined beneath his white lawn shirt. His jacket was ruined so he hadn't been able to put it back on. "Uncle George will properly tend to my ankle," she repeated. "You needn't wait around for him or my parents. I'll manage quite well with the help of my sisters and our staff."

He smiled at her again, his eyes crinkling at the corners. It was a miracle she hadn't melted into a complete puddle by now. Nicola had been right about her brother. He was charming, but Rose knew better than to mistake his politeness for anything more. "Are you that eager to be rid of me, Miss Farthingale?"

Lord Emory was experienced and sophisticated and knew how to go about in society. He ran with a fast crowd. Despite the unusual manner in which they'd met, she was ordinary in every respect and he probably considered her excessively boring. "Not at all, my lord. I have no wish to be rid of you. After all, you saved me and for that you shall always be welcome in the Farthingale home. But I suspect you've reached your limit of polite conversation and are eager to be on your way."

"Do I look as though I'm eager to be anywhere but here?" He was still smiling and she was still melting. *Drip, drip, drip.* Her little puddle would soon be a pond. With ducks swimming in it. And a swan or two gliding across it.

She cleared her throat. "Well, no. But you must find my conversation quite dull. You're too polite to show it."

The twins weren't nearly as polite. Having gobbled their ginger cakes, they sat fidgeting and bored until Rose took pity on them and gave them permission to return to the house. As they rose along with their governesses, Lord Emory also got to his feet. "Lily," he said with quiet authority, holding her sister back as the others walked ahead, "I'm curious about your stash of explosives. How did you come by it? May I see?"

She nodded. "I found a large pouch when we'd all gone down to see Uncle Harrison's regiment ship off for France last week. I tried to return it once I realized what it contained, but everyone was too busy to pay me any notice. So I brought it home. It's hidden under my bed."

"Under your…" Lord Emory's eyes rounded and his mouth gaped open for an instant before he seemed to recover. "I'm good friends with the regimental commander. Will you permit me to return it to him?"

If Rose could have jumped to her feet and hugged him, she would have done so. "An excellent idea, my lord. This is the perfect solution, and it can all be done quietly."

Lily frowned. "Shouldn't I tell Papa first? I've been meaning to show it to him, but he and Mama are always so busy lately I can't seem to get their attention."

"We'll figure it out afterward. Bring Lord Emory the pouch." Rose shook her head and released a groaning laugh as Lily skipped off. "Brilliantly done, Lord Emory. Thank you."

He chuckled. "And now, what were you saying about my being bored? Because I don't believe I've ever spent a more unusual afternoon."

"You're right, of course. I only meant that you don't strike me as a tea and cakes sort of gentleman."

"Is that the only reason you want me gone?" He arched an eyebrow, looking impossibly irreverent. "Or are you worried that I'll give your parents an accurate account of what happened today?"

Well, perhaps there was a little of that. "My ankle is bound, my gown is covered in soot, and the kiln is damaged. I think they'll suspect all is not as it should be. If you're worried that I'll understate the danger, rest assured the twins will not overlook a single detail. They'll probably embellish the story and have you dueling a marauding pirate or two at some point in their retelling."

He ran a hand through his hair and laughed. "I like your sisters, even though my eyes still cross whenever they stand together."

"Rolf has two more sisters," Nicola said, her own grin wide and her eyes revealing her triumphant joy in finally getting her and Lord Emory to meet. "The twins are the youngest, but there's also Laurel and Daisy. Laurel will make her debut next year and Daisy the following year."

"You all have floral names except for Dillie," he noted, nodding as Rose offered him more tea. He really was being quite attentive and polite, not at all impatient as Nicola had described him.

"Her real name is Daffodil, but she's not very fond of being called that. Yes, we're all named after flowers although our parents sometimes think they ought to have named us Nettle, or Thorn, or Bramblebush. We vex them at times."

He was smiling at her again in a charmingly seductive way that tempted her to rethink her decision to hobble into the house on her own. Why was it so important? Couldn't she pretend to be a delicate female in distress and feign endless gratitude when he lifted her into his manly arms and carried her inside?

The wind began to pick up and the white clouds suddenly turned gray, obscuring the sun. Lord Emory glanced up. The wind ruffled his blond locks, brushing them back to accentuate the strong angles of his cheekbones and firm jaw. "Looks like our run of good weather has come to an end. Miss Farthingale, let me help you into your home before the rain pours down and turns the dirt on our clothes to mud."

Pruitt must have also noticed the sudden change in the weather. He hurried out with two footmen to clear away the tea and linens. "May I help you, Miss Rose?"

Lord Emory moved possessively close. "I'll take care of her, Pruitt. See to the tables."

Rose regarded him curiously. Nicola wished for a match between them and had never been subtle in her desire, but Lord Emory's name was already linked to a recently widowed countess, a renowned beauty who traveled in his elegant circle. He reportedly was infatuated with her, if one were to believe the gossip rags, although he didn't seem to be the sort to be led about by the nose by any woman.

But what did she know about men? Or love?

Nothing, obviously. Her senses were still addled, for Lord Emory appeared to be interested in her beyond a casual concern for her injured ankle even though she knew it couldn't be so.

Shaking her head, Rose stood and carefully tested her injury by putting delicate weight on her foot. "Crumpets!" She winced as a lightning bolt of pain tore upward from her swollen toes and straight into her temples. "Very well, I'd be grateful for your help. I'll never make it into the house on my own without falling flat on my face." Her ankle was already throbbing and she had yet to take a single step.

He seemed relieved that she made no protest, but at the same time, his body tensed the moment he lifted her into his arms. Had she said or done something to displease him?

Was she too heavy?

Those ginger cakes were awfully good.

"Where should I set you down?" he asked, striding into the house with her nestled in his arms as though she were no burden at all. Apparently she was not too heavy for him and he seemed quite capable of holding her in his arms for hours.

She pretended to think about the question, for she was in no hurry to respond. She liked the solid feel of his arms and had an artist's admiration for the firm, masculine contours of his body. "The salon, I think. On one of the stools beside the fireplace."

"On a stool?" He frowned.

"Our clothes," she reminded him. "I'd hate to ruin my mother's new furniture. She took ever so long to find just the right shades of blue silks and brocades for the seat cushions and drapes."

Instead of doing as she suggested, he called to Pruitt to have one of the maids fetch an old sheet and spread it over the sofa.

"At once, m'lord," he replied without so much as batting an eyelash. Pruitt had been with the Farthingale family long enough never to be surprised by anything that happened in the household.

Rose remained in Lord Emory's arms until the task was accomplished, all the while itching to run her hands along the breadth of his chest and shoulders. She didn't think he'd understand the artistic purpose to her touch, but he also had an interesting face and well-formed limbs that merited further study.

She liked the shape of his mouth, but he would mistake her intentions if she lightly ran her finger across it.

He settled her on the sofa and then took a seat beside her because his clothes were as soot-covered as hers were and he couldn't sit anywhere else without dirtying the expensive fabrics. "Your shirt and jacket are likely beyond repair. Please allow me to pay for any damage."

His eyes widened. "No, Miss Farthingale. It isn't necessary."

"But—"

"Consider it my punishment for not coming to visit you sooner."

Her smile faltered. "Punishment? You were avoiding me? And now I've bored you to tears. Of course I have. Maybe that's your punishment."

Nicola leaped to her defense. "Rolf, you are delightful as always. Pay no attention to my beast of a brother."

He let out a soft groan that ended in a seductive growl. Despite her embarrassment, a tingle shot through her as her body responded to that very male, very animal sound.

"I didn't mean…" He ran a hand through his hair again. "I had a perfectly acceptable time with you, Miss Farthingale. The visit is not a punishment at all. Indeed, I plan to call on you tomorrow if you will allow it."

Nicola's eyes rounded in surprise and Rose could see that her friend was almost squealing with joy. She would have been excited too, but his meaning was obvious. He took no pleasure in seeing her. He only meant to stop by to ensure that his medical attention had done the trick and perhaps to report that the pouch Lily had just brought down was now safely returned to the regimental headquarters. "Lord Emory, you and your sister are always welcome here. But it isn't necessary. As I mentioned, my uncle is one of the most capable doctors in London. I'll receive the best care possible."

He nodded. "Then that settles it."

Rose nibbled her lower lip to stem her disappointment. *Fool! He offered to visit and you rebuffed him!*

What was wrong with her? She'd enjoyed his company and now he would never call on her again. Perhaps it was for the best. She liked him.

Probably more than was wise.

She felt the graze of his fingers against her forehead as he brushed back several locks that had fallen out of place. "I'll see you tomorrow, Miss Farthingale."

She glanced up, confused. "You will?"

He nodded. "There's a saboteur on the loose. I'll be staying close to you until we find him."

GET **THE VISCOUNT'S ROSE** NOW!

I would love for us to get to know one another! I hope you'll find me on my Facebook page, subscribe to my monthly newsletter, or connect with me on other social media channels that you enjoy. You can find links to do all of this at my website: mearaplatt.com.

—Meara

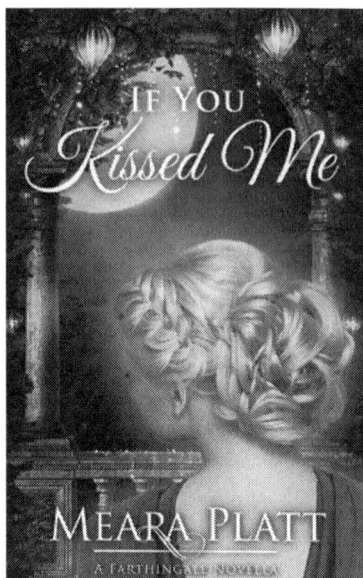

**Sign up for Meara Platt's newsletter
and you'll receive a free, exclusive copy**
of her Farthingale novella,
If You Kissed Me.

Visit her website
to grab your free copy:
mearaplatt.com

ALSO BY MEARA PLATT

FARTHINGALE SERIES
My Fair Lily
The Duke I'm Going To Marry
Rules For Reforming A Rake
A Midsummer's Kiss
The Viscount's Rose
Earl Of Hearts
The Viscount and the Vicar's Daughter
A Duke for Adela
If You Wished For Me
Never Dare A Duke
Capturing The Heart Of A Cameron

THE BOOK OF LOVE SERIES
The Look of Love
The Touch of Love
The Taste of Love
The Song of Love
The Scent of Love
The Kiss of Love
The Chance of Love
The Gift of Love
The Heart of Love
The Promise of Love
The Wonder of Love
The Journey of Love
The Treasure of Love

The Dance of Love
The Miracle of Love
The Hope of Love (novella)
The Dream of Love (novella)
The Remembrance of Love (novella)
All I Want For Christmas (novella)
Tempting Taffy (novella)

De WOLFE ANGELS SERIES
Nobody's Angel
Kiss An Angel
Bhrodi's Angel

DARK GARDENS SERIES
Garden of Shadows
Garden of Light
Garden of Dragons
Garden of Destiny
Garden of Angels

THE BRAYDENS
A Match Made In Duty
Earl of Westcliff
Fortune's Dragon
Earl of Kinross
Aislin
Genalynn
A Rescued Heart
Earl of Alnwick
Pearls of Fire (also part of Pirates of Britannia)

THE LYON'S DEN SERIES
The Lyon's Surprise
Kiss of the Lyon

A Lyon in the Rough

MOONSTONE LANDING SERIES
Moonstone Landing (novella)
Moonstone Angel (novella)
The Moonstone Duke
The Moonstone Marquess
The Moonstone Major

PIRATES OF BRITANNIA
Pearls of Fire

ABOUT THE AUTHOR

Meara Platt is a USA Today bestselling author and an Amazon UK All-star. Her favorite place in all the world is England's Lake District, which may not come as a surprise since many of her stories are set in that idyllic landscape, including her award winning paranormal romance Dark Gardens series. If you'd like to learn more about the ancient Fae prophecy that is about to unfold in the Dark Gardens series, as well as Meara's lighthearted, international bestselling Regency romances in the Farthingale Series and The Braydens series, as well as the Book of Love series, please visit Meara's website at www.mearaplatt.com.

Printed in Great Britain
by Amazon